BREATHING WITH TREES

Breathing With Trees

Book one in the Woodcoombe series

MIKE LAMBORN

Copyright

Dedication

For Sally, Emily and Toby, thank you for all the
love and laughter.
To all my friends, my love and thanks
for being there.
You know who you are!

'The tree which moves some to tears of joy is in the eyes of others only a green thing that stands in the way. Some see nature all ridicule and deformity...and some scarce see nature at all. But to the eyes of the man of imagination nature is imagination itself.'

~ William Blake, Letter to Doctor Trusler, August 1799

PROLOGUE

Afternoon, 15ᵗʰ May 2025. Lord and Lady Wood-coombe; Lewis and Charlotte, were in the drawing room having tea. It was unusually warm and dry for the time of year. The French doors were open, leading out to the grounds and the grassed Vale, the woods lay beyond. Charlotte was sitting, having given up reading her book, as Lewis bustled around her scrutinising the various paintings of the estate on the drawing room walls. She watched as he moved outside the French doors staring up and down the Vale, tutting and shaking his head, whispering under his breath to himself.

'What are you doing, Lewis?' Charlotte called, intrigued at what might be going on in her husband's head. Another scheme, an idea brewing, she guessed.

'Come here and I'll show you,' Lewis said, as he gulped his tea from a dainty cup rather than his preferred mug.

Charlotte sighed, put down her cup and book, and walked the few steps to stand by her husband outside.

'Right,' Charlotte said. 'What am I looking at?'

'See the pictures?' said Lewis, indicating to the walls inside.

'Yes, every time I sit in the drawing room, which is most days,' replied Charlotte, patiently.

'OK, now think of the largest one in the centre of the wall.'

Charlotte closed her eyes for a moment to best remember the picture, wondering what she was supposed to see.

Lewis pointed to his left up the slight hill of the Vale and asked, 'Now, what do you see?'

Charlotte quickly guessed this was a trick question. 'The same view as the picture,' she answered.

'Are you sure? That painting is three hundred years old, the latest from the mid-1920s.'

Charlotte was certain this was some kind of test, but not of what. Most pictures in the drawing room were scenes of the estate, mostly the Vale.

'I'll give you a clue,' Lewis said. 'What's above the trees? What's in the sky?'

Charlotte stared hard up the Vale while imagining the pictures she'd seen so many times before. What had she missed? Then she realised what Lewis was hinting at.

'Birds!'

'Yes,' said Lewis. 'It's almost the exact same view as depicted in many of the pictures in there.' He waved his arm towards the drawing room. 'So, what's the difference?'

Charlotte glanced at her husband oddly and then concentrated on the Vale in front of her. 'The birds are missing,' she said triumphantly. 'Only a very few, not the number any of the paintings seem to suggest.'

'Exactly,' said Lewis. Why are there so few now compared with the past? 'Is anything else different?'

Charlotte walked back into the drawing room and stood beneath the paintings. Lewis followed and stood behind her.

She pointed at a smaller painting. 'This one has a huge hedgerow,' she said. 'I don't know where that would be on the estate.' She moved to the next picture. 'This shows pigs and cows with long horns wandering the Vale and woods.'

'Yes, a hedgerow, but none now exist on the estate. And longhorn cattle and pigs once roamed the estate long before we saturated it with sheep.'

'So, what's the point you're trying to make?' asked Charlotte.

'We have paintings that show the estate at different times for over three hundred years. I have already verified most by looking at the estate diaries and accounts for the pictures' purchase dates.' Lewis moved to his left and tapped a smaller picture. 'What do you make of this?' he asked.

Charlotte took a step back and picked up her reading glasses before joining Lewis. She looked intently at the picture Lewis had pointed out.

'More tall hedgerows with clumps of scrub in front.' She paused, leaning in closer, pushing her glasses up to the bridge of her nose. 'Multicoloured flowers, loads of them.'

'Not flowers,' answered Lewis. 'Look more closely.'

'Ah, not flowers,' she whispered. 'Butterflies? Hundreds of them.'

'Yes, used to be an annual event. I've checked the

estate records and it mentions their arrival. I also checked with the curator and he confirmed the painting is called *Butterflies* on the payment entry in the accounts. It's not the only one either.' Lewis pointed at a similar size picture further along the wall. 'Painted by the same artist two years later.'

Charlotte looked and nodded in agreement. She slowly turned to face Lewis, taking off her glasses at the same time. 'What does this mean? We've never seen anything like that.'

'Exactly! Why don't we see them anymore?

'And the answer is...?'

'Different biodiversity, or to be more exact, biodiversity decline. In fact, when you look at the estate records you can clearly see that from about 1950 species decline as we keep managing the land and moulding it to our design. It's only now that we and others can see the unexpected outcome of our collective actions.'

'What do we do then? Go Back?' asked Charlotte, beginning to understand what her husband was saying.

'I don't think we can. Go back to when: 1700, 1850, or 1910? Impossible to know, but it is obvious that our current setup has changed the land for the worse and, therefore, the life within it.'

Charlotte nodded.

'Interestingly, we got rid of the sheep because growing the meadow grass seemed a better return as sheep prices had plummeted. The unexpected outcome has been the explosion in groundcover in the woods. We have seen the return of woodland flowers which the sheep would have eaten as soon as they showed, although deer are still a problem. This, with other unglamorous growth, brings in invertebrates, improves biodiversity, and attracts the birds, as you can see.' Lewis swept his arm, his hand open, across the wall of paintings. 'Revert back to woodland pasture, consider the reintroduction of longhorn cattle, pigs, beaver and other animals we haven't seen on the estate for probably a hundred years or more. They all play a potential part.'

'So, what's the plan? Rewild the whole estate?' said Charlotte, feeling quite excited by the prospect of change.

'No, not rewild, whatever that means. But make the land wilder to improve biodiversity, rather than continuing to mould the land to our ideal. Instead, let it breath, help it develop and evolve on its own, find its own natural balance, which will change over time and seasons. The Dutch have done a lot of work on this, as has Knepp Farm in West Sussex, not far from here, which has been on this journey for a number of years now. But we are very different. We own the estate. We don't rely on it for income. It's basically our private park, and, most importantly, we are more than wealthy enough to indulge in such a change. But it won't be easy. There will be problems and challenges, some people will be against change or letting nature just do its thing.'

Lewis took a deep breath. 'What do you think?'

Charlotte considered for a moment. 'We have the land, the money, the will and understanding. Perhaps we can show what can be done. Better than just talking about it.'

Lewis beamed. 'Exactly!' He stepped forward and

wrapped his arms around his wife and squeezed her lovingly. 'We'll have to talk to the family, because this is a long-term project and there is a lot to do. The next generation will need to carry this forward, and will probably be the ones that see the most benefit. Is Pen still in contact with Thomas, be great to see him back, I miss him, he's been away so long. We will also have to make some decisions about Pen's fiancé, Henry!'

Charlotte paused for a moment before answering.' Yes, Pen is still in touch with Thomas; they have always been very close. She tells me he's got a steady girlfriend now, and Pen thinks it might be serious, so that may pull him back. As for Henry I think that will play out with Pen without our intervention, we just need to give it time, no need to panic.'

'That all sounds hopeful. I have it on good authority Henry's family farm is in financial trouble, so Pen's trust fund would come in very handy, I've never liked or trusted that man. His reputation goes before him.

'Yes, dear, I know what you mean, but she has choices to make and I suspect Henry won't feature in Pen's future plans.' She waved casually across the paintings they'd just been discussing. 'This all sounds a lot bigger than I thought, but the land and its spirits will be pleased and thank us.'.

'Yes,' said Lewis, gently hugging her.

'I hope you don't do this to everyone who thinks this is a good idea,' she said, laughing and wrestling free from her husband's embrace.

~ 1 ~

Sunday 15ᵗʰ June 2025. Tom rubbed his eyes as he followed Fran up the stairs to the top floor flat, they had shared for the last two years, one of six flats on three levels in what would have once been a grand and spacious Edwardian mansion. A late party the night before and a boozier than expected late brunch had driven them mid-afternoon, tired and a little hungover, back to the flat to rest. Fran had made it pretty clear she needed to sleep. No wink or flirtatious, playful look over her shoulder suggested anything else as they scaled the stairs.

Tom followed her into their flat as she undressed on the move, clothes being stripped off and dropped on the floor as Fran rushed through the lounge. Tom's last sight of her was her hopping into the bedroom on one leg as she struggled to tug off her jeans. Tom entered the bedroom just in time to see Fran's final wriggling and settling under the duvet, and hear her sigh deeply as she stilled.

Tom was tired, but it was too hot to go under the duvet, too early to sleep, so he sat up on the bed, a pillow behind him so he would not have to endure the discomfort of the old, hard oak headboard. Tom smiled as he thought of how Fran would giggle at the way the headboard banged against the wall when they had sex and how she dismissed his attempts to reduce the noise. The sound must be heard next door and in the flat below at least. She said she didn't care, in her infectious way, and it had now become a running joke between them. The thought of her laughing about it made him smile again. But he was pretty sure if her parents were in earshot, she would have a very different response. Suddenly, Fran's father's face flashed into Tom's mind. The thought of her parents removed his smile. He was certain they didn't approve of him. Well, at least, her father, Charles, didn't. He always seemed disappointed when he grilled Tom on his prospects, and was only happy when he could humiliate or undermine him. Tom was sure if Charles knew the truth, he would change his tune, but probably be equally irritating only in a different way.

Tom dozed lightly, off and on. Unlike his girlfriend, he couldn't sleep. He sat upright next to the duvet-wrapped Fran and looked down at her face, veiled by her brunette hair. Tom peered harder at her to see if her eyes were open or closed; if she was really asleep or awake. As if in answer, she sighed and shifted slightly. Her closed eyes were revealed as her hair slipped from her face, also revealing her naked shoulder and neck, which she quickly, tightly covered back up. *Yes, asleep*, thought Tom.

Like the rest of the flat they shared, the bedroom was an eclectic mix of old furniture and worn carpet and furnishings, a faint echo of its Edwardian heyday. Shabby chic, Fran would tell him, and describe the flat and its contents to anyone who was faintly interested. But it had served the two of them well enough with no complaint for nearly two years, although it wouldn't be needed for a third. Time to move on. *Things will be changing one way or another,* Tom thought.

They'd talked about getting married, but not in any detail and hadn't discussed it with either of their families. That was the challenge. Would she fit into his family, their history? Sometimes it felt like a weight hanging on his fate and future that had prompted his leaving nearly eight years ago. As for her parents, there was no way they would consent until they understood the truth of his privileged background and future position. Prospects, as they would call them.

Tom understood their concern. She was their only daughter. They clearly loved her and wanted the best for her. Quite understandable, Tom reasoned, but they may well disagree with her about what that best might be! He just had to make sure he wasn't the cause of any rift. It would be a terrible weight between them, and they had enough to navigate without carelessly adding problems that could, with care, be avoided. Tom sighed into the room and felt the tension of future events and decisions tumble through his head and drop into his stomach like a cold stone dropping into a still pool.

It was another unusually warm June day in a week of unusual warmth that seemed set to continue. *Everything will be early on the estate*, Tom thought. The late afternoon sun sliced through the faded, thin curtains covering the bedroom window, illuminating the dust that hung hypnotically suspended in the still air and slashing bright blocks of random, geometric shapes of light across the carpet, bringing new life to the old, faded shapes and colours. Tom, fascinated, sat watching the shapes slowly shift and change as the sun moved west and at times briefly dulled, as the occasional passing wispy white cloud crossed the otherwise sharp, clear blue sky.

He didn't sleep but dozed. He couldn't believe Fran had wrapped herself so tightly in the duvet. *She must be baking*, he thought, but then remembered how she always complained of being cold. He thought back to their trip to Greece last year. The evenings had brought some relief from the heat, but Fran would always have her cardigan. Tom smiled to himself, reminded how he'd teased her about it.

He heard the vibration of the phone on the bedside table before its sharp ring fractured the calm of the room. Tom snatched the phone up, glancing at the screen, and saw it was Pen, one of his younger sisters. Fran turned over and sighed her annoyance at the interruption to her sleep.

'Hi, Pen, you, OK? Everything alright?' Tom asked, deciding not to whisper. She rarely rang and he hoped there wasn't a problem.

'Yes, fine thanks,' replied Pen. 'Just thought I'd call to go through next weekend. You are still coming? Bringing Francesca?'

'Yes, we're both still coming,' answered Tom.

Hearing her name, Fran's head emerged from the duvet, a drowsy, quizzical look on her face.

Tom, with the phone still at his ear, looked down at her enquiring face. 'It's my sister, Penelope.'

Fran smiled in response and let her neck and head ease back onto the soft bed and comfort of the duvet. Making sure an ear was clear so she could hear what was going on, she then shut her eyes again.

'Father's very excited,' Pen continued.

'Is he?' Tom said in surprise.

'Yes. You've been away, what, nearly eight years and he misses you, despite what you may think. We all do. He also needs your help—there's so much going on with the estate!'

'What do I need to know, Pen?'

Pen took a breath and began. 'Well. The estate is finally moving to be a charitable trust, wilding the estate and beyond. That's the main reason the royals are visiting in two weeks' time, so we can help wilding the royal estates. They are talking of using the charity status to get funds to buy new land to create corridors between current blocks of land. WPS Bank have already pledged fifteen million pounds to build the new lab on the estate, which will elevate Woodcoombe as one of the leading sites of research on northern woodlands. Introducing, sorry, reintroducing, certain species that used to roam the estate.

'Sorry, I forgot to mention the birds. Father was most upset that two buzzards were recently shot at the edge of the estate, so he's decided reintroducing birds should be part of the plan.'

'Who shot the buzzards?' enquired Tom.

'They think two likely lads from one of the sheep farms out to the east. They have a reputation for bird shooting. Duncan is investigating. I'm sure you remember him. His son Dan is sweet on one of the twins, Cath. He's a good lad, and nothing to worry about as long as they are careful, but that's an issue for me and Mum. Dan's been drinking at some of the eastern pubs, asking about bird shooting for sport and it seems everyone pointed at these lads.'

Pen paused to catch her breath. 'Duncan still looks after all the apprentices on the estate and Father's told him half this year's intake must be women. He's not happy so I've been asked to step in, which hasn't helped his humour on the matter. Meadow seed is a lucrative seller and the new American prairie meadow at the top of the Vale is already attracting a lot of seed enquiries. Trees are selling well and we need more plantsmen to keep up with the demand. Ironically, the biggest customer is the South West Fast Rail project. Ironic because they recently suggested the new line should come down the middle of the Vale, destroying half the ancient forest and cutting off Royal Dell. As you might imagine, Father was not impressed, and he politely told them to fuck off! 'Not going to happen!' Lastly, the two farms on the other side look like they might finally return to the estate, bringing it back to its original seven thousand acres. The scrubs are now clear of smallholders. Those are the headlines, Tom.'

'So, not much going on,' said Tom, laughing. 'Plenty for all of us to do! I assume Isaac is still about?'

'Yes, but you need to meet Kurt. He's been here now for

nearly eighteen months from South Africa. He's got experience in their national parks and conservation projects with big animals.'

'So, does Father want to introduce elephants at some stage? Make a change from sheep and be much more interesting. Scare the crap out of the sheepdogs though.' Tom chuckled to himself.

'Sheep have all gone. All part of the wilding of the land. It has made a huge difference already, trees self-seeding themselves, and the ground is covered in flowers and all sorts of life as it's no longer grazed to death.'

'All gone,' echoed Tom in surprise.

'Except for six. They no longer roam freely and mainly act as lawnmowers along the drive and around the house in fenced areas.'

'Lots to do then, I certainly won't be bored!'

They both laughed.

'Does your visit mean you're definitely coming back?' said Pen.

'Possibly, hopefully. Really depends if Fran likes the place.'

'I see,' said Pen, sounding slightly surprised. 'Didn't realise it was that serious. I'm sure she'll love the place.'

'I'm sure I will,' said Fran unheard by Tom.

Tom continued. 'As long as all the family behave and are not too weird on her first visit. There are plenty of other eccentric people around.'

'Yes, very true, you have a point. Our normal is not for everyone. I'll make sure everybody is on their best behaviour. But it is the summer solstice, so we will be out for the dawn on Saturday morning.'

'Solstice,' Fran quietly repeated from the duvet, eyes now wide open, listening intently.

Tom paused before answering Pen. 'Well, probably best she sees all our eccentricities. You never know how someone will react. I assume nothing has changed with the trees?'

'No, Mother and the twins now lead,' replied Pen. 'You won't recognise the twins; they are seventeen and no longer children, as I'm sure you'll quickly spot, but still mad as you might remember them. Do come back, Tom, otherwise I become heir and Henry won't marry me. He has no interest in becoming lord of the manor. He has his own family farm to run and worry about.' Pen's voice trailed off.

'I'm surprised Henry Campbell-Blyth doesn't want to become Lord of the manor,' said Tom. 'But that's why I left. The weight of expectation, and the history and responsibility, was too much. But I now have perspective and appreciate what the family has achieved over the last thousand years and I'm very intrigued about what we can achieve with the land going forward, especially when you look at the current state of the world, we all live in. '

'You sound like Father. He keeps saying the hardest decisions are soon to come. Sounds like you are coming back!' Pen almost shrieked with excitement and relief. Tom could sense a burst of happiness and her smile at the news. 'I'll work with you. So will Henry, even if he doesn't know it yet, and I'm sure Francesca will love the place and even the family eccentricities. Remember both Mother and Grandmother came new to the estate when they married into the family. Many have.'

'Very true.' Tom felt pleased he'd always been close to Pen, and it had been her he'd confided in when he'd left and who had to deal with the rest of the family on his behalf after his disappearing act. *Time to repay the debt*, he thought, and was pleased to do so. It felt right.

He always remembered Pen's last words to him before he left. 'You'll be back,' she'd said with the final hug and a kiss. He loved his sister and hoped this was a good omen for both of them for the future, although he found it hard to believe she was marrying Henry, who had always been a complete shit when they were younger. *Perhaps he's grown up and changed? We'll see*, Tom concluded doubtfully.

'Now,' Pen continued, 'I was hoping to talk to Francesca and give her some advice about clothes for the weekend. It's a girl thing!'

Hearing this, Fran wrestled herself upright, with the duvet clutched tightly across her chest, leaning slightly against Tom, who could feel the heat radiating off her.

'Good idea, I'll put her on if I can wake her up,' he said, grinning at the inquisitive face peering at him, with a hand held out for the phone.

Fran punched him playfully before reaching for the phone.

'Hello, Francesca,' Pen said. 'I'm Penelope, Tom's younger sister, everyone calls me Pen. Now, clothes for the weekend.'

'Great, lovely to talk to you, but please call me Fran.

Most helpful. Just wait a moment,' replied Fran, as she threw the duvet off and bounced her way off the bed and took the few steps to the large old wooden wardrobe, opening both doors with her free hand. 'OK, fire away,'

'It's baking here at the moment and will be this weekend, so no jeans, or just one pair in case. Loose, cool clothes are all you will need during the day, although a chunky cardigan might be handy when we are all up for the dawn on Saturday morning, as it could be slightly chilly at that time.'

'OK, let me have a look here,' said Fran as she bounced up and down in front of the wardrobe, plunging her hand in and pulling out items of clothing which she either pushed back in, placed on the chair next to the wardrobe or threw on the floor behind her.

'Don't worry about shoes for outdoors as we have every type in every size, as long as you haven't got giant or micro feet. Just bring your normal footwear.'

Tom watched Fran's strange, rhythmic, almost tribal, dance in fascination. *We're only staying two nights*, he thought to himself as the pile on the chair steadily grew in front of him, but he knew better than to say anything. Fran's bottom and long bobbed hair swayed to whatever rhythm was beating in her head. At times when she was sideways on, Tom saw her breasts had joined in the dance.

'Fran, a throwback to when everyone would have been working all day on the estate and needed a good wash and change in the evening – dinner is always semi-formal. Friday, just the family, guests and people from the estate, no workwear, so we dress up for dinner. Just smart, a cocktail type dress but not too much flesh. Saturday will be family and a few guests. Henry, my fiancé, will be there both nights. Be nice for you two to meet.'

'Yes, great. Do you have a wedding date?' asked Fran as she pondered evening wear blankly in the wardrobe in front of her.

'September this year, hopefully on the estate.'

'Hopefully?' said Fran without thinking.

'A few things to sort out and decide. Could make it a double wedding,' replied Pen.

'Not really sure about that, we haven't had any real wedding discussions as yet.'

'Quite understand but keep it in mind. You must get married on the estate. It's an amazing venue. They do it really well. And no problems with numbers. We've got nearly two hundred coming.'

Fran half turned to see if Tom was listening, only to see his soppy staring eyes, clearly not catching the comments. 'Sorry, Tom seems distracted at the moment.'

Tom coughed, now broken from his trance, and looked around, embarrassed at being caught out, especially with his sister in earshot. With a moment of desperation for something to make him look occupied on something other than Fran's rhythmic dance, he grabbed the book, dusty and long sat unread on his bedside table, and feigned reading the blurb on the back. He glanced up at Fran to see if he was out of trouble.

Pen laughed. 'Men! I could tell you some stories about Henry. Now, don't worry about the evenings. You can borrow something of mine. What size are you? I'm 5' 10', usually a ten or twelve depending on the cut.'

'Thanks, Pen. All my evening dresses are at home and not in the flat. I just need to pop round and get them, but if there's a problem it sounds like we're a similar size.'

'OK, great, look forward to seeing you next weekend. Can I speak to my brother again please? Thanks.'

'Bye, see you Friday,' Fran said as she passed the phone back to Tom who, having re-read the blurb, understood why the book had remained unread and unloved.

'Tom, last question. When are you planning to arrive?'

'About midday at Coombe Station. We will be travelling by train.'

'Obviously,' joked Pen sarcastically. 'I'll make sure there is someone there to collect you. Looking forward to seeing you both. Can't wait to get to know Fran better. She sounds fun. Bye bye, love you.' And with that Pen rang off.

'All OK?' Tom asked Fran, who had bounced back on to the bed and was now kneeling opposite him.

'Yes, great,' she responded with a smile and a shiver of excitement. 'Pen sounds nice. I'm really excited. What's the solstice? And why do we have to be up so early? Looking forward to meeting your twin sisters. Why by train, when we could drive? Not sure about a double wedding. But before any of this I have to visit home to get dresses for the evenings and we have to go tonight. I'll call Mum now. We can probably crash Sunday dinner. I'll drive.'

'OK, OK,' surrendered Tom, knowing when he was beaten. *Probably time I started introducing the truth to her parents,* he thought. The mention of Sunday dinner had made him feel hungry again.

'Good, I could do with a shower after I call them. You could probably do with one too,' she said with a wink and that cheeky look he loved.

As Fran called her parents, Tom's phone pinged with a message from Pen. He picked it up. It read: 'Really looking forward to next week. Don't worry, it will all be fine. Spoke to Father. He's delighted as is everyone else. The twins already have you married off, so beware! Just so you know, Noah and Naomi both back from uni. Loads of love to you both. Look forward to seeing you next weekend and an autumn double wedding. Ha ha!'

Tom smiled and grimaced as he read the text, replying simply, 'Thanks sis!!!'

Fran came off her phone. 'Seven o'clock for dinner, all OK.'

Tom offered up his phone. 'Read this,' he simply said.

'Who are Noah and Naomi? Will I be able to work on the estate now I've finished my degree? All sounds good.'

'I grew up with Noah and Naomi. Well, with a degree in geography and environmental science I think there will be many projects you would like coming up.'

'Good, I don't want to just swan about, like Lady Muck, as tempting as it sounds. Right, we need to shower,' said Fran. She jumped up and sprang to the bathroom, half turning and shouting at him, 'Come on, we don't have all day!'

Tom eased himself off the bed and walked briskly to the bathroom. *Things probably aren't so bad*, he thought to

himself, his sister's texted comment echoing in his head.
'Don't worry it will all be fine.'

~ 2 ~

Tom sat in the passenger seat. He'd prefer to drive, but it was Fran's car, a twenty-first birthday present from her parents last year. When he did drive, it seemed to be mostly when it was his turn to do the food shop, which often seemed to coincide with the need to fill up with petrol. He had on his best jeans, a white shirt and his brown leather deck shoes, no socks. Fran had said he looked smart, but also said her dad would never understand not wearing socks. *Lack of socks would probably be the least of his problems*, Tom thought to himself.

Fran eased into the driver's seat in her tight blue capri pants and multi coloured blouse, under which Tom had noticed she was, unusually, wearing a bra. *The parent effect,* he mused, as Fran glanced at him.

'I don't see why we don't drive next week. Be easier for all our luggage.'

Tom glanced back with eyebrows raised.

'Alright, my luggage,' Fran admitted with a grin and giggle, as she pushed the mini into first gear, pulled out and accelerated faster than Tom would have liked to the end of the road, ignoring the 20mph speed limit.

They needed to turn right across the traffic but the traffic was solid both ways. They were already late. It usually took about forty-five minutes to drive to her parents. The state of the traffic wasn't going to help to catch up. Fran revved the engine as she waited impatiently for a gap. Suddenly, she launched into a small gap across the oncoming traffic from her right, resulting in screeching brakes and blaring horns as she waited broadside across the road for another gap on the left.

For fuck's sake, thought Tom, *I really wish she'd drive a bit slower, she puts the fear of God in me!*

Fran ignored the noise and anger on her right, concentrating on getting into the flow of traffic now crawling slowly from her left. Tom watched the focused concentration on her face, her eyes scanning, looking for a gap. Suddenly, her face flickered and Tom instinctively braced as she screeched the car into the smallest of gaps. This was followed by more angry horns, shouting and waving of arms from the car now behind as she joined the slow-moving traffic.

'OK, we'll take the car next weekend, but only if I can drive.'

'Done,' Fran replied, smiling as the traffic crawled along.

'I'll text Pen now with the change of plan.'

'We're going to be late!' said Fran.

'Are we?' Tom replied in mock surprise. 'Shall we text your mother and let her know?'

Fran sighed, frustrated with the traffic and irritated by

Tom's sarcastic tone. 'Yes, we should,' she said wearily. The evening was not starting well.

Tom picked up Fran's phone.

'Do you want to dictate?' he asked.

'Dear Mum, really sorry we 're going to be late, traffic terrible. Don't delay your dinner due to us. I know Dad will get grumpy and too much red wine without food will not help!'

'Love, Francesca,' added Tom.

'Well remembered. Mum hates me shortening my name.'

'Hmm, but Lady Francesca Woodcoombe has a distinctive ring. Your mum will like that.'

'Christ, I hadn't thought about that.'

'Message sent.'

'I wonder how Mum will respond.'

The phone pinged a moment later with a new message. Tom read it out.

'Hi, Francesca, no problem, see you when you arrive. Drive safe. Mum xx'

'I'll reply with two kisses,' offered Tom. 'Your mum clearly hasn't driven with you much!'

'Fuck off, Tom,' Fran said, laughing. 'We'd still be waiting at the junction at the end of our road if you were driving. Remember, Mum has always talked better of you than Dad. Two kisses will be fine.'

'Gone,' announced Tom. 'Not that difficult to think better of me than your dad. He still wants to marry you off to one of the up-and-coming associates at his company. A trophy wife with an assured partnership future attached.'

'No, thanks, I'm no trophy. Anyway, I love you.'

Tom reached out and squeezed Fran's hand resting on the gear lever. 'Thanks.'

'And?!' said Fran in a slightly raised voice.

'I love you too,' responded Tom, with another squeeze of her hand.

*

They pulled up, fifteen minutes late, down the road from her parents terraced West London townhouse laid out over three floors plus basement. Tom spotted Fran's father's grey, shiny Mercedes estate nestling in the gloom of the weak and acidy street lights, low and long like a shiny alien ship. Fran's mother was waving from the front door at the top of the steps which led up from the pavement to the front door.

Here we go, Tom thought. *Showtime. Will it be a comedy or tragedy tonight?*

'Come in, come in,' said Wendy, Fran's mother, ushering them into the hall. 'Great to see you.' She gave Fran a hug and a kiss, before releasing her and swinging round to face Tom.

Now, the first awkward bit, Tom thought.

'You've been keeping her away, you naughty boy,' Wendy exclaimed with a set, thin smile, extending her arms out to Tom for his welcoming hug, a brushing of cheeks. He felt her downy, powdered cheek brush over his and was pleased he'd shaved and so avoided the unfortunate Velcro effect his stubbled face had had before. The polite, rather than loving charade, was completed with a meaningless air kiss, a performance perfected with her husband over years of dinners and functions with many, often once-met clients, strangers with whom she would chat and humour and who afterwards she would quickly forget.

As Wendy pulled away from the brief embrace, Tom felt relief to have completed it without incident, but the relief would be short-lived. Wendy, the polite and well-practised hostess, smoothly ushered them into the dining room, and Tom immediately spotted Charles, sitting at the dining table, intently watching the red wine he was swirling around in his glass, already looking annoyed.

Not a good sign, Tom decided.

'At last,' Charles said as they spilled into the room. 'What's the point of buying you a nippy little car for you to be late? Could have just bought you two fucking bus passes! Come on, sit down then, we can eat, at last!'

Tom pulled out a chair opposite Charles and, as he did so, Fran passed close behind him, heading for the chair next to him. As Fran passed, she whispered, 'Alright?'

'So far so good,' replied Tom.

Fran responded with a playful, loving squeeze to his arm as she sat down.

Charles scowled, as he hated such shows of affection. Tom noted he had never seen Charles or Wendy show any affection, which he thought was a shame and part of the problem. Everything with Charles seemed to be a transaction, had a price.

'Come on, let's eat for Heaven's sake,' said Charles, clearly annoyed, as Wendy passed out the loaded plates.

Charles waved a bottle threateningly at Tom, breaking his thoughts. 'Wine,' he asked.

'Yes, please. I'm not driving,' Tom said, lifting the bulbous glass for Charles to fill.

'You need a dress?' asked Wendy.

'Yes,' said Fran. 'We're meeting Tom's family this weekend, and I need to be smartly dressed for dinner.'

Charles smiled and Tom sensed Fran's father saw another chance to undermine and ridicule him.

'Where do your family live?' Charles asked, a mischievous smile creeping over his face.

'Woodcoombe Estate, south west past Guildford.'

'They live on an estate and dress for dinner, how quaint! We do our best here,' Charles said. For effect, he swept his hand theatrically around the room and across the table. 'We have an estate just to the north of us. I see no hint of such formality there and would never park the car up there, as I'm sure the wheels would be gone over night, if not the whole car.'

'Charles,' Wendy hissed, 'we all know what you're doing.'

'I'm just enquiring where my daughter will be going this weekend. You keep telling me I should take more of an interest,' he said to Wendy with an odd look on his face, before turning back to Tom.

'Where exactly is Woodcoombe Estate?' asked Charles.

'Roughly equidistant from Winchester, Guildford and Portsmouth, near Hazelmere,' said Tom.

'It's Tom's family estate,' interjected Fran, bored and clearly angry with her dad's line of conversation.

'You own an estate?' said Charles.

'Yes, King Ethelred granted the title and land, by Royal Charter in perpetuity, for saving his life.' Tom felt like a magician, producing a show-stopping trick out of a hat.

Charles sat blank-faced in surprise, absorbing what had just been said. He hadn't seen that coming.

'What exactly are you telling me?' Charles asked, breathing heavily, as his wide, wine-fuelled eyes stared alternately at Tom and Fran, his face a curious flushing red.

Tom raised his hand at Fran as he could sense her rising anger at her dad.

'Woodcoombe is a seven-thousand-acre estate that has been in the family since 998, when granted by the then King Ethelred the Unready. I am the heir and will inherit the estate and all the family assets, and Francesca would eventually become Lady Francesca Woodcoombe.'

'I guess for that to happen she would need to be your wife, and I don't remember you asking my permission. Or are we too lowly to expect such manners?' said a grim-faced Charles.

Fran couldn't remain silent any longer. 'It's my decision. I'm not a prize to be discussed or bartered for. I've already said yes and this weekend is about me meeting his family and better understanding what joining the family would mean,' Fran said angrily, her irritation clear to all.

Wendy looked shocked and stared at her open-mouth husband, who was going redder in the face, as she said, 'Our daughter, a real lady and living in a country house! It's like a fairy tale. Like William and Kate.'

'Oh God,' muttered Charles, unheard, under his breath.

Wendy smiled weakly, the stress of the evening show-ing in the lines on her face. 'Francesca, shall we go and sort out the dresses? You want to look your best. Leave the boys to talk.'

'OK, I can't eat any more,' said Fran, rising from her seat. 'Now both of you be nice, we will be back.' Tom and Charles couldn't fail to notice the warning tone in her voice.

As Fran passed behind Tom, she placed her hand on his shoulder, squeezing gently, her hand lingering until it was out of reach. It then gracefully trailed in the air behind her as she followed her mother, who clearly couldn't wait to get out of the room and had made a quick escape.

Charles dived into his food again, his knife and fork clinking on the China plate, the only noise interrupting the intense silence that the ladies had left behind. 'Eat,' said Charles, his mouth half full. 'It'll be completely cold before you know it.'

Tom looked down at the half-eaten plate of food in front of him. The gravy had already started to congeal and glaze, making a mystery of much it covered. Tom loaded a fork and was pleased to find more than a hint of warmth as it entered his mouth.

Tom and Charles sat in silence eating. Tom was pleased at the silence as he steadily worked through the plate.

Charles announced he'd finished with the ringing of his knife and fork being laid clumsily on his now empty plate. Charles drained the red wine from his glass, wiped his lips with the back of his hand and picked up the wine bottle to fill his glass, but to his surprise he found it empty.

'Finished,' Charles said indignantly, holding the bottle up in front of Tom. Charles tipped the bottle upside down and Tom watched a single red drop of liquid escape the neck and fall in slow motion on the white tablecloth.

'Fuck!' said Charles. 'Wendy won't like that!' He leant over and pulled the silver dish containing the condiments to cover the expanding red stain. 'White?' asked Charles as he got up from his chair, and took the few steps to pick up two fresh glasses and the cold bottle of white which was still shiny and wet with condensation from its time chilling. Charles walked round the table, placed a fresh glass in front of Tom and filled it with chilled, lightly golden liquid. He then swivelled on his heels, returned to his seat opposite Tom, and poured himself a generous glass.

'Cheers. Now, Tom, humour me if you will. I've met many country folk who are land rich but cash poor. Where do you fit in this?'

Tom took a deep breath as he ordered his thoughts. This was the moment! 'There are four main elements to the family fortune. The estate itself, which breaks even or makes a small profit, and will be moving to a charity status. Then we have a nineteen per cent shareholding in WPS Investment Bank which Father sits on the board of.'

Charles spluttered to life. 'My God, nineteen per cent! That's a lot of money! Let me think.' He paused for a moment as he ran rough numbers through his head. 'Yes. A very big number, and a huge competitor of ours.'

'The family was one of the primary investors when

it was set up in the mid-1700s. They'd made a fortune in commerce and trading. I did work experience with them before I went to uni and they are sponsoring my research, following my masters.' Charles had a strange expression on his face. Disbelief, Tom decided. 'So, no one will starve,' said Tom, with a smile to underline the position, enjoying the look of shock on Charles' face. 'We also have a long-standing, well-established property business, Coombe Property, with a mixed portfolio of land and property across the country built up over hundreds of years, and lastly, the fine art and jewellery the family have acquired over the centuries. We have a full-time curator looking after this.' Tom stopped and looked Charles in the eye. Charles would need a bit of time to process this, but Tom knew the pillars of wealth would satisfy even him, at least for a while.

'Does Fran know this?' said Charles.

'Broadly, but in no detail, and I doubt she understands the significance. Sorry, I forgot to add that each of us children, of which there are four, have a trust fund that can be accessed at the age of twenty-five, so none of us will be poor whatever happens.'

'Francesca's never mentioned any of this. It would have helped.' Charles paused. 'So, what now?'

'Visit to the estate, meet all the family. If this goes well, as it should, invite you and Wendy to visit. And then make plans as needed. There is plenty of good red in the cellar,' Tom said with a smile. For once he felt he'd finished a conversation ahead rather than angry and regretting what he hadn't said.

'Yes, yes,' responded Charles, a strange smile creeping across his face. 'Yes, very good. I look forward to meeting your family and the wine cellar in due course.'

Tom sensed a tone of approval. *Everything*, he thought, *everything is a transaction for Charles.* And he could not argue this was a good one for his daughter. *It's a shame he doesn't value her in the same way that she will be loved by me.*

The dining room door opened and Fran appeared.

'Tom, we're going now,' she said, walking briskly in and round the table to dutifully kiss her dad goodbye. On the way back, she grabbed Tom's hand and led him out through the hall, saying nothing until they were halfway back to the car.

'That went well.'

'Really!' said Tom in surprise.

'Yes, Mum says Dad needed to be told. She's delighted and he will come round.'

'Where are the dresses?' asked Tom.

'Don't worry, not forgotten. Mum's going to get them dry cleaned and drop them round on Tuesday evening.'

'OK, we can get an update on your father's thoughts and blood pressure then; his face went through a few shades of red.'

'Oh dear, I hope he's alright,' said Fran as she eased back into the mini to drive back to the flat.

~ 3 ~

Tuesday evening 17th June. Fran's mother delivered the dry cleaned and pressed dresses as promised on Tuesday evening. She phoned up to announce her arrival and said that she wouldn't be climbing the stairs to their flat. Fran dragged Tom down the stairs and out of the house to find Wendy loitering at the back of the car, boot open. The dresses were laid out across the long boot, bathed in the weak, acidy orange street light, plastic-shrouded spectres of evenings gone and those yet to come.

Wendy enthusiastically and briefly embraced Fran and then Tom.

'I'm so excited about your news, and I hope it all goes well. I look forward to meeting your family in due course, Tom.'

'Alright, Mum,' said Fran, irritated at her mother's gentle prod.

'Of course,' responded Tom, cutting across anything Fran's might say and possibly regret. 'In the next few weeks, I should think. We will be in touch soon with dates.

How's Charles? He looked a bit off-colour when we left on Sunday.'

'He's fine, he's just been under the weather; stress, I think. But Charles will never admit there's anything wrong.'

'So, he's OK then,' said Fran. 'Just unreasonable as usual.'

'I think it's fair to say if you had been more honest and forthcoming about things before last Sunday it wouldn't have come as such a surprise,' said Wendy, staring at Fran, with her thin, well-practised, diplomatic smile.

'So, it's my fault then! Fucking ridiculous!' said Fran. 'If he just took the time to get to know Tom rather than undermine him at every opportunity, we wouldn't be having this conversation now.' Fran bent forward and swept up the four dresses. 'Thanks for this, we'll be in touch when we return. Bye, Mum.' Fran planted an obligatory kiss on her mother's cheek, before walking briskly, with stamping feet, along the dim street back towards the flat.

'Oh dear,' Wendy whispered with a sigh as Fran stormed off.

'Don't worry, it will be fine,' said Tom. 'I think she's a bit nervous about the weekend, but she'll be OK.'

'Bless you, what do you think, Tom, same as Fran?'

Tom thought carefully before answering. 'I think we could all have acted a bit differently and avoided this situation.'

'Yes, quite so! We must all do better, going forward.' Wendy reached out and squeezed Tom's arm, then closed the boot of the car. 'Thanks, Tom. No doubt we will speak soon, hope the weekend goes well. Yes, we must all try harder,' Wendy said, getting back into the car.

Tom walked slowly back to the house and up the stairs, deciding what Wendy really meant was that he and Fran would have to try harder. Walking into the flat, he saw the dresses laid out on the table. Fran was sitting on the sofa, sobbing, with big tears rolling down her face. Tom knelt down to hug her.

'I'm so sorry, Tom, it's all my fault.'

Tom held her tightly. As he did, he could feel the shaking and sobbing steadily abate.

'It's not your fault at all, and it will all be fine. We'll work it out together.'

'Thank you,' Fran said her face blotchy and red.

*

On Wednesday and Thursday Tom noticed piles of clothes and stuff appear in various places around the flat. He couldn't believe how much Fran was thinking of packing. In a brave moment, Tom asked about the dresses. 'Two nights, four dresses, what's the plan?'

'I'm trying to pack. I doubt you will understand.'

'Probably not,' admitted Tom. 'Humour me.'

Fran sighed and put down a stack of clothing she'd been sorting. 'The plainest, simplest dress is for the first evening, after which I will have a better idea of what's appropriate or not for Saturday night.'

'I understand that,' said Tom. 'What's the most daring option for Saturday night?'

Fran walked over to the table and picked up a dress by its silver dry cleaning hanger and lifted its plastic covering. 'This one. It basically has no back; it drops down to the base of my back.'

Tom shifted in his seat with interest as she turned the dress to reveal the deep-scooped back. 'What do you wear underneath?'

'Not a lot!' Fran giggled.

'Christ, you might kill off some of the old boys from the estate wearing that. Pen would love it, but doubt she'd dare wear it.'

'At least they'll die happy,' said Fran, with a smile.

They both laughed loudly, the first time since Tuesday evening, their laughter finally dispelling the stress.

~ 4 ~

Friday 20th June. Tom dropped his single, long-owned, brown soft leather valise and suit carrier with his jackets for the evenings by the door of their flat. Fran struggled out with her two larger, well-packed, plump bags, reminding them both that they must not forget the dresses. Tom relayed the luggage down to the car. Lastly, Tom picked up the dresses, making sure they didn't drag or snag as he descended. Fran followed with her handbag over her shoulder and Tom's suit carrier, which was heavier than she'd expected.

'How many jackets do you have in there?' asked Fran, passing it to Tom.

'Three.'

'Three!' said Fran. 'Is there a risqué option for Saturday night?'

'Maybe.' Tom laughed, understanding the teasing and irony in her voice.

The journey from the flat to the estate would take about two and a half hours, with no stops, so Tom had decided they really needed to be away at roughly nine-thirty. To his great surprise they were, with no last-minute repacking panic by Fran, which made a change.

Fran teased him for driving at twenty miles an hour to the end of their road. Tom knew she would be commenting on his driving all journey, mostly saying he was going too slow. They navigated out of London's warren of roads and cruised down the not-too-busy main roads. One stop for coffee, taken away and drunk on the move, then another for the inevitable toilet stop.

'Not far now,' Tom announced as he suddenly remembered leaving all those years ago. Waking early in the dark, leaving Pen at the sitting room door, with a hug and a tear, then walking the path which was all that was left of the old road to Woodcoombe Village and the station. It was a cloudy, dry but warm day in early March. He remembered how surprised he was to see no one as he walked away. Even at the station he was alone, buying his ticket to London using the ticket machine, rather than the ticket office. It wasn't until a few minutes before the train was due that anyone else appeared on the platform, but no one he knew or knew him. Once on the train he experienced a wave of relief, a lifting of the huge weight that had been weighing him down for so long.

Jonathan Playly, an old school friend, had offered him a place to stay in the house he was renting with five other guys. Tom had the address but no idea how to get there. When he did arrive, Jonathan had looked at his single brown bag and asked, 'Is that all you've got?'

Tom slept on the sofa for the first month, then Jonathan asked Tom if he wanted to rent a room that had recently become vacant. He'd replied, yes, providing his allowance wasn't turned off. Tom eagerly embraced his new world, discovering gigs, clubs, beer, the occasional drug, and girls, all of which he enjoyed that summer to the full.

Tom had somehow got good enough exams to be accepted at Imperial College London to read Mathematics. He only told Pen he'd been accepted. He got a first degree after three years and the following summer he completed three months' work experience at WPS Bank, not difficult when your family is a main shareholder.

As Tom pulled onto the slip road, Fran said, 'Beautiful countryside,' as the sun-drenched panorama unfolded in front of them.

'Bloody heat will be a problem, if it doesn't rain the land you see will soon start loose its green sheen.'

Tom felt pleased to be returning. The stress he'd felt before he'd left all those years ago had not returned. He realised he was a different person now. The history, expectations and responsibility that had whirled around his head due to his accident of birth, now, like jigsaw pieces, slotted into place in his head along with the most important piece; the woman sitting next to him. Tom reached out with his left hand and squeezed Fran's knee.

'You alright?' Fran asked, turning her head towards him with a smile. 'You've gone a bit quiet.'

'I'm fine, thanks. Just remembering leaving, and I guess a bit nervous about returning.'

'Don't worry. We can be nervous together and, as you always say, it will be fine,' Fran said with a grin.

'I know it will be fine. We'll be going through

Woodcoombe Village soon. It's at the end of the ridge you can see running east on your right. The estate is the other side of the ridge and the Vale, as it's always been called, runs out southwest from the ridge.'

'Ooh, this is lovely,' Fran said as they entered Woodcoombe Village. 'It really is like a chocolate box cover. Pub looks nice.'

'Foresters' Arms,' said Tom. 'Owned by the family, tenanted out.'

'Cool, you own a pub,' said Fran with a smile.

The road narrowed as they approached a stone bridge at the end of the village.

'What's the river?' asked Fran.

'The Coombe. It rises on the downs to the north, meanders down to Woodcoombe Village then under the railway and into the estate, where the Cut, which takes runoff from the ridge, moors and scrubs feeds into it. The Coombe then runs through the woods before leaving the estate, running through Woodend and eventually to the sea near Chichester.'

'Is the Cut a river and what are the scrubs?' asked Fran, to prove her interest in what may well be her future home.

'The Cut looks like a river, but manmade a long time ago. It drains water that runs off the ridge and scrubs into the Coombe so it doesn't flood the Vale. The scrubs are poor land that run from the top east end of the ridge down to the Vale. It has always been tenanted to smallholders but it's a very tough place to exist and make a living. Pen told me there are no tenants left. There were only two hanging on when I went away. Royal Dell also has a small trickling stream running through it which also runs into the Coombe.'

'What's Royal Dell?' asked Fran, bored with rivers, and thought, smiling to herself, *Lucky they weren't heading for Venice.*

'It's where the family's fortunes really began, when King Ethelred formally granted by Royal Charter the 7000 acres plus of land and titles in perpetuity in 998. After Brandon Woodcoombe hid and protected Ethelred and his entourage in the Dell, since always known as Royal Dell, from a Danish raiding party who had landed near Southampton. Brandon ordered his foresters to protect Ethelred. All were expert longbow men. Legend has it the bowmen killed the Danish scouts as they entered the Vale. When the main party, on arriving, saw the scattered bodies at the mouth of the Vale, they decided not to enter and changed course. The Woodcoombe archers became, by order of Ethelred, the Royal Company of Archers. The skills and company have continued to be maintained in accordance with the Royal Charter. In 1068, however, the family lost roughly 1100 acres of the estate when the Normans rewarded two families, Clifford and Joseph, for their loyalty, with land.

'These two families, well, principally the Clifford's, went to court in 1952 to contest their legal right to the land. I can't remember all the detail but the final judgement was the land belonged to us as no documents were changed and there were no adjustments to the original Charter, but they said the land should stay with the Josephs and Clifford's on the basis of free tenancy as long as the families occupied the land, but they could not sell any of it and if they left, the land would revert back to the estate. The two farms are on the other side of the house, and that land is always referred to as the Other Side.

'As part of the Charter, Woodcoombe had to maintain and, when needed, make available the archers, who were basically the foresters and gamekeepers from across the estate, and they were allegedly present at the battles of Stamford Bridge and Hastings, and served in the Hundred Years War. As heir I am captain of the archers. It's still a condition of employment, especially with apprentices, that they practice and maintain the art on Sunday mornings. There's a strip of ground in the more southerly part of the wood called the range where the archers practice.'

'Wow, a lot to take in.'

'Yes, sorry, we're not short of history,' said Tom, pleased to find he felt proud, rather than embarrassed or weighed down by it as he had done before. 'And I haven't mentioned King Arthur yet.'

'What!' Fran said, in excitement.

'Legend has it he camped on the land when passing through on campaign. There's a specific field on the Other Side surrounded on three sides by a dry-stone wall, where Arthur allegedly camped, and one day might return.'

'Return!' Fran exclaimed again

'The Once and Future King will return at Britain's greatest need, so legend has it.'

'Can you use a bow?'

'Well, I could when I left, but they are not easy to use and you need a lot of strength.'

'Cool! What would happen if you didn't retain the archers?'

'In theory we could lose all the land and it would return to being a crown estate. But no one complains about maintaining it. It's part of the family and estate's history, heritage and tradition. OK, this is the village of Woodend.'

'Not as pretty as Woodcoombe. Do you own that pub as well?' asked Fran, pointing to her left as The Oak pub passed by.

'No,' chuckled Tom, 'we don't own The Oak. We bear right and then go over another bridge, nearly there.' Tom was surprised at how happy he felt seeing and describing the familiar sights of his home. It was good to be back.

The road rose momentarily as they crossed the bridge and Fran spotted the moving river below.

'Over the Coombe now it's left the estate,' said Fran with a smile, wanting to show she had been listening.

'Yes.' Tom was surprised he'd kept her interest. 'The high wall on your right is the bottom of the estate. That's the old gatehouse.'

Fran looked to her right and saw a grand, double-fronted, grey stone building with large, imposing, black padlocked metal gates at its centre.

'Here is the new driveway.' Tom slowed to turn right and waited a moment for a gap in the traffic before swinging into the estate.

'Here we are,' Tom said with a contented sigh.

The drive was guarded by a line of tall trees on each side, which formed a vaulted green cathedral roof of bough and leaf. The leafed roof almost seemed to glow from the relentless assault of the hot sun, and was every shade of green, flickering as branches rustled. At times, sunlight sliced through gaps, hitting the ground with bright rods of light, some permanent, some brief, coming, going, flickering as the leaf-tiled emerald roof flexed on the gently shifting boughs.

'Wow!' said Fran as they drove through the green cathedral guard, her voice almost a sigh. 'It's beautiful.'

'Yes, it is,' agreed Tom, smiling and happy with her first reaction to the estate.

As they left the tunnel of trees, they came to a small junction bathed in sunlight and heat, with a small collection of signs mounted on wooden posts stuck in the grass verge. Pointing left, the sign read 'Joseph's Farm', pointing straight up, 'Clifford Farm' and pointing right simply 'Woodcoombe'.

'The Other Side!' Fran waved her arm to the left. 'The two farms you mentioned,' she said, pleased she'd remembered.

Tom took the right turn, which snaked slowly up through the grounds, passing a group of men working in the heat amongst a stand of trees.

'That must be hot work,' said Fran as the road continued bending left gently uphill, away from the men. Fran suddenly became aware of how hot it was as the pounding sun streamed into the car. She blew out her cheeks as a building came into view. 'Is that your house?'

'Yes, Grade II listed and one of the best examples of a late medieval manor house, parts dating back to 1455.'

'Would we live there?'

'Possibly, although there are many other houses and cottages around the estate.'

'No, I think that will be fine,' said Fran with some glee.

'Well, family live there as well. Remember no matter how big it is, at times you seem to never be able to escape them.'

'Oh! I hadn't thought of that,' said Fran thoughtfully.

The imposing grey stone-built and grey-tiled roofed house now loomed up at them in all its five hundred plus years of glory. Blotches of moss and lichen brought some relief and contrast to the grey stone and tile. Three floors with a number of imposing stone chimneys thrusting up from the roof and what looked like a chapel attached at the far north end.

'The house used to have a moat surrounding it but that was filled in over a hundred years ago,' Tom said as he brought the car to a stop. 'OK, this is the original back entrance which is now used as the main entrance because of the drive. The original front door, which is exactly the same as the back, opens directly out onto the Vale which you saw glimpses of as we drove up to the house.' Tom stopped talking as he saw the familiar sight of Isaac sitting on the wall, not looking bothered by the heat at all.

'Who's that?' asked Fran, intrigued by the smartly dressed, wizened, grey-haired man now waving at them enthusiastically.

'Isaac. I'll let him tell you his story and it's quite a story to tell,' replied Tom.

~ 5 ~

Fran watched as the surprisingly spry Isaac moved effortlessly off the wall to open her door for her.

'Welcome to Woodcoombe, Francesca. Lovely to meet you, and great you've brought Thomas back.' Isaac made the slightest of bows as Fran unfolded herself from the car, finding little relief from the heat.

'Lovely to meet you, Isaac,' said Fran with a smile as they shook hands. 'Please call me Fran, everyone else does.'

'Including your mother?' enquired Isaac with a grin.

'No.'

'Thought not. Would you mind if I used your full name? It's just too nice to be shortened. I never, well rarely, call Thomas Tom.'

'OK, that's fine. How long have you been on the estate?'

'Over two hundred years, we came here as slaves.'

'Oh!' said Fran, not knowing what to reply. She flashed a sharp look at Tom who was grinning and shaking his head.

'Now come on, Isaac, tell the whole story or she will leave before we've even arrived,' Tom said lightly.

'Well, over two hundred years ago the then Lord Prentice Woodcoombe made it a clear stipulation with the bank that the family money should not be invested in any slaving ventures. Somehow this was overlooked and when His Lordship found out he immediately demanded his funds be withdrawn, but was told that was not possible. So, he asked for all the profit and investment from what had been a very successful venture to be paid into a separate account, which became known as the slave fund. Lord Prentice then went to the slave markets and bought all the slaves he could. He bought my great-great-great grandfather, his wife and their two children as well as two other families and a number of single men and women. They were all brought back to the estate, housed, fed and given a choice to be repatriated or stay on the estate or leave as free men or women. They were educated, taught English and looked after.'

'Crikey!' said Fran.

'Lord Prentice created the slave fund to support the slaves and their descendants, whatever choices they made. Many decided to leave. It was certainly a very difficult place for a black face then in England's green and pleasant land.' Isaac smiled at Fran.

'Your family stayed, didn't go back?'

'Yes, so green here. My forebears stayed and worked on the estate, as we have ever since. Lord Prentice became instrumental in the abolition of slavery; he took action to try his best to correct the wrong that had been done. He paid for the return of a number back to Africa, educated all who stayed and those who left but remained in

England. All left as free men with money in their pocket and a letter of introduction from His Lordship to help them start again.'

'Thanks, Isaac,' said Tom. 'So, we are not quite the terrible slavers you may have first thought we were. The slave fund still exists, but now it's called the less emotive 'education fund' and all the children on the estate have access to it.'

'Yes,' said Isaac. 'Paid for my children, Noah and Naomi, to go through university. They have just finished and returned to the estate. You should meet them. Thomas knew them both well.'

'What are they going to do now?' asked Tom.

'Naomi hopes to work or be an intern here with the new commercial manager; you probably haven't met her yet. Naomi studied Tourism and Hospitality at university and with the likelihood of the estate becoming open to the public more than its current three days a year, there should be plenty to do. Noah did Engineering and is waiting to hear from a wind turbine company. We'll see what happens.' Isaac sighed, pleased to talk about his children and the futures they might make.

'Fantastic, you must be pleased,' Fran said to the now silent Isaac.

'Yes, and it is nice to have them back, if only for a while. You've both just finished as well, is that right?'

'Yes, well, I have,' said Fran. 'I studied geography and environmental science, and it'll be great to put what I've learnt to good use here.'

'Fran, Fran,' was shouted from the door, followed by

the hurried arrival of a tall, slender, long-legged young woman with long, dark hair, tied in a ponytail.

'Fran. Sorry, Isaac, Francesca.' Pen stood in front of Fran not sure what to do.

'Hi, Pen, should we hug?' said Fran, feeling similarly awkward.

'Yes,' said Pen and, as they did, two more girls tumbled out of the door, one with the same straight dark hair as Pen, but cut a lot shorter, the other with a wild, strawberry blonde, loose, wavy, messy mop of long hair.

Pen turned. 'Meet the twins. Catherine,' she said, gesturing towards the curly blonde, 'and Jennifer,' with a gesture towards the dark-haired girl. 'More often known as Cath and Jen.'

Both rushed up to Fran together. 'Hello, great to meet you. You're very pretty. Are you really marrying Tom? Will you live here?'

'Stop,' said Pen in a raised voice. The twins fell silent and feigned sulky faces. 'If you don't, she'll get straight back in her car and take Tom away for good. I know you have many questions, but not as many as Fran will have this weekend so as you have already been *asked*—' Pen emphasised the word—'just stop.'

'Don't worry too much, please, I want to get to know all of you,' said Fran, amused and fascinated at the sibling rivalry she'd missed out on, being an only child.

'You've arrived.' They all turned, and an older, slender, elegant woman glided out of the door and headed straight to Tom and embraced him. Fran guessed it must be his mother, Charlotte, if she remembered rightly. She had

Pen's slim, tall figure but with same blonde hair as Cath's, although cut a lot shorter, with a few distinguished traces of grey.

Charlotte released Tom, but not before saying something quietly to him and kissing his cheek. She then moved towards the girls. 'Francesca, I see you've met Pen and the animals.' The twins rolled their eyes. 'I do hope everyone is behaving,' Charlotte said, looking at the twins.

'Yes, we're just getting to know each other,' replied Fran.

'Good, well, we can all help bring up your bags.' Then in a crisp, commanding tone, she said, 'Come on, everyone, look lively.'

Isaac moved towards Tom. 'Give me the keys and I'll park the car in one of the sheds.'

'OK,' said Tom, dropping the keys into Isaac's open hand.

Fran glanced at Tom, concerned at seeing Isaac climbing into her car.

Tom opened the back of the car and handed out the luggage, taking the precious evening dresses himself. He closed the boot and knocked on the rear window, which Isaac acknowledged with a wave before starting the engine and disappearing up the drive.

'You're in the Oak Room,' Charlotte said. 'We've done a lot of work inside while Tom has been away.'

Fran was pleased with the cool of the hall with its square flagstone floor providing a few degrees of relief from the heat outside. The stairs were dark wood with wide treads and a red-carpet runner. The banister rail's twisted design was from the same old dark wood and ran up the stairs, then continued around the first-floor gallery.

'Impressive, isn't it?' said Tom. 'The floor is the original house flagstones. The stairs were installed three hundred years ago. You can see to your right the original front door open to the Vale. Just to the right is the entrance to the dining room.'

Fran nodded, glancing over as she climbed the shallow stairs.

'Behind the stairs is the entrance to the kitchen,' continued Tom.

Fran looked about her in awe at the house, the grand entrance hall and its even grander staircase. *Home*, she thought, but didn't know what to say.

'I can see the sky,' said Fran, looking up.

'Lantern window installed by the Edwardians; it would have been very gloomy before then,' said Tom, admiring the light that flowed down the length of the hall's atrium.

'Spectacular,' breathed Fran, still taking it all in. 'How do you get to the second floor?' she asked as they steadily mounted the stairs.

'Via the back stairs, which are just down the corridor to the left. They used to be the servants' stairs, go to the second and third floors, but now used by everyone,' answered Tom.

The group turned right at the top of the stairs, along the gallery, and stopped at a white-painted wooden door with 'Oak' written in curly letters halfway down.

'Yes, Tom, it is your old room, but now completely refurbished and updated, as I'm sure you'll notice.'

They all entered the room and bags were placed down on the thick carpeted and rug-covered floor.

'Lunch is at one o'clock. See you both then,' said Charlotte as she ushered Pen and the twins out of the room. Suddenly, they were alone.

Tom looked around the room, slowly opening doors, exploring what had once been his teenage domain: a new ensuite bathroom with wet area and bath, a walk-in wardrobe and a small sitting room-study all attached to the bedroom the two of them now stood in.

'They have been busy,' said Tom, nodding his head in acknowledgement of the work carried out. 'Much better than the old, cold, smelly room I left behind!'

Fran quietly clapped her hands in front of her chest as she followed Tom around the room, excited by everything she saw.

'The decor in here is cool,' she said, inspecting the cream walls and the repeating pattern of branches and vines creeping up them and across the ceiling, finally surrounding the chandelier and ceiling rose centrepiece. 'Amazing,' she said with wonder.

'Cool, yes, but even cooler in winter. Unless they have sorted out the heating,' added Tom, running his hand along a new radiator hanging by the main door. 'Maybe they have!' he concluded with a shrug, now also studying the walls and ceiling. 'That's painted on, not wallpaper, and it does look like oak with vines and ivy running through it. Yes, amazing. I assume each of the other rooms with tree names are finished the same. They have been busy. But it needed doing.'

'Look at the view.' Fran gasped as she stopped hopping about, the initial excitement fading, and skated through the thick carpet to stand in the wide bay window which stretched almost the length of the room and looked out across the Vale. 'That's the Vale I assume?'

'Yes, and you can see the wood rising at the bottom of the slope from the house,' said Tom, walking up behind her and wrapping his arms around her, kissing the back of her head.

Fran wriggled to escape his embrace. 'Sorry, far too hot,' she said as she turned and kissed him on the cheek.

Tom checked the time. 'Lunch at 1.00 pm, in thirty minutes,' he said at the same time as there was a gentle knock on the door. 'Come in,' he responded.

The door swung open and in walked a short woman in her late fifties or early sixties, followed by a taller, slim, pretty younger woman in her early twenties.

'Mrs Cooper,' said Tom, smiling. 'How good to see you. Are you well?'

'Yes, thank you, very well, except for being older and stiffer. It's good to see you back, Thomas.' She turned to Fran. 'You must be Francesca. Pleasure to meet you,' she said offering her hand, which Fran respectfully took. 'Now, I'm the housekeeper for the house, and this is Jackie, one of the two assistant housekeepers, the other being Anna. Anything you need, just let any of us know. There's always one of us in the house, including overnight. Can we unpack your bags for you while you are at lunch?'

'There's really no need,' said Fran, feeling slightly embarrassed at the request.

'Well, those lovely dresses need hanging properly or they'll look like rags.' And with that Mrs Cooper waved at Jackie, pointed at the dresses and then at the walk-in wardrobe Fran had not long ago been admiring.

Jackie nodded, and smoothly went to pick up the dresses and hang them.

Fran felt awkward and embarrassed at someone her own age doing this for her.

'How's Mr Cooper?' enquired Tom, breaking the tense silence.

'He's well, thank you, but the nursery is so busy. He has two apprentices now but needs more help to keep up, especially as he can't really do the heavy lifting anymore and both the apprentices have day release for college.' She stopped with a sigh.

'Still live in Woodend?' asked Tom

'No, we have a cottage on the estate now, which makes things a lot easier for both of us.'

'Do you live in Woodend?' Tom asked Jackie as she closed the wardrobe door behind her, having hung up the dresses.

'No, sir, Woodcoombe Village, as does Anna.'

'Longer journey to work, I guess?' enquired Tom.

'Not really. There is still a path where the old road used to run from the estate to the village, and it's usually a lovely walk. If the weather is really bad, we call an apprentice to pick us up.'

'And I'm sure they are more than glad to do so.' Tom smiled as the memory of leaving years ago by the same route flashed in his head.

Was that a flirt? thought Fran.

Jackie smiled, turning to Fran. 'Lovely dresses, madam, especially the one with the low back. Not sure I would ever have the nerve or place to wear it.'

'Thank you,' responded Fran. 'Not sure I have the nerve yet.' They both laughed, but Mrs Cooper huffed, not liking the familiarity between the younger women.

'Lunch will be served soon. Plenty more people for you both to meet. Jackie, please stay and help with unpacking while they are gone. Francesca, if you need anything just let us know.' Mrs Cooper stared hard at Jackie and, as she passed her to leave the room, said, 'No gossiping.'

The bedroom door made a satisfying, soft but solid noise as it closed behind Mrs Cooper.

Immediately Jackie reached down and picked up one of Fran's bags, placing it on the bed, unzipping it.

Fran watched, slightly in horror, as tightly packed underwear exploded out on to the bed. 'I really can do that.'

'I've no doubt, you can, madam,' replied Jackie as she skilfully sorted out the freed, expanding clothing, 'but it's my job.'

'Oh, I see. Or do I?'

'Madam, there are few jobs round here and this is a good one. The pay's good and they look after you very well. Mrs Cooper is not getting any younger so there's a chance to become housekeeper in this grand house at some point. I understand your concern, madam, but please, let me do this for you.'

'OK,' said Fran feeling a bit deflated but not really knowing why. 'Sorry,' she added.

'Nothing to be sorry about, madam, I appreciate the thought.'

'Come on,' said Tom, opening the bedroom door for Fran. 'There's something I want to show you before we go into lunch.' He took Fran's hand and led her round the first-floor gallery to a plain arched opening. 'The back stairs,' he said as he led the way down the enclosed, anti-clockwise spiral stairs, still holding Fran's hand. 'Leads to the ground floor corridor, which runs the length of the house, joining all the rooms.'

'Oh,' said Fran. 'Where are we going?'

'The library. There's something I want to show you. More history, I'm afraid, but it's important.'

Fran nodded. *So much history*, she thought to herself. 'Well, I didn't expect a servant to pop up!' she quietly exclaimed. 'All a bit embarrassing, I thought.'

'Only for you, I think,' replied Tom. 'Yes, sorry, I should have mentioned it, but if I had, would it have made any difference? And we don't refer to anyone as servants. They are all staff. It's quite a difference.'

'I might not have embarrassed myself or Jackie,' Fran retorted.

'You're overthinking it. You were very polite and respectful and showed understanding when Jackie explained. Trust me, if you had had that conversation with Mrs Cooper, she would have given you very short shrift on the subject. Remember, we have a lot of staff doing all sorts of things across the estate and family businesses, and it sounds like we have more now than when I left. I imagine some will be at lunch.'

They came to the bottom of the stairs into the corridor. Tom walked to a door just to their right. 'Library,' Tom announced as he opened the door and held it open for Fran.

Tom followed and walked past Fran as she admired the walls of books. At the end of the room were two high windows with two large, comfortable looking leather wing-backed armchairs in the best light for reading.

Fran walked up to Tom, still looking around the room, taking it all in.

'The Royal Charter, *The Book of the Dead* and the Map of Souls,' said Tom as he stood by the square map chest that sat in the middle of the room.

'What!' responded Fran, with wide eyes.

Tom bent slightly and pulled out one of the thin document drawers. 'This is a copy of the Royal Charter granting us the lands and titles. It's a very good copy. The original is in the British Museum, and is thought to be the oldest such document still in existence.'

Fran tried to look interested, but she was feeling history fatigue.

Tom closed the drawer and pulled on white gloves, which Fran found intriguing, before pulling a very old book mounted on a wooden plinth on the top of the chest towards him; the *Book of the Dead*.

Fran peered forward to see what it was. *Sounds interesting*, she thought.

'In here is listed everyone who has died on the estate,' Tom explained. 'You can see here the last two entries for Isaac's wife and my grandmother.'

Fran looked, feeling it was all a bit strange, perhaps even macabre. Tom stepped back slightly and pulled open another document drawer.

'This is the Map of Souls. It shows where everyone in the *Book of the Dead* is buried in the Vale.'

Fran frowned, feeling confused. 'Buried in the Vale!' she said as she leant in, looking at the book and the map, trying to understand what it meant. 'For your grand-mother, what does WW mean?'

'Weeping Willow, and Isaac's wife is an H for Haw-thorn,' said Tom, pointing at the map.

'They're buried with these trees?' asked Fran, feeling a bit mystified.

'Not exactly. The tree is planted where they are buried. People can choose the tree they would like and it is grown ready in the nursery that Mrs Cooper's husband manages.'

'That's different!' Fran looked again at the book and the map. 'How many are buried then?'

'Well, the first was the first Lord, Brandon Wood-coombe, who was buried with an oak about a thousand years ago. The oak still stands. I believe over five hundred souls are buried in the Vale. Not all family. Workers and their families can request the same, as you can see from Isaac's wife.'

'Why?' asked Fran.

'What comes from the earth returns to the earth,' said Tom.

'What does that mean?'

'We believe the earth and all the life within it are im-portant and that we are part of that life and its cycle, not separate from it. So, it's a way of returning and honouring that belief and bond. Everything starts with the land. It's not compulsory.'

'I see, I think. It's all about the link you have with land and the life within it.'

'That's more or less it. It's a bit like the Buddhists think everything is interrelated and all life should be respected. So, on death we return a person's energy to the land and it will return in another form.'

'A person's energy?' said Fran, confused.

'Yes, the essence, consciousness of the person, their soul, spirit, if you like, lives on, released from its physical bonds by their passing.'

'Passing, do you mean death?'

Tom nodded. 'The solstice tomorrow is part of that link and respect to the land. It's nothing to be worried or frightened of. I actually now find it rather reassuring,' said Tom, smiling. 'Makes more sense than Heaven and Hell. It's old beliefs, magic if you like.'

'Not to some, it won't. I have to say it sounds a bit weird, hippies on steroids. Some must think it's all mumbo jumbo.' Fran laughed, but on seeing Tom's face drop added, 'But I will keep my mind open as I learn and understand more about it.'

'Thank you,' said Tom. 'It means a lot to many people here.'

They left the library and walked the short distance back to the hall. The walls and flagstone floor offered some respite to the swirling heat outside. The main door to the Vale was open and they could see the heat shimmering over the dry grass, a heat which leached into the hall, no breeze giving any relief. Fran was pleased she'd taken Pen's advice and dressed for the heat, in loose white cotton culottes and a light blue linen blouse, but she was still hot and aware she was a bit sweaty.

'Excuse me, please,' came a bright voice from the aproned, tray-carrying woman who had appeared from the kitchen behind the stairs.

They both stepped to the side nearer to the main door and heat.

They were thanked cheerfully as the tray was carried briskly through to the dining room.

'Lunch,' Tom said.

'Is it formal? Should I have changed?' asked Fran, a little irate, having spied her hair in the mirror and deciding it really needed a comb or tying up.

'No, no. It's very informal and open to everyone working in the house and a few out. It's usually an extensive buffet. Don't worry, there'll be plenty of people there I don't know.' Tom smiled and walked towards the dining room door. Fran followed, holding his hand, her grip, though, a bit sweaty, tightening with slight apprehension.

The room was bright, with large high windows allowing the light to stream in. The walls were stark white and with black wood beams set in the wall creating varying sized squares. Two big chandeliers hung from a thick black beam that ran the length of the room. The chandeliers' crystals refracted sunlight that played around the room and danced in the white squares and on the dark wood to the beat of the heat. The huge main table was set with many places on a crisp white cloth, some places taken, others vacant. A warm, friendly hum of chatter flowed around the room with the occasional word or laugh surfacing and floating in the voluminous space. The food was laid out on a long, old, dark sideboard. Only cold offerings, the day was too hot to consider anything else.

Fran noticed three young women in long, white full aprons serving and helping the hungry throng. Then out of the corner of her eye saw Mrs Copper standing by the door checking nothing was out of place.

'Can I assist you, madam?' Mrs Cooper asked Fran, having spied her and thinking she looked slightly lost.

'Thank you,' replied Fran. 'This is all new and very different to me.'

'Quite understand, madam, but nothing to be frightened of. Just think of it as a canteen for lunch like any workplace.'

Some canteen! Fran thought, with a momentary flash to the university canteen she rarely used. *Some workplace!*

'Now, what would you like?' asked Mrs Cooper, holding a plate. 'I can recommend the salmon.'

'With salad please, no potatoes, thank you,' said Fran with a smile, grateful to be rescued from her stage fright.

Mrs Cooper started to load the plate. Fran, standing next to her, pointed at a bowl of interesting beetroot salad she thought looked nice, which was duly added. Once complete, Mrs Cooper steered Fran to two empty places at the table, placed down Fran's plate and then pulled out the chair for her to sit down.

'Thank you, Mrs Cooper,'

'You're most welcome. Remember; if you need anything just ask.'

'Thank you, much appreciated,' said Fran as Mrs Cooper
turned to continue surveying the service of lunch.

'All, OK?' said Tom as he pulled out his chair to sit next
to Fran while juggling a plate, a glass of white wine and a
lively white bread roll that kept trying to escape.

'Yes, thanks.'

'You and Mrs Cooper friends now?' said Tom with a
smile.

'Best buds,' Fran said as she started to eat. *Better than
any canteen she could remember*, she thought. 'Is lunch provided every day?'

'Yes, during the week. Weekends, it's just family and
their guests.'

There was suddenly a ringing of clinking glass and
Fran saw Charlotte, Tom's mother, holding an empty glass
by its stem and tapping it gently with a knife to gain the
attention of the room.

'Lewis and the other men will be having lunch provided
at the lower stand where they are working, so they will
not be joining us today.' Charlotte sat down and the convivial hum of conversation and noise of eating returned
to the room.

'Would that have been the men we saw working when
we drove in?' Fran asked Tom.

'I guess,' Tom answered as he looked about for someone
to ask and confirm. 'Nick,' Tom projected across the table.
A tanned man in his late forties, Fran guessed, looked up,
pleased to see Tom, and immediately stood up. It was too

far to say hello or shake hands over the table so he pushed out his chair and walked round the table.

'Thomas, so good to see you,' said Nick as he and Tom warmly shook hands.

'Nice to see you, Nick.'

'You must be Francesca?'

'Yes, but please call me Fran.'

'Bet Isaac doesn't like that,' said Nick, laughing.

'Nick's the estate manager. You must have been here nearly ten years, I guess,' said Tom.

'Yes, ten years this year and never been busier, and we now have an expanding management team, who I was just talking to over there.' As he spoke, Nick turned and waved across the table. A blonde woman older than Fran, perhaps thirty, waved back and left her seat to walk round and join them.

'Hi, I'm Lucy Hayward, commercial manager, been here six months,' she said, briskly shaking hands with Tom and Fran.

'And what does a commercial manager do?' enquired Tom. Fran lent in slightly, also interested to know.

'I'm looking at how we might open the estate to the public more often than its current three days a year and also what else could be considered, like a small hotel or experience weekends.'

'I see,' said Tom. 'All important potential revenue with the plans that seem to be going on.'

'We also have a finance manager, Natasha, as well as an in-house head of legal, Kelvin, to make sure we don't all land up going to jail. But I can't see either of them here,' added Nick.

'Blimey, things have started to get very grown up since I've been gone,' said Tom. 'I assume we still use the family solicitors, Gilbert, Hays and Brookes?'

Nick shrugged.

'I think Kelvin came from there on some kind of secondment. I thought he would be at lunch. I only saw him this morning to talk about potential issues we need to consider if we open regularly to the public,' added Lucy.

Fran wondered if there was something more going on with Lucy and Kelvin by the

intimate, knowing tone with which she spoke about him. *Perhaps I'm overthinking again*, Fran thought. *Or perhaps not.*

There was a sudden rumpus at the dining room door as the twins made a late entrance. Fran spotted Mrs Cooper moving smoothly but quickly to head them off. 'Catherine, Jennifer, come and sit here please,' said Mrs Cooper in a raised voice.

Fran noticed they didn't argue and were sullen-faced as they sat down as directed. *You don't argue with Mrs Cooper*, thought Fran with a grin. She watched as she waved over one of the white-aproned girls. 'Now, ladies, give Gail your order and she will get it for you, and remember, be nice.' Both girls nodded and quietly spoke to Gail, who Fran thought had the slightest smirk on her face.

'Your father threw them out of lunch last week and told them if they couldn't behave and act civil, they could eat in the kitchen on their own when everyone had finished.

Told Mrs C to not tolerate any poor behaviour and make sure they are kept in line.'

'So, Nick, Father is still as sharp on manners as he always was.'

'Indeed,' said Nick, laughing. 'But it was quite a kerfuffle, which I think shocked a few new to the estate!'

The four parted and returned to their seats to finish lunch. As Fran sat down a voice over her shoulder asked, 'Madam, can I get you a drink?'

'Yes, please, do you have something soft? I really don't want any wine in this heat.'

'Homemade lemonade is very good. With ice?'

'Yes, please.'

The girl disappeared for a moment, returning with a tall tumbler of lemonade and ice which she placed to Fran's right.

'Thank you, what's your name?'

'Olivia, madam.'

'Nice to meet you, Olivia. Do you work in the kitchen?'

'Yes, I'm one of the assistant cooks.'

'Where do you live?'

'On the estate. My father's a forester and my brother an apprentice.'

Fran sipped the cold lemonade. She was tempted to wipe the glass's cold condensation across her face, but decided it probably wasn't the done thing and would also smear her make-up and make her look even more of a fright! 'Thank you.'

'You're welcome, madam,' said Olivia with a smile, before turning to attend to someone else.

Bloody hell, my parents will love this, thought Fran. *Need to make sure they don't get carried away.* A bit of reconciliation was needed before then as well, she realised. She felt a weight momentarily return to her heart.

'Madam.' A different voice was speaking over Fran's shoulder.

'Yes,' Fran responded, half turning to see who it was.

'Do you need anything?'

'Actually, this heat is boiling my head. You couldn't find a headband or similar so I can put my hair up?'

'Yes, madam, I'm sure we can help.'

'Thank you. Gail, isn't it? I noticed you serving the twins. Do you live on the estate, like Olivia?'

'No, Woodend, madam, so not far.'

'Do you like working here?' Fran asked, interested.

'Of course, madam, it was either here or The Oak. It's a good job and relatively well paid. They train you and, with so much change coming, no doubt there are opportunities for everyone. Give me a moment, madam, I think I have just the thing.'

Gail turned and walked away.

'OK, thank you,' said Fran, and returned to her food and the cooling lemonade as Gail disappeared through the dining room door. A few moments later she walked back in and came straight round to Fran.

'Will this do, madam?' Gail said, placing a black sports headband beside Fran.

'Yes, thank you, I'll get it back to you. You're usually in the kitchen, I guess?'

'Yes, madam, give it to any of the girls.'

Fran turned the headband over in her hand, thinking it was not exactly glamorous, but it would have to do.

Fran realised one of the twins, Jen, was standing next to Tom. 'Everything OK?' she asked.

Tom nudged Fran. 'Jen has suggested we all go to see Father who is working down the Vale on the stand of trees we passed coming in.'

'Sounds good,' said Fran thinking, *that's going to be warm!* 'I need to go to the bathroom first.'

'OK. We'll meet you in the hallway in ten minutes,' Tom said to Jen.

Jen clapped her hands and skipped away, walking back carefully round the table when she noticed Mrs Cooper staring sternly at her.

'Ready?' asked Tom.

'Yes,' replied Fran, pushing her chair back. They walked out of the dining room into the hall.

~ 6 ~

'The bathroom is just there,' said Tom pointing to a door in an alcove to the right of the kitchen entrance behind the stairs.

'Won't be long,' said Fran as she darted towards the bathroom. The floor and walls were tiled in small cream, blue, white and occasionally red coloured mosaic tiles that formed a swirling pattern on the floor and a repeat isometric pattern around the walls. *Victorian?* Fran wondered. The room was cool and brought relief from the heat outside, if only momentarily. She closed the door behind her, remembering to turn the lock, and took the three steps across the swirling floor to the white sink and wall-mounted mirror. *God, I look a wreck*, she thought. She picked up a flannel and towel from the wooden table to the right of the sink, ran cold water over the flannel and washed her face and neck, ensuring she didn't leave any smears or stripes of make-up across her face. *I think I've sweated most of my make-up off,* she thought, but at least she felt a bit cooler and fresher after the quick wash. She wiped her arms with the cool flannel, dried herself with the towel and then threw both into the wicker basket provided under the sink. She looked at herself in the mirror and sighed. *Nothing I can do now*, she thought. *There's no point reapplying any make-up if we're going out in the heat.*

She twirled the headband Gail had given her round her fingers. *How's this best going to work?* she wondered. Fran pulled the headband over her head until it hung limp around her neck then pushed it up to the top of her forehead and up the back of her head and above her ears, capturing her hair and raising it up off her neck. She looked at the result.

I look like something from an old keep-fit video or at best an extra from Fame! A refugee from the '80s, she chuckled to herself.

She could feel air now her hair was lifted and no longer insulating her neck. She took one last look in the mirror, winked at herself and walked back to meet Tom in the hall.

Tom was standing with the twins and Pen.

'That's a great idea,' squealed Cath, seeing Fran's hair. 'Like me, I guess ponytails don't work with your hair?'

'No,' said Fran, not really happy having her new look pointed out.

Tom looked at Fran. What has she done to her hair? he thought, but was wise enough not to say anything out loud.

'Pen, what are Father and the men doing?' asked Tom as the five of them slowly drifted towards the door.

'They're working on the lower stand, taking down and digging out all the elms. Disease has done for them. They hoped that, given time and a bit of luck, the tree would work out how to adapt and cope, as they can do, but they didn't and have become dangerous, so they are taking them all out. All the foresters and apprentices have been working on it for the last three days.'

'That's a shame, bloody hot work,' said Tom.

'Indeed,' replied Pen, taking a step nearer the door.

They walked out into the Vale and into the heat of the afternoon. The air was very hot and heat radiated up from the dry grassy and dusty ground. They strolled, steering right and walking down the Vale's gentle slope towards what had been the elm stand.

'Christ, it's hot!' said Tom, feeling his shirt start to stick to him almost immediately. *The girls don't look too bothered*, he thought as the twin's held hands and started to run down the gentle slope. *How can they do that?* he wondered, aware his face was wet and probably red from the sun. He really needed a hat.

'Not running?' asked Pen as she drew up to his left as they walked.

'How do they do it?' echoed Fran out loud, walking close on Tom's right-hand side.

'I love them dearly, but they are both a bit mad, especially Cath. They're probably getting ready to run down to the stand through the top meadow, which they love to do.' Pen stopped for a moment to wipe her forehead with the back of her hand, before taking three quick steps to catch up, shaking her head and swirling her long ponytail around in a vain attempt to find some cool air.

As Pen arrived back next to Tom, he said, 'Meadow, that's new.'

'Yes. The top meadow is four years old. The bottom meadow further down the Vale is three years old, part of the wilding work, and seed sales from both are good earners,' said Pen with a smile. 'A few minutes and we will be at the top meadow. It really is something to see and walk through.' Pen wiped her forehead again with the back of her hand.

'Beautiful,' said Tom as they stood at the top of the meadow, a tapestry carpet of colour, bobbing and swaying plant heads a foot or more above the parched ground.

'Various plants, rattle, daisy, buttercup, campion, plantain and others,' Pen said wistfully as she surveyed the waving and nodding carpet of colour. 'And some early cornflower. Probably the hot June has brought them on early.' She gave a satisfied smile at the scene in front of them.

Tom took Fran's hand as they stepped into the carpet of grass and wild flowers. He could hear the gentle hum of all types of busy flying, jumping, and crawling life working in the colourful swaying carpet.

'What do you think?' Tom asked Fran, whose hand slipped from his due to the heat and sweat.

'Beautiful, as you said,' she replied as she grasped his hand again, aware of both his and her own sweat.

They walked through the meadow, which was alive with life, the heat seemingly not bothering either plant or the meadow life. Squadrons of bees, gathering nectar, and low flying, skimming birds were unmoved by their steps through the colourful, fragrant carpet.

Tom raised his arm, letting go of Fran's hand, and pointed down the Vale over the meadow. 'There you can see the stand where the elms were and the men and machines are, and—' Tom paused, 'horses.'

'Horses!' repeated Fran.

'Yes, we keep heavy horses and use them around the estate. They are kinder to the ground than machines and often more practical in the woods.'

Fran nodded in recognition of what Tom had said and at the same time was walking slightly crouched with bent knees, trailing her hand through the meadow plants, amazed at the perfumed scent her hand released to swirl up into the hot air. Fran paused and stood up straight, luxuriating in the heady, lush scent of the combined meadow flowers and land.

Tom stopped briefly, half turned and waved to her to come on. 'Too hot to lounge in the meadow today, Fran. We're nearly at the stand and it looks like they have shade and will almost certainly have something to drink.'

Fran caught up with Tom and saw the line of gazebos set up beyond the meadow in a line next to where the elms had once stood. The men sat resting under them, escaping the sun, finishing the lunch brought from the house. Fran looked down at her clothes. To her relief everything looked fine; crumpled, creased and a bit dusty perhaps, but nothing embarrassing to worry about.

'You, OK?' asked Pen, who was a few steps behind.

'Just checking I'm not going to embarrass myself wearing thin clothes in this heat.'

'Quite understand,' said Pen as she walked round Fran checking for any signs. 'Just a small sweat line down your spine at the top of your blouse, but nothing to worry about.'

'Thanks,' said Fran.

The two sped up slightly and caught Tom, who now stood at the bottom edge of the meadow, his shirt hanging soaked with sweat on his back.

'Nearly there,' said Pen with a sigh of relief and another wipe of her forehead with the back of her hand.

The three walked towards the many men. The twins were ahead already, talking to some boys.

'Crickey, all the men are topless,' Fran said. 'Stripped down because of the heat I guess, hot work.' Fran was looking over at the twins and the young, tanned, muscular boys they were talking to. 'I can see why they hurried,' she said with a laugh.

'That's Dan, who Cath is seeing,' said Pen.

'Is that a problem then?' asked Fran.

'We hope not.' Pen's face slightly tightened for a moment.

Tom suddenly saw his father emerge from a group of resting men and walk towards him, pulling on his shirt as he did. Fran noted that he looked like Tom. He was around six feet tall, but broader and more muscular, and tanned from the outdoor work. He had brown hair, with what looked like the same wave in it as Tom but in the heat slicked down with sweat. *I need to get Tom working outside*, Fran thought, having seen the results in the men in front of her.

'Tom, Tom,' Lewis shouted with his arms outstretched now his shirt was on, but still unbuttoned and billowing out behind him as he strode purposefully towards Tom, just getting to him before Pen and Fran.

'Hello, son, how are you? Surviving the heat? I'm so pleased to see you.' He stretched his arms wide for a hug, but to Tom's relief decided against it and settled on a vigorous but damp hand shake accompanied by a broad laughing smile. Lewis paused and released Tom's hand, but kept the open smiling face as Fran and Pen caught up. 'You must be Francesca,' he said with a slight bow. 'A pleasure to meet you.' He held out a hand which Fran shook, holding the ends of his fingers to avoid the sweat. 'I'm sorry at my dreadful state. Third day getting the trees down and stumps out. I've told the men we will stop now for the day; it is Friday and most of the work is done. We had lunch brought down from the house and Isaac is bringing cold beer. You can get a lift back to the house with him rather than walk back up in this heat.'

'Is it always this hot?' asked Fran.

'The whole of June has been hot and dry. It's progressively got hotter as the month's gone on,' said Lewis, who paused, looking thoughtful for a moment. 'Each June over the last ten years has been progressively drier and hotter, but this year has been the worst. The meadow's early and the trees already look stressed. Luckily, we don't really have any crops to worry about and we won't replant the stand here until the autumn.'

'Global warming?' offered Fran.

'Certainly, contributes but no one really seems that interested. To most it just means more time on the beach and an earlier tan.'

'OK, Dad, let's not get all wound up on this now. It's far too hot and it's Fran's first visit.'

'Yes, of course, I'm sorry. You don't want to hear me going on about this now.' He shrugged and waved his hand around him for effect. 'But it does not only impact the estate, but everyone. Please, Francesca, call me Lewis. I believe you've met the rest of the clan.'

He was interrupted by the sound of an engine and a horn sounding three brief times.

'Beer!' said Lewis, turning towards the sound.

Fran saw all the men get up and walk towards the Land Rover. As it stopped, two men opened the tailgate with a metallic crash, pulled out crates of beer and started handing them out. There followed a rolling sound of bottles hissing as they opened, followed by appreciative sighs as the first cooling gulps were swigged and hit the men's dry throats.

'Here we go.' A huge man, in his forties, Fran guessed, around six feet five, wearing battered combat trousers and heavy working boots walked up to them. He was stripped to the waist, covered in sweat, very muscular and *a bit frightening*, thought Fran. Beer bottles were jammed between his fingers in his huge hands. He passed one to Lewis and then offered bottles to everyone else. Fran didn't normally drink beer, but the sight and thought of the chill of condensation offering a promise of cool relief was too much to refuse and she gratefully accepted.

'Good to see you, Thomas.'

'And you, Duncan, especially with this,' replied Tom, tipping his bottle in gratitude towards Duncan. 'Thank you.'

'No problem. Hot for all of us, whatever you've been doing.'

'Hot work, sir,' a smiling Isaac said to Lewis as he walked up to the group. 'Should roughly be two bottles each, so things shouldn't get unruly.' He smiled and looked at Duncan, who still had two unopened bottles stuck to his hand.

'Well done, Isaac. Can you run Tom and the girls to the house on your way back please?' asked Lewis as he tipped his bottle high to his mouth, draining the last drips of beer. Duncan automatically offered Lewis one of the precious spares he carried, which Lewis gratefully took with a nod of thanks.

'You guys ready?' said Isaac as he turned to walk back to the Land Rover.

'Yes,' said Tom, following Isaac, with Fran and Pen a few steps behind.

'We'll get in the back,' Tom said, helping first Pen then Fran into the back of the vehicle, before jumping in himself. Isaac slammed the tailgate closed and secured it before walking round to get in the driving seat.

Tom, Fran and Pen sat either side on the bench seating that ran along both sides of the covered space. A small window in the bulkhead between the front and back of the Land Rover opened.

'What about the twins?' asked Isaac.

'Leave them, they'll be fine,' replied Pen. The boys will run them back, if they don't walk.'

'Hold on tight, it will be a bit bumpy.' The small window snapped closed, Isaac started the engine and every part of the Land Rover immediately began to vibrate noisily and shake before Isaac pulled away.

It was bumpy and Fran marvelled at how Pen and Tom could sit in the bucking vehicle. They just seemed to sway in rhythm with every unpredictable bump. She had to steady herself by holding onto Tom's knee. Pen laughed and said something which Fran couldn't hear above the noise and vibration of the engine and the groaning suspension.

'We'll be on the road in a moment,' shouted Pen, which Fran acknowledged with a grin and a nod, as suddenly the jolting stopped and the ride smoothed.

Isaac stopped by the door Tom and Fran had arrived at only hours before. *Where does time go in this place?* thought Fran. They were all pleased to get inside the house and get some relief away from the heat.

'See you at dinner,' said Pen as she walked up the stairs with Tom and Fran.

'Seven o'clock?' asked Tom.

'Yes. If you need anything, Fran, just let me know via the house staff.'

'OK,' Fran answered, with a smile.

At the top of the stairs Pen turned left, Fran and Tom

right. 'I'm just down here in Meadow if you need anything,' said Pen.

Tom had already opened their door, kicked off his shoes and was undressing as he walked towards the bathroom. His shirt hit the floor, then his trouser belt was pulled off and thrown towards the bed. He paused as he stepped out of his dropped trousers and boxers and walked naked into the bathroom and under the large silver showerhead. Tom switched the temperature knob to cold and paused for a moment before flicking the shower on. The cold water, first a shock, then a relief, powered down onto him, making him catch his breath, but with the cooling relief his normal breath soon returned. He reached out for the shower gel to clean and dispel the smell of sweat he knew he had. Then he grabbed a towel and walked back into the bedroom while drying himself.

'Nice shower?' asked Fran, closing the main bedroom door, having watched Pen disappear into her room further down the corridor.

'Brilliant. Bit of a shock at first, but a relief to be cool and clean.' Tom was still drying himself as he walked across the room, dropping the towel to the ground before he fell naked onto the bed. 'A nap now I think, dinner at seven. What time do you need to start getting ready?'

Fran surveyed Tom's smelly, sweat-soaked clothes and wet towel strewn across the floor, and then looked at him. His body was slightly pink from the cold shower, with the exception of his sunburnt head, neck and lower arms. He laid out on the bed, ready to sleep.

'Five o'clock. Two hours should be more than enough. Shall I clear up your mess then?'

Tom sat up, looking irritated. 'I'll do it.' He jumped off the bed and picked up his discarded items by his finger-tips as even he had to admit they stank. He walked to the laundry basket, opened the lid and dropped them in.

'Done. I'll set my phone for five.' And with that he walked back to the bed.

He'll be snoring in a minute, thought Fran as she entered the bathroom, undressed and, like Tom before her, was soon standing under the showerhead getting ready for the shock of the cold rush of water. She caught her breath once and then luxuriated in the cool flow washing over her. She washed her hair, using shampoo and conditioner, wondering what damage the sun had done. She washed her body and then stepped out of the cooling shower to dry herself and immediately could hear the gentle heavy breathing, not quite a snore, of Tom laid out naked on the bed.

She was soon dry and walked back into the bedroom, dropping her clothes into the laundry bin, wrinkling her nose at the smell of Tom's sweaty clothes that wafted up from the opening and closing of the lid.

Fran now stood naked by the bed, finding comfort and reassurance in Tom's steady, deep breathing. She lay down next to him and gradually drifted to sleep, enjoying the feeling of her chilled, showered skin.

~ 7 ~

Fran woke with a start from a knock on the door. She slid off the bed, walked to the door and slipped on one of the thick white towelling robes hanging on the back, for the use of guests. Tom stirred with a snuffle and a snore. Fran watched him, still half asleep, getting up from the bed and rather unattractively scratching himself.

'For God's sake,' Fran said, both irritated and amused. 'Put this on. There's someone at the door.' She threw the other guest robe towards Tom.

The knock at the door was repeated and, at the same time, Tom's phone alarm burst into life. Tom slightly stumbled in his half-asleep state into the bedside table to turn off the alarm now blaring out. With it silenced, he quickly pulled on the robe, securing the two sides across his front and tying the belt round his waist. He then looked up at Fran and grinned.

Fran sighed and smiled back at Tom who didn't realise in his haste to don the robe he'd left his bits flashing.

Fran opened the door a crack, not wanting to expose anyone to Tom's unfortunate peep show.

'Sorry, madam, didn't mean to disturb you.' It was Jackie.

'No problem.'

'Does your dress for tonight need a press?' asked Jackie.

'No, it should be fine. They've all been dry cleaned recently and you kindly hung them up earlier.'

'If you're sure, madam. But if you change your mind, just let me know.'

'OK, thank you Jackie, and thanks for unpacking.'

'You're very welcome, madam.'

Fran watched Jackie walk towards Meadow and knock on the door, which opened slightly and then wider to let Jackie in.

'Fuck!' Tom laughed as Fran closed the door. He was standing in front of the full-length mirror, swinging his hips and looking very pleased with himself. 'What do you think?' he asked as he turned around, grinning.

'You need a bigger robe,' said Fran with a giggle.

'No wonder this is a problem,' said Tom as he pulled off the robe and, standing naked, checked the label. 'It's a small, is yours a large?'

'Possibly, it's very snug though,' giggled Fran. 'Right, I should get on, and do my hair. I guess you will only need ten minutes to get ready as usual?' She walked to the dressing table and sat down, plugged in her hair straighteners and started furiously brushing her hair.

'Shirt could do with an iron,' announced Tom. 'I'll call housekeeping.' He picked up the internal phone. 'Jackie will be round in a moment. She's in the process of collecting shirts and dresses for pressing and ironing.'

'That was her at the door a moment ago,'

'Bloody hell! I'm glad you didn't let her in,' said Tom, laughing, suddenly feeling self-conscious. 'We'd better swap robes before she knocks again.'

Fran sighed heavily to show her combination of irritation and frustration. Her hair was not going well. She stood up, took off the robe and looked at the label.

'Large,' Fran said as she held the robe out to Tom and they completed the exchange.

Tom then reached out to pull the still naked Fran towards him when there was another knock at the door.

'That'll be for you,' said Fran, smiling as he wrestled on the large robe. 'There, that covers everything.' A disappointed Tom took the shirt he wanted from the wardrobe and then strode back to the door, opening it slightly and sliding it through the gap to the waiting Jackie.

'All done,' said Tom, walking back towards Fran, who was now a picture of concentration, alternatively brushing and straightening her hair.

'Sorry, Tom, I need to get my hair done. No time for anything else.'

'Oh. OK. Understand,' said a deflated Tom. He plonked himself on the bed and picked up the television remote. 'I think there's football on.'

Fran could see him in the dressing table mirror and she thought he looked like a naughty puppy who'd been told no, all wide-eyed and disappointed.

Fran continued wrestling with her hair to a soundtrack of football blaring out. Tom got up to put on his boxers and socks.

'Wow, that's attractive. Don't let the staff see you like that,' said Fran with a giggle.

'What do you mean?'

'Have a look.'

A slouching Tom plodded up to the full-length mirror and stood admiring himself, making several different poses for effect. 'Hmmm, guess it makes you realise what a lucky girl you are!'

Fran laughed, feeling better now about her hair, which was finally co-operating. 'Yes, I am truly blessed.'

'Blessed are the loved,' replied Tom with a warm laugh, 'and I love you.'

'I love you, too.'

'Thank you,' said Tom, and Fran watched in the mirror as he came to stand beside her at the dressing table.

'Phwoar! How can any girl resist a man in ankle socks and baggy boxers?'

'Well, you're doing your best,' Tom replied with a half-smile.

'It's tough, I must admit, but if I am to be ready for seven and up at some God forsaken time in the morning...'

'Up at three-thirty, throw on some clothes, downstairs by three forty-five,' said Tom, grinning.

'Then I will need time to prepare and get my sleep, no matter how alluring you might look.'

'OK,' said Tom as he heard a knock on the door. He pulled on the robe again and opened the door just enough to slide the ironed shirt through the gap.

They left their bedroom at seven for the short walk to the dining room.

'Who will be there tonight?' asked Fran.

'All the family and key people who run the estate, many you've already met.'

Fran nodded in response, wondering how the evening would go and thinking, *I must leave at ten if I have to get up at silly o'clock tomorrow morning.*

They walked into the dining room to the gentle sound of small talk and the clink of glasses. 'Champagne?' asked a smart, white-aproned girl Fran didn't recognise, who was holding a tray of cut-crystal flutes from which sparkling bubbles streaming upwards.

Tom and Fran each took a glass and clinked them together, locking eyes for a moment, and took their first sip.

'You must be Thomas, and this your intended?' said a confident clear voice. 'The champagne is marvellous. My name is Fred, Fred Connell, Coombe Consulting, which I am guessing you've not heard of?'

Tom shook Fred's keenly offered hand. 'No, never heard of it, but not a big surprise. So much has changed. What does Coombe Consulting do?'

Fred stood up straight and took a breath. 'I met your father probably two years ago at a lunch and we got talking about all the plans he had, and I told him I work for a company that provides consultancy and project management for exactly what we discussed. After two months' further discussions, Coombe Consulting was born, with me at its head, and we project manage all the major change and development streams for the estate and family.' Fred paused. 'Your father's told me he wants you to join the board.'

'Has he?' replied Tom. 'Well, to be honest I haven't had

the chance to sit down with Father and discuss anything yet, but I look forward to talking again. What projects should I listen out for?'

Fred smiled. 'Project Scar, Project Crown and Project Sweet are the main ones at the moment.'

'Project Crown, is that the wilding of the Crown Estates which King Charles is leading?'

'Yes, it's not a very cryptic project name. Any ideas on the other two?' asked Fred, enjoying the pre-dinner game.

'Project Scar, who named it?' asked Tom.

'Good question,' said Fred, still with a smile, enjoying himself. 'Your father.'

'Then I would guess it's the South West Fast Rail project.'

'Correct,' said Fred, laughing. 'Well done again. And Project Sweet, as in sweet charity, is about obtaining charitable status for the estate, which, to be honest, we have very nearly completed. It does help having King Charles and his son William involved.

'Tom, can we talk about your research on natural resource economics and the algorithms you are creating? I believe WPS, who are sponsoring your research, want to use your work to measure the true environmental cost of all their future investment deals. Could be an environmental game changer, going forward,' Fred continued, looking serious now.

Tom smiled. 'Yes, I need to talk to the university and my partner about transferring the work to here.'

'Sooner the better. Rumours of the work and what it means are already circulating and there will be many who would want to steal the details so they can undermine any decision made using it. For example, we believe you'll never get any mining investment using your analysis. We also might need it to fight Fast Rail, but I think that will evaporate and they will cancel the new lines and change to an upgrade of the existing infrastructure, which makes much more sense for all sorts of reasons.' Fred looked serious, his smile now gone, as he talked business.

'Fine,' said Tom. 'We should talk further. Maybe not this weekend, but soon. Is that OK?'

'Yes,' said Fred. 'Let's talk soon. Have a great evening and I'll see you both in the morning, I guess?' His smile returned.

'Yes,' said Fran, pleased to be able to say something rather than just nodding as she tried to follow what was going on, 'but it's a very early start.' She yawned.

'Your first time?' asked Fred. 'It's quite an event and I have found each equinox and solstice I have attended quite moving—motivating.'

OK, thanks,' said Fran thinking Fred didn't seem like someone easily moved and he certainly didn't sound like he needed motivating.

'Dinner is served,' announced a smart, if a bit severe, Mrs Cooper dressed in black.

The throng quietened for a moment and then started to drift towards the table laid out with a crisp linen cloth, the best silver cutlery and a selection of crystal glasses at each setting. There was a deep red table runner running up the length of the U-shaped table, decorated with repeating gold embroidered trees, longbows and, Fran assumed, the family crest. Every so often along the table were ornaments of silver and crystal. Everything sparkled from the light of the chandeliers no longer refracting the sun which was now setting and only offering the occasional stray ray entering the room from the high windows as it journeyed down.

Magical! Fran felt Tom take her hand, and he smiled at her as they walked round the table to their seats. She then noticed place names at each seat for the first time and hoped she wouldn't be marooned on her own. To her relief her name was next to Tom's, seated on his right. All the family, except the twins, were at the top of the table. Fran looked at the place name to her right. NAOMI AMADI. Fran wondered if this was Isaac's daughter. Fran then saw the stunning, tall, young black woman, a similar age to herself, her shoulders bare, skin shining. Her black loose hair, hanging down to her shoulders, glistened in the light as she moved. She squeezed gracefully, but purposefully, behind the mainly already seated guests, exchanging greetings with many. *Her dress is amazing,* thought Fran; creams and greens wrapping and flowing around her as she moved. She stopped next to Fran.

'Naomi,' she said to introduce herself, while pulling out her seat to sit down.

'Hi! How are you?' asked Fran with a smile.

Naomi swivelled slightly in her chair to face Fran.

'Well, thank you, but I wasn't expecting this tonight. Father mentioned he'd met you. Forgot to mention it until five o'clock so all been a bit of a rush, and I did have other plans.'

'Sorry.'

'Not your fault, and it's good to meet you, Francesca.'

'Yes, I met your father and he mentioned you and your brother were home and back for the summer. Couldn't your mother make it tonight?'

'Mother died four years ago, but because he talks to her every day Father forgets, hence my late call. I'm back, my brother's still on his way, I hope to stay and work here. Should be plenty of jobs with so much going on. What about you, when are you moving in?'

'We haven't discussed a moving date yet. End of the summer? Before Pen's wedding, I would guess.'

'You'll be here before then.'

'What makes you say that?'

'This place draws you in and there is so much change and so much to do.'

'Oh,' was all Fran could think to say.

'You've met the family. Lewis and Charlotte are really nice. Charlotte would have been the same as you when she married Lewis, wide-eyed and new to it all, but she soon became a big part of everything and found she had the gift, which makes a huge difference.'

'The gift?' said Fran.

'You're out tomorrow morning for the summer solstice?'

'Yes.'

'You will see then. It's nothing to worry about. I'm guessing they will probably introduce you to see if you have any connection. I'm sure you will do fine.'

'Oh,' Fran said again, not really understanding or sure

what to say as questions and some confusion swirled in her mind.

'Don't worry, Francesca, there's absolutely nothing to fear, and you'll probably find it very interesting. Many find it uplifting. I certainly did and still do.'

'Will you be there? And please call me Fran.'

'Bet Father doesn't call you Fran. He wanted me to have a name that couldn't be shortened, so my brother, calls me Ni just to annoy the old boy. No, I'm not there tomorrow. Charlotte and the twins will guide you.'

'What about Pen?'

'She's a funny one. More going on there than meets the eye, and I have my doubts that the wedding will take place. Henry's a bad piece of work. He describes me as uppity and says I should know my place, with all the race connotations that go with that. He's only after her money in my opinion, which his family farm really needs, and I don't think he treats Pen very well, from what I understand. I really don't think she's happy. Keep a close eye on what goes on around her and I think you'll soon see what I mean. If Pen's there tomorrow she'll follow Charlotte and the twins. Much to her irritation, she doesn't have the same connection the others have.'

'I see,' said Fran,

'No, you don't, but you will,' said a smiling Naomi, looking down the table as the food began to arrive.

'You know Tom quite well, I understand,' said Fran.

'Ah, yes, I imagine my father dropped that into the early conversation with you? We grew up together and Father had high hopes of me and Tom. We had a bit of a teenage thing that lasted two months one summer, just before Tom went away. It was nothing, but Father saw it as closing the circle; we arrive as slaves and land up lady of the manor!'

'This is awkward,' said Fran, her mind racing.

'No, don't be silly, it's history and we've all moved on. Tom is with you now and I've been with my man, Spence, for four years. He may well come down and join me here. We really should be friends.' Naomi took a pen from her black evening bag, wrote something on the back of her place card and offered it to Fran.

'My number. Call me anytime this weekend if you are at a loose end.'

'OK. Thanks, I will,' said a confused Fran, taking the card, not sure if she should be pleased or not, but it was not the time or place to make a fuss.

Last to sit, at the bottom of the table, were the twins, supervised by the stern Mrs Cooper.

'Father told me they were in trouble,' Naomi said, amused. 'Quite a scene, I understand. They are fun and, to be honest, a breath of fresh air at times, but Cath can take things too far.'

Small plates of food started to arrive. *Like posh tapas*, thought Fran. She looked to the other end of the table where Pen sat, with Henry next to her. Pen looked up and smiled, and nudged Henry. Henry bowed his head. His gaze then moved from Fran to Naomi and his features hardened. He then leant close to Pen and said something while still staring at Naomi. Pen pulled away slightly, her face in a grimace, and playfully slapped Henry's arm.

He shrugged and leant in again and said something else, which made Pen stop still for a moment, her face frozen. *What did he say?* Fran wondered. Was that fear on Pen's face? Then Pen broke into a mock laugh and turned to talk to her mother to her right. Henry was still staring across the table and Fran glanced and saw Naomi returning his stare, unblinking and unflinching. Suddenly, Naomi broke eye contact and blew a theatrical kiss across the table. Fran looked over at Henry, his face tight and frowning, and watched him smoothly lift his arm from the table and sweep his thumb cutting across his throat as a mocking smile spread across his face. He then switched his hard gaze to Fran, his eyes widening, scanning her up and down, salaciously licking his lips before falling back into his mocking smile, mouthing 'Fuck you' across the table.

'Did you see that?' Naomi said. 'Told you he was a piece of work.'

Fran was stunned at what she'd seen. She didn't know what to say, but felt violated.

'You ladies alright,' said Mrs Cooper. 'I hope the foods alright? It's the first time Chef has prepared small plates; there are so many different dietary requirements these days.'

'It's all lovely,' said Fran as she reached for a plate in front of her.

Mrs Cooper lent over Naomi's shoulder. 'Terrible man,' she said quietly. 'He's a disgrace, but leave it with me.' Mrs Cooper stood upright and walked to the bottom end of the dining table, picked up a platter and slowly walked up the other side of the table, serving people as she went.

Fran and Naomi watched, intrigued, as she served what looked like ribs. Mrs Cooper paused behind Henry, smiling at Naomi and Fran as she asked Henry if he would like some. Henry nodded yes, but as Mrs Cooper went to serve the platter it slipped and deposited meat and sauce over Henry's shoulder, down his front and into his lap.

Henry jumped up in surprise. 'You stupid woman! It's bad enough sitting near them.' He nodded towards Naomi and Fran, his carefully oiled hair flicking out of place. 'You, silly bitch,' he shouted.

'That's enough!' said a deep authoritative voice. Lewis was standing, looking very unhappy. 'Accidents happen, Henry, I can only say how sorry I am.'

'That was no accident. I saw the old fool conspiring with those two over there.'

Tom jumped up. 'Henry, that's enough. I saw what you were doing. Pen, can I suggest you take Henry out and help him to clean up.'

Tom is clearly angry, Fran thought. Is that because he threatened me or because of Naomi? She felt very confused.

Henry jumped up, ribs and sauce sliding from his lap onto the floor. 'You never did have any taste, Thomas,' he half shouted, glancing again at Fran and Naomi as he pushed roughly past Mrs Cooper and rushed out of the silenced room.

Pen jumped up and followed, clearly upset.

As Henry and Pen left the dining room, Lewis spoke again. 'Please, everyone, carry on with dinner. Just an unfortunate accident. More wine for the table, please.' Lewis left his chair, walked round the table and squatted down behind Fran and Naomi. In almost a whisper asked, 'Are you both alright?'

'I saw what happened,' said Tom. 'The bastard is out of order.'

Pen caught up with Henry as he left the house and grabbed his arm. He instantly swung round and stuck her with the back of his hand. Pen yelped in surprise, staggered a step and stopped, raising her hand to her reddening cheek. The noise brought out two of the girls to see what was going on.

'You two can fuck off,' Henry shouted and the girls took a step back.

'Henry,' stammered Pen, 'why don't you come in and get changed? You can't go home like that.'

'Don't tell me what to do,' Henry spat, lashing out and striking Pen again with the back of his hand.

Pen rocked and this time fell back, coming to rest with her back against the wall.

'Please stay, don't go like this,' Pen said between sobs.

'No point,' said Henry, straightening up. 'Doubt there's much chance of a fuck now, unless—' he turned to the girls in the doorway, 'either or both of you would join us?'

The girl nearest to Henry said to her friend, 'Holly, go inside and tell Duncan to get out here quick, and then tell Her Ladyship.'

Holly did not need telling twice and quickly disappeared inside.

'Going for help, I guess,' said Henry, 'or gone to warm the bed?' He laughed.

Suddenly, the large shape of Duncan loomed out the door into the dimly lit road, his eyes latching onto Pen crying on the floor. 'What's going on here, then?' he growled.

'Nothing to do with you,' said Henry defiantly.

'What's been happening, Olivia? 'Asked Duncan. She was standing alone in the door.

'He hit Pen,' said a nervous Olivia.

'Don't believe that little tramp. No one in their right mind would believe her over me,' said Henry, his eyes bulging.

'My daughter knows better than to lie, unlike others here tonight. It's probably time you go...NOW!' said Duncan, in a loud voice.

'Your daughter,' said Henry, laughing.

'Time you went,' said Duncan, with a growl.

'When I'm ready,' spat back Henry.

Duncan stood up to his full height, just as Charlotte rushed through the door with Holly.

'No, Duncan,' she half shouted, as Duncan stepped forward towards Henry, his hands curling into fists.

'GO! Go, now! And don't think about coming back!' Duncan said to Henry in a threatening voice.

'I'm not afraid of you,' Henry hissed back.

'Then you are lot more stupid than I thought,' said Duncan as Henry started to walk backwards up the drive.

'This is not over,' Henry said, moving away quickly to find his car.

Duncan sighed and turned round once he was sure

Henry was moving off. He looked on, sadly, as Lady Charlotte knelt down to comfort the sobbing Pen.

'Duncan, can you please carry Pen up to her room. Olivia, can you find Jackie and Anna.'

Duncan bent down and easily lifted Pen. He then followed Charlotte back into the house and gently, slowly up the stairs.

As Charlotte followed Duncan, Isaac, Lewis, Tom and Fran appeared from the dining room.

'What's happened?' Lewis enquired urgently.

'It was Henry, I'll tell you later. I need to get Pen to her room,' Charlotte replied.

'OK, Duncan, when you are done could you and Isaac escort Mrs Cooper back to her cottage. Isaac, please first make sure Henry's car has gone and he has left the estate. Put someone on the main entrance to make sure he doesn't return later or any other nonsense he might think of.'

'Yes, sir,' said Isaac with a nod, walking up the drive with his usual relaxed, gait.

'I'll come with you.' Tom bent and kissed Fran. 'Sorry, are you OK, getting back to our room on your own,' he said, kissing her again.

'Yes, yes,' she replied, still confused and upset by what had happened to Pen. She hoped she was alright.

'Good idea, Tom, wouldn't do for Isaac to have to deal with Henry on his own,' said Lewis.

'He'll be gone,' Tom shouted back as he left to catch up with Isaac.

Back inside the house, Mrs Cooper wobbled into the hall on Naomi's arm.

'Don't worry, Mrs C, we will get you home shortly,' said Lewis with a warm smile.

Jackie and Anna arrived, and Lewis spoke to them. 'Jackie, can you go upstairs? Pen is not too well.' Jackie pushed past, not waiting for Lewis to finish and was running up the stairs. 'Anna, Mrs C is going home. Can you please look after the house, and ensure everything is locked and bolted.'

'Of course, sir,' responded Anna. 'I hope she is alright,' she said, looking with concern at a clearly upset Mrs Cooper. 'Still the solstice in the morning?'

'Yes, absolutely,' said Lewis.

Fran walked up the stairs, as the speeding Jackie overtook her and disappeared ahead. *She's worried*, Fran thought. Jackie paused as she met Duncan and Olivia coming back down the stairs having deposited Pen safely in her room. Fran noted a brief exchange of words as they passed, which seemed to spur Jackie on as she flew up to the landing and Pen's room.

'Good night, madam,' said Olivia as they passed, Duncan touching his forelock in a silent sign of respect.

As Fran went to open the door to her room, she saw Charlotte leaving Pen's room, looking worried, and decided she would pop along to Pen and make sure she was alright.

She padded along the landing to Pen's door and knocked lightly. There was no response, so Fran gently pushed the handle down and opened the door until there was enough of a gap to squeeze in. She froze, half in, half out of the room. The room was silent and dimly lit. Fran took a sharp intake of breath as she watched Jackie ease into bed next to Pen and put her arms round her, pulling her close and gently stroking her head like she was a small child, while talking quietly.

Fran backed out of the door silently, but suddenly Jackie looked up, locking eyes with the now retreating Fran. She held her gaze for a moment before returning her attention to Pen. Fran eased the door closed again and quietly scurried back to her own room in a state of surprise and disappointment she'd been spotted. Once in her room Fran sat on the bed for a short while replaying the events of the evening, then undressed and, feeling tired, slipped into bed. She quickly fell asleep despite everything that had happened.

~ 8 ~

Saturday 21st June 2025, Solstice. Tom's phone alarm trilled out into the still dark room. The very earliest hint of grey morning light edged round the room's heavy curtains, but not enough yet to chase out the blackness of night.

Tom threw the duvet off them both, announcing enthusiastically, 'Time to get up.'

'But it's still night,' said Fran, curled up in a ball on the mattress now the duvet had been rudely withdrawn. 'What time did you get back last night?'

'About eleven. Isaac and I checked Henry had gone, then I walked Isaac to his cottage and came back to the house. I had to raise Anna, who had already locked everything up, so that delayed me a bit. You were fast asleep. Need to be downstairs in five minutes,' prompted Tom.

'For fuck's sake! What a night,' complained Fran as she eased out of bed and began to dress. 'OK, won't be a moment.'

They left their room and went down the main stairs to meet the crowd gathering in the hall, its heavy wooden door already open to the dark Vale outside.

Fran recognised most of those gathered from the day before, including Tom's parents and Pen who was fussing around everyone, her cheek showing only the faintest bruise.

'You, OK?' asked Charlotte, placing her hand on Fran's arm in reassurance. 'Now you might find this all a bit odd, but just go with it. Nothing can hurt you; no harm can come from this. The twins, Pen and I will look after you so don't worry. Where are the twins? Late as usual.' She sighed in exasperation.

On cue the twins came tumbling down the stairs, their long hair flying in the air behind them, both pulling on cardigans as they crashed into the hallway and gathering crowd.

'At last,' said Charlotte. They stood in front of her, waiting to hear their mother's instructions, their faces clear and smiling, but with the usual hint of mischief. 'Now you two, make sure you look after Fran, please,' finished Charlotte with a reassuring smile.

'OK, thanks,' said Fran, smiling and taking a step away from Tom to stand with them. She saw Charlotte wave, and Pen and twins started to move gracefully towards the door and the dark outside.

'What size feet?' asked Cath as they looked at the pile of boots by the door.

'Five and a half,' replied Fran and was promptly passed a pair of ankle-length, green boots to tug on.

Fran then stood ready to leave the house, with a quick glance behind her to check Tom was not far. She saw him chatting with Fred, who they'd met the day before.

Tom must have sensed her looking across the now busy hall, as he looked up and waved, smiled and mouthed, 'I love you'. Fran felt a flash of warmth wash through her, and she returned the wave with a silently-blown kiss. She then turned and stepped from the light of the hall into the Vale's dark gloom and stood just behind the twins. It wasn't at all cold. *Surprisingly warm,* she thought, *no early morning chill.* There was no real need for the cardigans they had all decided to wear.

The light was oddly dull; still the black of night, Fran observed. She could see the horizon ahead with the merest suggestion of grey and blue tinting the edges of the black sky, still speckled in stars, which Fran thought looked like sprinkled diamonds. She'd never seen a night sky like it. In the distance a fractured golden loom of the sun shimmered, seemingly struggling to rise above the horizon and the black twisted profiled trees, failing to push out the stubborn night.

There was still just Charlotte, Pen and the twins with Fran outside.

Fran took a deep breath as Cath and Jen stood either side of her and each took one of her hands as the three started to walk forwards towards the growing sun's loom. Charlotte was not moving and Fran and the twins came to a stop in front of her after only a few steps, the heavy dew giving their boots a shiny, reflective gloss.

'Fran, you have nothing to fear. Just do what feels right. Most importantly, remember to breathe.' Charlotte leant forward with a loving, warm smile and gave Fran a gentle kiss on her cheek. Fran felt the warmth of Charlotte's breath, the soft kiss and her love. As Charlotte stepped away, Pen reached forward and reassuringly squeezed Fran's arm.

'Are you OK?' Fran said, returning the gesture with a concerned smile.

'Yes, and thank you for popping in last night, very kind of you,' said Pen. 'Jackie told me. Afraid I was out for the count after a sedative from Mum.'

'Yes, you looked asleep, and Jackie was taking good care of you.'

Pen glanced slightly nervously around her, leant in close and whispered to Fran, 'Talk later,' before squeezing Fran's arm again.

Fran smiled. 'Nothing to explain.'

Pen took her hand from Fran's arm, turned gracefully, almost in slow motion, and started to walk with Charlotte towards the struggling sun, the twins now either side of her, holding Fran's hands once more. Fran felt like they were gliding, not walking. Her feet didn't feel like they were moving, touching the ground or dragging in the wet, dewy grass whose beads of moisture were strung out like ribbons of diamonds, as if some of the stars above had fallen to earth and now resided in the grass's green universe. In front, Charlotte and Pen glided down the slight slope. Fran glanced over her shoulder and saw the others following, spilling from the hall into the last dark of night, as she walked towards the dawn light. Fran was disappointed she could not make out who was who and see Tom, but she had no doubt Tom would be near, which she was pleased about as she felt something important and exciting, but not frightening had begun.

As they walked, Fran saw the wood in front of them, tall dark interwoven limbs, looming and mysterious in the last stillness of night. Gradual grey light replaced the black, waiting for the season's first summer light to stream.

They didn't walk for long and, suddenly, they stopped. Charlotte turned and cast a glance across the arriving followers now standing, mixed and muddled, on the dewy ground.

Fran became aware of the twins singing a slow, sad lament. There were no words but the beautiful voices were calming, like a sad funeral keen. The twins rocked gently as they sang. Fran felt them gently squeeze her hands just as she realised, she was singing with them too. Fran somehow knew the song; something somehow remembered from a deep distant past.

Charlotte started in a gentle, effortless voice, not a shout or whisper, accompanying the singing of the twins and Fran. The singing drifted effortlessly, hauntingly, a zephyr of noise across the early morning stage of green and gathering new light. They all stopped in front of the largest tree. Charlotte's words were spoken not with a shout but a determined voice. No matter where anyone stood, they could hear her, clear and calm.

'We are all here to welcome the day, the first day of summer, to honour and thank the land and its life, for the season gone and the season to come, to offer our respect and thanks to all that has gone before and hopes for what is yet to come.' Charlotte stopped. The singing went on with Pen joining in with a rising effortless counterpoint melody in a soothing, not quite soprano, voice delicately overlying the twins' and Fran's lament with a more positive intent. The singing drifted lazily, soothingly across the people and land, absorbed by the trees. *Uplifting,* thought Fran, the music seeping into her, flowing like a liquid around and through her. She felt moved and emotional as if she might cry and she felt the first tear escape her already misty eyes. *Nothing could prepare you for this*, she thought.

Suddenly, they all stopped. Somehow, they all knew to end. *Something hidden in our DNA?* Fran wondered.

The trees stirred, the branches rolling upwards in unison in a rustling wave, numerous lights appearing, seemingly floating amongst the twisted boughs. Various colours, some close, some deep in the wood. The big oak in front of them seemed to sway and Fran thought she saw a bright light appear high in its boughs. Then, to her surprise, she heard a deep rasping voice.

'Welcome the summer but beware the poison in the ground and the fire in the air that bows to no season. We are the dying and few seem to care. Too much forgotten, too little remembered, everything denied. Most assuming that closeted behind glass, steel and stone they escape nature's long grasp and can continue their careless ways without regret.'

The deep voice, rumbling, ancient but clear and calm, vibrating the very air, paused then continued. 'I see the heir has returned. It's been a long time.'

Fran glanced sideways and saw Tom kneel and bow his

head. A sign of respect, she guessed. And although she didn't know why she knew it was the right thing to do.

Amongst the many, Fran also saw Isaac and Duncan and other weathered-looking foresters kneeling. She was sure Duncan had tears rolling down his face, which only swelled the tears rolling down her own.

The tree continued. 'You bring to us today a new life-force with a clear, open soul, and a brave, loving heart.' There was a pause. 'Come to speak with me.' And the oak's branches swayed outwards like arms beckoning Fran forward, creating an arch of leaves and branches at the front of the oak.

Charlotte nodded at the twins, who walked forward still holding Fran's hands, bringing her to the tree. 'Don't worry, just remember to breathe,' said Jen, as she and Cath gently placed Fran's hands onto the gnarled oak trunk. Fran was surprised. She'd expected it to feel rough, cold and damp, but instead it reminded her of laying your hands on a crumpled rug, not cold or damp but warm, soft and comforting, and she could feel a light heat from the trunk seeping into her hands. *It's like a dark woven tweed with flecks of colour from a moss, fungus and lichen palette on a thousand-year-old canvas of wood and life. How little I understand*, Fran thought.

'You have many questions, my dear, no great surprise. Like many, you've much forgotten and little remembered of other times and ancient things. We are both tree and man, we are one. Joined energies, one released by death, the other by the miracle of the exploding seed of life. Both nurtured and joined in and by the earth we all depend on and need. Combined together, watching for a millennia the world slowly forget. Breathe, it will help you remember what is forgotten,' said the deep, comforting, non-threatening voice from the tree.

Remember to breathe, echoed in Fran's head. She took deep breaths and suddenly felt a surge of relief and contentment better than any joint. The fragrant air from the trees entered her chest and lungs and seeped deep inside her. A rich, deep, not at all unpleasant smell and flavour of the earth, the tree and its leaves and the life within it. Fran felt refreshed, revived. Memories buried somewhere deep in forgotten corners of her soul, DNA now liberated, seeped back into her consciousness, together with an understanding of times long past and the symbiosis of all things living. She felt flashes of understanding as well as confusion and doubt.

'All who are here, man, woman, and tree, recognise our new friend, Francesca, someone of kindness of mind and soul. Welcome to summer to all who are here and to those who care and are joined by the energy of life, belief and understanding of the land. Thank you for the spring, but there is much to be done. Summer will bring more heat and flood, both tearing land and life. Too many naysayers denying our decline, forgetting that nature's long hand always finds ways to balance its books.' The voice paused and then, speaking directly to Fran, the tree said, 'Never fear the woods. They will always be your friend. They will renew and protect you always.'

Fran knew it was over and the twins removed her

hands off the tree and they took the few steps back to where they had stood before.

As the light on the trunk faded away it spoke one last time.

'Penelope,' said the oak. 'We feel your pain. Let love, life and hope be your guide. Live life as you would, not as others think you should. Don't let hate darken your light, which shines bright today.'

The great oak's branches swept back upwards.

Fran glanced sideways again to see that nearly all had taken a knee and most had bowed heads. Respect, love for the land and all its life. Fran began to understand, perhaps.

Pen's face was radiant, different from the face of fear and hate from the previous night, now full of joy, life and love.

Fran stood with the twins, half wondering what had happened, when she heard a deep baritone lament resonating from the wood. *The trees; they are singing*, she thought. Charlotte, Pen and the twins started to sing a complementary descant over the slow, deep rhythm set by the trees, a rising and falling brighter counterpoint of hope against the trees' almost funeral march.

Fran realised there were tears rolling down her cheeks. The sadness of a giant's demise had struck a note of sadness somewhere deep within in her. *How can this happen?* she thought. *How do we change this tragic ending?* There is a lot to do, she realised.

'Bless you,' said Charlotte as she put her hands either side of Fran's head, wiping the tears away from her cheeks gently with her thumbs and kissing her softly on her fore-head. 'Well done, you will be tired now and need to rest. It will take some days to make sense of everything that has been seen and said today. Talk to me at any time if you need any help. I was just like you on my first such visit.'

Suddenly, the sun burst over the trees into the Vale. The land lit up with the first rays of summer. The singing stopped and the trees all lifted to reach the sun and a new noise drifted across the gathered, thousands of leaves clapping like little green hands, a rushing noise like a gentle wave washing over fine sand.

'The trees are happy,' said Charlotte. 'They are pleased with the day.'

Fran looked around her and saw the joy of all present at the trees' celebratory sound.

'One, two, three,' counted Charlotte quietly and then began to sing a bright, uplifting song. Pen and the twins immediately joined in, and, to her great surprise, Fran found from somewhere deep she knew this song of hope and so joined in as the five of them turned and walked together back up towards the house.

The crowd moved as well and Fran started to recognise people. Lewis came striding up.

'Wonderful,' he said, embracing Charlotte, hugging Pen, the twins and finally Fran. *A family of love*, thought Fran.

'How was that?' asked Tom, standing behind Fran, who on registering his voice spun round and threw her arms round his neck and buried her face in his chest.

'I can't explain,' said Fran, her voice muffled from being buried in Tom. 'So much love and sadness, and yet also hope.' Fran realised she was crying again; she wasn't sure why, but different woken emotions were sweeping and swirling through her soul. Fran lifted her head from Tom's chest. 'I love you,' she half whispered, 'but I'm exhausted and need to rest.'

'You need to eat and drink first,' answered Tom, squeezing her close, almost lifting her off the ground.

Tom loosened his grip and Fran slid a small distance down his body, her feet planting firmly back on the ground from being on tiptoes. She saw Isaac smiling at her as he walked by, his face beaming in pleasure. Behind came the large frame of Duncan. The trail of his tears could still be seen down his face. As he passed, he slightly bowed and touched his forelock again in respect. As he straightened up, his face exploded into a huge smile. Olivia was tugging at his arm. He looked down and she offered him a hand-kerchief, which he took and wiped his face, now calm, still smiling with the joy of the moment.

Lastly, another man walked over. He was not as tall or bulky as Duncan but over six feet, dressed in grey combat trousers with a matching grey jacket, both with lots of useful-looking pockets, teamed with combat boots which gleamed, having been polished-black and shiny from the dew. He was square-jawed with piercing blue eyes topped off with slightly receding, close-cropped blond hair. He stopped in front of Fran. 'We haven't met. I'm Kurt, one of the senior foresters.' His Afrikaans accent sounded slightly harsh in the now still air. 'I've been here for nearly two years. Before that I worked all over Africa. I've seen many tribal rituals in my time and none have had the impact, connection or honesty of what I have seen here, and especially today. Thank you.' Kurt finished and walked on to shake hands and introduce himself to Tom.

He thanked me, thought Fran. *Wonder why. What have I done?*

They neared the house and Fran spied Naomi standing outside with Mrs Cooper on her arm, both enjoying the light and early heat of the new sun. As Fran neared, Naomi waved and brought her hand to her ear making the sign of a phone indicating she would call. Fran waved in acknowledgement of the message received.

As they neared the house Fran found herself walking next to Pen, Tom having been steered away by others into introductions and hellos.

'Can we talk later?' said Pen, looking sideways at Fran as they walked. 'It's complicated, but I think I see things a lot clearer now. There will be no wedding in September, which is the easy decision. Perhaps we could talk before dinner tonight?'

'OK,' said Fran.

'Great. Mother would like the two of us to join her for a glass of fizz before dinner.'

'OK.' Yet again Fran couldn't think of what to say.

'Duncan, Duncan,' called Pen and the huge frame turned and looked down kindly.

'Yes, madam.'

'Thank you for your help last night.'

'You're welcome, madam, I'm so sorry for what happened.' Duncan looked sad.

'Not your fault, Duncan. Please thank your daughter for reacting so well to what was happening.'

'I'll be sure to tell her, she's a good girl.' Duncan smiled and his face seemed to light up with pride talking about his daughter.

'Duncan, can I ask you a favour?'

'Of course, madam.'

Fran watched Pen dig her hand in her pocket and pull out a padded envelope which she handed to Duncan.

'Can you please arrange for this to be delivered to Henry at his farm; it's the engagement ring. Can it be delivered quietly with no fuss? I don't want anyone caught by him on his land. We all know what he can be like.'

'Indeed, madam, he won't be happy at the events of last night, and we both know he won't go quietly and there could be more trouble to come from him or his men. But I've got just the man to deliver this,' said Duncan with a smile.

'Thank you, who have you in mind?'

'Poacher John, he used to poach all round this region. Worked for Henry's family before he came here. He knows his way in and out of most places. He also knows it will hurt if he gets caught on Henry's land and that their men have no hesitation dishing out their often-harsh idea of justice.'

'OK. Thank you, but do tell him to be careful. If it's too much of a risk, abort.'

'Will do, madam.' And with a slight bow Duncan walked off.

'Could there be trouble?' asked Fran.

'Possibly, Henry will feel slighted by me and last night in front of everyone. He'll want the last word. He and his men are known for doling out violent retribution at times, so Duncan is right, Henry will not go quietly. And when he finds out about Jackie it will only add fuel to his fire.'

'You've made a decision then?' said Fran.

'I think so, but I'd like to talk it through with you, if you don't mind?'

'No, that's fine.'

'How about six o'clock in my room before we meet Mother?'

'OK, that should work. See you later,' Fran said as she left Pen and headed for the house, her bed and rest.

'Penelope, Thomas.' A voice drifted over the chatting crowd. Pen recognised it as her father and walked towards him. She arrived at the same time as Tom and they both stopped in front of their father, waiting to hear what he wanted.

'Can the three of us get together for a quick chat, please?' said Lewis, switching his gaze between the two of them. Pen and Tom nodded.

'Where's Fran? I lost her in the crowd as we got to the house,' asked Tom.

'Don't worry, she has gone to your room to rest,' answered Pen.

'Oh good, but she needs to eat,' said Tom.

'Don't worry, I'll organise a breakfast tray to her room and make sure she's alright.'

'Thanks Pen. That will be great,' said an appreciative Tom.

Lewis looked at his watch. 'Right, let's say eight o'clock in my study. Bring food and drink if you want.'

~ 9 ~

As Fran made her way back to her room, people kept introducing themselves to her. She was confused why so many of them congratulated her with beaming faces. She still wasn't sure what she'd done. She escaped into the hall, rushed up the stairs and sighed. Relieved to have left the crowd behind for the sanctuary of their bedroom, she sat, exhausted, on the side of the bed enjoying the quiet of the room. Her head was flopped forward, her hair falling limp over her face. Fran was focusing on her hands laid face up in her lap, fascinated to watch her life blood miraculously flowing through her veins. *There's so much I don't understand about life and death*, she thought. She felt her mind swirling with fragments of thoughts, floating and spinning, not yet making any sense. Something that morning had opened a long-closed door, hidden in her head, of things she did not know she knew, that now were let loose, but she didn't yet understand. *What did it all mean?* she puzzled, beginning to feel overwhelmed by tiredness that now laid siege to her mind and body.

Fran remembered the huge surge of sadness that had flooded through her from the trees, and now she felt sorrow tinged with anger for the timeless mighty presence that might be at its end. How could this be? Greed and arrogance raced into her head, her dad suddenly coming to mind, everything a commodity, everything a transaction. Everything a profit.

She then remembered the flood of love and hope that followed the sorrow, flowing from the people and trees as they breathed as one. *Where there's love, there's always hope,* Fran thought, wondering, doubting if her parents would ever understand and why it was important or even mattered. Her thoughts were interrupted by a knock on the door. She sighed heavily, leveraging herself off the bed, realising how drained she was, as she plodded lethargically across the room.

'Good morning, madam. Thomas and Penelope were concerned you might not have eaten. So, I've brought you a pot of tea, a jug of iced water and some pastries,' said Gail, offering up the tray in both hands.

'Thank you, yes, that will be great. I can't believe how tired and hungry I am. Please can you bring the tray in?'

'Of course, madam.' Gail walked into the room as Fran held open the door, shutting it once she was inside.

'Here, madam?' asked Gail, standing with the tray hovering over a table that sat beside one of the two big, plump, floral-patterned armchairs in the room.

'Yes, please,' said Fran, the tray reminding her how hungry and thirsty she was. She lowered herself into the comfy, enveloping seat, scanning the tray and feeling her body start to relax, even if her head still swirled around.

'It was good this morning, madam,' said Gail.

'You were there, with everyone else with the trees?'

'Yes, but not for all of it, too much to do in the kitchen and not my turn.'

'Not your turn?' queried Fran.

'Mr Balfour, Chef, lets two of us go if we are all working.'

'How many of you?'

'Four: Olivia, Holly, Michelle and me. Michelle never wants to go; she went once and decided it was the devil's work; pagan nonsense. So, she never went again. She and her family are very religious and attend church every Sunday. If she had seen this morning then she would probably want you burnt as a witch.' Gail laughed. 'Holly and Olivia were there the whole time. I saw the end as Chef said we were nearly done readying breakfast, and I could go. Never seen or heard the trees sing. Holly came back wide-eyed and tearful. She's new and said she's never seen the solstice before.'

'Please have a seat,' offered Fran.

'Thank you, madam, but don't tell Mrs Cooper. She is always telling us we must not be too familiar, which makes me smile when you think of Jackie and what might be going on there.'

'Going on?' Fran repeated, thinking about what she had seen the previous night as she poured the tea. 'Would you like a cup?'

'No thank you, madam.'

'Last night was terrible,' said Fran.

'He was lucky Duncan didn't tear him apart. Nothing more than Henry fucking Campbell-Blyth deserves. He is a bully and no good,' Gail spat out.

Fran raised her eyebrows in surprise at Gail's venom and language.

'When we serve him, he pushes his plates away so we have to stretch and lean across the table beside him, he then runs his hand up the back of our legs as we reach across.'

'Oh, God, how terrible,' grimaced a horrified Fran. 'What did you do?'

'Just walk away. But Mrs Cooper saw what was happening and tipped a glass of water in his lap which certainly upset him. Then Mrs Cooper made a point of always serving him, asking him to kindly pass the plate as it was too far for her to reach. He hated that, as it spoiled his fun.' Gail smiled. 'The best one was Holly, bless her. He slid his hand up her leg and she froze, then turned with such speed and ferocity, she caught his hand between her thighs, and she wrenched his arm and nearly spun him out of his chair. He didn't half squeal and he had his arm in a sling for a week, but he couldn't complain.' Gail laughed at the memory. 'I don't think it's the first time something like last night has happened between Pen and Henry.'

'What makes you say that?'

'There's been a few times she's stayed in her room for days at a time. I think he's hurt her before. Once we didn't see her for a week, but when we took trays in for her meals, she was clearly in a lot of pain down below,' Gail said cryptically with a slight grimace, 'and seemed to have trouble both sitting and standing.'

'Oh dear. Who looked after her?' asked Fran, wondering

what might have happened, thinking did she really want
to know, her face etched in concern at the thought.

'Her mother, Lady Charlotte. But Jackie spent most of
the time nursing her day and night.'

'Perhaps last night will be the final straw.'

'Maybe! If it is, Henry will not go quietly. His pride will
demand revenge. He's an arrogant, vindictive, nasty bastard. He's also certainly after her money. Strong rumour
is his family's farm, Long Farm, is bankrupt. I believe it's
up for sale.'

Fran raised her eyebrows in surprise again, remembering Naomi's comments the night before.

'There was an alleged rape,' Gail continued, 'some
years ago, which got swept under the carpet and came to
nothing, but there's little doubt he did it.'

'What happened?' asked Fran.

'Gave Rachel Provo from Woodend a lift home, but
instead drove her to one of his farm's sheds under some
pretence. His father heard her screams, interrupted whatever was going on.'

'Did she go to the police?'

'Yes. But they were useless and they kind of blamed
her. It was years ago, long before he hitched up with
Pen. Thomas would remember it. Not surprisingly it made
the local news and it was the main subject of gossip and
speculation for some time.'

'What happened to Rachel?' asked Fran, horrified at
what she'd heard.

'She now lives in New Wood, a small hamlet past
Woodend. Somehow, she managed to buy a house, many

believe paid for by Henry's father to shut her up. She seems alright, works in the ladies' clothes shop, Occasion, in Woodend.' Gail paused for a moment. 'We went to school together. We drifted apart after that, but I bumped into her a couple of weeks ago in the pub and we had a brief chat. I told her to look out for jobs on the estate.'

'That was nice of you,' said Fran.

'Thank you, madam, known her a long time so no reason why not, and her brother is an apprentice here already. Now I must go. Lots to do. Shall I bring you a tray at lunchtime?'

'Yes please, what's on offer?'

'Nothing hot, due to the weather.'

'Yes, please, something light with salad, but no potatoes, and could I please have some of that homemade lemonade as well.'

'Of course, madam.' They both stood up and walked to the door.

'Thanks for the chat. Wait a moment,' said Fran warmly as she darted into the bathroom and picked up the borrowed headband which had been washed in the shower and had now dried. 'Thanks for this,' Fran said as she handed back the headband.

'You're welcome, madam, thank you. It will go straight back in the gym bag. Ask me anything any time and I will certainly try and help,' said Gail.

'Thank you. I've so much to understand and learn,' Fran said, as Gail left the bedroom. Fran watched her smoothly descending the wide main stairs at a slight trot.

Fran went back to the chair, drank more tea and ate

another pastry then yawned, as tiredness started to overtake her. She needed to rest. She took off her dress and pulled on the larger dressing gown, which still had a slight pleasing smell of Tom, wrapped it round herself and snuggled into its soft embrace, before walking to the bed and, with some relief, curling up on top. Confused thoughts, the *Book of the Dead*, the Map of Souls, talking trees, singing songs she'd never heard before, drifted around her head as welcome sleep overtook her.

~ 10 ~

Tom walked into his father's study with a mug of tea and a half-eaten bacon roll. Pen was already sitting in front of their father's desk. As Tom moved into the room, he was struck by Pen's drawn and sad face. Then he spotted a new face he hadn't met before sitting on the left-hand side of the desk.

'Good morning, we haven't met, have we?' said Graham.

'No, we haven't,' said Tom, putting down his mug to shake hands. 'Nice to meet you and if you don't mind me asking, what do you do?'

'Of course. I'm Lord Lewis's, sorry, your father's EA, Executive Assistant. I basically make sure everything gets done, keep his diary and try and make sure he's in the right place at the right time,' Graham said, letting go of Tom's hand after a vigorous handshake and sitting down.

'So where is Father now?' asked Tom, glancing at his watch.

'He wanted to catch up with Fred Connell first. They're meeting in the library, but your father should be here any moment.'

Tom huffed as he picked up his tea and sat in the chair next to Pen to finish his roll.

There was a knock on the door, which then opened and Gail's enquiring face leant into the room. On seeing Pen and Tom, she entered the room and walked up to them.

'Just thought I'd let you know that I took breakfast up to Miss Francesca. She's fine, but clearly very tired. I would guess she's asleep by now.'

'Thank you, Gail,' said Pen.

Tom nodded and smiled his appreciation.

'She has asked for a lunch tray as well,' Gail added.

'Yes, very good, thank you again,' said Tom.

'A pleasure,' said Gail, before leaving the room.

'I hope this meeting with Father won't take long. I really should go up and see Fran,' said Tom, glancing purposefully at Graham.

'I'm sure your father will be here at any moment, but if you need to go, Tom,' replied Graham.

The door opened again and this time Lewis strolled in.

'Sorry to have kept everyone waiting, just wanted to catch up with Fred first,' he said as he sat down behind his desk.

'Father,' said Tom, 'I need to go and check on Fran, so hopefully this won't take too long?'

'We shouldn't be long, I want to bring you both up to date with what's going on,' said Lewis with a grin. 'So first we should be successfully registered as a charitable trust in the next few days. Therefore, the building of the lab and conversion of the old grain store can start in September as planned.' Lewis looked at Graham.

'Yes, sir, planning permission's all agreed, builders ready to go. But we still need to submit the plans for the visitor centre but need Lucy's report to go with it.'

'Christ, has she still not provided it? She's been at it for six months.' Lewis looked at Tom and carried on. 'Lucy Haywood is the commercial manager and has been brought in to look at future commercial opportunities if we open up the estate more to visitors. She came highly recommended with a great CV. How difficult can this report be?'

'I met her briefly at lunch yesterday,' replied Tom.

'More than we perhaps thought,' Graham said with a clear note of sarcasm, which Tom noticed with a wince.

'Perhaps!' said Lewis, frowning. 'Get me a meeting with her, please, and tell her I expect her to brief me in detail,' a clearly irritated Lewis ordered.

'Could Naomi help? She studied this at university, I believe,' interrupted Tom.

'Good idea, Tom. Graham, arrange a meeting with her before I see Lucy, please.'

'Yes sir,' said Graham.

'Right, more good news. South West Fast Rail project will be cancelled, as was the case with the high-speed lines up north a few years ago, and instead there will be a massive upgrade of the current infrastructure,' Lewis said with a smile.

'So, we have nothing to worry about now?' asked Pen, her face looking drawn and strained.

'No. The only way they could have brought the line through the Vale was to build a tunnel under the ridge, which would have added millions to the cost. So, it was unlikely they would have gone for that option.'

'Will there be an official announcement?' asked Tom

'Yes, next week in Parliament. So, by next weekend there will be two things to celebrate,' said Lewis, laughing.

'Thanks, Father, is there anything else? I would really like to check on Fran to make sure she is OK.' Tom sounded irritated and impatient.

'No, I think that's the main headlines.'

Pen half raised her hand. 'One thing from me. The wedding's off.'

Lewis's smile disappeared. 'So sorry, Pen, and sorry for being so insensitive after last night. Me ploughing on as usual with stuff that really doesn't matter. Silly of me not to think.' His face furrowed with concern.

Tom reached over and squeezed Pen's arm. 'You, OK? It's probably for the best.' He immediately regretted what he'd said, but it was the first thing that came into his head.

'Yes. I've been a bit of a fool about all of this. And, no, I'm not alright really,' Pen said, her face looking strained.

'Don't be silly,' said Lewis, his face still showing concern, his eyes a watery glaze. 'Love can make fools of any of us. But always remember we all love you and that will hopefully help to heal the wounds.'

'Thanks, Father,' said Pen as she got up and walked round to embrace him.

Lewis held his daughter tightly. He could feel her gently shudder as she cried on his shoulder.

Tom quietly got up to leave the room and motioned to

Graham to follow him. They both silently slipped out the study, quietly closing the door behind them.

~ 11 ~

Tom stood in the corridor, surprised at the number of people still moving about. They all looked happy though. *A good morning with the trees*, Tom thought, *cheers everyone up.*

'Tom, Tom,' a voice behind him called. He immediately recognised his mother's voice and turned to see her pushing down the passageway towards him.

'Do you have a moment? I'm having a quiet cuppa in the drawing room after this morning's theatre,' Charlotte said. 'I thought you were with your father; I was coming to interrupt,' she said mischievously.

'Left Father with Pen. Be warned, there's tears. I'm just off to check on Fran, she's going to think I've abandoned her,' Tom said as he made a step to walk away.

'She's fine and fast asleep. I've just spoken to Gail, so you have a wee bit of time. Fran needs her rest.'

'OK, OK,' Tom surrendered, stepping back and following his mother the few steps to the drawing room.

'Don't worry, I won't keep you long,' Charlotte said as she sat down and picked up her cup.

'Tea?' she asked, nodding towards the pot. 'Plenty in

the pot and still hot. I'm glad your father is with Pen, do them both good to have a cry. Your father's been very worried about Henry for some time.'

Tom silently poured himself a cup and then sat in the chair opposite his mother.

Charlotte watched him settle. 'Crikey, seeing you sitting there you look so much like your father!'

'Perhaps I should move then.' Tom shrugged.

'Don't be like that. I know he can be difficult, especially when he has an idea in his head, and can plough on no matter what anyone thinks. But he's a good man and hardly a day went by without us both wondering how you were doing. Jonathan's father let us know how you were and that you were alright.'

'So, you had a spy in the camp. I'll be having a word with Jonathan the next time I see him.' Tom laughed. 'But that explains how you knew to put my allowance up when I started to pay rent and bills. Thank you.'

'We just wanted to know you were alright and well, that's all. We were delighted when we learnt you had started your degree and equally when you got a first. Father even suggested turning up at your graduation ceremony to surprise you, but I said it might not be a good idea.'

'No, it wouldn't, as I didn't go,' said Tom, laughing.

'Oh, why not?' asked Charlotte.

'No one to go with really, except Fran. But in the end, we decided a nice day out, just the two of us, would be a nicer way to celebrate.'

Charlotte sipped her tea. 'Perhaps that would have

been a good time to get in touch, but we thought, as you'd finished, you'd possibly be coming back. How wrong were we. It's taken nearly another four years and here you are. So pleased to see you.' Charlotte looked at Tom for a positive reaction.

'It felt the right time and I thought I might actually be useful. My time in the real world also gave me perspective on our lives here and I quickly decided it was everyone else who is out of step with the world around them. My time at WPS confirmed that and influenced my postgrad work.'

'You know your father read your submission to WPS and insisted they back it. He sees it as important.'

'Even if he doesn't understand it,' said Tom.

'He may not have understood, but he could see you were passionate about it and since then Fred Connell has explained and reinforced how important it could be.'

Tom sat up straight in his chair, a look of surprise on his face at someone taking such an interest.

'Thanks, Mother. Yes, natural capital economics run through our system will give a fairer value to what happens on any business undertaking. Not only the price and profit of a tree cut down but a value for everything else lost when nature is impacted. It should help balance nature's books in our age of greed.'

'Sounds very exciting, but I'm not sure I fully understand,' said Charlotte.

Tom sat forward to try and explain. 'It's to ensure everyone understands the dependence of any project or business undertaking on natural resources, in respect of both supply of materials and services and absorbing waste and pollution. So, we measure and quantify the impact on natural resources, environment and ecosystems and land. We have a specialist team to analyse any plans; they survey the location, we then run all the data through the system Simon and I have built, carrying on from the work carried out in our masters'.

'The system generates a score and report. Ideally, the report should have a positive score which means overall the undertaking has a positive effect on nature. Hopefully, it will harness investments to ensure and accelerate nature's positive future. It ensures every natural element involved or affected by a business undertaking is understood and makes sure that nature in all its forms is recognised and integral to the plan. So, whatever the undertaking there should always be a positive outcome for nature. The mantra is: maintain, restore and enhance, in recognition of the planet emergency. We can't keep depleting natural resources with no thought or care, we must all strive for net zero at the very least.

'So, if you propose to build a mine, we take into consideration all these factors over the expected life of the mine to give a better idea of its value and absolute cost and requirements to be a positive undertaking, especially if the mine goes ahead on the basis that the mining company must pay for the replacement of everything lost or degraded so the mine's environmental impact is at least neutral.' Tom looked enquiringly at his mother, who slowly sipped her tea as she considered.

'OK, I think I see, but why would anyone let you

measure their project knowing it may well increase costs and make any investment or undertaking unviable?'

'Ethics. Everyone wants to do their bit following various COP and the deteriorating situation. Pressure from people and politicians. Ethical investment is now quite the thing. Like us now, and in the past, with slavery, many are putting caveats on what investment companies or pension funds can use monies for. WPS believe using this they can attract the green-ethical investor and they don't want to greenwash like so many still do. They see that being ethical will give them commercial advantage, a differentiator in a changing world with a big segment of green investors. For others, who traditionally have had no regard for the damage they do to nature, it could be very bad and costly news.'

'Is that why Fred Connell is so concerned about the security of your work?' asked Charlotte, looking worried.

'Yes, some will look to undermine the process. The sooner they get the details, the sooner they will start. It is more secure here than at the university. So, I need to go back to speak to my partner on this, Simon. He's a very good coder, a couple of years older than me. He builds all the clever stuff. I need him to move here to finish the project. I also need to see Fran's parents, and arrange a date for them to visit.'

Charlotte smiled, putting down her cup and clasping her hands together. 'I'll talk to Graham and get some weekend options for you. I take it no one mentioned next weekend?'

'No,' Tom replied shaking his head.

'We have King Charles, Camilla, William, Kate and the children coming. Charles is very interested in the wilding plans here and wants to talk about how we might help to do the same on the royal estates.'

'That's a step up in intensity of Father's plans.'

'Indeed!' said Charlotte. 'You have no idea what a royal visit means. It's been chaos getting everything done. A few times I thought Graham was going to explode.'

'I met Graham this morning. He does quite a lot, I gather?'

'God, yes, before he arrived, we, well your father really, and consequently us, were out of control. He sorts everything out and tells us what we need to know, such as next weekend there will be armed police in the woods. Your father said good and that he hopes the teenage village commandos decide on a bit of trespassing.'

Tom laughed as he imagined the lads from New Wood being stopped by armed police.

'He's gay, and he has asked if his partner, Stephen, can come to live with him here. We've said yes, if that's OK with you?' said Charlotte.

'Of course, what did Pen say? I can't believe Henry would be impressed.'

'She was fine, and Henry is not a problem now.'

'Terrible bloke,' spat Tom, his face showing a flash of anger when he thought back to the previous night.

'You don't know half of it,' said Charlotte, her face tightening as she spoke. 'He's hurt her before. She's a bit confused, and not sure what to do next, but she is very pleased you are back.'

'Confused about what?' asked Tom, looking concerned.

'Many things. Who she is, where she is going, what's next for her. I don't want to say too much, it's not fair on Pen.'

'Right,' said Tom, sitting up straight. 'I really should go and see Fran, or I'll be divorced before I'm even married.' Tom raised himself out of the chair, walked over to his mother and bent down to give her a kiss and a hug. 'Love you.'

'Love you, too, and so pleased to have you back. Can you tell Fran I will pop in and see her at about two o'clock. Remember I was the same as her once. New and equally confused.'

'Thanks, Mum, will do,' Tom said, squeezing her lovingly before leaving the drawing room.

~ 12 ~

Tom took the main stairs to the first floor. He reached their bedroom door and gently opened it, cautiously leaning in. He didn't want to wake Fran or startle her if she was already up and about. He saw her; a curled-up bundle on the bed. A blade of light cut through the gap in the still closed curtains, slicing across a corner of the bed and then the floor. As he walked softly towards her, he could feel the heat of the day easing into the room.

Another hot one, Tom thought, as he looked down at the sleeping Fran. It was no surprise to him that she showed no signs of the increasing heat, the thick dressing gown pulled tightly around her. He gently sat down beside her, enjoying the quiet of the room, but also noticing the gentle, almost calming murmur of voices outside drifting up to the room. He gently swept a loose strand of hair from Fran's forehead, and stroked her brow. She didn't stir. Tom wondered what was running through her head. He knew the morning's earlier experience could be quite confusing the first time for someone new.

Fran suddenly stirred and slowly unrolled from her

sleeping ball, stretching out to her full length along the bed.

'It's getting warm,' were Fran's first words before opening her eyes.

Tom stopped stroking her head, surprised she was complaining at being hot, something he'd never heard her say before.

Fran stretched again and rolled onto her side to face him then, blinking from her deep sleep, opened her eyes and looked straight at Tom.

'Hello, you,' she said, smiling, her face soft from sleep.

'Hello,' replied Tom as he leant over and gently kissed her forehead. 'How do you feel?'

'Much better now, but my head still feels like mush with lots of stuff whirling about.'

'Don't worry, it will settle down in a couple of days.'

'What happened? Did I dream it all? For a moment it seemed like I saw the world through a different, but somehow familiar, lens.' She sighed and yawned, stretching again, rolling on to her back. Then in one movement she sat up.

Tom reached out and took her hand. 'The world you're seeing must be somewhere. Something old, forgotten, an echo long past, or a distant memory. This morning just opened the door.'

'Yes, that's it, it was like an overstuffed cupboard of forgotten things that tumble out when you open its door. You look at the mess on the floor, recognising some and not others, but knowing they're all your things,' said Fran as she swept her hand over her forehead and then through her hair, shaking her head at the same time.

'Mother is probably the best person to explain. Like you, she came here new to everything. She said she'd pop in and see you about two o'clock today. Is that alright?'

'Yes, that would be good,' answered Fran. 'But what do you think?'

Tom paused for a moment. 'I think we still connect with old and ancient things. For us here, such things create a different consciousness, perception and connection with the world around us, beliefs the world outside our boundaries has forgotten sitting in towns and cities. Today challenged your accepted consciousness and perception of the world, you were shown a window into a different place that is just as real, just different, ancient and mostly forgotten, only remembered by most through fables and fairy tales.

'Remember what was said this morning.' Tom paused, dropping his voice as if reciting a prayer. 'Too much forgotten, too little remembered, everything denied. Most assuming that closeted behind glass, steel and stone they escape nature's long grasp and can continue their careless ways.'

'So, two worlds?' quizzed Fran.

'No, two consciousnesses each with different values, beliefs and priorities. In fact, when you think about it, there are multiple consciousnesses and perceptions of the world depending on your values and beliefs, driven most often by political, religious and economic beliefs and priorities. All just as valid, always overlapping, mostly co-existing, sometimes in tension, sometime clashing.'

'Thanks, that helps, but it's a lot to take in,' said Fran, her face looking intrigued as she wrestled with what Tom had said.

'So, when they said, 'Most assuming that closeted behind glass, steel and stone they escape nature's long grasp and can continue their careless ways'',' Fran took a breath, her face serious, 'perhaps my world or consciousness clashes with your world I have just seen?'

'I think that's fair. For example, trees are the biggest and oldest living entity in this country, but they get little to no respect or care. Few seem interested in what they really represent. Too often, business regards nature as a free or disposable asset and sees no reason to protect or maintain it. As in itself, nature in its broader sense doesn't fit anywhere in their economic model and doesn't represent or provide any shareholder value. But nature will always find a way back no matter where people hide. There's no escape. You can see that with the changing climate and weather,' Tom said, looking sad, but then felt Fran squeeze his hand.

'Thank you, I think I have a better understanding now,' she said, smiling. 'Now what's the time?'

'Ten-thirty,' answered Tom.

'Right, I'm exhausted and if I'm going to be at my best tonight I could really do with more sleep, so, why don't you fuck off,' Fran said, 'and let me sort myself out.'

Tom looked surprised. 'OK, I'll come back mid-afternoon if that's alright?'

'Yes, perfect. Sorry, I just don't see any point in you mooning around here while I sleep and fiddle about,' said Fran with an apologetic smile.

'No problem, Fran, I understand.'

Tom got up and backed across the room and, as he left Fran eased back down onto the bed and closed her eyes.

~ 13 ~

Fran was woken by a gentle but persistent knock at the door. She sat up, feeling a little drunk from sleep. She glanced at the clock. *Must be lunch*, she thought.

'Coming,' she said as she rose from the bed and walked to the door, feeling a lot better after a morning of rest.

Opening the door, she saw the happy face of Gail who was holding a tray. Gail swept in and exchanged the breakfast tray for lunch.

'Thank you,' said Fran, smiling, still holding the door open as Gail moved to leave with the finished tray.

'You're welcome, madam, anything else?'

Fran thought. 'Could I ask that lunch be cleared before two o'clock, Lady Charlotte is coming for a chat.'

'No problem and I will bring some tea; Lady Charlotte usually likes a cup.'

'Thank you very much,' said Fran as Gail left the room.

'You're very welcome.'

Fran inspected lunch, realising she was hungry and needed to eat. *Eat first, tidy myself up afterwards,* she thought.

Lunch was good; a beautifully light quiche with salad.

Just the job, Fran thought as she put her knife and fork down and guzzled the excellent lemonade. There was an hour until Charlotte was due to arrive, enough time to shower and wash her hair. But her thoughts were interrupted by another knock on the door.

'Come in,' Fran called.

The door opened and Jackie walked in.

'Sorry, madam, do you have a moment? I'm not interrupting lunch, am I?'

'No, not at all, I've just finished.'

'Just confirming you're OK to meet with Miss Penelope before dinner tonight, say six o'clock in her suite. Then you can go together to Lady Charlotte's suite before the three of you go down together to dinner at seven.' Jackie awaited a reply.

'Yes, I suppose that will be OK. But I thought I would be going down with Tom?'

'It's an old custom for the ladies of the house to enter last. Don't wear any jewellery as Her Ladyship will have the jewel cupboard open to find something for you and Miss Penelope to wear.'

'Oh, how exciting and intriguing.'

'Sorry, one more question, madam, if you don't mind?'

'No problem, fire away, please,' Fran replied.

'Miss Penelope is going to wear a new outfit tonight, she's had for a while, but *he* wouldn't let her wear it. It's a dark green with splits from ankle to thigh with the arms split from the wrist to the shoulder. The problem is the body is also spilt from the waist to under the armpit and there is a danger of gapping and flashing a boob as she moves about. We wondered how you dealt with this with your dress? As this would not be ideal at a family dinner, or any event for that matter.'

'I know exactly what you need,' said Fran as she got up and walked to the bathroom, returning holding a plastic envelope. 'Body tape, it will stick to you and the material.' Fran took out the tape and offered a piece to Jackie. 'You just cut it to fit. This should be more than enough unless you've got huge or heavy boobs. Or both!' she said, laughing.

Jackie shifted a bit uncomfortably on her feet, 'No, she has not,' she answered, looking embarrassed.

'Then that should be fine. Sorry, I didn't mean to embarrass you,' Fran said gently.

'Not your fault, madam, just me being silly.' Jackie paused and then continued slowly, unsure if she should. 'It was simpler when *he* was about, in so many ways. Now he's gone I don't know what will happen,' she said, her head bent forward staring at the carpet, kneading her hands nervously in front of her.

'Sorry, I don't know what to say, Jackie, other than I'm sure it will work out. If you do want to talk further, please don't hesitate to see me.'

'Thank you, madam, I really appreciate that. I'm sure you understand there isn't really anyone here I can talk to. Now I must go.'

'OK, I will see Pen at six o'clock.'

~ 14 ~

Tom leisurely wandered down the main stairs and bumped into his father in the hall.'Hi, Thomas, what are you up to?' Lewis enquired.

'I was actually coming to see you.'

'Well, I'm off to see Edward—Ted—Joseph to hopefully finalise and shake hands on the deal. Why don't you join me? Should be interesting, and we can talk on the way.'

'OK, that sounds good.' Turning, he followed his father out of the hall and on to the drive.

'You can drive,' Lewis said, smiling and tossing Tom a set of keys.

Tom looked carefully at the keys he'd juggled to catch while on the move. They looked very new. 'You haven't bought a new car?' said Tom, intrigued as the two of them strode up the drive side by side.

'You'll see in a minute; I think you will be surprised,' said Lewis, with a laugh.

They continued up the slight hill past the first shed and then turned into the second. Lewis led Tom to the far corner where something lurked under a grey car cover.

Lewis stooped by the dark shape and grabbed a corner of the cover. 'Ready?' he asked.

Tom nodded, feeling both excitement and anticipation.

Lewis pulled the cover. It slid easily off the shiny clean vehicle.

Tom gasped in surprise. 'You've actually bought this? All the old Land Rovers can't have died,' Tom said, still not believing his eyes.

'No, we still have enough old Land Rovers for the heavy and dirty work. You always complained all our vehicles were wrecks so I bought this with you very much in mind,' Lewis grinned. 'Those are your keys.'

They both laughed.

'Don't worry, Tom, I have a spare set, and I might borrow it when you're not about,' Lewis said.

'That seems fair,' said Tom, joining in with his father's mirth.

'In we get, let's go,' said Lewis, opening the passenger door and getting in.

Tom jumped into the driver's side and his eyes explored the spotless, new, shiny interior.

'Is this electric?' Tom asked in gleeful surprise.

'Yes, and I've had a fast charger installed which can charge two vehicles at any one time.'

Tom looked at his father. 'You're thinking of buying more?'

'Yes, anything bought from now on will be electric. You'd be surprised how much plant you can get now that is electric. Ideally, I'd like to have solar or wind turbines to generate the power but the permissions are a pain in the arse. So, more work to be done until we get self-sufficient.'

'That's brilliant,' said Tom as he turned the engine on and gingerly drove the new car out of the shed, turning silently left down the drive, passing the house towards Joseph's Farm.

'What's the deal with Joseph's Farm?' asked Tom.

'Ted Joseph wants to retire. He's in his seventies and the farm doesn't get any easier. I doubt he makes any money so he has spoken to me about a deal to pass the land back.'

'I see,' said Tom. 'That's four hundred and fifty acres, isn't it?'

'Yes, possibly a bit more. I've offered Ted a rent-free cottage, a pension, and jobs for his sons. But I'm not really sure what the sons want to do. They clearly don't want to take over the farm. So today we will see where we are.'

'What do you want me to do?' asked Tom.

'Nothing, just listen. This is a big deal after nearly a thousand years and it's important you are involved in what's going on, as you may be the one in the future who has to honour whatever is agreed today.'

'Oh, I see,' said Tom, glad to be included and pleased not to feel any pangs of panic or anxiety about the responsibility this imposed.

They quickly came to the crossroads with its staked wooden signs and Tom drove straight across, passing the sign for Joseph's Farm.

'What about Clifford's Farm?' asked Tom, glancing at the sign to Clifford's Farm as it flashed past.

'Rumour is it's in trouble. Yields are well down. He's filled the ground with so many chemicals he's managed to poison his own land. Top soil running off in heavy rains as he's joined too many fields together, got rid of all the hedgerows and inconvenient trees that hold the land together. He's also been dumping slurry from his dairy herd into the ditches between us and Joseph's land. But the last thing he will ever do is come to us for a deal.

'Henge Cottages,' said Lewis, waving his hand casually to his left as they passed a row of eight joined cottages which clearly needed work. 'They'll make a good addition to our accommodation across the estate. The farmhouse is a good size. Make a good home if you and Fran don't fancy living in the main house. All needs a lot of work and refurbishment.'

Tom nodded in acknowledgement of his father's words as he drew up in Joseph's farmyard. An elderly grey-haired man with a slight stoop and limp walked towards them from the house. Tom thought he was probably a similar age to Isaac, but all the years of farming had clearly taken their toll.

Lewis jumped from the car. 'Good morning, Ted.'

'Good morning, Lewis.' The two men came together to shake hands.

Interesting, thought Tom, all on first name terms as equals, no Lordship stuff. Tom stayed by the car as Lewis and Edward started to talk, noticing an elderly woman standing by the door of the large farmhouse. Ted's wife, Tom assumed; the two sons won't be far, he guessed.

Ted turned and waved to his wife to join them, and

she was closely followed by her sons, both looking a bit sheepish.

At the same time Tom was waved over by his father.

'Now, as I have said we will provide you with a cottage.' Lewis paused, looking at Ted's wife. 'One has just become available; one of the foresters has retired and is moving to Torquay to live with his sister, but it will need refurbishment work. Flora, shall I ask Penelope to get in touch with you to sort this out?'

Flora glanced up at Ted.

'Yes, that will be fine,' said Ted, looking at his wife and squeezing her hand with a smile. *She deserves some real comfort having put up with this for over forty years*, he thought.

'And your sons, what do they want?' asked Lewis sensing the deal was nearly done.

'Change of plan there. They have both decided on a new start in Canada, rather than work on the estate.'

'Fair enough, then I will give them each ten thousand pounds, to help them out,' said Lewis.

Lewis and Tom noticed smiles on the boys' faces as they stood, looking uncomfortable, a step behind their mother and father, listening to the negotiation.

'Fifteen,' replied Ted sharply with a smirk.

'Twelve thousand five hundred. Final offer,' Lewis responded, looking resolute.

'Deal,' said Ted, turning and smiling at his sons.

The two boys, in their late twenties Tom guessed, glanced at each other, clearly pleased. *So they should be*, thought Tom.

Ted threw out his hand to shake with Lewis and then stretched to shake with Tom. The deal was done.

Tom noticed his father made the effort to shake hands with both boys and Flora.

'I'll get this all written up and in a letter to you,' said Lewis. 'Flora, Penelope will be in touch with you about the cottage. Just one more thing. Do you have the farm's books and papers including the details of the Henge?'

'Yes, everything is in order for you to collect when you are ready,' answered Flora.

'All the Henge stones are behind the barn,' Ted said, waving to the building that stood at the bottom the steep hill. 'One of my biggest regrets is taking it down and planting Henge Hill, a nightmare to plough and harvest. Should never have listened to Clifford, it never paid, and it's certainly been a lot more trouble than it was ever worth.' Ted looked at Lewis. 'I guess you will restore the Henge. What will you do with the hill?'

'Yes, restoring the Henge is probably the first job. Return the hill to meadow, I would guess,' said Lewis as he stared at the top of the hill.

'Good,' said Ted, offering his hand again to Lewis.

'Sorry, we must be off,' said Lewis, breaking from the latest handshake and stepping towards the car.

'Yes, I think we are done. Thank you, sir, very much,' Ted said as Tom and his father climbed back into the Land Rover.

Tom reversed carefully, turning the car to drive back. 'Job done. Thought it was a bit cheeky asking for more cash for his sons,' said Tom.

'Yes, job done,' said Lewis thoughtfully. 'I don't blame Ted pushing the money for his sons. To be honest, to get the land back I would have paid a lot more. It's much less than it would have cost us in a year to house and employ the boys. I might just agree to the fifteen thousand Ted asked for.' Lewis paused. 'Be good to get Henge Hill restored, it's a national monument and should never have been taken down.'

They were both silent for a moment as Tom drove back.

'Is Pen alright?' asked Tom, thinking about their earlier meeting that day.

'Yes and no. We both had a good cry, and I think given a bit of time, love and support she will be fine. She also has some thoughts on what she would like to do, which is great, to be honest it's a bit of a relief. I was already taking measures to protect the family assets from that fool Henry. Now we are back to business as usual.'

They passed the house and Tom parked back in the shed and theatrically put the keys in his pocket, which made his father laugh. They then walked back to the house, side by side.

'What about lunch? We can talk some more,' said Lewis, beckoning Tom to join him in the dining room.

Tom paused and looked at his watch. 'Mother's seeing Fran at 2.00 pm,' said Tom.

'Well, I'm meeting Naomi at 1.30, but that still gives us plenty of time for the two of us to have bite first and continue our chat,' said Lewis, at same time placing his hand on Tom's shoulder and playfully steering him towards the dining room.

They were late for lunch, and it was just the two of them in the dining room. Lewis did nearly all the talking, which suited Tom as he got a big download of his father's thoughts and plans, giving him much to think about and consider. The future wilding of the estate, the future of the estate and the need to act, not just talk about the issues that need addressing and finally, how he hoped Pen and Tom would manage most of the estate-based projects.

They were interrupted by Graham entering the room.

'Naomi's arrived for your one-thirty meeting, sir. She's waiting in your study,' he said.

'OK, I'll be there in a moment,' said Lewis as he drained his wine glass and stood up, turning to Tom. 'So glad we had the chance to talk today. Have a think about what we discussed and let me know your thoughts.'

'Will do.' Tom yawned, feeling tired from the early start and a couple of glasses of wine with lunch, thinking it wasn't much of a discussion. But he was pleased to have caught up with so many of his father's concerns and thoughts.

'I think I will go and sit in the drawing room, look at the pictures you mentioned and then go up and see Fran when I'm sure Mother has finished.'

'Good idea. You can catch a small nap. Your mother will probably be up there for the best part of an hour,' said Lewis with a laugh and a playful slap on Tom's back.

~ 15 ~

Once Jackie had gone, Fran sat and thought for a moment about how tricky this must be for both Jackie and Pen. She wondered how the family might react, but she felt sure Charlotte, and others, must know or at least suspect, so perhaps it might not be the shock they thought it would be. Fran got up and decided to shower and wash her hair even though Jackie's visit had eroded the time before Charlotte's arrival.

When finished in the shower, Fran dressed in a baggy lounging outfit she usually reserved for stay-at-home, hungover Sundays. She sat at the dressing table with brush, hair dryer and straighteners to wrestle with her hair again.

At ten to two there was a knock on the door. *Must be Gail*, thought Fran. 'Come in,' she called.

There was a slight pause and then Gail sailed in with a breezy 'Hello,' carrying the tea tray with one hand. She quickly swapped it for the finished lunch tray. 'How's the hair going?' she asked.

'OK, thanks, I think for once I'm winning,' Fran replied, laughing.

'Anything else, madam? The teapot has a cosy on to keep it hot. If it does need refreshing just call and I'll bring up a fresh pot.'

'Thank you, Gail, no, nothing else,' said Fran as she got up from the dressing table. 'Let me get the door for you.'

Fran held the door open for Gail to leave with the larger tray. Closing it behind her, Fran walked to the middle of the room and sat in one of the comfy chairs, wondering what she wanted to ask Charlotte. Fran had only been considering for a moment when there was another knock on the door. *She's early!* Fran thought.

Opening the door, she found Charlotte standing smiling, dressed exactly as she had been at dawn.

'Come in. Please, come in,' said Fran, opening the bedroom door wide with one hand, the other waving vaguely into the room.

'Lovely to see you, I hope you are alright?' Charlotte said, stepping forward to give Fran a hug and a kiss on the cheek.

Fran responded with a kiss and gentle squeeze. 'We have tea,' she said, pointing to the tray and moving towards the comfy chairs.

'Lovely, the girls here know me only too well.' Charlotte smiled. 'I drink gallons of the stuff, especially in the afternoon. I'll be mother.' And Charlotte sat and leant over the tray at her side, pulled off the tea cosy, which made her giggle for some reason, and set up two cups and saucers. 'How do you like it?' she asked.

'Dash of milk, no sugar, please,' said Fran.

In a moment Charlotte leant towards Fran and offered

her a cup and saucer. Thin tendrils of steam rose from the cup, proving its heat, which disappeared as Fran moved the cup and eased further into the comfy chair.

'What was it like for you when you first came here?' asked Fran, blowing on her tea, which was still too hot to drink.

Charlotte sighed. 'I came here all unknowing thirty plus years ago. I met Lewis when I worked for a company he used to visit. He was very smart and polite and always took the time to chat to the staff in the general office while my boss kept him waiting. He visited roughly once a month. When I saw his name in the diary, I would always make an extra effort to look my best.' Charlotte paused and looked quizzically at Fran who was laughing,

'What's so funny?' asked Charlotte.

'I was the same with Tom, sorry Thomas. Made an effort if I thought he would be about.' Charlotte waved the correction away. 'Funny how things don't really change.' Charlotte joined Fran's laughter, nodding in agreement.

'Then,' Charlotte continued, 'on one visit Lewis asked if I would like to join him for lunch after his meeting as he preferred not to eat alone. Obviously, I said yes. I popped in to tell my boss before I left and he told me there was no rush to return, so after a very pleasant lunch Lewis got me a taxi back to the office at three-thirty in the afternoon. On my arrival my boss immediately called me in, asked how it had gone and if he had spoken at all about the business they had going on. I said no, which was quite true. My boss looked disappointed but said I could have any time off I needed if he invited me out again.' Charlotte paused to drink her tea. Fran was sitting forward, intrigued to hear more.

'Well, I thought I would hear from Lewis soon after the lunch—we seemed to really get on—but I heard nothing, and he didn't come to the office again for another two months. Then, a few days before Lewis was due in, I got a note from him asking if I would like drinks and dinner after his late afternoon meeting at our office. I sent a note back and said I'd assumed he'd forgotten about me as he hadn't been in touch since the lunch, and I wasn't sure I was free.'

'Playing hard to get, good for you,' said Fran.

'He called me the next day,' grinning, Charlotte carried on. 'Problems on the estate had kept him from London for far too long and he was really sorry and, yes, he should have been in touch, and he really hoped I could make dinner as he was looking forward to seeing me again. So I agreed.'

Charlotte went to refill her tea cup, her face soft and happy at the memory. She took a quick sip of tea before she carried on.

'Dinner was amazing and at the end he said he'd arranged a car to take me home, he would get a taxi back to his hotel. Before I got in the car we kissed and I admit I was tempted to join Lewis in his taxi back to his hotel.'

'You little minx.' Fran laughed in mock shock.

'That's nothing to what my parents would have called me if I hadn't made it home!'

They both laughed.

'More tea?' asked Charlotte. 'The pot's still hot.'

'Yes please,' said Fran as she leant forward offering her empty cup, which wobbled slightly in the saucer as she passed it.

Charlotte poured Fran a fresh cup as she continued. 'Well, after that I didn't have to wait long for him to get back in touch. Lewis wrote to me to see if I was free for lunch the next week. I said I would meet him at the restaurant. When we met, we kissed again. Over lunch he told me about the estate and said I must visit some time, which I remember sent a shiver of excitement down my spine.'

'A bit different to Tom and me. Burgers and lager, a greasy kiss and the option of a rickety sofa bed I found easy to resist.' Fran laughed to herself, thinking she couldn't imagine having this conversation with her own mother.

'After the lunch Lewis sent an invitation asking if I would like to join him for dinner at his hotel when he was next in London.'

'Uh-oh,' said Fran, her eyebrows raised in mock alarm.

'I told my parents I was staying with a friend from work. Well, the rest is history, and we married a year later. You really must get married here, Fran. It's a wonderful place. Five years later I had Tom.'

'How old were you when you married?' asked Fran.

'Twenty-three. We were engaged for about a year,' said Charlotte, looking curiously at Fran's hands. 'So, a similar age to you. No engagement ring?' she enquired.

'Not yet. I'm not that worried; we just haven't got round to it. Yes, I am twenty-two. Did you feel pressure to have children?'

'No, not really, but I quickly realised there was an

expectation to carry on the family line. I hadn't planned on more children after Thomas and Penelope. But I decided it would be nice to have one more. Twins were a bit of a surprise, but I won't lie, I had plenty of help. That's one thing you can always be sure of here.'

'If Tom hadn't come back would that have been a problem?'

'No, not in itself. The problem really was that terrible man Penelope was going to marry. Lewis had started to take steps to limit what he could do to the estate and family business, but at least we don't have to worry about that now.' Charlotte's face had tightened slightly at the mention of Henry, but she quickly relaxed again after a sip of tea.

'Must have been a worry. What do you think she will do now?' asked Fran.

'Surprise us, if she is honest with herself, as was said to her this morning. Let love, life and hope be her guide, live her life as she would, not as others think she should, don't let hate darken her light.' Charlotte stopped, her face relaxed and almost serene at the mention of what the trees had said.

'Ah, the trees,' breathed Fran almost in a whisper

'I believe Tom has shown you *The Book of the Dead* and the Map of Souls and explained their meaning?' said Charlotte.

'Yes, but it's all a bit confusing.'

'Well, that's not surprising. Tom has thrown you straight in, which I think is a good idea as it's something important that you need to understand, living here and marrying Tom.' Charlotte looked straight at Fran, unblinking.

'The joining of energies is hard to take in. Tom said it's similar to Buddhist beliefs.'

'Yes, that's a good way of thinking about it. Death is not the end. Your energy passes into another form.'

'Your energy? I have none at the moment,' Fran said, not meaning to be funny, but it made Charlotte laugh.

'Think of it as your soul, your essence, your character, the things that make you, you. The energy that drives your desires,' said Charlotte. 'The joining of life energies with the trees keeps us connected to the land and gives the trees a voice they did not have before. I know it's hard to take in. I was the same. And I would guess after this morning you are exhausted and confused?'

'Yes,' was all Fran could think to say.

'Don't worry, it will all slot into place in a few days and your energy will return, and over time you will make sense of things. It hasn't changed or hurt you in any way, just opened a window to ancient things you had forgotten, but which were always there buried in your mind. Your mind must be supple. You picked up the singing today. I think the challenge is that we really have to listen to what the trees have to say as they are better connected to the land and what is happening than we are and they've certainly been around a lot longer than any of us.

'I remember the first time I walked to the trees early one morning with Naomi's mother and Isaac's wife, Jane. When I laid my hands on the tree and breathed in, it was like...' Charlotte paused, 'sliding into a hot enveloping bath with your favourite fragrance. I found it very sensual; the warmth spreading over and through my body, heating my skin, with every breath an increased feeling of connection with something I had forgotten, but at the same time I somehow knew. Old magic, as Isaac would say.'

'Yes,' said Fran. 'Like something forgotten, suddenly remembered, but still a bit of a surprise. Do you have a tree selected?' said Fran, not sure if she should ask.

'Yes, English cherry.' Charlotte smiled. 'A beautiful tree with blossom and fruit. I like the idea and find comfort that my essence will live on through such beauty.'

Fran wrinkled her nose. 'I don't think I'm quite ready to make that decision yet.'

'You have plenty of time to consider all of this and there are many here who can help, so don't worry about it. Try and relax. There's no reason to fear it.'

'Yes, thank you. I think I understand better now, but I can't imagine my parents doing so in any way,' Fran replied, thinking how her dad would laugh and think it was all tosh and nonsense.

Charlotte sat up straight. 'We have to be careful who we tell about all this. As you say, most would not understand. There's a big difference walking in the woods to connecting and talking with it. Before I forget...' Charlotte said, her hand delving into her pocket. She leant forward, holding out a piece of folded paper to Fran. 'Dates for your parents to visit, from Graham, Lewis's assistant. I have underlined those I think are the best, when you and your family would be the only guests.'

'Thank you,' said Fran, taking the paper and glancing quickly at the dates listed.

'I will see you later for a glass of fizz before the three of us go down to dinner. I will have the jewellery cupboard open. I'm excited as I think I have just the set to go with your dress, from what I have been told.'

'That's exciting. A set of jewels sounds interesting,' an eager Fran responded.

'The cupboard is basically a walk-in safe where all, or most, of the family jewellery is kept. It has to go back in and be locked before we all go to bed. Jackie will make sure they are returned to the safe at the end of the evening. Sorry you can't take them home with you.'

'That's a shame,' said Fran, laughing, eager to see what Charlotte had selected.

Charlotte laughed as she stood up. 'Insurance requirement, I'm afraid, we have to advise them every time we take any of the major items off the premises.'

'What's a major item?' asked Fran.

'Any collection of items worth more than one hundred thousand pounds. The collection I hope will work for you was bought in Paris, in the 1920s, by the then Ladyship. The matching set is Cartier and the most valuable we have.' Charlotte smiled at Fran's obvious excitement.

'I can't wait, it's so exciting,' said Fran, trying not to sound too enthusiastic, but knowing her face was betraying her.

'Right, I must go, if there are any concerns or problems please come and talk to me. I will always make time.'

Charlotte walked towards the door, Fran following.

They hugged before Charlotte left. Fran closed the door behind her and leant her back against it, thinking how good it had been to talk and she looked forward to their next meeting. She glanced at the piece of paper still held in her hand, scanning the dates, and deciding three weeks' time might be the best. She sighed, deciding her dad would probably moan at any date.

~ 16 ~

Tom was woken by a gentle jab in the ribs as he napped on the sofa in the drawing room. He'd initially looked at the pictures on the walls his father had spoken about over lunch and had indeed noticed the difference to how things were today and had been in the paintings, quickly understanding what his father had meant about wilding the estate and giving nature its chance. But he quickly realised he needed a sleep as planned. He'd always liked the room. It had a calm atmosphere which made you relaxed. He understood why his mother could often be found in here in the afternoon, with a book and a pot of tea.

He was jabbed again with a bit more force, and he opened his eyes in surprise.

'Hello, you.'

Tom blinked, expecting to see Fran, his eyes telling him he was wrong.

'What are you doing here?' a confused Tom spluttered.

'Your father told me during our meeting you were in here having a rest. I've been wanting to have a chat and thought this might be a good opportunity.' Naomi smiled as she took Tom's hand and sat next to him on the settee. 'There's something I need to know,' she said as she held his hand in hers, palm up. With her free hand, she gently ran her index finger slowly up Tom's wrist and across his hand to the tip of his fingers.

'What are you doing?' Tom stuttered, drowsily, not understanding what Naomi was doing or why.

'There's something I—we—need to know.' Naomi ran her finger down Tom's lower arm for the third time.

'Need to know what?' asked Tom, a hint of panic in his voice.

'If there is still anything between us?' Naomi said as she stopped stroking his hand, instead lifting it and holding it to her breast.

'What the fuck are you doing?' Tom, now frightened, blurted out.

'When you left all those years ago, I waited for you to get in touch. I mooned around for a whole month sure you would call or message me. My brother told me I was mad. What does he know?' She paused, reflecting. 'Probably has more sense than me. I'd worked out you'd most likely joined Jonathan Playly in London. In the end I messaged him. He told me you were fine and relieved to be away from the estate, so I cried a lot and started to work out what to do next. But now we are back and I have to know if you felt a spark like me?'

She started to move Tom's hand gently and slowly over her breast. Tom looked on in complete confusion. He could feel her smooth skin under her thin blouse, then her nipple moving under his fingers as Naomi slowly moved his hand up and down, all the time smiling, keeping eye contact.

'NO!' Tom almost shouted as he pulled his hand away sharply, breaking eye contact at the same time. 'We were just kids that summer. I'm in love with Fran. I'm going to marry her.'

'Well done,' said Naomi with a forced smile, trying to hide her disappointment. 'I just wanted to be sure. There's clearly no spark in you for me.' Her normal smile returned.

'You are mad! How far would this have gone? What would have happened if someone walked in?'

'It would have gone as far as you wanted. If someone had come in it would be just more gossip, which this place thrives on. Am I mad? I don't know. I just wanted to know before it all becomes too complicated for us both.' Naomi leant back in the settee, shrugged and relaxed her shoulders, and sighed. 'Sorry!'

Tom sat up. He didn't know what to say. Naomi looked like she might cry.

'We were just naïve teenagers, hardly lovers, holding hands and fumbling around, little sense in our heads, having a good time. I'm sorry if you expected more or if I let you down.'

'Is it because I'm black?' said Naomi with an edge in her tone.

Tom sighed. 'Christ, no. Never entered my mind. I don't know why you would ever think that. When I was in London, that summer it seemed like a dream, like a good book that clings to your mind. I had realised we were going nowhere; it would never last. We seemed to want different things. You're right I should have spoken to you before I left, to explain, but I thought you felt the same. You always seemed to be so casual about us. I do love you, but like a sister; a dear friend.'

'You passed the test. Fran's very lucky. You should be pleased. Yes, you are right, I wasn't very clear. My first love and romance left me very confused and I didn't know what I wanted. Still friends then, I hope, if I haven't ruined that. That would be stupid but typical of me. Sorry to put you through this.'

Tom took Naomi's hand and squeezed it. 'Sorry, I have to go. I do love you, just not the way you wish.'

'You go, I'm going to sit here for a few minutes,' said Naomi with a weak smile.

Tom got up to leave, considered giving her a kiss, but thought better of it. He walked away and left Naomi to her thoughts.

~ 17 ~

Standing in the passage outside the drawing room, Tom took a deep breath then blew it out hard, feeling some stress of the moment easing. *What the fuck was all that about?* he thought as he walked to the back stairs. He never realised that that summer had meant so much to her. They were just kids. Memories crept into his mind of long sunny days, hot summer nights, naïve fumbling and clumsy sex, thoughts he hadn't had for years. The memories made him smile, but he worked quickly to bury them again, as they didn't help his current dilemma. Clearly, it had all meant a lot more to Naomi than it had to him. If he had known or realised, would it have changed his plans? No, it would have only complicated things and probably landed up in a messy end, with both of them hating each other. At least now they were friends, although that might be a bit strained now.

But it had meant something to her, and still did, he thought, feeling a mixture of confusion and concern and, for some reason he couldn't comprehend, guilt. *Does it change anything now?* he wondered. Only if he wanted it to, he supposed, as he climbed the stairs to the first floor. He had passed the test, as Naomi had said, and she was a difficult woman to resist. *But I rejected her.* The thought calmed him. He would be feeling a lot worse now if things had progressed, and wracked with guilt and even more panic about what it all meant.

Tom paused by their bedroom door, taking a moment to compose himself before entering. He looked at his watch. Three forty-five. Fran would be expecting him back any time now.

Another deep breath, then he raised his hand to open the door. He felt it was all in slow motion. *Is this how panic and guilt works?* he wondered as he pushed the door open and walked into the room, telling himself nothing really happened, nothing had changed. So, why was he having to convince himself?

'Are you alright?' a concerned Fran asked as he entered.

'Yes, I'm fine. I had lunch with Father then went to sleep in the drawing room, as you were seeing Mother. Slept heavily and longer than I had intended as I was tired from the early start. Woke heavy-headed with a bit of a fright.'

'You poor thing. I was just wondering where you were and then, like magic, you appear. Why don't you try and go back to sleep? You've got hours until you need to be ready. I'm seeing Pen at six o'clock, and I can make sure you're awake before I leave, which will give you time to sort yourself out,' Fran said with a sympathetic smile.

'Good idea,' said Tom, as he sat heavily on the bed. He pulled off his shirt and lay down.

'Let me help,' said Fran, tugging his trousers down.

'Oh,' she said in surprise. 'Not everything is tired by the look of things.' She giggled as she pulled off her top and stepped out of her baggy lounge trousers.

'What are you doing?' said Tom for the second time that afternoon.

'Well, I haven't paid you much attention this weekend,' Fran said playfully as she sat astride him.

*

What an afternoon, Tom thought, as Fran said, 'Sleep well,' with a kiss, before heading to the bathroom.

'I will,' Tom whispered as he rolled on to his side and closed his eyes to sleep in the late afternoon heat.

Fran returned to sit in the comfy chair with a magazine she had found on a shelf. She could hear Tom's slow, deep, slightly rattling breath. She was tempted to sleep but she had done her hair and it wouldn't be that long until she would need to dress for the evening. She was soon bored of the magazine full of pictures of wellington-booted pretty young things leading groomed animals, picking fruit or making jam. *Was this the life ahead of her now*? Fran wondered, knowing she would need something more.

Time slipped by. She found the tea was still warm enough for another cup. Then, at five-thirty, she decided it was time to get ready for the night ahead.

On the dressing table she had laid out black pants and black tights which she slipped on. She had already cut the body tape to size, but was a bit of a fiddle once the dress was carefully put on. Lastly, she put on black heels. She stood, checking and admiring herself in the long mirror. It seemed funny not wearing any jewellery, but she was intrigued and excited by what Charlotte had for her. A last quick brush of the hair and a squirt of hairspray. *Ready*, she thought, walking over to the bed and gently shaking Tom by his shoulder. She leant forward and said, 'Time to wake up, Tom.'

Tom stirred. Clearly, he had been in a deep sleep. He opened his eyes and looked at Fran. 'You look amazing.'

'Well done, right answer,' said Fran.

'Two right answers in one day, that's pretty good for me.' Tom's words slipped out before he realised what he was saying and he had a sudden flash of unease.

'What was the first one?' Fran asked innocently.

'Just something I said to Father.'

'Pen and I are seeing your mother before dinner to get jewelled up so when you next see me, I should sparkle.'

'You always sparkle,' said Tom with a grin, the panic dissolving.

'You're on a roll today, Tom. Three right answers in a day, even if the last one was corny, but very sweet.' Fran kissed him again. She glanced at her watch. 'Now I must go, see you at dinner.'

'Yes, see you later,' said Tom.

Fran waved as she walked through the bedroom door.

Tom sat upright, feeling out of breath, not liking the panic his answer had induced. *God, I must be careful and act as if nothing has happened,* he told himself. It was six o'clock, so plenty of time to be ready by seven, even if he did need a shave and shower. He wondered what jewels his mother had lined up.

~ 18 ~

It took Fran moments to walk the short distance to Pen's room. She knocked gently on the door and heard a faint 'Come in,' accompanied by what sounded like giggling. Fran opened the door and saw Pen and Jackie standing together in the middle of the room, both with smirks on their faces.

'Pen, your dress is amazing, the green really suits you.'

'Thank you. Give us a twirl, I've heard so much about yours,' said Pen.

Fran swirled round once as she walked to the middle of the room.

'Brilliant, it's everything I thought it would be and I think what Mother has chosen will look great,' said Pen. 'Sorry, we were just sorting out the body tape which is a bit of a faff, but I think we have got there now. It seems to work well.'

'You wouldn't know it was there, not a crease or a ruck,' said Jackie as she smoothed Pen's top with her hands.

'OK, Jackie, thank you, that's enough,' said Pen, a little flustered as Jackie smoothed over her breasts. 'Thank you, Jackie, that will be all for now. I need to talk with Fran.'

Pen looked a bit embarrassed as she waved Jackie away. Jackie looked a little hurt at being dismissed this way.

'Yes, madam, of course.' Jackie paused by the door before leaving. 'Can I please remind you both that whatever jewels you are wearing must go back in the strong room tonight. So please call me when you get back to your rooms and I will ensure their return. Have a good night, ladies.'

'Please have a seat,' said Pen, leading Fran across the room. They both sat down. Pen kneaded her hands lying in her lap, which gave away her nervousness. *Or perhaps embarrassment,* Fran thought.

'I've made a decision,' said Pen, her face now looking determined. 'I'm going to move out of the house and into a cottage on the estate. Father has agreed on a new role I have created, which will keep me busy.' Pen took a deep breath, a look of relief taking over her face and she stopped kneading her hands.

'Good for you, I think that's a brilliant decision,' said Fran, with a smile.

'And I'm going to ask Jackie to join me, not as staff but as my partner.'

'Have you asked her yet?' said Fran. 'You sure it's not too soon?'

'No, not yet. I just haven't found the right moment or words.'

'Are you worried what she will say?'

'No, neither do I care what anyone else might think.'

Fran laughed quietly.

'What's so funny?' demanded Pen.

'When I saw her earlier this afternoon, your mother said she expected you to surprise everyone and, as you were told this morning. 'Let love be your guide'.'

Pen leant back in her chair. 'Mother told me some time ago I must make a decision. I had already decided I couldn't marry him, I just didn't know how to end it, but he solved that problem last night.' As she spoke, Pen touched her cheek that now showed no sign of the blow. 'Now I've decided to see if I have a future with Jackie. Mother won't be surprised as she told me I can't have both him and her. Everyone else might be a bit shocked but will get over it and carry on as they have before. I'm not the first person in the family to run off with a member of staff, so it's not the first such scandal. Although I think I'll be the first lesbian, or perhaps, more accurately, bisexual. How are you? A lot to take in on your first visit.'

Fran smiled. 'Certainly is. Both Tom and your mother have explained, but to be honest I'm still trying to get my head around everything.' Fran sighed. 'I appreciate it's very important, but it's such a lot to take in and process.'

'Yes, I understand that, and last night's performance must have made you wonder what you are signing up for, joining this family. I can assure you things are usually a lot calmer and duller. Just give it time for all the stuff you've taken in to settle in your head. I promise it will all makes sense in the end.'

'Thank you,' said Fran. 'Anything you think I should do?'

'Next time you're here, go for a walk in the woods with Isaac. He will help show you what it all means.'

'Good idea. We'll be back in a few weeks with my parents.' Fran's face tightened at the mention of her parents.

'Is that a problem, then?' asked Pen, looking concerned.

'I don't know. They won't understand talking with the trees but will certainly enjoy lording it in the house. The big difference is they don't really show much emotion. I am overwhelmed by the love I've seen this weekend. I feel quite humbled, but wonder if I really have the compassion and empathy everyone here seems to have for each other, the land and the life within it.'

'The question is, do you want to; the trees clearly think you have the capacity and they are rarely wrong. You connected so well,' said Pen, trying to reassure her.

'I think it's being buried under a tree of your choice that I struggle most with. To be thinking of your death, hopefully so far away, seems so weird. Macabre!'

'Just different ways, mostly forgotten. One way or another everyone returns to the land in your world and ours. Not right or wrong, just different.'

'Two worlds, as Tom said,' said Fran, her face relaxing.

'And you have the chance to straddle them both if you choose. We all must, in some way. We have to recognise the world outside the estate, we cannot live in isolation, as tempting as it is at times. It will adjust; change your balance in time.'

'Have you chosen a tree?' asked Fran.

'Yes, an ash, which is already growing in the nursery. I feel quite comforted that my energy will carry on and not just evaporate. It won't be the end, but a change, my essence will carry on, add strength and help give voice to the earth.'

'Like going to Heaven?'

'I guess, as some believe, but I've never heard anyone talk from Heaven telling us what it is like. Here the connection in life is continued in death. It's a change, not an end. This may sound weird but sometimes I visit my ash and lay a hand on it to welcome it into the world. Sometimes I'm sure I feel a warmth as if it recognises me.'

'I see, I think,' said Fran thoughtfully.

'We should be going to see Mother,' said Pen as she stood up. She started to shake her shoulders and shimmy. 'Everything still holding, nothing falling out.' Pen laughed.

Fran stood up, joining in the shaking and laughter. 'But I wouldn't start dancing like a looney and testing it too much. On a night out to a club at uni, I was wearing a loose cut away top, a bit risqué, and used tape. It was a hot and sticky and, while dancing like a madwoman, the tape lost its stick. All a bit embarrassing, but I had my trusty cardigan with me.'

They both laughed their way to the door and out into the hall, turning right to Charlotte and Lewis's rooms

~ 19 ~

Tom showered and shaved and now, dressed in his new dogtooth blazer, he stood ready to go down for dinner. He glanced at the clock. *Six forty-five, time to go*, he thought. Must be down and seated before the ladies arrive.

*

Charlotte opened the door. 'Come in, come in. You both look fabulous, but we don't have much time before dinner.

'Fran, this is an old tradition, from when there used to be house parties here most weekends the ladies would always be clapped into dinner. It's an excuse to dress up and get the jewels out; the mostly female staff like seeing the dresses and jewels, we'd thought it would be fun with you visiting this weekend, we probably only do this a couple of times a year.'

'The twins don't take part?' Fran asked

'No, Jen thinks it's a nonsense and an anachronism we best forget and Cath just doesn't take it seriously. Shame, it's just a bit of fun, but we'll see what they think when they are a bit older.' Charlotte turned to her personal maid. 'Sophie, a glass of bubbly for everyone please. Penelope, I have picked out these diamonds for you, they will go well and reflect the green.' Charlotte led Pen over to a table where jewellery had been laid out on velvet mats. Fran followed and inhaled sharply when she saw the size of the diamonds Charlotte had picked out and was now hanging round Pen's neck.

'There, they look great. There's a matching bracelet and diamond drop earrings,' said Charlotte, pointing at the table, before turning to Fran with a smile. 'Don't worry, you haven't been forgotten. Follow me.'

Fran followed Charlotte into what looked like a cupboard, but once inside found herself holding her breath in surprise, surrounded by shelves of jewellery of all colours and shapes and styles; everything you could imagine and more, reflecting, shining and shimmering under the small room's bright downlights. Fran stood still, wide-eyed.

'The family jewels, well, those that aren't in a museum,' said Charlotte, waving her hand across the shelves for effect.

*

Poacher John stood at the side of the drive waiting for his lift. He then heard the distinctive sound of one of the Land Rovers clanking its way down the drive towards him. For the hundredth time he checked he still had Penelope's envelope in his pocket, which he patted once he'd confirmed it was still where he'd put it.

*

Tom walked into the dining room, which was its usual calm, white-clothed, glittering best, took a glass of champagne from the silver tray and moved towards the hors d'oeuvres, realising how hungry he was.

Duncan and Isaac were standing talking with their respective daughters, Olivia and Naomi, who were accompanying them tonight

*

'Now, Francesca, I have something special for you. I've never seen these worn before.' Charlotte swept her hand across a red-jewelled set and smiled.

'They're beautiful,' said Fran, almost in a gasp, feeling overwhelmed by the almost glowing jewellery she was about to wear.

'Rubies with pink diamond surrounds and clusters with silver and platinum mounts made in the 1920s by Cartier, the most valuable jewels we have. Made for a flapper's then-fashionable flat chest and bought by Lady Clara Woodcoombe when she visited Paris,' said Charlotte. 'They call this the tail. It was designed to hang down the front almost to the waist. The necklace is a bit heavier than any of the others but, as you'd expect, beautifully balanced. I thought with that dress you could try and wear it the other way round so the tail hangs down your back.'

*

The Land Rover came to a juddering stop and John opened the door to get in.

'Who the fuck are you?' he demanded as he put one leg in.

'Eddy Provo. Duncan said you needed a lift so I volunteered. Nothing else to do tonight.'

'Are you old enough to drive?'

'Yes, nineteen. I've been an apprentice for two years now.'

'Sorry, I didn't recognise you and thought Dan might be driving me.'

'No, he has other plans,' said Eddy with a soppy grin.

'OK then,' said John, now fully in the vehicle. 'Through New Wood, take the lower road then into St Mary's Lane and park up in either of the first two parking bays in the woods on your left.'

'Right-o, sounds straightforward enough,' said a still grinning Eddy. He crunched the gears and they lurched forward to leave the estate.

'For fuck's sake,' muttered John, as he was thrown around by the lurching, grinding gears.

*

'Perfect,' said Charlotte, taking a step back once she'd secured the necklace around Fran's neck.

Fran could feel the tail touching the bottom of her back.

'Now stand here, use this hand mirror to see your back in the full-length mirror behind you,' said a beaming Charlotte. 'It's spectacular and exceeds my expectations. So pleased it works. You'll need Thomas to hang the tail over the back of the chair when you sit down.'

Fran didn't know what to say. It reminded her of when she would dress up as a princess as a small child, but this was real.

'Incredible, beautiful, thank you so much, it's such a privilege to wear this,' Fran said, touching the equally jewelled counterbalance to the tail which sat on her chest.

'It's a pleasure. These things need to be worn, not

locked away or in a dusty museum.' Charlotte, paused and pointed at another shelf. 'These are the matching brace- lets and earrings. I'll help you put them on.'

'There are a lot of beautiful things in here,' said Fran as she scanned the other glistening treasures, trays of rings, watches, and other jewels.

'Quick,' said Charlotte, pulling a tray out from the shelves. 'What's your favourite ring?'

Fran, distracted, stared at the sparkling red and pink jewelled bracelet now on her wrist while her index finger hovered over the rings, awaiting her decision. 'That one,' Fran said, dropping her hand to point.

'Good choice,' Charlotte answered with a smile.

*

Lewis arrived, picked up a glass of fizz and went straight over to speak with Tom.

'I'm going to say a few words tonight,' he said. 'Wel- come Francesca, give out some good news. Will she be alright with that? Been a bit of a weekend for her.'

'Yes, should be fine, just keep it short please.'

'OK,' said Lewis, smiling. 'We'd better sit down. The ladies will be down soon. Nice jacket, by the way.'

*

Sophie helped Charlotte with her jewellery for the night, slotting and pinning a silver and diamond tiara carefully onto her head. She already had an enormous jewelled brooch pinned to her dress.

Charlotte looked around at everyone with a contented smile. 'We shine. We sparkle.' She laughed, raising her glass. 'Oops, one more thing,' she said as she disappeared back into the cupboard, quickly took the ring Fran had chosen, put it into a velvet ring box and popped it into her clutch bag.

*

'Why do they call you Poacher John?' asked Eddy as they chugged along.

'What?' asked John above the straining noise of the Land Rover.

'Why do they call you Poacher John?' repeated Eddy.

'Well, when I was a lot younger, there was a very popular American television show and everyone said I looked like a character called Trapper John. So, people started to call me Poacher and the name has stuck ever since.'

'You looked like a TV star, cool,' said Eddy grinning. 'And did you actually poach?'

'What do you fucking think?' replied a now irritated John.

'I guess, yes.'

'Back then you could have a great side-line poaching from whoever you weren't working for. Now, it's not so easy and probably impossible to make it pay against the risk. It could be dangerous back then, as if you were caught you usually got a bit of a kicking, which wasn't so good, and Long Farm was one of the worst.'

'Is that where you are going tonight?'

'Yes, if this fucking car can actually get us there.'

'Anything to do with last night?'

'I've been asked to deliver something quietly; I have no idea or interest of what it is.' John patted his pocket again where the envelope was hidden.

*

Gail knocked on Charlotte's door and entered. 'Everyone is seated and waiting for you,' she announced, holding the door open. 'You all look amazing,' she said with a broad grin.

'OK. Ready, ladies?' Charlotte cast her eye over Pen and Fran who both nodded, each taking one last glance in the mirrors near them. 'Show time, let's go!' said Charlotte as she downed the last of her champagne.

'Madam, I hope you don't mind, many of the staff have gathered at the stairs to see the three of you come down,' said Gail.

'No problem, Gail, it's Fran and Pen they have come to see and they both shine tonight, as they always should,' Charlotte said, glancing over her shoulders at Fran and Pen walking side by side as they neared the main stairs.

*

Naomi leant over to Olivia. 'They'll be here in a moment. Can't wait to see their dresses.'

Olivia glanced at the dining room door. 'Yes, I've heard a great deal about Miss Francesca's dress, but Miss Penelope also has something new,' Olivia replied, clearly excited.

'I think, from the sounds of it, Miss Francesca's will steal the show,' said Naomi.

*

Eddy steered into the first wooded parking bay in St Mary's Lane.

'What now?' asked Eddy.

'You sit here until I'm back. You don't move, whatever

happens, got it?' John almost snarled, his face set to the task ahead.

'How long do you think you will be?'

'Should be back in two hours.' John glanced at his watch. 'Seven-twenty; it will be properly dark in the woods within the hour, so providing there are no problems two hours should be more than enough, but if I don't appear in two, wait for three before you do anything. It might just be I have had to make a detour to get back.'

'So, wait for three, then come and look for you,' Eddy said, concentration etched on his face.

'No, you drive back and find Duncan. Tell him exactly what's happened. He'll know what to do,' said John.

'But I can handle myself and might be able to help if there's a problem.'

'No, go back as I have told you, if I'm delayed or rumbled it will probably involve Bull, the Long Farm foreman, who would even give Duncan a run for his money in a scrap, and Quill and Stanic, Bull's two goons. You wouldn't stand a chance, son, and no point two of us getting hurt. Only make things worse.'

'OK,' said Eddy, looking a bit downcast that his help had been turned down.

John leant forward, reached back and drew the knife from the sheath on his belt. He rolled the familiar, smooth, mottled bone handle in his hand and the freshly sharpened, cleaned, silver blade shone brightly.

'That's a knife,' Eddy breathed in admiration.

'For the dogs if they are let out. But if it comes to it, I will cut Bull or his goons to get away.'

Eddy said nothing as he watched John hold up and roll the shining blade in the last of the day's sun before he sheathed it back in his belt, opened the door and stepped out.

'Remember what I've said,' said John. 'Good lad.'

Eddy nodded as John shut the door and headed into the woods. Sighing heavily, he then put in his earphones and settled down to wait, rolling the conversation around in his head.

*

Charlotte paused at the top of the main stairs and turned to Fran and Pen.

'We have an audience, so let's not disappoint.' She pointed at Pen to take the left and Fran the right side of the staircase. 'And do a twirl on the way down as the girls have come to see the dresses, they've all heard so much about.'

Pen and Fran only had to take half a step sideways to get in position as instructed and then followed the slowly descending Gail. Fran could see nearly all the staff were either gathered below in the hallway or above along the first-floor gallery.

Fran was suddenly aware of Pen doing a turn, her arms extended. Fran swallowed. *Hard enough wearing heels,* she thought, *now she had to twirl around.* She raised her arms, one hand grabbing the rail to her right, turning and swapping hands as soon as she could to ensure her balance. Fran caught Pen's grinning face and she bowed her head and then gracefully crossed to Fran's side of the stairs.

Crikey! thought Fran, as she let go of the rail, and, as gracefully as she could, copied Pen and moved to the left.

Fran heard a gentle rippling applause from the watching crowd which continued as they all descended to the hall.

'Beautiful,' clapped Mrs Cooper. 'All of you. So lovely to see.' Her face beamed.

'Lovely to see you, Mrs Cooper, you're looking well. Sorry about last night,' said Pen.

'Don't be so silly,' said Mrs Cooper, dismissing Pen's remark with a wave of her hand. 'I saw you all this morning, welcoming the summer. Naomi insisted I rested for the remainder of the day, and here I am tonight,' said Mrs Cooper with a smile.

Next to Mrs Cooper stood Jackie, who had clearly been crying. Pen paused in front of her, took her hands and kissed her on the cheek, saying something that Fran couldn't catch even though she was standing by Pen's side. Jackie's face lit up, and she replied to Pen but, again, Fran couldn't catch what was said. A happy Pen leant forward and kissed Jackie's cheek again. Fran was aware of whispers and nudges from the gathered staff and wondered what had been said.

Charlotte smiled at the two young women as they followed Gail to the dining room door.

*

The sun seemed to be racing to set, but John still had enough grey light, even amongst the trees and scrub, to help him move up through the woods to the Campbell-Blyth farmhouse. If he remembered rightly there was a path and cover all the way up to the side of the house so once he'd got there all he had to do was check the coast was clear and then pop out and push the letter through the door. It would then be an easy walk back to Eddy, and a beer on the way home, he decided.

*

Eddy had his eyes closed, and opened them in surprise at a brisk tap on the window by his head.

'Who are you?' asked the bloke.

'I'm Eddy and I'm waiting for a friend.'

'Aren't we all,' said the bloke with a crooked smile. 'Are you new? Are you on the WhatsApp group? Do you know if anyone else is coming?'

Eddy was very confused. 'No, I'm picking up a friend who will be a while.'

'Each to their own, but this is a popular spot,' said the bloke, grinning and turning as another car pulled in. 'Here she is, she may have brought a friend,' he winked at Eddy. 'Must go, wander over if you want to watch.'

What is going on? Eddy said to himself as a lady got out of the car with a dressing gown on. The bloke was opening the back of his van and pulling his top off.

The inside of the van had a dull light on. Eddy looked away as the bloke pulled off his tracksuit bottoms and the lady peeled of her dressing gown. Both now naked, they stepped into the van.

Bloody hell! What's going on? Eddy thought with alarm. There was another tap on the window. Eddy swivelled his head to see a blond-haired woman, whose age was difficult to tell.

'First time?' she asked. 'Me too. Why don't you just come and watch?' She stepped away and her dressing gown fell open. *Lucky it's warm*, thought Eddy, not sure if he should look or not. 'No, thank you, I'll stay here. I'm waiting for a friend.'

Blondie stepped forward again, holding the dressing gown closed across her body.

'Well, I could join you for a while if you like,' she said with a smile, holding her dressing gown tightly closed.

'No thank you, you're very kind, but I'm happy to stay in here on my own, thank you.'

'Whatever, each to their own,' she said as she turned and walked towards another car that had just arrived.

'Fucking hell. John will never believe this. I seem to be parked in dogging central,' Eddy said out loud to himself as people flitted about from car to car in various states of dress or, more accurately, undress.

*

Gail paused by the dining room door and glanced back. 'Ready?' she asked. All three nodded.

Gail walked in first. 'Ladies, gentlemen and guests...the ladies of the house.' Gail then stepped aside and held the dining room door wide open and Charlotte entered with a well-practised elegant glide to the sound of clapping. Next to enter was Pen and the clapping went up in volume. Fran followed last. By now, everyone was standing and clapping, and she saw Charlotte and Pen shining in the light of the room. All a bit strange, but Fran had to admit she was beginning to enjoy being centre stage. *Nearest thing I'll get to being on the red carpet*, she thought as she did a final twirl.

*

John got to the house quicker than he expected,

'Cody. Perry. Here, boys.'

Fuck, the dogs are out, thought John, instinctively reaching behind him to check his knife.

'Good boy, Perry, now in you go.'

House dogs, breathed John with relief as he heard Cody being called again.

Then John heard the unmistakable sound of paws padding up behind. John was now kneeling on one knee in the bushes at the side of the path. He swivelled to peer behind into the dark, at the same time taking a firm grip of his knife, although he'd noticed no barking from either dog. Suddenly, he could hear footsteps and panting moving up behind him. Close now, the dog had his scent. Then the deep brown eyes and lolling tongue of the panting chocolate brown Labrador was next to him, emerging from the dark, sniffling and nuzzling him, tail wagging. *A happy chap*, John thought.

'Cody,' was shouted out again, John guessed from the house. John stroked the dog and then gently pushed it on towards its home. It walked two paces and then, as only Labradors can, looked back with its big mournful face.

'Go on,' John urged quietly and, to his relief, the dog did. 'Good boy.'

John heard then a yelp from Cody.

'You come when I call you. Will you never learn?' John heard shouted and then the house door slammed shut.

*

Tom walked from his seat and offered Fran his arm.

'You more than sparkle, you exploded into the room like a thousand suns.'

'Thank you.' Fran smiled, feeling slightly giddy from the excitement on an empty stomach and a gulped glass of champagne. They passed Naomi who was on her feet and she reached out to give Fran a hug as she went by

'Star of the show in every sense. Fab dress,' Naomi said.

'Thank you,' was all Fran could think to say. Then she remembered her tail as Tom steered her to her seat.

'Tom, can you please ensure my tail is over the back of the seat and I don't sit on it.'

'Of course,' said Tom as he leant forward and lifted the jewelled tail, lowering it gently as Fran sat down. 'All done,' Tom said as he sat down.

*

Eddy was getting a bit concerned, having passed the stage of finding the goings on around him funny.

Blondie had returned, her breasts slipping out of her dressing gown as she asked if she could to get into the cab with him. Eddy had again politely declined.

He looked at his phone. John had been gone barely an hour, so no quick escape.

Two more cars turned in and stopped and, to Eddy's horror, suddenly lit the parking area with blue flashing lights. Police spilled out.

Eddy watched as everyone was rounded up, many quickly dressing as the police moved about.

Another tap on the window and a policeman grinned as Eddy wound it down.

'Good evening, sir. Could I have your name and address please?'

'Why? This is nothing to do with me.'

'Really, sir? Then perhaps you could tell me what you are doing here?'

'Waiting for a friend who's in the woods.'

'Really, sir, and what is their name?'

'John. He's looking for the dog which ran away when it was being walked this morning.' Eddy knew that none of what he said sounded very convincing.

'OK, sir. But I still need your name and address. Don't worry, it will only be a caution.'

Eddy sighed and his head dropped. 'Alright. Alright.'

*

Fran was sat between Tom and Isaac. Charlotte was next to Tom.

Charlotte leant past Tom and spoke to Fran. 'You, OK? You look sensational. Wearing the necklace, the wrong way round, really works and you wear it so well. You'll be the talk of the house for some time to come.' As Charlotte eased back to her seat, she grabbed Tom's hand and thrust into it the ring box she'd put in her bag earlier.

Tom looked at it a bit bemused and went to open it only for Charlotte to say, 'No!' She clutched his hand, dragging it with the box away from Fran's gaze to between her and Tom.

'Open it carefully so Fran cannot see,' Charlotte whispered.

Tom carefully opened the box, then shut it quickly, putting it in his jacket pocket.

'She chose it when we were putting on the jewellery. She really should have an engagement ring; it was your grandmother's and I'm sure she would be delighted for Fran to have it.'

'Thank you, thank you so much, I'm sure she will be love it,' said Tom with a big smile as he squeezed his mother's hand.

*

John moved forward to the corner of the house. He was still hidden by scrub. Lights from the big farm sheds opposite the house gave some light. John looked left and right, and listened for any sound. All clear. He pulled out the letter and checked the way was clear again, then stepped out quickly to the front door and dropped the letter through the letterbox. He turned straight round and knelt at the side of the house in the cover of the scrub he'd just left, then ran back along the side of the house and listened. No noise. He breathed again. Then he heard an angry shout from inside the house and the front door being opened. 'Get out, get out, Cody, you fucking stupid dog!' And he heard a yelp as a dog was roughly expelled. John immediately stood and ran, crouched, through the scrub along the side of the house back into the woods, back towards the car.

*

The policeman took Eddy's details. 'You're a way from Woodcoombe. Why would you walk your dog's here when you have acres of land back there?'

'Give the dogs and us a change,' Eddy offered, unconvincingly.

The Sarge looked equally unconvinced and waved to his colleague.

'Can you bring Bob over please, now you've got his details.'

The policeman nodded and, holding the bloke from the van by the elbow, steered him over.

'Here you are, Sarge, Bob,' the policeman said with a laugh.

'Now, Bob, do you know this man?' asked the Sarge.

'No,' said Bob, looking very bedraggled. 'He was here when I arrived. Thought he was a new member, but he never left his car. Although Mabel,' Bob nodded towards blondie, 'tried to tempt him out, but he would have none of it, said he was waiting for a friend. He's nothing to do with us, not even on the WhatsApp group.'

The Sarge sucked in his lips as he thought, then returned his attention to Eddy.

'Can I see your phone please, specifically WhatsApp?'

Eddy did as he was told and passed the phone to the Sarge with WhatsApp open and watched as he scrolled through the chats, checking deleted and archived messages as well.

'Nothing here, son, I'm going to give you the benefit of the doubt this time,' said Sarge as he passed Eddy back his phone with a smile.

'Thank you,' said Eddy as he sighed with relief.

*

Dinner was served amongst a happy hum of chat and

occasional laughter. *Altogether a lighter evening than the night before, with just the family and a few others*, thought Fran.

'How have you found us, Francesca?' asked Isaac.

'Well, there's been a lot to take in and understand.'

'Yes, we have some unusual ways. The main thing is how do you feel, what have you found here that would make you stay or come back, what's in your heart?'

Fran thought for a moment. 'It's certainly been emotional. Sorrow, shock, love, and hope all in a day. As Tom has said to me, the consciousness and values of the world here are very different to the world I'm used to. Yes, I will be back and I'm looking forward to understanding more, getting involved and finding ways I can help.'

Isaac's face was relaxed and smiling as he turned slightly to face Fran.

'Well said! I'd have been surprised if you said you understood everything, it takes time to understand and appreciate, our different, odd, many will think, ways of living with the land.'

'Someone suggested next time I'm here I walk the woods with you.'

'Great idea, you can meet Jane, my wife. She would love to meet you.'

'Hawthorn?' said Fran. 'Thomas has shown me the Map of Souls.'

'Well remembered, young lady,' said Isaac with a laugh.

'Thank you, I think I'm beginning to understand,' said a smiling Fran, feeling pleased with herself.

*

John moved quickly, well, as quickly as he could. *Not as spry as I was,* echoed accusingly through his head, as he felt himself sweating and his breath heavy and rasping. 'I'm too old for all this,' he said out loud to himself as he stopped, bent forward, his hands on his knees. As he waited to cool down and his breath to return, he listened intently for any sound of pursuit. To his relief there was none, no shouting or barking. But then he heard the padding sound of a dog again.

Fuck! John thought. Dogs got my scent. Then the same chocolate brown Labrador emerged from the dark, tail wagging, tongue lolling, enjoying the game. It padded slowly up to the recovering John, nuzzling him with his nose.

John put a hand out and stroked him behind his ears. The dog moved closer.

'I'd guess you'd be Cody,' John said as he stroked the dog's flank and felt him flinch. 'Was that a kick then, you poor boy?' John continued, stroking the dog's neck, and Cody moved nearer, glad of attention and a level voice.

John stood up, his breath returned, and he no longer felt quite so hot. Cody looked up at him mournfully, wide-eyed, walking round him, continuously brushing his legs.

'Come on then,' John quietly urged Cody as he started to move again back towards the car.

Cody seemed to bounce along next to John as they moved through the wood, tail wagging constantly, clearly enjoying the game.

John saw the various cars and lights where he'd left Eddy. instinctively he stopped and knelt on one knee in the shrubbery for cover. Cody stopped next to him and sat down, panting slightly, tail still wagging happily, rhythmically slapping the ground.

'Easy, boy,' John said as he placed a hand on Cody to calm him. 'Fuck! Wonder what's going on here?'

John stood up slowly and moved carefully to the edge of the wood. Cody lolloped along slowly behind.

John saw Eddy standing by the Land Rover next to the Sergeant. John strained forward to be sure of what he was seeing. Sergeant Bennett. *What the fuck has the boy done?* thought John, trying to understand why there was such a crowd. He decided there was nothing for it and he slowly stood up and walked out, with Cody plodding along beside him at heel, to find out what was happening.

'Good evening, Sergeant Bennett, haven't had the pleasure for some time.'

The Sarge and Eddy turned at the voice.

'You've found the dog!' Eddy exclaimed in surprise.

'To be more exact, boy, the dog found me,' a slightly confused John replied while he stroked Cody.

'You lost the dog this morning, I understand?' said the Sarge.

'Yes, he chased after squirrels and got lost in the woods,' said John, hopefully guessing the story Eddy had laid. 'Walked here this evening hoping he would pick up my scent and return as he is probably hungry now.'

Sergeant Bennett narrowed his eyes and ordered the other policemen, 'Search the rim of the woods for anything suspicious.' The Sarge then looked at John. 'Need to make sure you're not up to any of your old tricks.'

'I've retired, Sergeant.'

The Sergeant said nothing, just shook his head slowly in doubt.

The policeman who'd been checking the perimeter returned with a shake of his head.

'OK, you can both go,' Sergeant Bennett said, turning away.

'What's been going on here?' John called out to the retreating Sergeant.

'One of Big Bob's evenings,' said Sergeant Bennett, laughing as he made his way back to his car.

'Fucking hell, and I thought I was too old. Come on Eddy, well done, let's go.'

*

Lewis tapped his wine glass. The convivial hum and laughter subsided as he stood up.

'Good evening, everyone, don't worry, this won't be a long speech. Hopefully, just some good news to share with all here.' Lewis paused, looking at the expectant faces. 'I'm delighted to confirm that the South West Fast Rail project has now been cancelled, so no line will be coming through the Vale. But they still want the contract for planting trees and hedgerow, but now along the current upgraded lines, which will create wildlife habitats and corridors from here to Land's End.' There was a ripple of applause, and a palpable sense of relief across the room. Lewis continued. 'We will officially be a charity next Monday so the first stages of building work can start as planned. The second stage, visitor centre etc, hopefully will follow and I'm delighted to confirm that Naomi will be helping with the plans.' Another ripple of applause. Naomi was smiling broadly at her mention, Isaac looking very proud.

'All here know next weekend we have some very special guests, which will hopefully give us the opportunity to expand our work here to other estates and lands. Today Thomas and I agreed with Ted Joseph the return of his farm to the estate after a thousand years.'

More applause.

'Lastly, Penelope has spoken to me about the value of the community we are all part of here and I have agreed that she will set up and run a Woodcoombe community team to look after everyone.'

There was enthusiastic applause although no one really knew what this meant, but they wanted to show their support for Pen after the drama of the night before. Pen stood up and waved down the applause and cheers.

'Thank you all, you're too kind. I'm sure you're all wondering what the community team will actually do. Well, to be honest we are still deciding, but it will be there to work for the good of all here and the community beyond. Finally, news for everyone.' She glanced a bit nervously at her mother and father. 'I have decided to move out of the house and live on the estate and I'm delighted that Jackie has agreed to join me, but not as my maid or housekeeper.' Pen made a slight bow and sat down, to more applause.

Lewis was still standing. 'Sorry, one more thing, I'd like to formally welcome Francesca to the family. I sincerely hope she has survived the weekend, that we haven't frightened her off and that we will see her again very soon.' Lewis raised his glass. 'Francesca.' The room stood as one and repeated the toast.

Fran wasn't sure what to do but as everyone sat, she remained standing up, without a clue of what to say.

'Err,' she stuttered, searching for words. Tom took her hand hanging by her side and squeezed it. 'Thank you, yes, I look forward to coming back. I still have much to learn and this world is very different to the one I know, but I think I am slowly understanding, so thank you all for your patience now and in the future.' Fran paused, then raised her glass. 'To all of you. Family and friends.'

Everyone stood up and raised their glasses. 'Family and friends,' rang out across the room with some emotion as they made the toast. When they all sat down, Isaac remained standing and he started to recite in a clear emotional poetic rhythm.

'We give our fealty to lord, liege and land.

Our blood runs deep, strong and true in root and vein.'

Duncan stood and passionately joined in the last two lines.

'By the bow, by the land, we stand united, until the end.'

Lewis, Tom and Kurt stood up, joining Isaac and Duncan in a triumphant last line.

'By our blood and the spirits of man and land our promise is made.'

All five men cheered loudly at the end, raising their glasses, and everyone applauded.

Naomi leant over to Fran. 'That's the promise of the bowmen,' she said with a smile.

Fran nodded her thanks to Naomi, feeling the emotion

of the promise sweep the room. Even Naomi had a tear in her eye.

They all cheered and Isaac shouted out, 'Now!' and the promise was chanted again. Everyone was standing caught in the promise's spell. Fran stood as well, holding Tom's hand in awe at the passion and emotion in the room. Everyone, even those serving, joined in and Mrs Cooper came in on Gail's arm to join them. By the end there were few dry eyes in the room and the passionate emotion fuelled a shouted cheer at the end.

*

John and Eddy climbed back into the Land Rover.

Cody sat on the ground looking up at John wide-eyed and mournful, tail wagging.

'Come on then,' said John, smacking his thighs in encouragement.

Cody jumped and scrambled into the cab with John helping to pull him in. He sat on John's lap, excited, trying to lick his face, tail slapping from side to side. John spoke gently and calmed him down and slipped him carefully into the footwell with Cody resting his head on John's lap.

'You know the Sergeant?' Eddy asked.

'Yes, I've had the pleasure in my poaching days,' said a thoughtful John, thinking back.

'Do you know Big Bob?' Eddy grinned at John.

'Vaguely, he's a bit of a local legend, but the police and council don't like his escapades. Upsets the tourists.'

Eddy started the engine and the Land Rover shook and squealed. The truck again juddered and lurched, as Eddy drove off. Cody started to howl.

'Now you know how I feel in this fucking wreck of a truck,' said John as he calmed Cody down.

Eddy smiled, glancing at Cody. 'Is poaching always this easy?'

'First time I've had any animal surrender.' John laughed, stroking Cody. eHeHe looked thoughtful. 'Provo, where have I heard that name before?'

'My sister, Rachel, was attacked up there about eight years ago,' Eddy spat out through clenched teeth.

'Of course, how stupid of me. Terrible business, no wonder you were so keen to get up to the house.'

'Yes, but probably just as well you made me stay in the truck, I would have only done something really stupid,' said Eddy quietly—well, as quietly as he could over the noise of the straining Land Rover.

'Don't worry, son. Revenge and comeuppance always come to those who deserve it and often comes in the most unexpected way, so be patient and be smart. We could share the dog if you like. He can live with me, but perhaps you could help exercise him. Just needs a good home and some love and attention, like any of us.'

'Yes, I'd like that,' replied Eddy. 'We'll be back soon.'

'I was thinking of stopping off for a beer. But probably not wise with the dog, all we need is to run into someone from Long Farm who recognises Cody. We can get a plate of food and a beer at the house. And the kitchen will have food for the mutt.'

'Probably sensible,' replied Eddy. 'I appear to have escaped Mabel so I shouldn't push my luck any further.'

'Nothing to fear from Mabel,' said John, 'We went to

school together about a hundred years ago.' He smiled. 'She started dancing at The Oak pub when we were still at school, which caused a bit of a fuss. The girls who danced there were either beginning or ending their careers and for Mabel, it's now definitely the latter, although last time we spoke she said she'd definitely retired.'

'Have you...?' Eddy enquired casually.

'Mind your own fucking business, you cheeky little runt, but for the record, no. But I've always got on with her well enough and would call her a friend. She left for London and a glamour modelling career. Every man in the country over a certain age will know her; she was a regular in the red top newspapers, and appeared on television as a glamorous assistant on game shows. Returned a couple of years ago, lives in Woodcoombe Village. She's not a millionaire, but she's done alright, seen her in the Foresters a few times. Used to happily watch her dance at The Oak in our younger days. Surprised she's mixed up with this lot, she must be bored. Perhaps I'll give her a call and make sure she's alright.'

Eddy wrinkled his nose, 'Lucky for her you're just reaching your prime.'

'Cheeky bugger,' said John with a laugh, enjoying Eddy's company now.

'They have wet T-shirt competitions at The Oak on Thursdays instead of the strippers now.'

'So, I've heard, how does that work?' asked a curious John.

'Girls are given free white Oak pub T-shirts then squirted with water and the girl who gets the loudest cheer gets fifty quid and free drinks. If there's a lot of girls there's a second and third cash prize. It becomes pretty chaotic. It's a bit mad.'

John laughed. 'I wouldn't want my girl up on stage wiggling about and flashing her stuff. All a bit sad if you ask me and not exactly a step forward for the ladies. Not much dignity or self-respect in that.'

'Some girls have complained, but others seem to love it. Fifty quid is more than a day's money for many, plus there's free drinks for all of them, more drinks if you win,' said Eddy. 'I'll take you down one night if you like.'

'Fuck off, they'll think you've brought your grandad out for a treat.'

There was a pause and they then both laughed loudly, Cody joining in with a friendly howl.

*

After the drama of the promise, the dining room settled back into its relaxed hum of talk and chatter. Most were tired from the morning's early start, the evening's good food and fine wine only adding to the drowsy feeling.

Catherine left her seat, walked round the table and stopped behind Charlotte.

'Mother, I'm going to bed now, so goodnight.'

'Say good night to your father and others before you go,' said Charlotte as she gave Cath a goodnight hug and kiss.

Cath turned towards Tom and Fran. 'Goodnight, Tom, so pleased to see you back. Fran, lovely to meet you, can't wait until you come back, and we can really talk.'

Cath then went over to say goodnight to Lewis and left the room. Fran noticed Charlotte and Pen exchange looks as Cath disappeared, and Fran wondered what the concern was.

~ 20 ~

Dan woke with a start and instinctively looked at his watch. Eleven thirty-five. *Shit!* he thought to himself, I should really have gone an hour ago.

Cath lay asleep next to him on her side facing him, her arm stretched across his bare chest, her strawberry blonde hair splashed over her pillow and framing her face. *Like a halo*, Dan thought.

He had a choice. Go now or go back to sleep and wait until the morning. Cath had asked him to stay all night many times. But he could probably still sneak out now before the house was locked up for the night. If he waited until the morning, there was little chance of getting out unnoticed and that would only mean trouble for them both and especially Cath. Dan smiled to himself, remembering Cath had said she didn't care who knew and he had no doubt many of the staff in the house already did.

He decided and eased himself out of bed, careful not to disturb Cath. He gently held her outstretched arm, which had just been holding him, and moved a pillow underneath it as he lowered it down.

He dressed quickly, noticing her smell still on his skin

with a smile. He glanced back down at Cath as he pulled his T-shirt on. *Yes,* he thought, *it would be good to wake up with her and lounge in bed for a while.* He slipped on his jacket and shoes and crept to the door. He gently opened it and listened. No one seemed to be around and he eased himself out, quietly closing the door behind him. *Back stairs*, he decided, *the main stairs are too bright and there's no chance to hide.*

Dan walked down the corridor round the gallery to the plain arched opening and, as quietly as possible, began to descend the spiral stairs, listening hard for anyone coming the other way. He came to the ground floor corridor without incident and headed towards the main door. Suddenly, there was a sound behind him and Dan moved quickly to hide behind the main stairs.

Fuck, they were locking up the main doors to both the Vale and the drive. He thought quickly. He could use the midnight window in the corridor, famous for those who were late and needed to get out after the house was locked up for the night, but if he used it now it would be unlocked and, in the morning, it would be spotted and there would be an enquiry as to why it was open. Dan dismissed the idea of going back and getting Cath to lock the window after him; too much fuss. The only route open to him was through the kitchen whose door was just behind him. The foresters' door was always available, but you never knew who you might meet in the kitchen. Dan decided he really didn't have a choice and turned to go through swing doors to the kitchen. He paused as he heard voices ahead. As he quietly descended the few steps to the kitchen, he could see the lights were on and he heard someone sounding like they were talking to a dog. Dan had to go forward. There was no point going back and so he stepped through the short, dark corridor towards the kitchen light.

Then he heard the swing doors behind him flap open and closed and brisk steps behind him.

'Out of the way, whoever you are, please, tray coming through,' said Holly, briskly carrying a large tray out in front on her.

Dan pushed himself against the wall as Holly passed. *Perhaps I should go back*, he thought. But this was his only way out now.

'Here we go boys, dessert! And there's someone skulking in the corridor, no idea who it is,' Holly announced to John and Eddy who longingly scanned the tray of unused desserts from the evening's dinner.

'Whoever you are come in and have something to eat, you fool. Walk in under your own steam or I'll send the dog to flush you out,' John said, winking at Eddy.

'That's if we can drag him away from his food,' said Eddy.

Holly laughed. 'Never seen a dog eat so much; must be hungry,' she said, turning to see who would appear in the light of the kitchen, the chomping of Cody eating the only noise as the three of them waited for the mystery guest to appear.

Dan stood up and stretched. He knew he had no choice, but better caught by staff here than family in the main house.

'What the fuck are you doing here?' said John as Dan appeared timidly, his eyes adjusting to the kitchen lights.

'Overstayed his welcome, I would guess,' chimed in Eddy with a broad grin.

'Bless him, you've been locked in.' Holly smiled. 'Now Dan, come and sit down, you hungry? We have a few mains as well as puddings, what do you fancy?' She turned to John and Eddy. 'Now, you two, don't you go giving him a hard time.'

John looked thoughtful. 'Dan, if you're in the house for the reason I think you are, you're playing a dangerous game for you and whoever you might have been visiting, which isn't hard to guess.'

'Food?' asked a smiling Holly.

'Please,' replied Dan, wondering if the kitchen really had been a wise choice.

'Chicken, ham and egg pie. Sorry, it will be cold now.'

'That will be good, thanks,' a subdued Dan replied.

'Eddy,' said John, 'pour young Dan a small beer. He'll need something to wash the pie down with.'

Eddy got up, took a beer glass and walked the three steps to the barrel sitting on its stand at the end of the kitchen.

'Now, lad,' said John, leaning towards Dan. Holly hovered, not wanting to miss a word. 'You had better be clear of your intentions if you are going to carry on with whatever you're up to. Does your father know?'

'He suspects and keeps telling me to be careful and that if I play fire don't be surprised if I get burnt,' Dan replied between mouthfuls of pie.

'Too fucking right. Sorry, Holly, for my French. Duncan knows what he's talking about. Hero or zero, it's up to you and whoever to decide.'

'I didn't know 'fuck' was a French word, but I'm not surprised,' mumbled Holly.

'For fuck's sake,' breathed John, raising his eyebrows while Eddy giggled at what Holly had said.

'How's the dog doing?' John asked Eddy with a slight snarl.

'He's finished his food and he's looking sleepy,' said Eddy, standing over the dog.

'Better get him out and home before he shits in the kitchen and falls asleep.' John looked at Holly. 'I don't think shit is a French word. They say *merde* if memory serves me right.' He spied Eddy laughing again. 'Can you please take Cody tonight? Bring him out to the range in the morning and I'll take him from there.'

'I'll walk with you, if that's alright,' said Holly. 'Just leave your dirty plates tidy on the side and they'll be cleared tomorrow. Any desserts not eaten in the bin, please, and the pie in the fridge.'

'OK,' said John. 'You two go carefully.' He winked at Eddy, which Holly didn't see, and John was sure Eddy blushed.

Suddenly, they all looked towards the entrance to the kitchen, having heard the doors to the hall swing energetically.

'Evening all,' said Lewis as he emerged, smiling, into the kitchen light.

'Good evening, sir,' said John, slightly rising from his seat.

Eddy and Dan mumbled similar, touching their forelocks briefly in respect.

Dan felt himself go hot and cold with Cath's father now standing in the kitchen. *Could it get any worse? Perhaps I should have stayed with Cath until morning,* Dan thought to himself.

'What are you lot all up to this late?' said Lewis as he took a seat.

'Can I get you anything, sir?' asked Holly.

'Don't worry. I can make myself a green tea. Anyone else like a hot drink?'

'Tea please,' replied John.

'Are you sure, sir? It won't take me a moment to do,' said Holly.

'No, no, you get home. You've already had a long night with dinner this evening, now go,' said Lewis, smiling.

'If you're sure, sir?' replied Holly picking up her coat.

'Yes, go! I can make tea,' Lewis gently commanded. As he stood, he filled the kettle and took two mugs off the shelf.

Cody, intrigued by the new voice, padded round the large wooden kitchen table and nuzzled Lewis's leg.

'Hello, boy, where did you come from?' Lewis bent down and gave Cody's neck a good scratch then stroked his flanks, feeling him flinch. 'Something wrong with his ribs?'

'Yes,' said John. 'Don't think it's too serious, just bruising.'

'So, how come you have him?' asked a now curious Lewis.

'Miss Penelope asked me to deliver something to Long Farm which the boys here helped me with tonight.'

Dan felt some relief. He now had an excuse as to why he was in the kitchen at midnight.

'Yes, Penelope told me. Go, OK?'

'Mission accomplished with no casualties, but Cody here seemed to take a liking to me when he found me in the grounds. I didn't poach him, he came willingly, kind of surrendered. From what I heard, hiding by the front door, they don't treat him too kindly.'

'OK, very good, I'll tell Penelope. Get the dog to the vet for a check. Our vet doesn't deal with Long Farm. Charge it to the house account. Keep the dog on the estate, we don't want a scene with that idiot Henry over this.' The kettle boiled and Lewis filled two cups. 'How strong, John?'

'Builder's, please.'

'You'll never sleep,' said Lewis, laughing.

'Don't you worry about me, sir, I will sleep like the dead.' John turned in his seat. 'Now, you youngsters, get going home, and I'll see you boys on the range tomorrow morning.'

With relief, Dan followed Eddy and Holly out of the forester's door, making sure the key code door lock clicked and locked.

'You lucky fucker!' said a grinning Eddy to a serious-faced Dan, 'I thought you'd had it when His Lordship walked in. Your face was a picture.'

'So, did I. I nearly shit myself when I saw him. I thought

he had me bang to rights.' Dan sighed. 'But John saved me. That was good of him. I'll have to find a way to pay him back.'

'Buy him a couple of pints, he'd like that.'

'That's a good idea,' said Dan with a smile, feeling a bit more relaxed now he was out of the house with a solid alibi in place.

*

Lewis slid the steaming mug in front of John and sat down. 'How do you find Dan, John?'

John looked up and met Lewis's gaze. 'He's a good lad, will be a very good senior one day, like his dad. Bright lad. You rarely have to tell him anything twice and he always asks sensible questions. Respected by the other apprentices, a bit of a leader I would say. Cracking bowman as well.'

'And he helped you tonight?' Lewis pressed gently.

'Yes, why do you ask?'

'Charlotte thought he might have met up with Cath tonight, and she's concerned.'

'Why?' asked John, feeling he was being talked into a corner.

'Like any mother, doesn't want to see her daughter hurt or make a mistake she might regret. Had enough worry with Penelope, which she understandably doesn't want repeated.'

John smiled. 'I know Duncan has warned him to be clear on his intentions. We also discussed it briefly tonight before you came in. I think he's very clear of the issues for him and her.'

'Thanks, John, that's very helpful, and you must think something of him as you didn't give him up when I came strolling in, even giving him an alibi.'

John coughed. 'I don't know what you mean, sir,' he said with a wry smile.

'You're a good man, John, and it says a lot that you helped him out. I will certainly keep you in mind when I need a reliable wing man.'

'Thank you, sir, anytime, just let me know. Eddy's a good lad as well. Had to think on his feet tonight and did really well. I have no children, sir, but I spend most of my time with the apprentices watching them grow up. Seems to me a big part of the job is to let them make mistakes, but make sure they learn from them and console and help them when it all goes wrong, which it does for all of them at some time. Only way they learn and grow into the men we want.'

'Thank you, John. I don't disagree, but Charlotte might not quite see it that way.' Lewis stood up and picked up his mug, 'Right, I'm off to bed, need any help here before I go?'

'No, sir, I'll finish my tea, clear up as Holly instructed and then be off myself. Goodnight.'

~ 21 ~

Sunday 22nd June. Ted Joseph woke up as usual at four-thirty with no prompting. Not even the dark and cold of winter let him sleep. As usual he crept out of bed, dressed and heard Flora sigh as she shifted, enjoying having all the space. She would wake later and, as always, have breakfast ready for him and his two sons at eight.

Today was different. After agreeing to return the farm to the estate the day before, he decided he would take his favourite walk, perhaps for the last time. The stairs creaked as he descended, a repair he'd put off for years, but could now forget. Ted entered the kitchen. The dogs stirred from their basket with the expectation of an early walk. Ted ushered them back to their bed. Today it would just be him and his thoughts. The dogs looked sulky as Ted pulled on his boots and decided on his old tweed jacket rather than the heavy waxed coat. It would be warm again today, even this early in the morning.

As he stood up, he placed his hand on the old, brown, leather suitcase sat atop the kitchen table. It looked worn and well-travelled, the leather various shades of brown. Stains of wear. A wedding present, Ted remembered, that despite its worn look had not travelled anywhere but lived in the attic which let in the weather and played home to many birds. It contained all the farm accounts and diaries, which Flora had always maintained. They would have been bankrupt years ago without Flora's diligent work keeping the bank at bay. His only regret was that there had never been enough money left to use the suitcase for the holiday it was intended for, and his wife deserved, although he knew he would have grumbled at leaving the farm even for a day. Flora never moaned and always supported everything as best she could. In their early days she would be out, sweating, helping in the fields, bringing in the harvest, cutting and bailing hay, herding the cattle; all tiring work, but she never complained and would make sure there was always food on the plate. His only contribution to the suitcase was the detailed plan of the Henge when they'd taken it down and cleared the top of Henge Hill. He admitted to himself it should never have been done. It had been there for probably two thousand years or more and there was magic about the place.

Ted patted the suitcase and walked out of the kitchen door to the farmyard, which was still in shade from the hill, but as the sun rose and travelled west it would flood the yard by midday.

Ted glanced up Henge Hill, then walked to fields that ran from its bottom to the boundary ditch, road and hedgerow with the estate his land would now be joining. He ducked between the two rails of the wooden fence that separated the field from the farm buildings and yard. He laughed as he looked at the field with its crop poking through its covering of various grasses, white clover, plantain and other plants that his neighbour would kill with pesticide as he considered them all weeds and useless. Most of his fields looked like this and always had done, but it was now called regenerative farming and was quite the thing, but to Ted it was simply the way he and his forefathers had always worked the land. He could see no good coming from pouring chemicals into the earth year after year.

He walked to the hedgerow at the bottom of the field, a wonder of life. The morning dew gave everything a shiny gloss that sparkled in the bright early sun. The webs and leaves shimmered and held droplets of dew, refracting the day's new light. Bees were already busy and the birds flew skilfully in and out of the hedgerow. The day was already alive with sound and movement. Life!

He'd been told many times to cut down the hedgerow to increase the size of the field, increase production and yield. He'd decided it would make little difference and wasn't worth the loss; coexistence had been his answer, which for many years had made other farmers laugh, as they seemed to treat their relationship with nature like some kind of war, that had to be won at all costs. Ted paused for a moment, closed his eyes and let the day and land wrap around him. He breathed in deeply the smell, taste and sound of the land and its life. He could feel the sun gently heating his back. He sighed and opened his eyes to see the sun turning the morning dew to light, wispy strands of mist that hung still and delicate, dancing a few feet off the ground.

Ted continued walking, seeing the signs of nocturnal

animals. His movement gave breath to the floating threads of dew mist, making them twist and dance. He bent and passed through the fence to the next field with a bit more difficulty as the thin hedgerow was starting to spread. Once through, Ted stood tall and stretched. The field looked much the same as the last. *He could*, he thought, *have combined the two*, but it would have destroyed the new hedgerow he'd been training for the past four years, and was it really worth it? Ted walked slowly to the bottom of the field watching the birds skilfully swoop to and fro above him. Then ahead of him, he saw three fox cubs playing in the long grass and summer flowers, rolling, tumbling around, their red coats damp and shiny from the dew. They heard or smelt him and all three froze.

Two turned and raced back into the hedgerow. One stood firm, his nose in the air as Ted continued walking. 'Hello,' he said as he got near. The fox cub decided it had had enough, lost its nerve and darted away to join its siblings safe in the depths of the scrub. Ted laughed as he walked by and kept smiling as he saw the ancient drystone wall and his favourite place.

He loved the touch of the ancient wall as he laid his hands on it to climb over, comforting, solid and strong, a constant in a mad world. A thousand years old, quite likely much older. He made up his mind he would still check and repair the wall even when they'd left the farm. White Lady's Field lay behind the wall which bordered three sides of the field with a deep ancient hedgerow on the fourth. It had a sea of meadow flowers from the seeds Ted had scattered from the bag Isaac had given him last summer. A glorious floor of nodding heads and swaying stems rose above the green ground cover. Ted began to walk across to inspect the wall on the other side. As he moved, he thought he saw something white flash by in the corner of his eye. When he turned to look there was nothing there and he shrugged and carried on. Halfway across the field he saw a figure clamber over the opposite wall and land clumsily in the field. Ted immediately recognised Reginald Clifford from Clifford Farm. Clifford waved his arm and stick in the air as his portly frame swayed ungainly across the field. 'You there; what are you doing? You're on my land.'

Ted walked towards Clifford and soon they stood only a few feet apart.

'Ah, it's you, Joseph. Understand you're giving up. Can't say I'm surprised. Still, I'll soon have these walls down and plant a decent crop,' said Clifford, a gleam in his eye.

'It's not your land whether I'm here or not. Never has been and never will be,' spat out Ted.

Clifford roughly grabbed Joseph's arm. 'You fool, you think you can stand in the way of progress.'

Clifford shook Ted and Ted instinctively grabbed Clifford with his free arm to help keep his balance.

'You're bloody lucky I'm not with my dogs. They'd soon see you off my land. I guess you're responsible for these stupid flowers that now infest the place. I'm going to spray weed killer on them this afternoon,' said Clifford.

'No, you won't!' Ted shouted back, 'You've already ruined enough land with your poisons. You'll not do the same to this field, which you perfectly well know is not yours.' Ted shook Clifford hard by the arm, noticing how fleshy and soft his arm was under his coat. *Long time since he did any proper work on any farm,* Ted thought.

Something white flashed by their side, up the field.

'What was that?' Clifford said as both men glanced sideways. Nothing to be seen.

'We are in the White Lady's Field,' replied Ted with a laugh.

'I suppose you believe that nonsense, a Lady to protect a field once used by King Arthur. Probably an ugly old crone, hung or burnt as a witch, who some Victorian decided should be venerated,' said Clifford, still pushing Ted about.

'Ugly, I don't believe that's true.'

The two men stopped struggling and turned their heads up the field towards the soft voice. They saw a beautiful woman dressed completely in white with bare feet, floating just above the grass, casting a luminous white light.

'Who the fuck are you? You know you are trespassing,' shouted an angry Clifford.

'This is not your land,' the Lady went on, 'or your land,' she said looking at Ted. 'One of you cares, one of you doesn't. You each know which one you are. Perhaps today one pays the price, one gets his reward?'

Clifford stood open-mouthed, realising, as Ted already had, that their boots were now firmly stuck in the ground, which had somehow become sticky and thick with mud. There was no escape.

The White Lady smiled she looked at Clifford. 'So, you know Arthur and his knights did camp here for almost a week and held court. This was then deemed by Merlin as one of the possible places the Once and Future King could one day reappear. I vowed to look after this field in life and I was buried at the top of this field. You can see the stone, which one of you cleans every so often,' she glanced at Ted, 'and now I am a spirit of the land and still protect this place as Merlin intended.'

'It's still not your fucking land,' snapped Clifford, struggling to move his boots which were now firmly stuck.

'I will ask the land,' said the White Lady. 'Let the land be the judge.'

'What nonsense,' said Clifford under his breath.

She turned quickly and stared hard at Clifford, her face still glowing white but somehow darker, eyes and features now sharp and menacing. 'I hear everything you say and think. You'd best be quiet; with the damage you've done over the years.'

The Lady knelt and put her ear to the ground, muttering something neither man could understand.

She then stood up and placed a hand on each man's shoulder and said, 'Be still and let's hear what the land and its spirits have said.'

The two men froze and stopped their struggle to pull their boots from the mud. Ted noticed that despite kneeling with her ear to the ground there was no sign of any mud on her anywhere. He didn't know why but he felt calm, no fear.

'The land says you both belong to it,' the White Lady said as she floated again above the ground. She raised her hands above the wide-eyed men's heads, clapped her hands three times and then stood back, and looked at the two pairs of empty rubber boots sticking out of the mud, which was now dried hard, laughing as she twirled gently and faded away into the morning light.

~ 22 ~

Maria Campbell-Blyth stood in the kitchen ready to cook breakfast. Her husband, Tyler, walked in.

'Just put some coffee on, be ready in five mins,' said Maria. 'Any sign of Henry joining us this morning?'

'I heard him in the shower. Well, I assume it was him, I'll give him a shout.'

Tyler walked to the wood-panelled door, which hid the entrance to the stairs. 'Henry,' Tyler shouted, 'joining us for breakfast?'

'Yes,' came the echoing reply from above. 'Be down in a minute.'

Tyler turned to his wife, who had heard the reply as she placed the large, dark, well-used pan on top of the range.

'Hope he's cheered up. He's been in a foul mood since Friday night,' said Maria as she took eggs, bacon and sausage out of the fridge.

'I'll do the toast,' said Tyler, moving to the kitchen counter. 'What's that?' he said, seeing the blue envelope on the windowsill addressed to Henry.

'I don't know. It was on the floor this morning. Must have been delivered during the night.'

'Perhaps that's what set the dogs off once we got them in. Still no sign of Cody, I guess?'

'No, I checked if he was waiting by the door as soon as I was down and called him, not a sign.'

'He can't have gone far and will be back when he's hungry.'

'I guess the letter is from Penelope. I think they had a row on Friday as Henry was back rather than staying there the night and he's been foul ever since.'

'Let's hope everything is still going to plan, or we will have to sell. Been invited, summoned, to a meeting at the bank next week. We don't have enough cash to pay the wages at the end of this month the way we are going.' Tyler sighed with concern as he focused on slicing the bread and loading the toaster.

'Have you told him the farm is up for sale? And you have a buyer?'

'He knows it's up for sale,' said Tyler as he stretched up and took down the toast rack from the shelf above his head, 'but I don't believe he thinks I would really sell and, no, I haven't told him we have a buyer.'

Maria nodded in response as she took the envelope from the windowsill and placed it where Henry always sat at the sturdy, wooden kitchen table, then returned to large pan on the range, now full of breakfast.

'Morning all.' Henry swept into the kitchen. 'Any sign of Cody?'

'No,' Maria and Tyler replied together.

'He'll turn up, stupid dog. Coffee ready?'

'Might have helped if you hadn't thrown him out on

the end of your boot. Coffee just done,' said Maria, taking down three mugs.

Henry sat down and looked at the letter staring up at him.

'You going to open that?' said Tyler, sitting down and placing two mugs of coffee on the table.

'Coffee first, I think,' Henry said, his face blank, not sure what Pen might have written after Friday night. His father couldn't help but notice the tension in Henry's face as he stood up to get the toast and see if he could help his wife.

'Once you've done the toast you can take yours and Henry's breakfasts,' said Maria, not picking up either Henry's tension or Tyler's concern.

Henry put down his mug and carefully picked up the letter.

'Who delivered this?' he asked into the room as breakfast was placed in front of him.

'No idea. It was on the floor this morning, so I guess it was hand-delivered,' Maria replied.

Henry ran his nail along the edge of the letter and took out the note inside. They all heard the light metallic twang as the ring pinged off the table and hit the quarry tile floor and bounced several times.

Henry watched in shock as it bounced across the floor, as he recognised it immediately. He slowly opened the letter.

Tyler bent down from his seat and stretched to picked up the ring and held it up.

'That's not a good sign.'

'It's over,' said Henry as he threw the one page note across the table. 'The stupid bitch!'

'That's enough, Henry,' Maria interrupted as she sat down at the table with her plate before Henry could say anything else.

Henry sat sulking; his face drawn. 'Five million and share options.'

'What?'

'That's what her trust fund was worth, Dad, and she had even agreed to leave Woodcoombe and live here.'

'Well, it doesn't look like that's going to happen now, so that plan has gone up in smoke.'

'It's not my fault.'

'Then whose fault is it, mine?' Tyler asked in exasperation.

'You run the farm, and now it's bankrupt, so you tell me.'

'You've got a bloody cheek, son. You have always treated this place like a hotel and the farm like your personal money machine. How much have you spent on your plan to woo your way to that trust fund, let alone any other inheritance that might come her way?'

Henry looked blank, his face frustrated and angry at the same time.

Tyler continued, 'Plus the money spent getting you out of the shit eight years ago and keeping you out of prison.'

'So, it's all my fault?'

'Usually is, but you expect all of us to quietly rally round and sort it out for you, don't you?'

'He is our son,' said Maria, looking upset. 'Eight years

ago, was a misunderstanding that got out of hand, but we managed to sort it out.'

'At a price of seventy-five grand for the house and her silence plus a wedge of cash for Sergeant Bennett to let things slide. So, let's say a hundred grand then, plus the money you've spent wooing the Woodcoombe girl.

'Afraid we've run out of rope now; the bank won't be bought off any more with excuses and promises of future monies via you. We have a buyer for the farm at the asking price, which the bank, when I see them next week, will probably insist I take or foreclose. Although,' Tyler rolled the ring, held up in his fingers, 'we should get at least get ten thousand back on this, which might buy a bit of time, but not long, and it won't solve the problem.'

'If you sell, where will we live and what will happen to all the staff?'

'Me and your mother have already found a place in South Devon with a few acres of land so I can still play at farming.'

'What about me?'

'Well, son, it's time you found your own way and made your own living. We can probably let you have some cash to get yourself started.'

'Very fucking nice of you.'

'That's enough, Henry, keep a civil tongue,' said Maria, playing with her breakfast.

'Son, like most people your age, get a job, earn a living.'

'How long have I got?'

'I'd guess two, maybe three months by the time the farm sale and our purchase go through.'

'OK, that gives me time to get sorted out. Any idea how much money I might get when everything is done?'

'Around twenty thousand, possibly a bit more, have to see; not enough to retire on, I'm afraid, son.'

'Guess you'll be taking the dogs.'

Tyler looked around the kitchen. 'Well, dog at the moment, we seem to have lost one.'

~ 23 ~

Tom and Fran woke at the same time as the sun lit their room with slices of warm light through the gaps in the curtains. Tom stretched out with a slight groan, throwing off the duvet at the same time, while Fran lazily, elegantly, uncoiled herself from the tightly wrapped bedding she'd nested herself into.

'Shall we have breakfast in here today?'

'Yes, be nice to ease into the day and actually have time to talk, rather than constantly being on show to everyone else,' said Fran as she swung her legs out of bed and stood up.

'What would you like?'

'Something light; fruit and yoghurt. And green tea.' She disappeared to shower.

Tom called the kitchen. 'No problem, be up in ten minutes,' he said as he moved the small table into the window bay so they could eat and talk while looking over the sun-drenched Vale.

Fran reappeared, her head wrapped in a towel, and sat down and gazed down the Vale.

'It's been an incredible couple of days but I'm pleased

to be going home. Did last night really happen? It was like being the princess you play at when you're a child, it was like a dream, magical. Pen's news was certainly a showstopper.'

'And you were a party-starter.'

'Your mother was right, Pen certainly surprised everyone. She was very brave. I hope Jackie's OK now the news is out?'

Tom looked puzzled. 'Sorry, I didn't fully understand what Pen meant.'

'Really!' said an exasperated Fran, eyebrows raised. 'Pen wants to be more independent, and Jackie is joining her as her partner, not staff.'

'Oh, I didn't see that coming!'

'Well, you probably haven't spoken to or seen her as much as I have in the last two days, and it seemed pretty obvious.'

'She never mentioned it before.'

'Probably worried what you might say, while she decided what to do about Henry and the future course to take.'

'Did Mother know?'

'Yes, we discussed it obliquely when we met. Pen and especially Jackie, I think, will need plenty of love and support until everything settles down.'

'Pen never mentioned it to me, bet Mother's having fun explaining that to Father.'

'Do you think it will be a problem?'

'No. Once he understands he'll be fine, it will just be the surprise. Like me, I doubt he saw this coming. Henry won't be happy; she dumps him and then moves in with a woman. His pride will be further hurt. It could push him over the edge.'

'Good, he deserves it. If you ever acted like him, I'd probably stab you or something.' Fran laughed as there was a knock on the door. 'Ah, breakfast,' she said as she jumped up, her towelled head wobbling as she headed to open the door.

Tom got up and quickly retrieved the ring case from his jacket pocket.

Gail entered, carrying a large tray. Fran then took the plates and pots from the tray and placed them on the table.

'Thank you, Gail.'

'You're welcome, madam. Can I just say you looked incredible last night, like a film star.'

'Thank you.'

Gail left and Fran sat down, beaming at the compliment.

Tom stood and then knelt next to Fran's chair and offered up the ring box.

'Should have really done this some time ago.'

Fran looked confused and a bit flustered. 'What's this then?'

Tom opened the small box and Fran gasped. 'That's the ring I picked out last night. It's beautiful.'

'Yes, you can thank Mother for this, she said you should have a ring and I told her you would want to choose. Mother said leave it to her.' Tom paused and swallowed nervously. 'Will you marry me? Do you still want to after this weekend?'

'Yes, yes, you silly boy, I still want to marry you.' She leant forward and kissed him on the lips. 'But please give me space to acclimatise to this place and everything about it. I will also want to be doing something useful and meaningful, not just be wafting around the house.'

'The ring was my grandmother's and I'm sure she would be delighted for you to have it.'

'Would I be able to meet her and have a chat? Isaac is going to take me to meet his wife in the woods next time we're down.' Fran giggled. 'Listen to me; talking with spirits and trees and not thinking anything odd about it. I think I might be slowly understanding.'

'You certainly have the connection. But it's never certain how people will react.'

'I can't think about a wedding at the moment and certainly not this year. Spring or early summer next year feels right.'

'OK. No problem, have a think about it, and I guess talk to your mother. I'm sure she'll have a view. Next year sounds good, gives us time to move and settle in.'

'She certainly will have a view. When she sees the ring, I'd be amazed if she doesn't ask if we have a date in mind. Did you take pictures last night? I'd like to pop in on the way home and get the date sorted for them to visit.'

Tom felt slightly anxious. 'Just a quick visit, not staying for dinner or anything?'

'No, you're safe. I'll give Mum a call before we leave, just pop in to show her the pictures and the ring.' Fran lifted her left hand and admired the ring at arm's length.

'Beautiful,' she whispered to herself. The sun glinted off the large diamond centre piece.

'Now, what else do we have to do before we hit the road?'

'Say goodbye to Mother and Father. And I do need to go to the range and talk to the lads about open day, which is looming up.'

'I'm not going to stand there watching you play bow and arrows for hours.'

'OK, we'll drive round, I should only need half an hour, then we can be off.'

'Deal, as long as I can drive.'

'Done. I'll find out where Mother and Father are and then as soon as we are ready, we can get going. By the way, you can leave anything you don't want or need to take home here as this will be kept as our room until we decide something more permanent.'

'Does that include washing?'

'Yes.'

'Fantastic!' said Fran as she packed. 'If this is our room for a while the bed needs mending.'

'What's wrong with it?'

'It doesn't make a noise like the one at the flat.'

'I'll let you deal with maintenance team on that one,' Tom said, pleased to hear her cheeky humour again after the busy and, at times, confusing weekend.

~ 24 ~

Fran and Tom breezed out of their room and down the main stairs with one light bag each.

Tom's parents were having breakfast quietly in the drawing room and the couple found them in their dressing gowns sat round a small table with the French doors open to the Vale.

Tom knocked and walked in. 'Hope we haven't disturbed you but we wanted to say goodbye and thanks for a great weekend.'

Fran bounced round Tom. 'And a big thank you from me.'

Charlotte stood up and embraced Fran. 'Don't worry. It's been wonderful to meet you, and we look forward to seeing you again, soon I hope?'

'Three weeks' time looks best for my parents.'

'OK, that's great, could you liaise directly with me on the details, rather than via Tom? It will probably be easier.'

'Yes, OK, will do.'

'By the way, nice ring,' Charlotte said in Fran's ear as she gave her another hug.

'Thank you, it's beautiful, thank you so much, I'm very lucky.'

'You're worth it. I see great things,' said Charlotte as she gently kissed Fran's cheek.

'Straight home then?' asked Lewis as he hugged Tom before stepping forward to hug Fran.

'No, we're stopping off at the range to see the guys quickly and discuss the open day in August. And popping in to Fran's parents.'

'We have the ex-chief of the defence staff, General Sir Eliot Rawlings doing the inspection so we need to have something good,' Lewis said to Tom. 'And I guess you need to see if you can still pull a bow?'

'I'll be fine,' said Tom, trying to convince himself.

The car had already been brought down to the house and they threw their bags casually into the boot.

'I'll drive round to the range while you phone your mum, then you can drive the rest of the way.'

'OK, but there's no signal,' scowled Fran looking at her phone.

'It'll come back as we drive to the range.'

Tom drove down the drive but turned off left just after the elm stand where they had seen the men working when they arrived.

'Now, the visitor centre is planned to be built on your right. Like the laboratory it will rise curving from the ground, a sculptured, flowing building which will look like it's moulded to the land. It will be glass-fronted with an arching living roof of grass and wild flowers which will anchor it to the ground.'

Fran said nothing as she looked at the empty space, trying to picture what it might look like.

Tom continued. 'Up ahead you can see the old grain store that will be converted to living accommodation, principally for those working at the laboratory which will be to the left of the grain store. Got a signal yet?'

'Yes,' said Fran as she scrambled with her phone to call her mother.

'Hello, darling, everything alright?'

'Yes, Mum, we'll be on our way home soon and wondered if we could pop in, just for a cuppa.'

'That would be lovely, your dad will be out, but that doesn't matter.'

Tom couldn't help but feel happier hearing that Charles wouldn't be around.

'Mum, I have a date for you and Dad to visit, three weeks' time. Arrive Friday afternoon, leave some time Sunday.'

'Is that from the 11th to the 13th?'

'Yes, Mum, is that OK?'

'Should be fine but your father will moan as he always does when he has to take time off work.'

Tom drew the car to a stop.

'When your parents visit, I was thinking of coming down a few days early. There's something I need to do. Is that a problem?' Tom asked.

'No, no problem at all.'

They got out of the car and Fran immediately saw the foresters and apprentices standing in a ragged line, the ones at the front raising and firing their bows. Most seemed to be stripped to the waist, a quiver of arrows hanging from their belts. They held bows, the bow arm protected by a leather brace. The young apprentices looked bulkier, more muscled, as if they had been in the gym. Most of the older foresters were lean and muscular from hard work. Duncan looked massive, like a giant in a children's book. *Have to get Tom fit once we're here*, thought Fran, *I think lean will be better.* They all looked hot even though it was only just past ten in the morning. *Must be harder work than I thought*, decided Fran.

Tom was greeted warmly by the archers and with laughter and a firm slap on the back from Duncan. Tom was passed a bow and a quiver of arrows. Isaac ushered Tom to the front as Tom pulled his brace onto his arm. Fran stepped forward a few paces to look down the range and saw a collection of targets at different distances and more people lurking around. *Looks dangerous down that end*, she thought.

'Company,' Isaac called out clear into the warm air, 'into sections.'

Fran watched as the archers grouped either with Isaac, Duncan or Tom.

'Captain's section front and middle, others to the flanks,' Isaac continued. Again, everyone moved.

Fran thought Tom looked a bit lost as archers gathered round him. Fran noticed Duncan had mostly apprentices with him, including Dan, his son, gathered to Tom's left. *I'll have to invite the girls down, they'd love this*, she thought. She noticed Isaac talking into a walkie-talkie as he walked up to Tom and his middle section.

'You OK, captain?' Isaac asked Tom. 'Captain's section always takes the centre and holds its ground.'

'Thank you, Isaac, I do remember some things,' said Tom, slightly irritated.

'We've upgraded the training since you've been gone. It's now a lot more fun. Got the idea when I saw golf buggies on television made up like golf balls. Thought they'd be a good target.' Isaac spoke into the walkie-talkie again. 'Bring out the horses and be ready to go.'

Tom looked at Isaac, confused.

Tom then heard the rumble of quad bikes and saw some strange looking machines roll onto the range.

'Armoured quad bikes completely covered in an armoured shell, all painted with French cavalry colours and coats of arms. Much better than static targets. Five good hits and they are deemed out. The drivers are all safe and all mic'd up.'

'Blimey, that must have been fun creating.'

'Yes. We had a few close calls in the early days figuring it out. The key was making sure the armour would always at least slow the arrow. The drivers have quite a gap between them and the outer skin. They wear helmets and protective clothing just in case an arrow does get through with any force.'

'Even Duncan's arrows?' Tom asked as he glanced over at Duncan, who was flexing the bow and string, which was noticeably bigger than anyone else's, with both arms as he warmed up to face the charge and at the same time talked quietly to the apprentices standing with him.

'Rupert is just as strong. Between them it's like they

are firing missiles. The quads tend to aim at your and my sections as the firing's not so heavy, but allows Duncan to fire at their flanks.'

Isaac and Tom nodded at each other.

'Ready!' shouted Isaac. This was greeted with a roaring cheer and raised bows. He stepped back to his section and lifted the walkie-talkie one last time. 'Charge!'

Fran heard the revving of engines straining and saw the strange painted ball-shaped vehicles start to rumble and race down the range.

'Stay back whatever happens, don't move from here,' said the man in a high vis jacket near Fran, who had just noticed Holly standing holding a dog. Fran sidled down next to Holly.

'Exciting, isn't it?' Fran said, nudging Holly gently with her arm.

'Yes, madam, I've never watched before, but Eddy asked if I would look after Cody while he trained.'

'I didn't think there'd be this much to it.' Fran bent down and stroked Cody who was watching the action very carefully.

The whining of the quads was getting louder. They weren't built to carry the weight of the armour and you could hear their engines straining.

'Three hundred yards!' shouted Isaac, 'Hold, stand steady, wait.'

Isaac was greeted with shouts and roars of pent-up tension waiting to be channelled into the bows and their strings.

'Two hundred yards!' shouted Isaac. 'Archers, plant your feet to the land!'

All the men took their stance, holding their bows ready, arrows notched and poised.

'By the land we stand a promise made will now be kept.'

As one, all the archers replied to Isaac.

'By the bow, by the land, we stand,

Strong, united, until the end.'

'God, can you feel it?' Fran exclaimed, almost shouting at Holly.

'Feel what?' replied Holly, confused.

'The air, it's alive,' said Fran. *The spirits and elements have been called, the promise is a living thing, it's alive, not just words*, Fran thought in awe tinged with a flicker of fear.

'Land, anchor the bowmen firm to the ground. Air, bring wind to take their arrows keen and true; air, give them clear sight. Spirits, keep their hearts and belief strong, one day their actions might matter more than today's practice fight,' Fran said under her breath as she closed her eyes. She raised her arms and concentrated on the energy that she felt and could see behind her closed eyes—flowing, rolling, intertwining waves; the yellow of the air, green of land and white of spirits. *How do I know this, what am I doing?* she thought as she watched the energy flowing out around the men and down the range, swirling, turning and twisting together. With concentration, and conducting with her raised arms, she wove the elemental forces into her requested spells, and for a moment Fran was at one with those ancient forces that flowed around her making her spell, answering her call.

The trees shook. Fran opened her eyes and saw Isaac looking straight at her. He nodded. He had felt her spell.

'One hundred yards; loose arrows,' shouted Isaac, throwing back his head as he did, his eyes wide with the fight.

A cheer rang out and Fran saw all the men ensuring their stance was strong and anchored to the land. They pulled and suddenly the air was filled with the sound of arrows being let fly from the bows, cutting and hissing through the air, singing strings and a hissing sound as arrows split the air, all accompanied by a roar from the men and their growling as they strained to fire again and again. The arrows kept flying, their friction heating the air, the men all sweating and glistening from their efforts.

Crikey, the girls have got to see this, Fran said to herself as she watched the men fire, notch new arrows then pull and fire again.

Tom was breathing heavily as he pulled a fresh arrow from his quiver. With a sigh, he notched it to the bow and, with gritted teeth, prepared for the effort of firing again.

Fran closed her eyes and searched for the spirits' energy again. 'Spirits, give the captain, whose soul is true, the strength to do his turn.' She opened her eyes and saw Tom grinning, not grimacing, as he energetically pulled, loaded and fired another arrow.

'Are you alright?' asked Holly.

'I don't think I've ever felt better.' Fran laughed and bent down to stroke the howling Cody, whispering in his ear, 'Shh, you're no war dog, be calm and quiet, you have nothing to fear.' Cody looked up, wide-eyed, relieved, stopped howling and lay down with his paws stretched out in front.

Fran looked down the range to see the hurtling-coloured eggs one by one come to a halt with many arrows protruding from them. As the last one stopped a huge cheer rang out.

'Cease firing,' shouted Isaac. 'Recover arrows.' There followed whooping and shouting as the men went out to recover spent arrows that they could use again.

Fran walked towards Tom. 'That was amazing.'

'Glad you enjoyed it; I was struggling a bit then suddenly got a second wind,' said Tom, flexing his arm muscles, which screamed from the effort.

'You can thank this young mage, who gave you strength, saved your blushes and gave our arrows the wind. You can come again, well done,' said Isaac. 'When you're next here we will definitely walk, talk and see what other skills you have hidden away.'

Tom looked confused as he rubbed his sore arm and saw Fran blush a bit.

All the bowmen were returning, having recovered their arrows.

Duncan walked up and slapped Tom on the back. 'Pretty good for a soft city boy.'

Everyone laughed.

'Not as surprised as me,' replied Tom, realising there might have been a little bit of magic involved, but he'd take the credit as it came. 'Thank you, everyone, fantastic practice. You all scare the fuck out of me.' There was a ripple of laughter and howls from the apprentices standing at the back. 'We need to think of the display for open day. We have a high-ranking general doing the inspection, so we need some ideas,' said Tom.

'How about a battle re-enactment?' suggested Duncan. Behind him the apprentices cheered.

'Good idea, take a bit of planning, sorry, have to go. Thank you. See you all in a few weeks back on the range.' Tom went to turn to go as Fran pushed forward; all the bowmen looked at her curiously.

'This is great for you boys, but what about the girls?' There was a chorus of laughter from the men. 'I know we can't pull the bows, but we could be shield maidens. We could carry extra arrows and I'm sure there's other things we can do.' The laughter was replaced by muttering and chatter.

The idea is planted. Let the spirits let it grow to a roar, Fran thought.

'It's an interesting idea. In the past there were shield maidens, why not now?' said Isaac, addressing the men as much as Fran. 'We'll consider how it might work.' His eyes scanned the men, no one laughing now.

'Now we must go,' said Tom, giving his bow and quiver to the man next to him, walking briskly, taking Fran's hand and moving to the car.

~ 25 ~

'God, I'm exhausted after that,' said Fran as she settled into the driving seat. 'Fancy sharing the driving so I can have a nap?'

'Not sure I can drive at the moment. My arms are knackered after firing that bow.'

'Even with my help,' said Fran, grinning.

'The trouble is, you have to be careful with spells. There can be unexpected consequences. You helped me to continue firing, but the consequence is the muscles in my arms are now worn out. See how I am when we are halfway home and then maybe swap?'

'OK.'

'There is a serious side to this and it's important you spend time with Isaac to learn. Any change you make with a spell has to be paid for somewhere else in the elemental world.'

'Bloody hell, I never thought about that, how do you know so much about it?'

'Isaac and John would take us out when we were children and tell us about the old ways and beliefs. I think my grandmother, whose ring you have, could channel and make spells. Occasionally, she would talk about it. It was like telling us fairy tales.'

'Could it be this ring, that used to be hers, that brings the magic?' Fran waved her left hand in the air.

'I don't think so, I don't think it works like that. Isaac would be the best person to ask.'

'Or I could ask your grandmother when I go to woods when we next visit.'

'Yes, you could. Turn left here. It's the avenue out.'

Fran swung the car into the avenue of trees that had welcomed them when they arrived only two days ago. Now, as then, they stood tall, closing out the sky above and, as Fran drove to the exit to the main road, the trees opened up and bathed the car in sunlight.

'The trees are saying goodbye,' said Tom.

When Fran got to the end of the drive, she stopped the car, jumped out and faced back up the drive, now all bathed in sunlight. She stretched out her arms again and bowed in thanks. As she stood, she brought her hands together on her chest as if in prayer, closed her eyes and said thank you. In answer, the avenue of trees shook and closed together again with just shards of sun piercing the green canopy, the same as when they had first arrived.

Fran got back into the car.

Tom looked at her, opened-mouthed. 'I've never seen anything like that before. Are you alright?'

'Yes, I feel fine, quite invigorated in fact. Don't feel tired now as I did before. Let's go.' Fran switched on the engine and drove out of the estate.

~ 26 ~

The traffic was light and Fran was soon speeding back to London.

'Think my arms are feeling better. Fancy a coffee and then I take over?'

'Are you sure? I'm feeling OK. Why don't I continue on to my parents and then you can drive home. A coffee sounds good though. I'll pull off at the next services.'

They didn't linger long at the services. They gulped their coffees and were soon back on the road.

They arrived at Fran's parents, and Tom jumped out of the car.

'You're keen,' said Fran, surprised, as she followed him to the front door.

'All that coffee. I really need a wee.'

Fran knocked at the door. There was a pause with Tom jigging from leg to leg with an anxious, slightly strained, face as he waited for the door to open.

'Hello, Wendy, sorry I really need to use the toilet,' Tom said as he rushed past, pleased to miss the always awkward hello embrace.

'Of course,' said Wendy, stepping back to give Tom room to get by.

'Sorry, Mum, too much coffee on the drive up,' said Fran as she hugged her mother.

'No problem, happens to all of us from time to time.'

Fran and Wendy walked into the sitting room.

'I have news,' said Fran, holding out her left hand.

'Oh my God! What a ring. It's beautiful. Look at the size of that diamond. Must have cost a fortune.' Wendy paused. 'Congratulations,' she said while inspecting Fran's bejewelled finger. 'So, any thoughts on an actual wedding date?'

'We're thinking May or June next year, on the estate, which is an incredible venue. You'll love it.'

'How exciting, dear. You can show me when we visit. Tom, I hope everything is alright?'

Tom had been trying to quietly enter and sit unnoticed, hoping his arrival would not draw any comment.

'Thank you, yes, fine.'

'Come in and sit next to Francesca.' Wendy waved and Tom carefully stepped past Wendy's legs and joined Fran on the sofa.

'Beautiful ring, Tom,' said Wendy.

'Thank you, it was my grandmother's. Been in the family for a long time, I believe.'

'Tom, show Mum the pictures of last night.'

Tom took out his phone and passed it to Wendy. Fran was bouncing gently on the sofa, remembering the magical evening.

'It's an old tradition. The ladies of the house enter dinner last and are clapped in,' said Fran.

'How lovely, darling. So, you are a lady of the house?'

'Yes, Francesca is considered one of the family, next we need to decide where to live,' Tom answered.

'What are the options?' said Wendy.

'Live in the main house or take a place on the estate. We haven't really discussed it in any detail yet,' Tom said, glancing at Fran, who shrugged, not sure what to say. 'There's an old farmhouse that is becoming available. But it needs a lot of work, and everything will need doing.'

'How exciting,' Wendy said, looking at Fran.

'Yes, Mum, but as Tom said we haven't discussed it yet and we currently have some lovely rooms allocated to us while we decide.'

'Rooms?'

'It's a suite; bedroom, bathroom, and study'

'Sounds very nice.'

'It is, but maybe not what we want long term. We haven't discussed it yet.'

'I'd love to help you to figure it out when we visit.'

'Good excuse to have a nose around the estate,' threw in Tom, which was met with indignation from Wendy.

'Just trying to help, Tom.'

'Of course, Mum, but still, it's a good opportunity to have a look around,' Fran said, mirroring Wendy's shocked look.

'It looks a very glamorous evening. I prefer the green outfit, whose is it? It's a bit more subtle.' Wendy returned her attention to the phone. 'Who are the other two in the pictures?' she asked, tipping the phone towards Fran.

Fran got up and bent down next to her mother. 'That's Penelope, one of Tom's sisters, in the green. That's Charlotte, Tom's mother.'

'Lady Charlotte?' added Wendy.

'Yes, but they don't use their titles with friends and family, in fact they don't seem to use their titles much at all.'

'Oh,' said Wendy, sounding disappointed. 'The costume jewellery you have on looks a bit much, dear, makes your outfit look a bit tacky.'

'Thanks, Mum!'

'Sorry, darling, I'm just not keen on the outfit. Not sure it's really appropriate and makes you look a bit cheap.'

'For your information, Mum...' Fran paused, taking a breath. She could feel anger and frustration rising. 'That is the most expensive jewellery set in the family collection; 1920s Paris Cartier, emeralds and pink diamonds. How much are they worth, Tom?'

Tom was reluctant to get drawn into the conversation, as he could see this visit, like so many others, was not going to end well. But he now had no choice.

'I believe the set is valued at around half a million pounds. They were loaned and on display at the V&A 1920s' fashion exhibition last year.'

Wendy sat with her mouth open. 'Well, that's a bit different. Perhaps I was mistaken, maybe they just don't photograph well. So how much is the ring worth?' Wendy asked.

Fran rolled her eyes, looking at Tom.

'I don't know for sure,' said Tom, 'but I would guess high five figures.'

'Fuck!' said Fran, looking down at her ring hand now resting in her lap. She'd never thought what it might be worth. *Did she care?* she thought.

'We don't need that sort of language, thank you, Francesca,' said Wendy with a look of disdain. 'I hope you didn't talk like that this weekend?' Her mouth broke into a thin smile. 'Your father was impressed when he noticed your family, Tom, on the latest *Times* Rich List just behind the Duke of Westminster.'

Tom sighed. 'Yes, I believe we are allegedly about nine billion, the duke just over ten, but I doubt anyone is counting. It's not a competition or a race as far as we are concerned. We're lucky the hard work was done by our ancestors over the last thousand years.'

'Mum! Surely the important thing is I'm marrying the man I love, and happier than I have ever been. For God's sake, why is it always about money? It's always a trans-action with Dad. Did he just want to know I'd made a good deal? Better than him hoping to marry me off to one of his young stars. Bet he's gloating about it at work.'

'Francesca, you're being silly now and your father wouldn't be very happy if he heard you talk like that.'

'Like I give a fuck!' Wendy sat up, shocked at Fran's reply, 'Tom's family welcomed and included me, but didn't ask or make any comment on my background.'

'Why would they, darling? They have enough wealth not to worry about someone like you.'

'Sorry, Wendy, I don't know what you mean, someone like her? Everyone welcomed Fran for who she is and how she behaves. We tend to measure people not by the size of their wallet but the size of their heart. My mother chose the jewellery for Fran as she knew about the dress. I can assure you if it was anyway inappropriate, she would have said. In fact, she said it was great to see glamour return to the house, rather than the line of black dresses usually on parade. Both my mother and grandmother came into the family as outsiders so she knows very well how hard it would have been this weekend for Fran being introduced to all of us and our different ways.' Tom, paused and took Fran's hand, before looking back at Wendy. 'They'll welcome you and Charles in exactly the same way. And your daughter looked stunning last night, like a princess, and you really should be proud of her. As I was. She has been amazing all weekend.'

Wendy huffed, clearly irritated. 'Tom, are you suggesting I'm not proud of my daughter? I hope you're not. We've done everything for her.'

'I'm sure you have, Wendy, but perhaps forgot the simplest and most important thing.'

'What's that then?'

'Showing your pride and support with love. You really should be proud, she will do great things, we have no doubt.'

Wendy sat red-faced, her mouth opening and closing, but no words came out.

'Come on, Tom, we're going,' said Fran, standing up.

'I've had enough. Mum, I'll be in touch to finalise the details of the visit with you.'

Wendy stood up. 'Sounds like the two of you might be ashamed of us and not think we're good enough to meet Tom's parents.'

'No! It's just everything seems to centre on money. You changed your tune a moment ago quickly enough when you knew what the jewellery was worth.'

Fran had Tom's hand and dragged him with her as she headed for the front door and back to the car, leaving her mother gawping after them on the step.

'Well, that went well,' said Tom. 'Their stay is going to be fun.'

'Not sure 'fun' is the word I would use,' Fran replied as she and Tom got back into the car. 'You'd better drive, Tom, I'm in no state to be behind the wheel.'

'Sorry,' said Tom, breaking the silence as he drove back to the flat, 'but felt I had to say something. I'm fed up with the way they treat you every time we meet up with them and you land up upset. Oddly, I don't mind when they pick on me.'

Fran was staring ahead as if in a trance. 'You're right, they've always talked about how much they've spent on the best school, or best of everything for me, how it's such a good investment in my future. Why can't they just be pleased? I have no doubt they meant the best and loved me in their own way, but they seem unable to show and share the love they must have somewhere for each other. Often, all I wanted and needed was a hug. At times that would have been worth more than any amount of money they spent.' The tears slipped down her face.

~ 27 ~

Monday, 23rd June. Lewis sat in his study. He'd just finished a catch up with Kurt and had to listen to all the issues Kurt was encountering around licences, permissions, government agencies and others around the introduction or reintroduction of different species to the estate. The practical issues were pretty straightforward, but the different permissions and their processes were proving a minefield to navigate. He'd finished by saying he needed help with the formal stuff and they needed to make a better plan.

Lewis was frustrated but smiled as he scanned an article on the successful introduction of the European bison in Kent. He thought about sending a copy to Kurt but was concerned it might push him over the edge. *Kurt is right*, thought Lewis, *we do need a better plan and a think about how we run the project.* Talk to Fred, he decided.

There was a knock on the door and Graham came in and broke Lewis's thoughts on bison.

'Sir, I have Detective Inspector Hazel Collins and Sergeant Bennett to talk about the disappearance of Joseph and Clifford. And I have Isaac and Flora Joseph outside who would also like a word.'

'Thank you, Graham, yes, I remember you told me the police were coming. Could you find out if Isaac and Flora have something new to add to the disappearance? If they have, they may as well share it with me and the police at the same time.'

'Yes, sir,' said Graham as he left the room, returning in a moment and showing the police in.

Lewis stood in front of his desk, ready to greet them.

'Nice to meet you, Inspector,' Lewis said as he thrust out a hand.

The plain-clothed inspector shook hands enthusiastically. 'Nice to meet you, sir, I wish it was under different circumstances.'

'Indeed, how can we help?'

'We'd just like to go through the details of yesterday to make sure we have the order of events right and have not missed anything.'

'No problem.' Lewis addressed Graham, who had been standing quietly at the back. 'Graham, could you please ask Isaac and Flora to join us.'

Graham slipped out with a nod.

'Sergeant Bennett, sorry, sir, I assumed you two had met before?' said the Inspector.

'Yes. We know the Sergeant well; he's been the law around these parts for quite some time. Good morning, Sergeant, hope you are well.'

'Yes, thank you, sir, just being a bit run ragged by the royal visit next weekend.'

'They have a couple of road closures to man,' the Inspector said in a clearly sarcastic tone and Lewis saw the Inspector and the Sergeant glance at each other. *Clearly no love lost there*, thought Lewis, *Bennett won't like anyone poking around in what he's been up to.*

The Inspector broke eye contact with Bennett. 'The Sergeant has done a great job, I understand he's pretty well stamped out poaching and rustling without any arrests or convictions following his great community work,' the Inspector continued in the same sarcastic tone.

'You're not local, Inspector?'

'No sir, my accent gives it away I guess, Birmingham born and bred.'

'How do you find yourself here, out of the smoke and into the green?'

'I got promotion, but no jobs in Birmingham, nowhere else keen to take me on. I was given a couple of options and this seemed the best, nearest to home so I can pop back and see my family from time to time.'

'Welcome, Inspector, I hope you will like it here, if there is anything we can ever do to help please don't hesitate to get in touch.'

Sergeant Bennett shifted a bit uneasily, realising his quiet life might be coming to an end. He stood trying to calculate when his police pension might be due. A good few years, he regretfully concluded.

'Inspector, I have asked Isaac and Mrs Joseph to join us. We can then go through all the detail and I think Flora...' Lewis took a step forward and took Flora's hand and quietly said to her, 'I'm so sorry for what's happened,

I know it's no consolation, but what we agreed with Ted still stands. Don't worry, we will look after you.'

'Thank you,' said Flora looking up from the floor. 'That's a big worry I can now forget.' She glanced at Isaac who was standing close next to her.

'You'll be fine, Flora, we will all be watching out for you, you have more friends than you know,' said Isaac softly.

'I don't know what you have to add, but are you happy to tell us and the police at the same time?' asked Lewis, still in a low voice which the Inspector and the Sergeant couldn't quite catch.

'Yes, but I'm worried they will thank I'm mad; I had a visit from the White Lady.'

'I see,' said Lewis, smiling and nodding knowingly, glancing at Isaac.

'You'll be fine, Flora, it's the Inspector who will have the issue, not us. Just tell her what you told me, alright?' Isaac stooped down slightly so he could look into Flora's downcast face. 'Alright?' he repeated. 'I believe you.'

Flora shivered nervously. 'You believe and understand the old ways, Isaac. OK, I will tell them.'

Isaac and Lewis looked at each other and nodded.

'I think we're ready to go, where do you want to start, Inspector?'

'At the beginning. Sergeant, please get everything down.'

Bennett huffed slightly as he took out his notebook and pen.

Isaac watched Bennett's discomfort in amusement.

Been a while since he's taken any notes or done anything by the book, he thought.

'Now, Mr Joseph got up at around dawn,' said the Inspector, turning to face Flora.

Isaac nudged Flora; she looked up. 'Yes, every morning he was up early, rain or shine, sometimes with the dogs, sometime on his own. He would walk different parts of the farm, but his favourite route was along the bottom of the farm to White Lady's Field, and I'm sure that's where he walked yesterday morning.'

'That's where we found his boots. Clearly, he didn't return,' said the Inspector.

'No, he is always back for breakfast with the boys at eight, who will have done the milking and feeds. For all forty years of our marriage, it's been the same. He has a clock in his head that wakes him up. He tries his best not to wake me but I'm always aware he's getting up.'

'And your two boys went out to look for him.' The Inspector was stroking her chin thoughtfully.

'Yes, they went and checked the most likely places he would have gone.'

'Including,' the Inspector paused, 'White Lady's Field?'

'Yes.'

'But they didn't notice the boots stuck in the ground.'

'No, they would have just looked over the wall then checked the ditch, no reason to walk the field.'

'That's what both lads' statements say, Inspector,' butted in Bennett.

'Thank you, Sergeant.'

The Inspector took a step nearer to Flora, still stroking

her chin.' And when your lads came back you called Woodcoombe?'

'Yes,' said Flora, dropping her eyes to the floor again, not enjoying being questioned yet again.

'I took the call,' volunteered Graham from the back of the room. 'I spoke with Mrs Joseph and then with His Lordship who said the foresters and apprentices would all be at the range.'

'Thank you...'

'Graham,' added Bennett, his interruptions clearly irritating the Inspector.

'Isaac?'

'Yes, ma'am.' The Inspector smiled. She liked being called ma'am.

'How did they get the message to you?'

'Short wave radio; I use it for the training. We'd pretty well finished, so we divided up areas to search and sent everyone out, to meet outside the main house once done.'

'Thank you, Isaac. You getting all this down, Sergeant?

'Yes, ma'am.'

'Good. Tell me, Isaac, what is 'the training'?'

'Longbow practice, you should come and see it.'

'Sounds interesting, I will.'

'So, no one found anything, Isaac.'

'No, ma'am.'

'I understand Thomas, your son, sir, left before the search started?'

'Yes, about five minutes before I got the message.'

The Inspector turned to Lewis. 'Could I have your son's contact details? Just routine, you understand.'

'I understand. Graham, can you please pass Thomas's details to the police.'

'Thank you. Now I understand there's some fresh information?'

'Yes,' said Isaac as he led Flora gently to stand by the desk next to Lewis, facing the police. 'Just tell everyone what you told me earlier.'

Flora looked up at Isaac. 'But she...' Flora whispered to Isaac looking at the Inspector, '...won't understand and they'll think I'm some kind of fool.'

'No, they won't, trust me.' Isaac squeezed her arm.

The Inspector walked forward and spoke gently. 'Mrs Joseph, tell us what you know and we can see if it helps us.'

Flora took a deep breath as she pulled herself up straight and looked the Inspector in the eyes. 'I had a visitor last night.'

The Inspector leant forward, curious at what she might be told.

Flora continued. 'The White Lady visited me and said Ted had returned to the land and I would see him again when the Henge was back in place and Arthur was resting quietly.'

Flora stopped. Bennett rolled his eyes.

The Inspector stood up straight, thoughtfully scratching her ear. There was a silence in the room as everyone waited to see what she would say. 'Sergeant, can we get the White Lady in for questioning, please.'

'That will be difficult, ma'am, as she's been dead for some time,' Bennett replied gleefully.

The Inspector swung round sharply and stared at

Bennett. 'Dead, Sergeant? But Mrs Joseph has just told us she spoke with her last night.'

'How did the White Lady speak to you, Mrs Joseph?' Bennett asked.

Flora glanced at Isaac, who nodded to carry on. 'In a dream as real as if she was standing here now.'

'Thank you, Mrs Joseph, very helpful. Is there any way I could talk to the White Lady to see if I can understand what is going on?'

'Possibly,' said Isaac. 'Tomorrow morning.'

'What time?'

'Earlier the better, but shall we say seven o'clock? Meet in Joseph's farmyard and wear sensible shoes. The ground will be wet from the dew.'

'Sergeant—'

Isaac cut in before the Inspector could finish. 'No, you must come alone, if you want the best chance of meeting her.'

Bennett was going to say something but seeing the Inspector's face decided better of it.

'Isaac,' the Inspector snorted, 'I decide how we will do this.'

'Not if you want to meet the White Lady.'

The Inspector put her hands up in surrender and noticed Bennett sniggering. 'OK, have it your way this time. But if you're wasting my time...'

'I will do my best to get what you want,' said Isaac with a slight bow.

'Well, I think that's it then,' said Lewis, clapping his hands together. 'Just to remind you, Inspector, the royal security team are a bit jittery about the disappearance so we really need it resolved or they might force us to cancel next weekend.'

'I'm well aware of that, Your Lordship, they're leaning on me to sort this out as well.' She looked hard at Isaac. 'You had better not be mucking me about, my friend.' With that the Inspector walked out, waving for Bennett to follow.

'Are you sure about this, Isaac?' asked Lewis with a concerned face.

He nodded. 'I think I can sort this out tomorrow.'

'Was that alright?' asked Flora Joseph quietly.

'Yes. Shall we get some tea?' said Lewis, smiling kindly, although he wasn't sure what he was smiling about, but Isaac had never let him down before.

~ 28 ~

Tuesday, 25th June. Isaac leant on the fence at the edge of Joseph's farmyard. He understood why Ted would have loved the walk at this time. Everything was fresh, calm and peaceful, full of early morning life. The silence was interrupted by the arrival of the Inspector being driven by Bennett. *He won't be happy playing chauffeur and being up at this time of the morning*, thought Isaac. The Inspector got out of the car and Isaac was pleased to see Bennett was not joining her.

'Good morning, Isaac.'

'And a glorious morning it is, Inspector, probably similar to when poor old Ted set out two days ago.'

'Sergeant Bennett has tried to explain to me what this is all about. Myths, legends spirits, magic and King Arthur—a bit different to my old beat. The only magic there was chemically induced.'

'Hopefully, when we've finished this morning, you will understand more. Shall we go? It's not far.'

Isaac and the Inspector climbed through the fence. Along the way Isaac explained about the hedgerow and pointed out its varied life bustling around in the morning light.

The Inspector was captivated and took a keen interest in everything Isaac said and showed her.

Soon they reached the drystone wall of White Lady's Field and Isaac helped her over.

'What was that?' the Inspector exclaimed as Isaac dropped into the field behind her.

'What did you see?'

'A flash of white in the corner of my eye.'

'Ah, the White Lady is about.' Isaac crouched down, placed one palm on the ground and closed his eyes. 'I call on the White Lady to show herself.' He opened his eyes and stood up and saw the Inspector staring wide-eyed in surprise at the beautiful woman dressed completely in white flowing robes with delicate bare feet who seemed to be floating just above the grass, casting a luminous white light.

'Who summoned the White Lady?'

'I did, My Lady.'

'Are you,' she said questioningly, 'the mage I felt the other day weaving spells on the range? How disappointing, I was expecting more.'

'Not me, My Lady, another; new, and just finding her way.'

'Whoever it was certainly has the gift. Is this her who stands before me now?'

'No, it is not.'

'Then whoever it was I would like to meet.'

'Not today, but I promise I will bring her. Today we need to talk with you about something else.'

'Those men? There have been many visitors here digging and prodding the ground since they were taken that morning.'

'Taken!' said the Inspector.

The White Lady looked at the Inspector. 'Yes, one had shown some care and had a good heart, one had not and showed no respect for the land. They both knew which they were. One got his wish and reward; the other couldn't escape the land's long grasp for his careless ways.'

'What happened to them?' asked Isaac.

'They were taken back by the land from where we all come from and all eventually return.'

The Inspector looked confused.

'We all come from the earth and, one way or another, we return. One was tired and ready for his spirit to return, the other frightened as he knew the damage he'd done.'

'Spirit?' said the Inspector.

'Inspector,' Isaac said, 'the land takes the energy, spirit and soul back and it joins or is reborn.'

'Let me show you,' said the White Lady as she raised her hands and clapped three times.

Isaac flinched as he knew it was a spell and equally that the White Lady could be mischievous.

'The Grey Man.' The White Lady waved. Suddenly, a grey figure materialised in the air next to them. It shimmered and looked wispy as if made of smoke.

'Ted!' exclaimed Isaac in surprise.

'Ted Joseph? Do you have any idea how much trouble you have caused?' said the Inspector.

The Grey Man turned slowly to face the Inspector and Isaac. 'It was my time, I was tired and ready, so here I am back with the land where it all begins. Tell Flora I'm sorry; she will understand. And tell her we will walk together again soon.'

The Inspector reached forward but her hand passed through the smoke that was now Ted Joseph the Grey Man.

'Don't touch!' Isaac half shouted. 'You should never touch a spirit unless invited, you never know what it might do to you.'

The Inspector withdrew her hand with a sharp jerk as if scalded by hot water, a concerned look on her face as the hole she'd created in the floating Grey Man's body was filled and repaired by the wispy swirling smoke that floated around the shape that was now Ted.

'The Grey Man will be seen at the Henge when it's re-built. Put a stone to his mortal being at the bottom of the hill so his wife will always know where to find him and not have to climb the hill.' The White Lady went into a slow spin, her dress trailing lengths of misty fabric as she turned. As she slowed, she clapped her hands three times, giving the Grey Man a shallow bow as she stopped. Isaac and the Inspector watched him dissolve and disappear into the morning light and he was gone.

'Where'd he go?' exclaimed the Inspector.

'Back to the earth.'

The Inspector looked confused.

'The Grey Man is still new to his form; he needs to build strength and understand the power his new form has.'

'Where is the other man?' asked the Inspector, her head already spinning from everything she'd heard and seen so far.

'Good question,' said the White Lady. 'Come and look here.' She stepped a couple of paces, bent down lightly and swept her hand across the green ground. The Inspector and Isaac watched curiously as the grass cleared to reveal Reginald Clifford, caught under the transparent ground as if imprisoned under a sheet of ice, his face contorted in anger and fear, pressed tight against whatever force was holding him down as he struggled vainly.

The Inspector looked away. 'That's horrible, he looks like that painting. What's it called? Ah yes, *The Scream.*'

'His energy will be used to help repair the land. But as you can see, he can't accept his fate, which only make things harder for him. If only he'd used such energy for the best.' The White Lady sighed.

Isaac stepped away from the image of Reginald Clifford, shaking his head. 'White Lady, you have their energy, their souls, their very essence. What about their bodies?'

'They will rot in the ground.'

'Could we have the bodies? That will stop people trampling and not respecting your field.'

'Where do you want them?'

'In the ditch behind the field,' said Inspector, pointing. 'We can then do all the necessary stuff from the road and not disturb you anymore.'

Three claps above her head. 'It is done,' said the White

Lady. 'You seem more worried about the vessel than the wine. How very strange.'

'Thank you,' said Isaac.

'Don't forget to bring me the new mage. You promised. You know I will remember.'

'I won't forget,' said, Isaac with a slight bow.

'Come call me again if you need my help. You have a good soul and are a wiser and stronger mage than you believe,' said the White Lady as she dissolved into the light.

'She's gone,' said the Inspector.

'Her essence is still about; you just can't see her. Let's check the ditch.'

They walked to the bottom of the field and peered into the ditch; two bodies bobbed lightly in the murky waters.

'There you go, Inspector, case solved. Death by misadventure. This water is toxic poison from Clifford's Farm so you have cause of death.'

'Yes, and I can give Bennett a hard time for not finding the bodies before.' They both laughed.

They took the road back past the main house and what was the elm stand, down to Joseph's Farm where Bennett was waiting, comfortable in the car with his flask of tea and half-read newspaper.

They arrived at the junction at the top of the drive.

'I'm this way,' said Isaac as he turned left to walk away.

But suddenly the Inspector started to laugh, which stopped Isaac in his tracks. 'Working in Birmingham I've seen many dead people and death from many causes and methods, mostly messy. But never seen any spirits or ghosts or seen or felt anything like today. Although we did have one bloke who beat his wife to death and then claimed she was haunting him. Hung himself somehow in his cell in the end. He did make a dreadful mess of her, so probably deserved whatever he got, but I shouldn't say that. Perhaps that was the wife's revenge?'

'Extreme events can sometimes stop the soul resting and its energy might seek revenge or resolution, so possibly she haunted him to death and then she could rest?'

'Guess we'll never know, but if my report had said 'haunted to death', I'd be lucky to be giving out parking tickets now. Seen people buried; but usually in concrete. Once the family of a drug dealer decided to leave him in a pillar supporting a road. A rival gang had concreted him in. They put a plaque on the pillar and had a remembrance service, all a bit strange standing under a flyover listening to a service, as cars sped overhead.' She laughed again. 'I'm pretty sure the people who buried him were there. The contractors were so pleased they didn't have to drill him out, they laid on a buffet after the service under the road which made the whole event even more surreal. It's a strange old world, but I can honestly say I've never seen anything like today before; still not sure what to make of it all. You live and learn. Thank you, Isaac.'

'You're welcome, Inspector. Keep your mind open, especially if you're thinking of sticking around. There are many ancient things here that are still part of our world.'

'One more question, Isaac; what's a mage?'

Isaac, paused. 'Those who practice magic, a spell caster, in touch with ancient things. It's where the word magician comes from.'

'Should I ask Bennett to dust off the ducking stool, get the stake in place and firewood ready?'

Isaac didn't answer, just waved and walked away with the Inspector's laughter at her joke ringing in his ears.

~ 29 ~

Tom had already spoken to Simon a number of times about moving to the estate to finish the project. Now it was just finalising the details.

While the project was Tom's idea and concept, it was Simon who had built the code and made the system a reality. They met at university. Simon was a few years older than Tom and had had a successful career before university as a coder in the games industry, but had decided he would get some qualifications to allow him to work in other industries and combine his gaming experience with the usual systems, program delivery and functionality. 'Sex it up', as Simon would so often say. Tom had been surprised when he agreed to work with him. Simon had loved the ambition and ecological aspect of the project which certainly appealed to the hippy part of Simon and his girlfriend, Emma. 'We will stick it to the man', Simon had said, although Tom was not really sure what he meant by this.

'We're going to the estate next week, on the 9th and will be there until either the 13th or 14th.'

'OK, Tom, I'll travel down on the 9th. I'll get the train and be there at about three o'clock.'

'We will be there by late morning. I'll come and pick you up at the station.'

'Thanks, I'll have a few bags. Would you have room for some stuff when you drive down?'

'Should have, probably depends how much Fran loads up. Shall I pop round Tuesday evening and pick it up?'

'That works, probably best you take the laptops and hard drives etc, be dreadful if they got lost while I'm travelling and juggling bags.'

Tom went a bit hot and cold at the thought. 'But everything's backed in the cloud, isn't it, Simon?'

'Yes, but it will also be stored locally, along with all the concept testing and trials we did in the early days.' Tom thought Simon sounded far too calm about losing any work. Simon didn't believe there was a security issue, but had decided spending, perhaps, six months in the country rent-free, at someone else's expense, would be fun and a definite upgrade on the grotty, South London room he had been renting.

'Why don't I take all the kit in the car; it must be quite heavy. If you have too much to carry with you on the train, get it delivered and charge it to the estate. Shall I ask Graham to get in touch to organise?'

'That's a great idea as I'm moving out so everything has to go. Yes, ask him to call me. Can I just check that the office is ready as I specified?'

'Yes, Graham has confirmed it's all done. When do you

want to set up and test it, as I'll make sure Graham is there in case there are any problems.'

'Shall we aim for the Wednesday afternoon we arrive? It'll beat having to do the unpacking. Shouldn't take long, just be a matter of plugging in the laptop and making sure everything connects up. It either will or won't work, but should be OK, it's all pretty straightforward stuff. Sorry, Tom, I know we discussed this, but it is OK for Emma to visit and stay from time to time?'

'Yes, let's get set up that afternoon, then we can crack on as we want. No problem, Emma can stay whenever she wants. Just inform me and the housekeeper.'

'Just so you know, Tom, I've finished all the latest build and coding, and the core algorithm functionality and operation should be done, so it's back to testing again. If it's all OK, I can move on to the reporting functions and outputs as well as refining the UX and UI.'

'That's great,' Tom replied as he remembered what UX and UI meant; user experience and user interface. 'Let's chat when we're both there and I'll have a think on the testing. We could do with a live case.'

'Nearly there, Tom, feels like we are on, or at least near, the last lap and the finish line is in sight.'

'Yes, feels like all the really heavy lifting has been done, and as long as the core algorithms are complete and pass testing it should all work.'

'Of course, it will fucking work, have some faith.'

'I do! OK, See you Tuesday evening, Simon.' Tom rang off, feeling a flash of excitement that after two years they might be nearly there. *Then the fun begins*, he thought.

~ 30 ~

'Hello, Mum.'

'Hello, Francesca, how are you?'

'I'm fine, thanks, just wanted to call and say sorry about the other day when we popped round. It all seemed to get out of hand.'

'Yes, I'm sorry as well. I was a bit clumsy with what I said about your dress. It was just a surprise to see you wearing something like that, not something I would choose.'

'Not to worry, no harm done.'

'I hope not, but you both seemed pretty upset. I thought it was only your dad who had the knack of upsetting you, but that skill seems to have rubbed off on me.'

'Doesn't matter, I wanted to call and confirm the details for the weekend.'

'We're still invited, then?'

'Don't be silly, of course you are.'

'It's funny, Francesca, your dad actually seems to be looking forward to it.'

'Crikey, is he alright?'

'Well, I finally got him to the doctor's last week and they confirmed the stress is not doing him any good.

They did a load of tests, we're awaiting the results, but his mood has lightened in the last few days and he's even mentioned retirement and suggested a long cruise might be a good way to start.'

'Wow, get it booked before he changes his mind.'

Wendy chuckled. 'We'll see. Arrangements for the weekend?'

'Yes, sorry, got side-tracked. We're going down on the Wednesday. Tom has some work stuff to sort out and Simon who works with him is arriving then. You and Dad come on Friday as planned but you can arrive whenever you like, just message me your expected ETA.'

'OK, darling, what clothes do we need for the days and evenings?'

'It'll be hot and dry and unlikely to change. On the Friday evening the plan is a barbeque, which will be very relaxed. On the Saturday a family dinner, which will be semi-smart, so for Dad, a jacket, but no tie. The ladies will be in cocktail dresses.'

'Will we be clapping you in?'

'No, it should all be very relaxed, just family and close friends. For outside, sensible shoes, and clothes for walking in the woods. I want to show you around the estate. All in all should be a very relaxed, casual weekend.'

'OK, thanks, dear, I'll put your father's dinner suit away, might have to take him shopping. No! I will just buy him what he needs as I usually do, or he'll be wandering around all weekend in his ancient blue blazer, which has seen far too many nights out.'

'We've decided we will stay in the suite of rooms we

have for the moment until we've settled into the estate. Tom's given notice on the flat, but we have until September to get out, so we just have to decide when to make the final move.'

'Sounds exciting!'

'And also, a bit frightening. It's a big change.'

'But it's what you want, isn't it?'

'Yes, I knew this moment would come, but it's still a bit daunting. But they do have an apartment in the West End which Charlotte uses for London trips, which we will be able to use to see friends, and it is beautiful on the estate.'

'Sounds like a good problem to have to me, darling. I guess you can have friends to stay.'

'Yes, you're right and, as you will see when you visit, there's plenty of room for guests. I'm going to get some of the girls down.'

'Have you seen Juliet recently? I bumped into her mum the other day and she asked how you were.'

'Seeing her and some of the others the Tuesday evening before we drive down.'

'Is that wise, darling?'

'Probably not, but Tom can drive the next day. Sorry, Mum, have got to go. If you have any questions just give me a call, otherwise see you on the 11th.'

'Yes, will do, looking forward to it. Goodbye.'

~ 31 ~

Cath left her room where she'd been sitting quietly after two tests had confirmed the news. She'd sat wondering for some time about what to do next and decided it was best to see her mother. To her surprise she felt calm, happy should anyone have asked, but she wondered if the reality had sunk in.

Charlotte, as she often was in the afternoon, was in the drawing room with a book and a pot of tea. The French doors were open to the Vale and as Cath slid silently into the room, she could see the fading grass outside and the dusty air shimmering gently in the continuing heat.

'Hello, Mother,' Cath said gently.

Her mother looked up in slight surprise, her concentration on the book broken.

'Catherine, come in, is everything alright?'

Cath walked slowly and sat with a plonk into the chair opposite her mother.

'You're looking well, dear, this weather suits you better than me. You don't seem to mind the heat or burn as you might think you would with your fair skin. I might have to find somewhere else to sit and escape to in the afternoons, too many people know I can be found in here.'

'Oh, sorry, would you like to catch up some other time?'

'No, dear, you're here now and I will always make time for any of you if you need to talk. How can I help?'

'I have some news I want to discuss with you.'

'Good or bad news, my dear?'

'Well, good, I think, but I probably haven't thought it through completely.'

They were both silent for a moment.

Charlotte wondered what it could be. Cath seemed calm and looked happy, so Charlotte dismissed some of the potential issues which were racing through her head. It was just very unusual for Cath to want to discuss anything.

Cath was wondering how to tell her mum.

'So,' Charlotte broke the expectant silence that hung in the room. 'Catherine, what do you want to discuss?'

Cath sat up straight and took in a deep breath. 'I'm pregnant. Done two tests today and they're both positive.'

This was one of the options Charlotte had dismissed, as she thought there would be an air of panic, not the happy, calm Cath who currently sat in front of her, now with a look of relief on her face at having shared her secret.

'Oh, do you feel alright, dear? Dan's?'

Cath looked straight at her mother. 'Yes, I feel fine, yes Dan. There has been no one else.' Cath dismissed the second question with a clear tone of irritation.

'Does he know?'

'No, not yet, I wanted to speak to you first.'

'What do you want to do?' Charlotte asked, picking up her tea cup.

'What to do?' Cath echoed. 'Keep it, the news has made me feel so happy I can't think of not having it or giving him or her away.' Cath finished with a small shudder at options she'd not really considered and now easily dismissed.

'Catherine, we will support you, whatever you want to do, and thank you for telling me. I think there are a few things to do. I'll make an appointment with the doctor to check the test is right and everything's OK. I suggest you find Dan and share your news and see what he has to say. Once you've done that, I will tell your father, if you would like me to?'

'I'll talk to Dan and then we can talk again. Perhaps Father could talk to Duncan in case he gets in a rage with Dan.'

'Yes, that might be a good idea, but I'm sure everything will be fine. We'll work it out whatever happens. We love you, dear.'

'Thanks, Mum, I love you too. I'll talk to you soon. We were being careful, but sometimes I guess you get carried away.'

'Quite understand, dear, you may not believe this but I was young once.'

Cath didn't respond and an awkwardness fell between mother and daughter. Cath got up, kissed her mother and walked out, looking and feeling relaxed and happy to have shared the news. As she left, she put her hand in her pocket, pulled out her phone and hit the call button to talk to Dan.

'What do you want? I'm working.'

'Sorry, Dan, I know, but there's something I need to talk to you about as soon as you can.'

'Sorry, Cath, I'm covered in shit at the moment as I'm digging out the ditch on the borders of Clifford's Farm, where they found the bodies of Joseph and Clifford. Don't know how they missed them before.'

'How terrible! At least they know what happened now.'

'Accidental death. One of the coppers told us they're not looking for anyone else, they reckon the two got into a bit of a tussle and fell in the ditch and couldn't get out. The mixture of chemicals and dumped slurry did them in.'

'How horrible!' Cath pulled a face. 'But I do need to see you as soon as possible.'

'Of course, princess, as soon as I'm clean.'

Cath loved it when he called her princess, often he called her 'his princess from the big house'.

'Call me when you're clean.'

'OK, better get back to clearing the mess in this ditch so the police can do their thing. Bye. Love you.'

Dan rung off. Cath sighed. She didn't know what to do with herself, so she walked back slowly and thoughtfully to her room to await Dan's call.

*

Charlotte poured a fresh cup of tea and couldn't stop thinking about Catherine's news. She couldn't settle back into her book, her mind racing about how this might play out. *Dan's a good lad, he'll be a good addition to the family, but they are so young. Perhaps this is what Catherine needs, something to anchor her. She seems happy enough, well, at the moment, but it won't all be plain sailing.*

Charlotte closed the French doors and called the doctor to make an appointment. As she finished the call Lewis walked in.

'Who were you on the phone to?' Lewis enquired casually as he sat and poured himself a cup of tea.

'The doctor, dear, Catherine came to see me a little while ago.' Lewis looked up with concern.

'Everything alright?'

'Yes, women's things, just going to get it checked out to put her mind at rest. It's not serious, quite normal. Made an appointment with the doctor for tomorrow.'

'That's good.' Relief showed on Lewis's face. 'Hate it when there's anything wrong with any of them.'

'Nothing to worry about, dear,' Charlotte said, lovingly running her hand through her husband's hair.

*

Cath sat in her room, not sure what to do as she waited for Dan to call back. She was pleased Jen wasn't about; she was busy studying for exams. Cath was sure her sister would pass, then she'd be off to university in the autumn and gone like Tom, but hopefully not for so long. Cath wondered how her twin would feel about becoming an auntie, and what her reaction might be. She bet the first thing Jen said would be, 'I told you to be careful'. Cath was amused at the thought of Jen's probable anger or indignation, which would not last long, and then she'd give her twin a big hug and ask lots of questions.

Bored with watching the clock on her wall turn slowly, she stood in front of the mirror looking at her stomach. She took a cushion and held it against her, then tucked it under her shirt to admire her prospective round shape. A thought occurred to her. *Fuck! I'm a twin!* She grabbed another cushion and pushed that under also. *God, I'll be enormous.* She eyed her new profile at different angles, before pulling out the pillows and throwing them on the bed, pleased to see her trim figure back, if only for a while. Names suddenly came into her head. Boys, girls. A trickle of names came to mind, but nothing stuck.

Then her phone rang. Cath glanced at the clock. The call was earlier than expected.

'Hi, I managed to get away.'

'Brilliant.' Cath hopped about as she said it.

'Where shall we meet, should I come to your room?'

'No.' Cath thought it unlikely they would talk much if he did, and that was how the current situation started. 'Come to the French doors to the drawing room, I'll let you in.'

'I'm already on the move so I'll be there in ten.'

'See you then.'

'Love you, princess,' said Dan as he ended the call. Cath still had her phone to her ear even though Dan was gone. 'Love you, too, and hope you still will after we've talked,' she whispered into the ether. No one heard.

Cath let herself into the drawing room and, as she had expected, there was no one there. Her mother had returned to her room. She opened the French doors, hoping that Dan might already be there, but there was no sign of him. She stood inside unable to settle, frustrated she didn't feel the same calm as she had earlier when she'd talked to her mother.

She didn't have to wait long for the familiar shape of Dan to appear between the doors. He entered the room and Cath embraced him.

'So, what's so important?' said Dan, looking a bit pensive.

'I'm pregnant,' Cath blurted out. It hadn't been how she intended to tell him, but any other words eluded her.

Dan said nothing for a moment, a look of surprise on his face.

'Are you OK?' he asked, concern in his voice, hugging Cath.

'Yes, I feel fine, in fact never better.'

'Good, who else knows?'

'Just you and Mother. I had to talk to her first. She's arranging for me to see the doctor.'

'Why, is there a problem?' said Dan.

'No, just to check everything out.'

'Can I come with you? I want to support you in all of this.'

'I don't see why not; I'll talk to Mother.'

'Well, I am the father,' a rather indignant Dan said before he softened and hugged Cath again. 'So, what will we do, get engaged, married, live together?'

'Sorry, Dan, I haven't really thought about anything further than telling you today.'

'My father brought myself and Olivia up on his own after my mother walked out when we were young. It's a tough job for one parent, even with the help your family gave him.'

'And you haven't turned out too bad, Dan,' Cath added squeezing him again.

'I want to be part of this, princess, you shouldn't have to do this alone.'

Cath's phone rang.

'Mother,' she said, raising it to her ear. 'OK. Tomorrow ten-thirty. Dan would like to come...I'm with him now. Yes, all OK. We're getting engaged then we'll see how everything else pans out.' Cath took the phone away from her ear for a moment and looked at Dan. 'Mother says congratulations.'

Dan smiled and felt relieved and pleased Charlotte hadn't questioned the engagement or that he could join them at the doctors.

'Thank you, Charlotte, now the tricky bit, telling everyone.'

'Did you hear that, Mum? I'll put you on speaker.'

'Yes, I'll talk to your father this evening. I'm sure he'll be fine, but he will want to speak to you both as well. What about your father, Dan?'

'I'll tell him and Olivia over dinner tonight, I guess. I'll let you know how it goes.'

'Dan, would you like Lewis to talk to your father, maybe tomorrow?'

'Let's see how it goes tonight, Charlotte. If it goes badly, I might also need the doctor tomorrow!' Dan said half joking, but they all knew what Duncan's temper could be like.

'OK, Dan, let us know as soon as you've spoken to your father, if you're still alive. Tomorrow, we need to leave at ten o'clock. Could you drive?'

'Yes, no problem, I'll meet you at the house at ten o'clock.'

'See you tomorrow if we don't speak before. Bye.' And Charlotte rang off.

Cath put her phone down and looked hard at Dan. 'Don't worry, it will all be alright.'

'I know,' he said as he stood up to leave with a deep sigh. 'I'd better get home.'

'Call me later and let me know how it goes.'

With a final hug and a kiss, Dan disappeared back out of the French doors.

~ 32 ~

Dan walked back slowly to the cottage on the estate he'd lived in since he was born and shared with his sister, Olivia, and his father. All of them worked on the estate. He was pleased Olivia was off and cooking dinner for all three of them. *Might temper any anger from his father,* he thought. *Must get Cath a ring, I have some savings. Perhaps they could get a cottage on the estate, or would they expect him to move into the big house? He didn't know. Boy or a girl?* He decided he didn't care as long as everyone was alright.

'Hello, mate, you look like you've got the weight of the world on your shoulders.' said Eddy as he bound up and slapped Dan on the back.

'Just been to see Cath.'

'She alright?'

'Pregnant!'

'Oh fuck, how'd that happen?' Eddy slapped Dan again with a big goofy smile on his face.

'Don't be an arse, Eddy. This isn't a joke.'

'Well, I have some news as well. My sister Rachel is coming to work on the estate, as a housekeeper below Anna and Jackie, but I can't believe Jackie will be working for long in the house if she is shacking up with Penelope, and Mrs Cooper must be due to retire sometime soon.'

'Good news for your sister. Will it be nice having Rachel about?'

'Suppose so, haven't really thought about it.'

'How's it going with Holly and the mystery dog, Cody?'

'Nothing going on with Holly, she just likes helping out with the dog, that's all.'

'You really are an arse. Everyone can see how she looks at you. Although what she sees is beyond all of us.'

'Fuck off, Dan! There's nothing in it.'

'Then you really are as stupid as you sometimes look. Now I'm off to tell my sister and dad the good news about the baby. Wish me luck.'

'Good luck, mate. If you need to talk or need anything, just give me a shout any time.'

'Thanks mate, appreciate it. Where you off to now?'

'Picking up the dog from Holly, meeting her in the garden at the Foresters'.'

'For fuck's sake, and you think nothing's going on. By the way, I might need you to be best man in the future.'

'Really? What an honour. Thank you, I won't let you down, promise.'

'I know, mate. Please don't discuss my news with anyone for the moment.'

'Your secret is safe with me.'

'I very much doubt it, you arse. Have a good evening. Bye.'

'And you, mate.'

Dan walked into the house and immediately smelt

dinner cooking. *Very useful having a sister working as a commis chef and going to cookery college,* Dan thought. When Olivia wasn't about, which was often, he and his father took turns cooking, with variable results.

'Hi, Olivia.'

'Hi, you, where've you been?'

'Up at the big house. Cath wanted to see me.'

'Oh, anything wrong?'

'Yes and no, I'll explain over dinner.'

'Dad's having a shower, he'll be down soon. Why don't you pour you and Dad a beer. I'll have a white wine. What were you doing today? Your clothes stank. They're now on their second wash. Hopefully, that will get rid of the smell.'

'Police wanted part of the ditch dug out where they found the bodies so four of us landed up to our waist in shit and whatever else is in there. The police took lots of samples, don't know why.'

'You must have been working with Billy. I saw—actually smelt— him when walking home. All the muck had dried on him in the heat and he looked a state.'

'Yes, with Billy.' Dan was interrupted by his father entering the room.

'Ahh, a beer, good, thanks. Just what I need, cheers.'

Dan picked up his glass and raised it, smiling at his dad, trying to gauge his mood, which at first glance seemed pretty good.

'You seem in a good mood,' said Dan.

'Well, I managed to avoid digging shit today, so that's a good thing. Also think we've sorted out the open day.

Been talking to Viking re-enactment groups all day and they seem keen.'

'But surely we can't use the longbows.'

'They will need depowering and you can get special rubber-tipped arrows that don't do much harm.'

'Sounds cool.'

'Agreed with Isaac we will have shield maidens. Still need to decide what they will do. Thinking one for each bowman. So, thirty plus girls in all.'

Olivia turned from the stove. 'Don't see that being a problem. I'll do it, so will many of the others.'

'Well, Isaac will put something out very shortly with the details and we are going to muster on the range a week Sunday.'

'When Thomas and Francesca are visiting,' said Olivia. 'Now, sit down, dinner is ready. Beef stew with dumplings and there's a fruit pie in the oven.' Olivia was always amazed at what and how much the boys ate. No matter the weather, no matter how hot, it still had to be solid hot food. Meat and a fruit pie was a favourite combination. They would never tolerate a salad or vegetarian. *Must be all that working outside,* she thought, as she sat down and mopped her brow.

Duncan and Dan took turns to fill their plates and, despite their usual hungry appetite, there was plenty left for Olivia, who didn't want much. She was hot, and had been all day with the weather and the kitchen, and just really wanted a shower and to watch trash TV with a cold wine and some chocolate.

'I'm getting engaged,' Dan blurted out, between mouth-fuls.

His father and Olivia froze still at his announcement.

'Congratulations, Dan,' offered Olivia with a beaming smile.

'Congratulations, son. What prompted that move?'

'Cath is pregnant. I'm going with her and Charlotte to the doctor tomorrow morning.'

The dining room was silent. The tinkering of cutlery on plates and gulping of beer between mouthfuls of food had gone. Dan and Olivia looked at their father, waiting for what he might say or do next.

'Good lad, you're doing the right thing. There'll be things to sort out in time. How do you feel?'

'Cath seems really happy about the situation and we're very fond of each other.'

'*Fond!* But do you love her? Because fond ain't good enough, boy!'

'Yes, Dad, I love her and she loves me.'

'Then that's good enough. It won't be easy at times, but love will see you through.'

'Thanks, Dad.'

'No, thank you. A grandchild! What better surprise, what a present!' said Dan's father, beaming like his daughter.

'And I will be an aunt.'

'Enough talk now,' said Duncan. 'Time to eat. Another beer I think, Dan, please.'

*

Charlotte had retreated from the drawing room to

their bedroom with her book. Lewis came in to wash and change for dinner.

'You look happy, dear,' said Charlotte.

'Yes, it's a good day. The royal visit this weekend will go ahead now they have found the bodies and think they know what happened. Pen let me know that Kurt's wife and child finally have their visas sorted and can now join him. Talking to Isaac and Duncan, we seem to have solved what to do on the open day.'

'What's the plan?'

'Re-enactment of the Danish raiding party chasing Ethelred. Should be quite a show.'

'Sounds good, dear.'

'How are you, any news?'

'Well, yes, how do you feel about being a grandfather?' Charlotte said.

'Blimey, Thomas isn't hanging about!'

'Not Thomas dear, Catherine.'

'Oh, I see, with Dan?'

'Yes, of course.'

'Well, they're very young, but Dan's a good lad. Is Cath alright?'

'Very calm, and seems very happy. Oddly, I think this might be good for her. We're seeing the doctor tomorrow morning just to check things out.'

'Your call this afternoon when I walked in, you knew then?'

'Yes, sorry, my head was still spinning and I couldn't think of the right words.'

'Fair enough, quite understand, my head was still full of estate business.'

'It always is,' Charlotte said under her breath. 'They're getting engaged,' she continued brightly.

'That's good. Obviously, we will give them all the help they need.'

Charlotte's phone rang.

'It's Cath, I'd better take it.'

'Hello, dear.' A pause. 'Oh, that's good, Duncan and Olivia.' Another pause. 'I'm with him now, all OK I think.' Charlotte glanced at Lewis as she spoke. Lewis nodded and smiled. 'Just Jen and Pen, not sure if Jackie's joining us tonight,' Charlotte continued. 'OK, I'll tell him. See you at seven. Bye. She turned to Lewis, 'That's good, Duncan seems alright about it, but perhaps you could talk to him tomorrow?'

'Yes, good idea. Should I say anything over dinner?'

'No, Cath has said she will announce it tonight herself. As Olivia knows it will be through the house in a flash. Juicy gossip, won't be a secret for long.'

'Might stop them talking about Pen and Jackie, which would do them a favour,' said Lewis thoughtfully.

*

Jackie did join the family for dinner. She was obviously nervous. It was a big change for her to get used to, from being staff to family. Charlotte hugged Jackie and Pen when they arrived and told Jackie she was pleased to see her and she was a very welcome part of the family.

Cath was quiet, mulling over her announcement. She decided she would wait until whoever was serving was in the room as well. Typically, her father had news about the estate he felt compelled to share. *Good news about Kurt's family*, Cath thought. Once her father had stopped talking, Gail started serving dinner, and Cath decided this was the time, but as she composed herself Mrs Cooper walked in to check service was alright. Cath was just about to say something when her mother asked Mrs Cooper how she was, and started a short conversation. As soon as they'd stopped Cath jumped in.

'I'm getting engaged!' Cath almost spat out before anyone else could speak.

The room went quiet. Gail paused serving for a moment before smoothly continuing. All eyes were on Cath.

'That's all a bit sudden,' said Jen, sitting next to her.

'We thought with the baby, it was a good idea,' replied Cath with a broad grin.

'You're pregnant!' exclaimed Jen her eyes wide. 'I told you to be careful!'

'I knew you'd say that,' Cath replied.

Jen leant over and gave Cath a hug and a kiss. 'Love you, I can't be angry, you mad thing.'

Jackie leant gently over to Pen. 'Do you think we might have children some day?' Pen didn't reply straight away. It was something she'd dismissed from her thoughts, but seeing what it had done for her sister, she whispered back to Jackie, 'Let's talk about it.'

'Champagne, I think, but just a small glass for you,' said Lewis, nodding at Cath.

Gail left the dining room to get a bottle, ready to burst with the gossip she'd heard.

~ 33 ~

Gail burst into the kitchen. 'Catherine is pregnant!'

Chef and Michelle both looked up in surprise.

'Dan?' asked Michelle as she continued to busy herself with dessert.

'Yes. They want champagne. Michelle, could you help with the glasses, please?'

Michelle looked up at Chef.

'That's fine, dessert looks nearly finished. Well done, nice work.'

'Thank you,' Michelle said as she took off her apron and went to get the champagne glasses and take them upstairs. As she did so Gail pulled a chilled bottle from the fridge.

'Gail,' said Chef, 'please remember to replace the bottle in the cooler. You never know when they want one. Big weekend coming up.'

'Yes, Chef.'

Gail followed Michelle back up to the dining room, meeting Mrs Cooper in the hall muttering to herself and shaking her head.

'You OK, Mrs Cooper?'

'Just a bit of shock. I still think of the twins as babies, although I know they're quite grown up. It's all change. Where will it end? Perhaps I should just retire?' she said with a sigh.

Lewis led the celebratory toasts and jokingly told Cath off for making him a grandfather and feeling old. To which everyone laughed, Cath and Jen, both telling him he was.

*

Next morning, Olivia was on the breakfast shift and was surprised at how the news had travelled. She was sure everyone she passed gave her a knowing look as they said good morning. When she entered the kitchen Chef asked if everything was alright. Holly gave her a hug.

Dan, walking to get the car, passed all the men standing waiting for the day's jobs to be allocated and they broke out in spontaneous applause. Isaac came over and shook his hand.

*

The doctor's appointment was very uneventful. It confirmed Cath was pregnant and that everything was OK. It was too early to tell if the baby was a boy or a girl, which Cath found a bit disappointing. She didn't know why.

The drive back was as quiet as the drive there, until Charlotte asked, 'Have you two thought of living arrangements?'

'No,' answered Cath. Dan was silent, just listening as he drove his precious cargo. 'We haven't discussed it yet.'

'Tom and Fran are going to stay in the house until they

find their feet, then decide. You two could do the same. We have plenty of room.'

'We'll think about it, Mother. Thanks.'

~ 34 ~

Thursday, 26th June. There was a meeting for everyone on the morning before the royal visit. Lewis spoke, then a representative of the King, and finally Ms Rogers, a plain-suited woman who was in charge of arrangements and security.

The royals would arrive together in two cars plus escort on Saturday morning and leave early afternoon on the Sunday; the exact departure time was still fluid. A full itinerary had been agreed for the visit. The security lockdown would begin in earnest on the Friday morning and continue until they left on Sunday. Armed police would be patrolling the estate, guided by foresters as needed. An area would be prepared in case a helicopter was needed for any reason. They would also be using drones to patrol the perimeter. Local police would be closing and patrolling roads bordering the estate for the duration of the visit.

Bet they fuck that up, thought Poacher John, who would be helping to guide police around the estate, which he found amusingly ironic as he'd spent most of his time when actively poaching trying to lose them.

Ms Rogers, who was giving the update, scanned the

staff in front of her, as ever with any royal visit, she was confronted by keen and excited faces. 'I believe you are already aware that from tomorrow morning, for security reasons, it's been agreed that staff can no longer come and go from the estate as they please and if you live off-site make sure you have arranged your accommodation here for Friday and Saturday nights. If this becomes a problem for anyone you will need to see me. You will be able to find me in the OP's room. Graham, I believe, will tell you where that is.'

Graham coughed to get Ms Rogers' attention.

'Thank you, Graham.'

'The office next to the library,' said Graham in an important voice.

'One more thing from me. You will see armed personnel other than police, quite possibly in army greens. This is just additional security. You do have the King of the country visiting and his heir. Any questions?' Ms Rogers finished.

A hand at the back went up.

Ms Rogers strained to see who it was. 'Yes?' she questioned in a clipped tone.

'Can we still have longbow practice on Sunday morning?' one of the apprentices asked.

Ms Rogers didn't seem to know what to say and looked relieved to see Lewis move forward.

'Yes, practice will go ahead as usual. In fact, the King and Prince seem keen to see their Company of Archers in action and I'm sure both will want a go. While I'm on the subject, as some of you will know, we are introducing shield maidens. I think Isaac is putting a note out with the details.'

Graham coughed again. 'Just need to run off copies and hand them out, but if any of the ladies want to turn up at the range on Sunday you will find out more.'

Lewis looked at Ms Rogers. 'If there are no more questions?' he said, before pausing for a moment. No response. 'Then thank you, everyone, for your understanding and help with this important visit. That is all. Any further questions or problems, you all know what to do.'

'Thank you,' said Ms Rogers, turning to Lewis. 'Can someone brief me on what exactly happens on Sundays with the longbows? I'm not sure we've understood this properly.'

~ 35 ~

Monday, 30th June. Tom's phone rang. 'Hi, Dad. How'd the weekend go?'

'Well, thanks, I think. They arrived about eleven. Can you believe it, a couple of local police manning road closures weren't keen to let them through, caused a right kafuffle and a lot of shouting from the royals' security team. After that, it was pretty much plain sailing. I had a long chat with Charles before lunch; he wanted to know more about the wilding plans. I introduced him to Kurt who, it turns out, met his father some years ago when he worked for a conservation charity in Africa. Charles wants to keep a close eye on what we and others are doing and already is thinking what he might potentially do on royal estates. He also thinks at some point he will be able to gather other estate owners to agree some common goals.

'After lunch we all went to the woods, led by Isaac who greatly praised both land and tree, showed us all sorts of creepy crawlies, birds and things, which everyone loved. Managed to talk to Charles and William in the evening, which was good. William has very similar views to Charles, but I would say is a bit frustrated at the speed things move and that the talk too often outweighs action. Sunday church, then they visited the range. Interestingly, they were both unaware of the archers' royal connection, but I don't think Charles will forget.

'There was a bit of fuss with Poacher John. When he was guiding, he had a bet with one of the soldiers he was escorting, who said he could out stalk him in the woods. Poor chap didn't stand a chance and John put an arrow in the tree two feet above the soldier's head, clean shot. His mate, who was refereeing the contest, hit the deck when John's arrow struck the tree and, as a reflex, raised his weapon into a firing position, so John put an arrow in the ground about three feet in front of him. In the end they all laughed, but the soldiers weren't happy. Their officer was furious, said they shouldn't have been fucking about. Which was said out of earshot of the King and Prince, who were both fascinated with what had happened.'

'Can't wait to hear the full story from John,' said Tom.

'I've heard it. It's worth a listen.'

'So, all went well then?'

'Yes, apart from a bit of tension between the royals' personal staff and our house staff, just wanted things done a bit differently.'

'Bet Mrs Cooper didn't like that?'

'No, but Anna dealt with it all very well, so it wasn't really a problem.'

'Is Mrs Cooper slowly passing over the reins?'

'I think so. Sorry, I am assuming you know Cath's news?'

'Yes, Pen spoke to me and Fran has been talking to

Mother about next weekend, when Fran's parents visiting. Is Cath alright?'

'Remarkably so. Your mother thinks it could be a good thing; give her some focus. From what I've seen so far, I would agree.'

'What are Cath and Dan going to do?'

'Still under discussion.'

'We will be arriving Wednesday, as will Simon to set up our new office. Fran is going to spend the afternoon with Pen and Naomi.'

'Charlotte told me you were arriving a few days early. That will be good. See you in a couple of weeks.'

'Will do, Father, bye.'

~ 36 ~

Tuesday, 8thJuly.Tom dropped Fran off at the restaurant where she was meeting the girls, before driving round to Simon's, telling her he could pick her up later. She'd initially told him no, then remembering they were travelling to Woodcoombe the next morning, decided a lift home at a sensible time was probably a good idea, so she asked Tom to pick her up about ten-thirty.

Tom drove to Simon's, following the sat nav. After knowing Simon for four years, working closely for two, he realised he'd never been to his place before. Simon had said he lived in a room jammed with his junk with just enough space to eat, sleep and fuck.

Tom pulled up at the address as the sat nav announced he had reached his destination. At first glance, the tall, terraced building looked similar to Tom's, but perhaps not quite as well maintained. Tom found the front door open and realised the building was not flats but rented out as individual rooms, resulting in odd corridors leading off from the stairs. He climbed to the third floor to room fourteen, which he found down a badly constructed, plasterboard corridor in need of repair. Tom knocked on the door and it quickly opened and Simon beckoned him in.

'Welcome,' said Simon, theatrically sweeping his hand across the empty room.

The room was bare except for the mattress and four bags. The carpet was threadbare, dotted with stains of various grimness and size. The curtains hung limply, thick with dust, with no discernible colour. The walls were marked and dented with rectangular lines, a reminder of old pictures and posters, the only relief to the fading grubby, magnolia-coloured walls. Tom guessed the two larger bags were for him.

'All the stuff to go to yours was packed and picked up this morning,' said Simon. 'Means you can see my domain in all its glory. I know it's pretty shit, but if you think this is bad you should see the shared bathroom, just down the corridor. Thinking about it, don't!'

'Did you have much to send?'

'Important things: gaming computer, gaming chair, TV, stereo, tech stuff, as well as a load of records, CDs and books. There's some other shit I will probably throw out when I get to yours and have time to sort it out.'

'You hungry?' Tom asked, his tummy rumbling.

'You're not expecting me to cook, I guess? I did have two electric rings, a toaster and a small microwave in that corner.' Simon, pointed and Tom noticed burn marks on the wall and, worryingly, on the ceiling. There was also the greasy grime of spilt food on the ragged carpet, which looked like it might be moving. 'But I gave them away today. To be honest they were all in a shit state.' Simon looked slightly embarrassed about the state of the room, then noticed Tom looking at the carpet.

'Ah,' said Simon. 'See you've found my pets. They moved in about a month ago, when the heat started. Tried to get rid of them, but they're tenacious little fuckers.'

'Shall we go out and eat? My treat,' suggested a shocked Tom.

'Café around the corner is good,' replied an eager Simon.

'Let's go then,' said Tom, heading for the bags.

'No, leave them here while we eat. You don't want to leave anything interesting in your car, especially when it's dark.'

Tom was relieved to escape from the room as he followed Simon out. They met a few people on the stairs coming in as they made their way out of the house. Simon stopped and talked to a stunningly attractive, statuesque girl who gave him a hug and a kiss before they continued, with some relief, out onto the street.

'Who's she?'

'Rio, she's been here longer than me. Originally from Brazil, hence the name. Don't know what her real name is.'

'Friend?'

'Yes, and in the past more,' Simon said with a sigh, shrugging his shoulders.

In five minutes, they arrived at the café. It wasn't very full. They sat in a booth and looked up at the menu hand-written on boards above the counter.

'What can I get you, gents? Hi, Simon, you haven't been in for a while.'

'Hi, Toni, been busy.'

Toni took their orders and quickly brought up the teas they had asked for. She lingered.

'So, what are you up to?' Toni asked Simon, ignoring Tom, as if he wasn't there.

'Working on the usual coding stuff. This is my boss.'

'Hi, boss,' said Toni with a wiggle. 'Give us a job?'

'What do you do?' asked Tom.

'Depends on what you want,' she said, coyly turning back to the counter to get their food. She placed two plates down in front of them.

'Toni's a computer whizz, and a bit of a hacker. Part of the Green Gnome Collective, which I guess, Tom, you've never heard of, but she could do a lot better if she had the chance.'

'Thanks, honey,' said Toni, running her hand down Simon's arm. 'The collective is an eco-group. You may remember Petroleum X, that was us. It was basically whistle-blowing, using information we were given, but it caused Petroleum X a lot of embarrassment and raised many questions on how they did business.'

Tom didn't know what to say.

'Sorry, we don't have any jobs at the moment, but you never know.'

'Fair enough,' said Toni as she turned to serve another customer.

'Seriously!?' said Tom, once Toni was out of earshot

'You need to loosen up, Tom. She may not have a degree or gone to the right school, or any school, but she's dynamite with a computer. She is really very nice.'

Tom and Simon chatted about the project and the work still to be done. Several times Simon dropped in how useful Toni could be to move things on.

They finished eating and Tom paid the bill in cash with a twenty-pound tip for Toni, which brought out a big smile and a thank you.

Tom and Simon strolled back to the flat.

'Simon, Toni a friend?'

'In the past occasionally more, but just a friend now.'

'Like Rio?'

'That's right, just friends. I'm with Emma now and very happy, trying my best not to fuck it up for a change. One of the reasons I agreed to move down to yours was to keep me out of trouble.'

'You can get in as much trouble in the country as in the city, so be warned,' replied Tom, amused.

They got back to Simon's flat and each carried a bag down to the car. They were heavier than Tom had expected. At nearly ten o'clock, Tom climbed into the car having said his goodbyes to Simon, telling him they could discuss Toni next week when they had everything set up and had agreed everything that needed doing.

Should get to the restaurant in about twenty minutes, nice timing to pick Fran up, Tom thought to himself.

On arrival, Tom decided he would go in and say hello, rather than message Fran. The restaurant was busy but the burst of laughter from a table at the back gave Tom a clue where to find the girls. They'd finished eating, and were on cocktails, clearly not their first. Fran saw Tom crossing the floor towards them and stood up and waved.

Tom had met her four friends before. Fran explained one couldn't make it as she was ill, bloody virus! They stood up, one by one, some more glazed and unsteady than others and gave Tom a hug and a kiss.

'Must go!' Fran suddenly announced, picking up her bag and cardigan. 'You all must come and stay. I'll be in touch, love you all.' Fran then went round the table kissing and hugging each of her friends before she left. One of the women made a show of holding Fran's left hand, inspecting her ring closely and giving it a mock polish before giving Fran back her hand and letting her go.

Fran was still waving as she went through the door of the restaurant into the street.

'Where's the car?'

'Just around the corner,' Tom replied leading the way. 'A good evening? Did you have much to drink? You seem surprisingly sober for a night out with the girls.'

'Great to see everyone before we move. A few drinks, but I really didn't want to be suffering tomorrow, so just a bit tired now. I need my bed.'

They got into the car and Tom drove them home.

'You, said before we move. I assume you mean to the estate? Do you have a date in mind?'

Fran shifted wearily and looked at Tom. 'You're going to need to be there with Simon now he's moved so let's just get on with it. Let's say the week after my parents visit.'

'OK, we can start getting organised this weekend. I'll talk to Graham. Do you want to mention this to my mother and everyone else?'

'Yes. no problem. I'm seeing Naomi and Pen tomorrow

afternoon. When are you setting up the office with Simon? By the way, what was Simon's flat like?'

'Shit! It's a room, not a flat, with a shared bathroom that sounds like a biohazard.'

'That's not very nice, Tom. I'm sure it wasn't that bad.'

'Trust me, truly awful!'

'Oh, no wonder he was so keen to make the move to the estate.'

'What are you doing with Naomi and Pen?' Tom asked quietly.

'Promised to catch up with Naomi last time we were down. She's meeting me at two o'clock after lunch at the house and we are going to wander down and meet Pen at Henge Cottages as they or the farmhouse might be an option for us.'

'Possibly, but they all need a heap of work.'

'Yes, Pen mentioned that, but it's still worth a look.'

'Be interested to hear what you think,' said Tom, thinking he would be quite happy living in the main house. 'You should have a closer look at Pen's and my parents' rooms so you get an idea what we could have built for us.'

'Good idea,' replied Fran. She hadn't thought about that as an option, although she guessed Tom would like to stay in the main house, which did have a lot of advantages, now and in the future.

'Home,' announced Tom as he parked and turned off the engine.

They walked slowly up the ever-steep stairs to their flat.

'Would you like a drink?' asked Tom.

'Could I have a green tea, please, and a large glass of water.'

'Of course, you go to bed and I'll bring them in.'

'Thank you,' said Fran, brushing past Tom and kissing him as she headed to the bedroom.

Tom stood waiting for the green tea to brew. He'd left the bags he'd collected from Simon's in the boot of the car. You couldn't see them but he still had a nagging feeling he should bring them inside, just in case. You never knew.

Tom carried the drinks into Fran, who was already in bed sitting up, flicking vaguely through a magazine.

'Here you go,' Tom said as he put the drinks on her bedside table. 'Just popping down to the car, as I left the bags in there I picked up from Simon's.'

Fran said nothing, just rolled her eyes as she sipped the tea.

*

Tom slung a bag over each shoulder and mounted the stairs back to the flat. His legs soon started to burn and he could feel himself sweating. The bags cut into his shoulders. With relief he placed them next to Fran's packed bag and, Tom, assumed, new outfit hanging from the picture rail in the hall.

He decided to have a quick shower after his stair work-out. When he finally got to bed, Fran was already securely wrapped in the duvet, purring gently, submerged in sleep.

~ 37 ~

Wednesday, 9th July. Next morning, they set off just after nine. Fran was quiet. There wasn't much conversation, just polite rumbled mutterings between them. Suddenly, Fran almost shouted, 'Coffee. Stop!'

Tom swerved towards the pavement. Fran jumped out, pausing long enough to ask, 'Do you want anything?'

'No, thanks. I'll get something when we are out of London.'

Fran didn't wait to discuss or question, but closed the door and walked briskly into her favourite coffee shop, appearing a few minutes later with a large takeaway cup and a brown bag containing breakfast.

As she jumped in Tom started the car, ready to continue the journey.

'Do want a slurp?' offered Fran holding up her cup towards Tom.

'Yes, please.' Tom accepted the cup, enjoying the aroma the cup threw out before he'd even tasted the coffee. He took a gulp and immediately wished he'd said yes when offered. He passed the cup back and saw Fran had torn the bag apart to reveal a crumbly croissant now lying in her lap.

'That's going to make a mess.' Fran hated her car to be messy

'I know, but I need something. I will clean it up.'

Tom didn't answer, focusing on driving and getting out of London so they could stop and he could get a bite and a coffee of his own.

'So, you're seeing Naomi and Pen this afternoon. That should be fun.'

'Yes,' said Fran as she chewed her breakfast. 'I'm seeing Isaac Thursday morning, going to join him as he walks the woods.'

'Good, he's the best person to tell you about the gifts you have and how you can use them.'

'To be honest, Tom, since we've been back, I've pretty well forgotten all that stuff.'

'It's still all in there somewhere and you clearly have a gift.'

'Supposing I don't want the gift, just want to be normal?'

'Talk to Isaac about that and also Mother. She, like you, came from the outside, as you know.'

Fran nodded and sipped her coffee as Tom drove.

They arrived at the house just before twelve. They were greeted by Anna, who carried Fran's new outfit as they went to their room.

'Been a few changes, madam, since you were last here,' said Anna.

'Crikey, that was only a couple of weeks ago!'

'Mrs Cooper is starting to take a step back and I'm picking up many of her duties.' Anna said looking happy at the news. 'A new girl has started, Rachel Provo. She will principally look after yourself and Master Thomas, but also help elsewhere as needed. Sophie, Lady Charlotte's maid, will also be helping more generally around the place. For the moment, Jackie remains working as a housekeeper, but I don't know for how long. We expect to take on two apprentices. Running the house is getting ever more demanding, especially with the increase in visitors.'

'Wow! We have a maid,' Fran exclaimed. 'Do we really need one?' The same embarrassed feeling she had had on her first visit washed through her again.

'Think of it like this, madam, we allow you to get on with your things and it's a good job for us locals; there aren't many of those about.'

'Sorry, just I find it tough to get my head around that I even need a maid to look after me.'

'Not just you, Master Thomas, madam. They have many other duties around the house. Rachel will also look after your parents next weekend and I'm sure you'll both have other friends visiting.'

'Crikey! My parents will give poor Rachel the run around. They'll love it, and won't have any embarrassment at all.'

'I'm sure it won't be a problem. I bet we've had more demanding and difficult guests than your parents. Sorry, madam, if there's nothing else, I must get on.'

'Just my outfit for Saturday could probably do with a press.'

'No problem, it'll be collected and done before then,' Anna said cheerfully as she left the room.

Fran, now alone, spun round the room, waiting for Tom who was delivering the two bags of kit to his and Simon's new office. She stood in the bay window looking down the Vale, wondering what it was like here when the weather wasn't boiling hot. She scanned the trees down the shallow hill towards the river and, for the first time, felt something, a brief connection and flash of energy as if the woods were saying hello, reminding her that they were still there, waiting for her. She broke away from her thoughts and walked into the centre of the room as Tom came in.

'You ready for lunch?' he asked breezily.

'Yes, I think I am.'

They left their room, and Tom took Fran's hand as they descended the main stairs.

'We have a maid; Rachel Provo,' Fran said.

'When Graham was helping me with the office, he told me there have been some changes. A few issues were highlighted in the running of the house with the royal visit last weekend. More resource needed in housekeeping and kitchen.'

'I've heard of Rachel Provo before, but can't place her,' Fran mused.

'Rachel was Henry's alleged rape victim years ago.'

'Yes, I remember now.' Fran was annoyed she hadn't immediately made the connection.

They walked into the dining room and it had the same friendly buzz of conversation as at her first lunch. But no Mrs Cooper, instead Anna stood overseeing service. Fran recognised Olivia, but not the other girl manning the buffet table.

Fran chose a light lunch and sat next to Tom. Nick, looking stressed, began talking very animatedly to Tom as soon as he sat down. Fran scanned the room. Some faces she recognised, others she did not. Unlike last time, no one seemed to be taking any particular notice of either her or Tom, which was nice.

At ten to two Tom leant over and whispered in her ear. 'Simon sounds like he's going to be a bit early, so I'm going to drive to the station now.'

'OK, see you in our room before dinner,' said Fran. She watched him leave the dining room and noticed Naomi bobbing into the hall, so decided to leave as well.

'Hi, Naomi, I'm ready if you are?'

'Yes, let's go.' Naomi led the way, out onto the Vale. Fran put on her white, wide-brimmed hat to help combat the continuous sun.

'Very film star, with your glasses and hat,' said Naomi admiringly as she led the way down the Vale towards Henge Cottages.

'I usually love the heat, but this is too much for me,' said Fran. 'Wonder when it will stop?'

'Father told me June has got hotter and hotter over the years, but in the last three years it's really got too much; excessive. It usually ends by mid-July, with a big rainstorm and brief flooding as the weather system changes. Then the weather returns to something near normal, although still warmer and dryer than average.'

'Doesn't the heat bother you?'

'No, not as much as some. Probably has something to do with my heritage. Father, Isaac, goes out every day in a jacket and doesn't break a sweat. But he hates the cold, like me.'

They walked in silence, skirting the meadow, watching the bees and butterflies swimming through the waves of gently nodding flowers. Fran breathed in the perfume of the meadow. It was just as sweet as the last time and she imagined lying down in it and bathing in its thick, fragrant breath.

'How far is it?' asked Fran, now feeling the heat.

'We pass the meadow, past the elm stand you saw being taken down last time you were here, follow the drive to the Joseph's Farm. About fifteen minutes, I guess.'

They passed the avenue out of the estate, past the wooden signs Fran had only seen before from the car directing you to Joseph's, Clifford's or Woodcoombe. Then they saw the line of pretty cottages and Pen sitting on the steps of one in the shade.

Pen stood up when she saw them coming.

'Henge Cottages,' Pen said. 'Part of Joseph's Farm. Seven cottages, the central five two bedrooms. The ones on each end are three beds. I've managed to find a builder, a father and son—builders are so very hard to find at the moment—and they arrive from Newcastle mid-July to start work. They're going to live onsite, in their van. Jackie and I are going to move into a two bed. Both the three bed ones are taken, one for Kurt, now his wife and child when they finally arrive, the other for Doctor Sara Azar and her two sons. She's interesting, Iranian. Trained in the US and Germany, worked in hospitals in Iran, then she and her husband, an engineer, were denounced. He was arrested and is believed dead, she escaped with her sons overland. One of her sons has been blind from birth.'

'Thanks, Pen. Is there much work to be done?' asked Fran, still absorbing all that Pen had said.

'Everything! The good thing is they are pretty well watertight, apart from a little damp, also Flora Joseph, and I think Dan and Cath, want one of the cottages, so they're going fast, which is no surprise.'

Fran looked towards the farmhouse.

'Is that where Flora lives now?'

'Yes, with her two sons who are supposed to be off to Canada, but no one seems to know when. The farmhouse needs loads of work as well, but at least it has power and water connected, which none of the cottages have.

Fran, if you're thinking about the farmhouse, no work will happen on it until all the cottages are done and Flora moves out, which she won't do until the boys have gone.'

'OK, thanks, I've got the picture.'

'I'll arrange to catch up with you and show you the options in the main house.'

'That would be great. Perhaps tomorrow afternoon, if that works for you?'

'Meet you after lunch,' Pen replied. 'At the bottom of the main stairs at two o'clock?'

'That would be great, look forward to it,' replied Fran, already deciding certainly the cottages and probably the farmhouse were not going to work for her and Tom.

Naomi and Fran left Pen sitting back in the shade as she waited for Jackie to join her.

'Thought we might at least have looked inside,' Naomi said as they walked back the way they had come

'Three bed might have worked, but others have a greater need, so apart from being nosy I didn't see the point.'

They continued to walk back, no words spoken, just the oppressive afternoon heat that seemed to have gained its own substance as if the heat had congealed the air and made it thick.

The crunch of their sandals was interrupted as Naomi announced, 'Spence and I have broken up,' breaking Fran's thoughts about where to live and the heat, as sweat trickled down her back.

'I'm sorry to hear that. He was supposed to be joining you here?'

'Yes, for the summer, but he changed his mind and said I must come back to London.'

'You want to stay here?'

'Well, I did the report for the visitor centre planning application and I've asked if I can run it. Whatever happens now I have a job here, which is what I wanted.'

'Wish I had a job. I will need something to do,' sighed Fran.

'Speak to Pen when you see her tomorrow. She's collating all resources for the estate, current and future.'

'I will. Is Pen's job getting bigger?'

'Looks that way, the estate is a business, after all, with an ever-expanding number of employees. The lack of resource management has finally caught up with them. They got in a bit of a mess letting go of Lucy Haywood, who came in as commercial manager to set up the visitor centre, but couldn't provide a report to support the planning application. Landed up having to pay her off when, in reality, she just wasn't very good.'

'Quite a job Pen's got, then.'

'There's something else, Fran.' Naomi slowed slightly and looked sideways at Fran. 'I have a terrible confession to make, please hear me out.'

'I'm listening,' Fran said.

'After Spencer and I broke up, I was a bit all over the place for a while. Pen had told me how serious you and Tom were and I felt terribly jealous. So, when I bumped into him the other week, I made a point of flirting with him. I admit, at that moment, I wanted to split you up.'

Fran stopped and stared at Naomi, whose eyes were fixed unblinking to the ground.

'Tom pushed me away with no hesitation and, believe me, I can be very persuasive.'

Fran had no doubt about Naomi's persuasive powers as she listened with a feeling of dread.

'Nothing happened,' Naomi continued. 'He—he pushed me away,' she repeated. 'Not a flicker of interest. I'm so sorry, it was a silly, stupid thing to do. When it comes to men, I don't seem to make good choices or decisions. Years ago, Tom was my first and really only love and I wanted to know if he still had any feelings for me. Finding a boyfriend is easy, finding the right one is hard. Every time I seem to get let down. It can't all be my fault.

'I was finding it difficult seeing you together and you becoming part of the family, when part of me has always felt it should be me not someone else. Tom was very clear, we are friends and nothing more, which I now accept and understand. Although I've probably fucked that up with both you and him.' There was a quiver in her voice as she finished and Fran thought she looked very sad, certainly not the confident, proud, determined woman she was used to seeing. Naomi shuddered as she failed to hold back her tears. Fran took the few steps between them and embraced Naomi as she cried.

'Are those tears for Tom or you?' Fran asked

'For me; I've made such a mess of things. I never seem to learn my lesson. And a bit for Tom and you, as I really don't want to cause any trouble between you.'

Fran squeezed Naomi before releasing her. It was too hot to hug anyone for long. The dread in Fran's head was disappearing and, to her surprise, she felt a wave of sorrow for Naomi. She looked weak, broken. Or was she mistaken. *Could this just be a grand charade?* Fran wondered. *Only time will tell*, she decided, stepping away.

'You're so lucky,' Naomi sobbed.

'I know,' said Fran, understanding Naomi's anguish, as she imagined what it would feel like if the situation was reversed.

'God, I must look and sound a state and I feel so stupid. I'm such a fool,' Naomi said as she stood up straight, wiped her eyes and shook her head. 'Fuck, it's hot and getting upset doesn't help. How about a swim?' The Naomi Fran knew was returning.

Fran looked surprised as Naomi started to stride off.

'Come on,' Naomi said, turning as she walked, tears still in her eyes.

'I don't have a costume or a towel.'

'You don't need a costume and you'll dry in a moment in this heat.'

'OK,' replied Fran, not sure what to think as she attempted to keep up with Naomi, who was now on a mission.

They skirted the bottom of the meadow and crossed the small strip of fading green Vale grass before getting to the river. They walked into a collection of tall willows, their leafed branches hanging like curtains, the small leaves fluttering gently with the faintest whisper. Swallows swung to and fro, cutting curves across the cloudless blue sky. They walked into the shaded centre of the willows and Fran noticed a large pool under the willows' wide arms nestling beside the River Coombe which was quietly running fast.

'We can dip in the pool. Don't go into the river. It goes too fast now and you don't want to wash up naked further downstream,' said Naomi with a laugh as she started to undress, completely unfazed.

Fran suddenly felt very self-conscious. Then she heard a voice.

'Don't worry, dear, it's quite safe in the pool, but unfortunately the river runs too fast to bathe safely these days, which is a shame.'

Fran swung round to try and see who was talking, but no one was there.

'If you're shy,' the voice continued, 'is this better?' Branches dropped to form a wider denser screen around the pool.

Fran realised it was the tree. *How stupid of her,* she thought. 'Harriet?' she asked. W for Willow she remembered from the *Book of the Dead*, Tom's grandmother.

'Yes, dear, I've been looking forward to meeting you.'

Fran glanced at Naomi who was now standing naked, waiting for Fran.

'Don't worry, she can't hear us, unless I want her to. I can sense the tension between you. Let me see...' The voice sighed and paused. 'Ah, no surprise: Thomas!' Another pause. 'Always remember you are the now, she is the past and...and I only see you in the future, so you have nothing to fear on that account. If you can allow it, she will be a really good friend, like her mother, Jane, was to me and still is.'

'Hawthorn!' Fran interrupted. 'How do you know?'

'Yes, hawthorn. I can see glimpses of the future; I'm a poor seer. Forgive her today and she'll stand with you forever. I sense, in the future, you will need each other for a purpose I cannot see. Remember, I was like you when I married Maxwell, all those years ago. And I was great friends with Naomi's mother, although like you two it perhaps didn't start well. Just give everything time, dear, and I promise everything will all make sense and come right. Any time you want to talk, sit under the willows and I will come to you. Now swim, the pool is cool and quite safe.'

Fran felt a sense of relief wash through her as she walked to stand next to Naomi's piled clothes. As she undressed more branches slid down, obscuring her further to anyone who might stroll by.

'Thank you,' Fran said looking up into the heart of the tree, which shook briefly in response.

Fran, naked, shuffled self-consciously to stand next to Naomi facing the pool. It looked clear and cool. *Perhaps cold,* thought Fran, *after the heat.*

'Best just to jump in, it's a slight shock at first, then relief,' said Naomi, taking a step to the edge. She took a deep breath and jumped in upright feet first.

Fran watched her disappear into the water with a satisfying small splosh, just the bubbles rising to give away her presence. Fran realised she was holding her breath, waiting for Naomi to surface. To Fran's relief, Naomi's head appeared, her black hair sparkling with jewels of water which sprayed off as she shook her head and took a breath.

'What's it like?' asked Fran.

'Wonderful.'

'Cold?'

'No, a relief. Jump!'

Fran took a deep breath, moved forward and felt her toes curl over the grassy edge. Then she jumped feet first into the pool, arms tight by her side. She felt the cool relief of the water wash up her body as she entered and sank. She wondered how deep it was and if her feet would meet the muddy bottom. Instead, her descent soon slowed and she became aware she was moving upward. She paddled gently with her arms and legs and broke the surface with a slight gasp for breath, in response to the water's cooling effect. She wondered how deep the pool was and how far she had sunk.

Naomi was floating a few feet away and splashed Fran playfully. 'How's that, now you're in?

'Amazing, so refreshing, my skin is tingling.'

They floated and wallowed in the pool, laughing and splashing each other, like they were lifelong friends. *Not yet,* thought Fran, *we will see, time will tell.*

A while later, Fran went to the side to climb out.

'Not like that. You'll slip and slide on the mud. If you do get out, you'll be covered in dirt and have to jump back in to clean up,' said Naomi, who was now upright in the water, her arms in the air. Fran watch as a branch came down from the willow. Naomi grasped it and was gently lifted out of the water. Fran watched Naomi's athletic body slowly lift from the pool, the water sliding off her shining skin as she rose, running down her legs and dripping off her toes. The branch then moved over the bank and gently lowered her onto the ground.

'Arms up,' Naomi commanded. 'Don't worry, it's quite safe.'

Fran grasped the branch and hoped she'd enough strength to hang on, regretting she hadn't been to the gym for so long. She then felt herself being gently lifted, the water falling away from her as she escaped the pool's grasp and, in a moment, she was standing next to Naomi on the grass. The air was warm, but her skin still held the cool of the pool.

Some branches above them parted and the sun streamed in, bathing them in warmth to dry them off. They dressed and, giggling, walked out from under the willow's dome back into the unrelenting sun and heat. Fran turned and took Naomi's hand.

'Bow,' Fran simply said and they bowed their thank you to the trees and spirits who had welcomed them. The willows stretched and shuddered in recognition.

They walked up the Vale and the house gradually came into sight, first the chimneys rising into the blue, then the roof, as they ascended the slight hill of the Vale.

'OK if I leave you here? I need to go this way,' said Naomi, pointing uphill to the right. 'Our place is up near Coombe Village, but handy for the Foresters' Arms. You OK getting back to the house?'

'Yes, can't really miss it,' said Fran, taking a step towards the chimneys and roof that looked like a strange ship sat on top of the shimmering heat of the land. As she walked, the rest of the house came into sight. The coolness of the swim now disappeared which was disappointing, but the relief, however short, was good, and she would definitely visit again.

~ 38 ~

Simon was thirty minutes early, although he didn't know how he'd managed it. Tom was on the platform waiting as Simon's train pulled in and he spilled out onto the platform, looking around, lost, unsure of where he was.

Tom waved and Simon looked relieved to see him and visibly relaxed as he collected himself.

'How many stops at empty stations does this train make?'

'You must have caught the slow all-stations train. It goes a different route to the fast one. Sweeps up all the small village stations, many of which only get one train a day and even fewer passengers.'

'And they all look the same. Everything's so green.'

'Welcome to the country, my friend. Shall we go?'

Simon nodded, picked up his bags and followed Tom out of the station to the car.

'I thought you might have picked me up in a horse and cart,' Simon said as he put his bag in the boot and walked round to get in the passenger seat.

'Could have done, didn't realise you wanted the full country experience. Maybe when Emma comes down.'

'She'd love that. So, this is Woodcoombe Village,' said Simon. 'Looks like the picture on the lid of the fancy biscuits I buy my gran. She'd love this.'

'She can visit as well, if you like.'

'Maybe, be nice. She pretty well brought me up. My parents split when I was five and I went to live with Gran. She never gave up on me despite my few ups and many downs.'

Tom glanced at Simon. His face was serious, reflective, and slightly sad.

'Yes, she'd love this,' Simon repeated thoughtfully as they drove to the estate.

They drove up the entrance avenue with its guard of trees.

'Fuck! Is that your gaff?' Simon said as the house came into view.

'And yours too now,' Tom added.

'Fuck! This is a bit of an upgrade to the place I left.'

'I should hope so!' said Tom. They looked at each other as Tom brought the car to a stop and laughed loudly.

'I'll take you to your room first, then the office.'

'Sounds good,' Simon responded as he continued to look up and down the house before him in disbelief.

'Good afternoon, sir,' Anna said as she walked out the main door with Rachel a step behind her.

'Hi, Anna, and you must be Rachel. Nice to meet you. Have you met Fran yet?'

'Hello, sir. No, I guess I'll catch her before dinner

tonight,' Rachel said as she stepped forward and shook Tom's hand.

'Ladies, meet Simon.'

'Hello, ladies, nice to meet you,' Simon said, looking uncertain as to who they were.

'I'm Anna, housekeeper, and this is Rachel who will look after you during your stay, Mr...?'

'Fuck! Sorry. Do I need looking after? Call me Simon, everyone does,' Simon said looking confused.

'Remember,' said Tom, 'I've seen the state of your last place.'

'That's fair, if harsh,' replied Simon, with a broad grin on his face.

'Rachel will make sure you know how everything works here. Right, shall we show Simon his rooms? Anna, could you let Graham know we will meet him in the office in fifteen minutes, please.'

'Of course, sir,' said Anna as she strode back into the house.

'This way please,' gestured Rachel, leading Tom and Simon into the house. 'We'll take the back stairs as Mr Simon is on the second floor in a mini suite.'

Rachel opened the door to Simon's rooms and led the way in.

'All your stuff is here. I can help you unpack, if you like?'

'Where's the bed?' asked Simon, running his hands over his boxed possessions as he walked through the room.

'Your bedroom and bathroom are through there,' said Rachel, pointing to a half-open door at the end of the room.

Simon, in surprise, walked through the door and Rachel and Tom couldn't help laughing when they heard Simon's response on seeing his bedroom.

'Fuck! I must stop saying that, sorry.' Simon returned to the reception room shrugging his shoulders, a look of shock on his face.

'This is all for me?'

'Yes, for as long as you stay.'

'I never expected anything like this, I don't know what to say, thank you.'

'You're welcome, I hope you enjoy your time here. We'd better go and meet Graham at the office.'

'Mr Simon, if you need anything or have a question, just pick up the house phone or ask any of the staff you might see wandering around,' Rachel said as she led them out of the rooms down to the office.

Graham was already there and shook hands with Simon when he walked in. 'Hopefully, you shouldn't have any issues with anything. It all worked fine last weekend and their requirements were surprisingly similar to yours.'

'Who was here last weekend?' Simon asked as he looked up from connecting a laptop.

'We had royal guests, and this was the ops room,' said Graham.

'Fuck! Sorry. Who was here?'

'The King and Queen, William, Kate and their children,' said Tom.

Simon looked up again. 'Fuck, oops sorry. Right, I think we are ready.' Simon sat back in his chair his finger poised over the keyboard. Graham rolled his eyes. 'Three, two, one.' Simon hit the keyboard and looked hard at the screen. 'We have lift off, Houston, all systems looking good. Could someone turn on the big screen, please.'

Tom reached over and turned on the screen on the wall. Suddenly, it came to life, showing Simon's laptop screen.

'Perfect!' Simon said as he started to shut everything down. 'Brilliant, thank you,' he said to Graham.

'You're welcome.' Graham leant forward with two keys in his hand. 'One for each of you. I do have spares, if needed.'

'Do we really need these?' said Simon, shaking his head. 'I'm only going to lose the key or forget to lock up. I thought the idea was just being here was safer than the university?'

'True,' Tom said. 'Why don't you get yourself sorted over the next few days and we can catch up Monday and discuss work plans and everything else.'

'OK, Tom, sounds good.'

Graham's phone rang. 'Yes, OK, not a problem. Sit her somewhere and let me know. I'll be down shortly.'

'Problem?' enquired Tom.

'No, I don't think so,' Graham said as he moved from looking at Tom to Simon. 'Seems you have a visitor, Simon.'

Simon looked up, surprised and confused at the same time.

Graham continued, enjoying the brief suspense. 'Emma, she wanted to surprise you.'

'Fuck!' Simon said. 'I told her I'd be in touch once I'd settled in.'

'Not a problem?' said Tom looking at Graham.

'No, sir,' Graham replied. His phone buzzed. 'Emma is in the sitting room with Rachel.'

'OK, Simon, if we're all done here, let's go down and see her.'

Tom and Simon left the office and turned left towards the last door in the corridor for the sitting room. It was bigger than the drawing room, situated at the end of the house, with big windows and doors that opened out to the Vale, with a large television, big settees, an open fireplace and heavy curtains to help keep the room warm in winter. A comfy room for lounging, but surprisingly not used very much.

Tom and Simon walked in. Emma jumped up and half ran at Simon, flinging her arms around him.

'This is amazing. I didn't believe it when the taxi swung in here. I was convinced there must be a mistake, but then Rachel told me you arrived a little while ago. I hope this is not a problem, me crashing in unexpectedly?'

Simon looked at Tom, as Emma hung round his neck, nuzzling his cheek. 'No, not at all, Emma, pleasure to see you, although normally a bit of notice would be helpful.'

'Sorry,' said Emma, now standing next to Simon.

'No, it's really not a problem, stay as long as you want.' Tom wondered if he should have said that. 'And you have the pleasure of helping Simon unpack.'

'Thanks, Tom, I hope this really is OK, and you're not

just being nice about it,' Simon said quietly with a rare serious face.

'Really, it's no problem, and Emma, I can promise his room is a definite upgrade from the slum he left.'

'Slum!' an indignant Simon exclaimed.

'Can you find your way back to your room, Simon?'

'Yes, two flights up the back stairs.'

'And if either of you need anything just pick up the house phone. I'll pop in later to make sure you're both OK,' said Rachel as they all left the sitting room.

Tom walked with them up the back stairs, leaving them at the first floor to go to his own room. Fran was already back and showered, sitting with music on, looking at her phone. Tom told her about Emma's surprise arrival and suggested they go to the Foresters' Arms to eat with Simon and Emma and invite Pen and Jackie, Cath and Dan. Fran thought it was a good idea, but asked if Jen might feel left out. Tom said he would invite all of them although he doubted Jen would come—exams!

'I'm phoning Mum,' Fran announced.

Tom mockingly dived for cover and scurried into the hall to phone round about the evening. When Tom had finished, he crept back in and found Fran looking deep in thought having finished her call.

'Everything alright?' Tom asked gently.

'I don't know, Mum's not very happy with Dad. Probably nothing, just their usual ups and downs.'

'They're OK for the weekend?'

'They'll be here about two in the afternoon. Dad has to do a call in the morning; that's really pissed Mum off.'

'I'm sure they'll be fine once they get here,' Tom said, hoping he was right, 'so don't worry. We're all set for tonight. Meet bottom of the main stairs at seven. It's about a half hour walk. I've reserved a couple of tables outside.'

'Everyone coming?'

'All except Jen. She's revising, last exam. Naomi will also be joining us. She'd already had plans with Pen and Jackie tonight.'

'OK, quite a crowd, shame about Jen.'

'Yes, have you met Rachel?'

'She popped in and picked up my outfit for Saturday night, to press. We had a brief chat; she seems very nice.'

~ 39 ~

Tom and Fran met Simon and Emma at the bottom of the main stairs.

'Let's go, everyone else is meeting us at the pub,' said Tom as he led them out, turning left up the Vale. 'It's about a thirty-minute walk. We go to the top of the estate and pick up the old road.'

The evening was warm. Tom laughed to himself as Fran carried her trusty cardigan. Heat radiated out of the ground.

'What was that?' Emma exclaimed.

'Bats,' Tom said. Fran winced, tightening her grip on Tom's hand, and looked up at the small dark darting creatures weaving speedily across the evening sky. 'They live in the old chapel. They're protected. They won't do you any harm. There's a couple of owls who nest in the front of the chapel as well.'

They continued walking.

'Is that another meadow?' asked Fran.

'It's the new prairie meadow, North American grasses and flowers,' said Tom.

They found the old road, which was mostly unmade. It

used to lead directly to Coombe Village from the house, but was closed a long time since but remained a path mostly used by staff of the estate. Tom remembered Pen letting him out of the sitting room French doors and hugging him goodbye all those years ago. He'd walked up the Vale to the old road which took him to the village and station, then London. It felt like another life now. It was good to go— *and equally good to be back*, Tom thought.

The path took them along the top of the estate, over the wooden footbridge to cross the cut, which Fran noticed was bone dry. They could see the village on their left start to light up as the day faded to dusk. On their right the woods stood, the tightly clustered trees at their heart already dispelling the light and bringing darkness to the woods' heart. Fran felt a brooding presence from the wood. Not threatening. A pulse, deep, ancient, pervading.

'What does Rachel do?' asked Emma.

'She is one of the housekeepers and looks after Fran and me and our guests. She has other tasks. It's a big house to keep going,' said Tom.

'So, what does she *do*?' continued Emma. Simon nudged her as they walked and Emma shrugged. 'We—you—need to understand,' Emma said quietly to Simon.

'Emma,' said Fran, 'I know it's difficult, I'm still getting my head around it. Part of her job is to look after us, make sure we're comfortable. She'll organise your washing and all that sort of stuff. I guess all the things your mum might have done for you.'

'She's a servant, in other words,' Emma said with slight contempt.

'No! She's an employee, who is paid a good salary and overtime as needed and gets paid holiday and other perks with the job,' said Tom.

'Sorry, I just want to understand,' said Emma.

'Understood,' said Tom, 'but sometimes people are quick to make the wrong assumptions. I would suggest you have a quiet chat with Rachel, that will put your mind at rest.'

'That's what I did when I first arrived here,' said Fran. 'It really helped get my head around how the place works.'

'OK, thanks, I'll do that. She organises washing, brilliant. Simon, we'll need to get you new undercrackers. The ones you have are a bit shredded and you might need to change them more often. You can't expect the poor girl to handle the ones you've got, especially if you've worn them for a week.' Emma wrinkled her nose up for effect.

'Fuck off, they're not that bad,' said Simon. 'They're just worn in and comfy, and I do change them regularly.'

'Worn in! Worn out!' Emma exclaimed.

'Must be love,' Fran whispered to Tom, amused at Simon's discomfort at discussing his underwear.

Suddenly, the pub came into sight. Twinkling lights peeped through the trees and hedges in front of them, the gentle, friendly sound of talking and laughter floating in the evening air. There was a small gate which let them into the pub garden from the path. Tom saw Cath sitting with Dan, waving from two tables pushed together. There were lots of hellos and introductions as everyone sat down. Tom walked inside and up to the bar.

'Good evening, sir,' said a cheerful voice from behind the beer taps.

'Good evening. I booked the double table outside.'

'Yes, sir.'

'Can you charge everything to this, please,' Tom said as he passed a credit card over the bar.

'Of course, sir,' the barman said as he read the card. 'Are you one of the family?'

'Yes—Tom.'

'Colin,' said the barman as he reached over to shake hands. 'Nice to meet you. Been managing here for three years. Heard you were back.'

'Colin, please pay for the drinks of anyone you know is from the estate on this card as well.'

'Yes, sir. Could be quite a bill.'

'I guessed that. Thank you,' said Tom, turning to walk back outside.

Pen, Jackie and Naomi had arrived and sat down, and the warm sound of chatter lay thick over the table. Tom noticed Rachel sitting at another table with some others. He recognised Poacher John, a girl from the kitchen and a lad, but couldn't think of their names. *Your father would know who they are,* echoed through Tom's head.

As Tom squeezed into the space left for him next to Fran, Colin appeared with a tray of drinks.

'Thanks, Colin, can you include that table in the bill please?' Tom asked as he nodded to where Rachel and John were sitting.

'Of course. More drinks to come, I'll take the food order in a minute.'

'Thanks.'

Tom noticed Pen walk over and talk to John and decided to join her. Fran was deep in conversation with Simon and Emma.

'Good evening, John,' said Tom.

'Good evening, sir. You know Rachel, this is her brother Eddy, an apprentice and Holly who works in the kitchen.'

'I was just thanking John for ensuring the engagement ring was returned to Henry,' said Pen.

'Any problems?' asked Tom.

'Only poor Eddy got spooked by the wildlife while he was waiting for me.' John chuckled at an uncomfortable Eddy who was shifting in his seat uneasily, hoping John wasn't going to go into any more detail, especially with Holly sitting next to him, holding his hand for the first time. To his relief, Cody chose that moment to stir under the table and make an appearance.

'Hello, boy,' said Tom as he bent down to make a fuss of the dog. 'He's new?'

'An escapee from Long Farm. The three of us are sharing looking after him. He's been checked by the vet. The poor boys had a bit of a rough time, on pain killers at the moment as his ribs are badly bruised. Possibly cracked, X-ray wasn't clear, but he'll be fine with a bit of rest and love,' said John, now making a fuss of Cody who was nuzzling his legs.

'Now, all your food and drinks will go on my bill,' said Tom.

'Thank you, sir, are you sure?' said John.

'Absolutely,' insisted Tom, hearing John announce he

thought the steak would be good, as he and Pen walked back to the double table.

Fran was now talking to Cath. Emma and Simon were deep in conversation with Naomi. Jackie reached out and took Pen's hand as she sat back down. Dan was sitting alone nursing his beer. Tom sat down opposite him.

'All OK, Dan?'

'Yes, just not used to all this.'

'I guess things have changed pretty quickly for you?'

'Just a bit,' Dan said as he took a swig of his beer. 'Still adjusting.'

'Have you decided on living arrangements?'

'I think so, I'm moving into the main house and then we will take one of the Henge Cottages.'

'Good decision, but living in the house isn't that bad. I appreciate it's a big change, Fran and I have had the same conversation. Being in the main house will be good when the baby comes, plenty of help.'

'Well, the cottage won't be ready before the little one arrives, so we don't have to make a final decision now.'

'Welcome to the family. Don't worry, it will all work out,' said Tom as he raised his glass to Dan.

'Thanks,' said Dan, managing a grin and raising his glass also.

Cath spotted Fran was only on soft drinks. 'Not drinking either, Fran? Anything you want to share?'

Fran looked confused for a moment and then realised. 'No, nothing to share. I'm walking the woods with Isaac tomorrow, so I'm keeping a clear head and hopefully will not be too late tonight.'

'I'll not be late as I'm already tired,' said Cath as she patted her tummy.

Trays of food arrived and caused a brief pause in conversation as everyone ate, but the chatter and clinking of glasses quickly returned.

At ten-thirty Cath got up and started to say her goodbyes. Dan, now talking with Eddy and Holly, reluctantly also readied to leave.

'I'll walk back with them,' Fran said to Tom.

'OK, I'll come with you.'

'No, you should stay, I'll be fine. I'll be with Cath and Dan.' Fran kissed Tom on the cheek, picked up her cardigan and went to stand with Cath to wait for Dan. Pen and Jackie, hand in hand, also joined them.

They went back through the gate back onto the old road. Dan had Cath's arm to ensure she didn't trip on the uneven ground, which Fran thought was very sweet. There was little moon, but just enough to help see their way. The village, now on their right, was all twinkling house lights with the occasional set of headlights sweeping down its streets. As they walked past the woods, now a deep black wall against the darkened night sky, Fran felt the same brooding force she'd felt before. *I'll see you tomorrow*, she thought, as if in answer to the woods' call. Pen caught Fran's arm.

'I can feel the woods, they're calling,' she said.

'Tomorrow,' Fran said to Pen and they both felt the pulse from the wood slip away.

The noise and light from the pub garden gradually faded away, replaced by the silence of the night, interrupted only by the noises of the wood; of animal and creaking bough. The black sky above the Vale opened out with a sheet of stars glittering and shimmering around a silver slice of moon. They all stood and looked up in awe at the sky's treasures lighting their way. Fran glanced at the wood framed by the star-studded sky and the now black Vale floor.

Whoosh; something swept gently by, ruffling the night air.

'Owl,' Dan gently called.

The bird glided past them effortlessly on its soft brown and white feathers and three feet of wingspan; silent, just a whisper in the night, slicing the warm night air with hardly a sound, out of the wood across the Vale before landing on a fence post and bending to eat what it had caught.

'Beautiful,' Fran said out loud.

Everyone had stopped, first mesmerized by the sky and then the majestic owl.

Now on the Vale the house stood lighted up like a ship on a wine-dark flat sea. A beacon. *Home and bed,* thought Fran, feeling tired now.

'I hope we're not locked out,' said Cath.

'Don't worry, I have my key,' said Pen, 'but the doors should still be open and the house knows people will be back late.'

'I'm the duty housekeeper tonight,' said Jackie.

'How come?' asked Pen.

'My turn. Poor Anna hasn't had a night off since before the royal visit. Sophie is covering until I get back.'

It didn't take long to reach the house and the door to the Vale was still open. Everyone said goodnight. Jackie announced she was going to the kitchen to get a cup of tea. Pen went with her.

Fran checked she had everything ready for the morning and then was soon in bed, wondering what the next morning with Isaac would hold. What did she want to ask? She checked her alarm was set one last time before curling up to sleep.

~ 40 ~

Thursday, 10th July. Fran woke to find Tom fast asleep, half undressed on top of the bed. She'd not heard him come in. Before she left, she nudged him and he stirred and held his head.

'Should have walked back with you last night. Christ, my head hurts,' Tom moaned, his head seeming to pound with every breath.

'See you later. Hopefully, you'll feel better by the time I'm back.'

Fran went to the dining room, bumping into Dan who was coming out.

'Morning, how are you?' asked Fran breezily.

'Good, thank you, ma'am. Better than some, I would guess,' Dan spluttered, a bit embarrassed.

'Please call me Fran. After all, we are practically re-lated. Ma'am makes me sound like some distant maiden aunt and a hundred years old. And yes, just left Tom with his head in his hands.'

'Sorry, still getting used to all this, can't get used to calling His Lordship and Her Ladyship by their first names either. Can't believe how nice everyone has been, but it's all a bit surreal. Tom won't be the only casualty this morning, free bar only leads to trouble.'

'It's a big change for you and Cath. I understand you're thinking about one of the Henge Cottages?'

'Yes, Cath seems keen, but the baby will be here long before they are ready, so we are looking at changing Cath's rooms around, she has so much space. Probably much better being in the main house with the little one. What about you and Tom?'

'I think we will land up in the main house at least for the immediate future. I'm seeing Pen this afternoon to discuss things. How's your dad?'

'He's fine as long as I do the right thing. Lewis had a chat with him, which was good. After the work's finished on Cath's rooms, I will move in permanently. Rachel, the new girl, is going to have my room at the cottage. It's a bit of a trek for her to and from New Wood every day.' Dan shrugged. 'So no going back. Sorry, must go. Work!' Dan said, taking a step out of the door.

'Everything alright at work?'

'They gave me a hard time at first but now I'm just the butt of a few jokes. Nothing more than I would say to anyone if the roles were reversed. Dad sometimes growls at everyone if it looks like it's going too far, so all OK, thanks. There'll be a few sore heads this morning, which will be fun.'

'Have a good day.' Fran smiled and patted his arm.

'Thanks, Fran, and you,' Dan said, as he walked out the door.

Fran had a quick breakfast. She asked Gail for a pot

of tea and breakfast to be delivered to Tom at about ten o'clock and warned her he might well be grumpy.

Fran waited for Isaac outside the hall door to the Vale. She didn't imagine he would be late. *It's hot again*, Fran thought, *will the weather ever change?* She found it hard to imagine what the place would be like cold, with rain and dark clouds scudding across the sky.

'Good morning, Francesca.' Isaac's arrival interrupting her musing on the weather.

'Good morning, Isaac, how are you?'

'I'm well, thanks, better than some I've seen this morning. Shall we walk and talk?' he asked, moving past her with his usual rolling gait, towards the woods.

Fran took a few hurried steps to catch up.

'You asked to walk with me today, how can I help?' Isaac continued as they strolled slowly side by side across the scorched brown Vale.

'Tom and Charlotte have tried to explain things to me, but I still have a lot of questions and would like to understand a little better. Perhaps you could help me?'

'Be happy to help.' Isaac paused. 'Let's go back a little. Over two thousand years ago, everyone lived by the land and its cycles. People considered themselves part of the natural system which they relied on to live and survive. They worked with the land and nature was respected, revered and celebrated. Because they were so close to it, they recognised the need to be good ancestors. They realised the land and the life within it had its own spirit, energy and magic, although they couldn't define it. So, myths and legends grew. All of them have a grain of truth somewhere even if now it's corrupted.'

Fran was quiet for a moment as they continued across the Vale.

'OK, I understand that. How does the estate fit in?'

'Because the Vale and estate have been isolated and owned by the family for probably the last fifteen hundred years at least, it's retained its own unique relationship with the land, maintaining many ancient beliefs, such as recognising and celebrating the year around the land's natural rhythm of changing seasons, such as the solstice as you've seen.'

'It can't be the only place like this?'

'If there are others, we haven't found them. I think the reason my ancestors stayed is because they had a similar relationship with the land and its spirits in Africa, so they automatically connected to the beliefs here.' Isaac paused. 'The spirits of the land want to connect with you because, as was said at the solstice, you have a clear and open soul and a brave, loving heart. That's the reason you can connect and understand the magic that's locked, hidden somewhere in your soul. It's an understanding and ability inherited from distant ancestors, from when they were close to the land, that enables you to connect now to the land and its spirits.'

'So, it's something that's always been in me, like a skill or talent I never realised?'

'Sort of, we all come from the land originally, and the beliefs would have been commonly understood and

followed, even if not everyone could connect to the spirits and

elements. But such memories and beliefs have become
buried, forgotten, as people left the land to live in towns
and cities.'

'I'm beginning to see,' Fran said thoughtfully.

They came to the edge of the woods and stopped. Isaac
faced Fran and pointed at the woods.

'Tell me, Francesca, what do you see?'

'The woods,' said Fran, irritated by what seemed a facile
question. 'Trees! I see the trunk, branches and leaves.'

'Yes, but that's only part of the wood. You're pointing at the overstory, the crown and bulk of the tree that
stands in the air above the ground, but that's only one
part of it.'

Isaac walked into the woods and waved his arms across
the ground, brushing the scrub and bushes. 'This is understory. The scrub and plants that grow at ground level are
equally important. And possibly most important of all is
what happens hidden under your feet in the underwood.
Remember, everything is connected.'

'Underwood?' repeated Fran to herself, feeling confused.

'Let me show you.' He stopped in a small clearing and
knelt down, gesturing to Fran to do the same.

'The real magic is under your feet. Everything returns
to the ground, even the ash of the funeral pyres thrown
to the winds settles into the earth eventually. All history
is held underground by the earth. It's where some of the

most amazing things happen. Now place your hands flat on the ground and open your mind.'

Fran watched Isaac sweep away loose debris from the ground in front of him and then spread his hands flat on the grass and close his eyes in concentration. Fran did the same.

She allowed her mind to open. She first felt a gentle heat coming from the ground, a welcoming warmth like when she'd placed her hands on the oak at the solstice.

'What do you feel?'

'The land's heat. Its energy, I guess.'

'Good, you're connecting, what can you hear?'

Fran struggled with her thoughts. It was a strange feeling, trying to listen so hard.

'I hear mumbling voices.'

'Spirits talking, floating, 'Isaac said. 'What else can you find?'

Fran strained to hear and see and discovered the pulsing, living white threads spread as far as her mind's vision. She first heard their rhythm before she saw their delicate silver threads leading in all directions.

'I see living threads of beautiful silvery white and can feel their beating rhythm,' Fran breathed, enchanted and intrigued by what she was seeing and hearing.

'Ah, the threads that hold the earth together. A living entity, bigger, older than the trees above, fungus and its threads, veins of life. Francesca, you've found the wood wide web.'

'The what?'

'The wood wide web. The living fungus and its threads

spread and connect and join all roots together. They join with the buried, hence why our blood flows through root and vein. The underwood. A network that communicates and helps everything, cooperates. Provides warning and information, shares energy and food, can create solutions to disease. An old, dying tree will transfer its energy to the young tree nearby to help ensure its survival and the continuation of its kind. It's a collective life support system that spreads across the whole wood and is part of the wood. The overstory, understory and underwood are all connected, are one living thing, more plant than animal but sentient life, although different to what is usually described as life on earth. Search for more threads.'

Fran looked for the threads Isaac had described. She sank further down and out into the new subterranean world. As her mind navigated further, she saw with wonder thousands of silver threads running in every direction, binding, joining everything together into a single life force, buzzing and carrying their messages, energy and antidotes across the wood.

'I see the white, almost silver threads. They're quite beautiful, almost luminous in the ground. I can sense the energy running through them, it's both constant and urgent at the same time.'

'Excellent,' said Isaac as he stood up, and Fran sat back on her heels, lightly rubbing her hands together to brush off the dust from the ground before she stood as well.

'The web couldn't save the elms we saw being cut down on my first visit here?'

'No, the web's system seems to be most effective when

there's a mix of trees and each brings its own unique strength and capabilities. But funnily enough the seeds from the elms taken down seem to have evolved and look to now be more resistant to the disease that killed their parents. But we will be planting a mixed wood and keeping it messier than it was to allow a good understory to grow in autumn to help make the new stand more resilient.'

'And the people buried under trees? Tom told me about the almost Buddhist karma.'

'Well, Francesca, you've just become aware of your past life with the land by triggering your connections. That's your karma and the consequence of this will influence the nature of your direction going forward. Those buried with trees tend to join, anchored, with the tree they have chosen and are planted with, their karma, and combined they give the wood and land a voice that many could do with listening to. But I doubt many would understand or heed.'

'Such as Tom's grandmother, Harriet, and the willow.'

'Yes, and my wife, Jane, and the hawthorn. Jane told me you'd been to the willow for a swim with Naomi. Jane would like to meet you some time. Spirits not planted with trees, the unanchored, add their spirit, energy and essence to fuelling the web, an equally living thing, a different, but no less important karma. The connection of the overstory, understory and underwood web is probably collectively the oldest and largest life, bigger than any elephant or whale, but equally endangered.'

'How far does the web stretch?' Fran had been unable

to find an edge when she followed the threads of life reaching through the ground.

'We don't know, but the land is very undisturbed so the chances are it's very wide. When the lab is built one of the planned projects is to investigate the fungus, its threads and the web. They did a lot of research on this in Canada a while ago, which identified the collective nature and size of the wood wide web in a forest there, but left a lot of questions unanswered. Your skills, Francesca, could be useful.'

'So, when the land's disturbed, the web is disturbed?'

'Yes, it's very delicate. Deep ploughing can rip it up and break the web. Broken, weakened, disconnected, it rarely has enough time in the current world to recover and mend. The land becomes poorer as a consequence, hence the need to add so many chemicals to wring food from the land.'

'I see. How am I able to do magic?'

'I think you know. You bend and weave the key elements: fire, water, air, earth and spirits. It's this friction when you weave them that creates the energy for you to cast a spell. It's a skill more than a science, something you feel, you sense.'

'Yes, I see the elements as long fluttering lengths of fabric, like flags, twisting and turning, red, blue, yellow, green, white; I see them in my mind's eye and weave them together to get the magic I need.'

'But you must remember every spell has a cost.' Isaac looked serious; his usual amiable smile gone. 'You are re-arranging the order of things. If, say, you cast a spell to save Tom's life, the spirits would demand another life in exchange, so a life would be taken at random to save Tom's because a life was due at that time.'

Fran looked thoughtfully at Isaac. 'That's quite heavy stuff and scary if you do something without thinking.'

'Spells are serious things, Francesca, don't let anyone tell you different.' Isaac's face lightened. 'No problem with what you did on the range the other Sunday, minor stuff.'

'Thank goodness.' A relieved-looking Fran glanced at him.

They walked out of the woods onto the Vale, back towards the house.

'There is a sixth element.' Isaac paused.

Fran looked at Isaac, intrigued.

'Dark matter. The element that can't be seen, so you would have to feel it. It holds the universe, planets, stars and this earth in their place and permeates, seeps into our bodies, the earth, everything.'

'Is it a bad element? How should I consider it?'

'It's transparent, invisible. It's something else perhaps we should explore one evening, sooner than later. Night is supposed to be the best time to find it. If you can weave that element in any way, you will be quite exceptional.'

'Have you ever found dark matter?'

'No, I am a very average mage. I can feel when you're working and could help you channel if needed. You have so much more capability than anyone I have ever seen and we've only really just started.'

'What do you think I can do?'

'You could certainly be leading the solstices soon.'

'What about Charlotte and the others?'

'Charlotte was like you when she arrived, found she had a buried gift once she connected with the land, but nowhere as good as you, Francesca. You have so much potential, you could be Merlin's child.'

'Isn't he something to do with King Arthur?' Fran breathed; intrigued and worried.

'Yes, the Once and Future King. Legend says that Merlin or his representative will be here ready for his return.'

Fran went quiet as she thought what that might mean. 'Is King Arthur coming back? It's just a story, a fairy tale.'

'Remember what I said. Every myth and legend has at least a grain of truth.'

'How could I be Merlin's child?'

'It's more a figure of speech, a metaphor. It's his capability, not his family tree. We will see. It's just a legend, nothing to worry about.'

Fran wasn't so sure as she saw Isaac chuckle to himself thoughtfully.

'I also promised to introduce you to the White Lady. She will be able to answer many of the questions now floating in your mind. But that's also for another day.'

Fran nodded, not really sure what she'd been told.

'Isaac, how would you sum up what all this means, with the land and the life within it?'

'It's about considering yourself part of nature, respecting it and working with its rhythms. Being a good ancestor, leaving the world at the very least no worse than you entered it. In this time, that means being a conserver, not a consumer devouring the land and its assets with no consideration to the damage, but I don't have much faith in the world doing the right thing. I think nature will extract its revenge. Maybe it already is. We see the weather changing faster and faster every year, not just here but all over the world. In a few weeks the weather will break if it runs as it has the last few years, and we will have a short spell of heavy rain and flash floods again. A once in a hundred-year event happening every year: nature's revenge, all of our own making, but nobody seems to care or want to listen.'

They continued walking slowly in silence from the wood back towards the house. Isaac looked happily around the Vale and back at the woods, pausing occasionally to watch the swifts and house martins cutting and weaving patterns through the hot blue sky above the Vale between the green of the wood and grey of the house. Fran was deep in thought at what she'd heard today. Somehow it all made sense to her and she felt comfortable with this new world, though she wondered what was next.

'Thank you, Isaac,' said Fran, nodding sincerely. 'I'm starting to understand, I think. Thank you for this morning and I look forward to whatever the future holds.'

'You're welcome, Francesca. We'll talk again. Call me if you have any problems or questions.'

'A favour, Isaac. My parents are visiting this weekend. Could you give them a tour through the woods? Something gentle.'

'Of course, when?'

'Saturday morning?'

'Eleven o'clock? I have breakfast with Tom's grandfather, Maxwell on Saturday mornings. He was lord before Lewis. He lives with his nurse in the old gatehouse.'

'That will be fine, meet you at the hall door to the Vale?'

'Yes, see you then. Bye, Francesca, if you have any questions, you know where to find me.'

'Thank you, Isaac, I really appreciated today.'

Isaac walked down the Vale with his usual swaying gait bringing his own rhythm to the day. Fran, still thoughtful, made her way back to the house, wondering what state she would find Tom in.

~ 41 ~

Fran entered the house to find the kitchen staff buzzing about setting up lunch. *It never stops for them*, thought Fran, walking up the stairs to see what state Tom was in.

At least he's out of bed, Fran thought as she entered their room. Tom was slouched, almost horizontal, snoozing in one of the comfy chairs. She saw the tray she'd asked to be sent up, with the addition of a jug of iced water. Fran sat opposite Tom and poured a glass, realising how thirsty she was. *Must keep drinking in this heat*, she reminded herself. Tom stirred and opened one quizzical eye without moving from his prone position.

'You're alive?'

'Barely.' Tom grunted and shuffled himself more upright in the chair.

'We're seeing Pen at two.'

'You go, you don't need me there.'

'Are you sure?'

'Yes, it's what you want that counts.'

'OK, if, you're sure. I need to have lunch first. Are you coming down?'

'No, I can't move. I've already asked for lunch to be brought up, then I'll sleep and hopefully feel better by this evening.'

'As long as you're OK for tomorrow, when my parents are here. If you're not you'll be in big trouble.'

'Understood,' Tom said with a wry smile.

'See you later then. Wouldn't have thought I'll be more than an hour with Pen.'

'OK, see you later.'

Fran left Tom and went down for lunch. She saw Simon and Emma sitting looking a bit self-conscious in the dining room and went to join them.

'Hi, Fran,' said Emma as Fran walked up. 'Are we OK being in here?'

'Yes, you're fine.'

'Just feels so weird, a bit odd.'

'I know what you mean, I felt the same when I first came here, a few weeks ago. What have you two been up to this morning?'

'We were a bit slow getting up after last night, got down here a bit late for breakfast, but managed to sneak in, went for a walk then back for some unpacking,' said Simon, leaning forward over the table.

'This place is amazing,' said Emma, beaming.

Simon nodding enthusiastically in agreement. 'But hot!'

'Yes, the heat outside seems unrelenting. But the heat-wave is everywhere, there's no escaping it.'

'Global warming?' said a knowing Simon.

'What the fuck would you know?' mocked Emma.

'I do listen and watch the news occasionally and

everyone seems to post and blog about climate change now,' said Simon.

'I understand the estate records and diaries show something is changing with the weather. I'm told the weather will break soon with heavy rain and possible flooding,' Fran said.

'Good afternoon, can I assist anyone with lunch?' said Holly.

Simon and Emma looked a bit flustered at the request.

'Perhaps if you could come up to the buffet you can decide what you both would like. Nothing hot, due to the weather,' Holly said.

Fran nodded at Simon's and Emma's enquiring faces and they got up and followed Holly to view the lunch offering, returning in a few minutes, Emma with a modest plate which Fran liked the look of, Simon with a bulging plate.

'Madam, what can I get you?'

'I'll have the same as Emma, please, but without the potato salad.'

'Certainly, madam.' Holly walked away.

'It's all a bit formal and proper,' Emma half whispered to Fran with a serious face.

'Emma,' Simon said between mouthfuls of food. 'Don't start.'

'I know it takes a bit of getting used to, I found it difficult at first. It's just the way they do things here; very traditional. Have a chat with any of the girls if you get a chance, they all seem quite happy and looked after.'

Emma didn't look convinced, but accepted what Fran

said reluctantly and began to eat. 'It's just odd, last night we were laughing and drinking with Holly and her fella, Eddy, and now it's like she's never seen us before.'

'Yes, I know, they are pretty formal and all the staff are trained not to be too familiar, but you will find they are quite talkative if you get them alone. They all love a bit of gossip,' Fran said, looking at her watch.

'Sorry about Emma, Fran. She thinks she's working for the revolution. Up the people!'

'Here you go, madam,' said Holly as she put a plate in front of Fran.

'Thank you, Holly.'

'You're welcome, madam.' And Holly turned with a smile from the three of them to assist someone else at the buffet.

'How come she gets your lunch and we have to go and choose?' asked Emma pointedly to Fran.

'Because I'm family and a lady of the house, but I'm normally quite happy to queue with everyone else.' Fran felt a bit embarrassed at what she'd said and could see Emma wasn't very impressed.

'Be careful what you say, Fran, or you'll go on Emma's list and when the revolution comes...' Simon didn't get to finish as Emma elbowed him hard in the ribs.

"Lady of the house', what does that mean?' retorted Emma.

'One day I will be Lady Francesca when Tom takes over from his father, Lewis.'

'Fuck, that's cool,' Simon wheezed out through a mouthful of food. Emma slapped his arm playfully, but with meaning. 'Sorry, I'm trying to stop using that word all the time. Didn't we meet a Lewis at breakfast this morning, Emma? He seemed really nice.'

'Very likely that was Tom's father, and yes, he and his wife, Charlotte, in fact the whole family, are very nice.'

Everyone was quiet as they ate.

'Anyone need a drink?' asked a returning Holly.

'Lemonade, please,' replied Fran.

'Sounds good, same for me,' said Emma.

'And you, sir, a beer?'

'No, that's probably not a good idea, something soft, please.'

'Three lemonades then.'

Holly returned a moment later with three glasses of lemonade which she placed on the table.

'Did you get home alright last night?' Fran asked.

'Yes, thank you, madam, Eddy walked me back to the house. The sky was amazing, so many stars. I stayed on the top floor, too difficult to get home.'

'Are your parents OK with that?'

'Yes, madam. I'm going to see if I can get a room on the estate, the journey to and from home is a pain.'

'Couldn't you work nearer home?' asked Emma, sitting up.

'Not much work around here and this is a good job. There are lots of opportunities.

Rachel is taking Dan's room when he moves into the main house.'

'Yes, I bumped into him this morning and he mentioned that.'

'I hope he's alright about it.'

'I think he's fine; he's got other things to think about.'

'What opportunities do you have here?' Emma pointedly asked. Simon rolled his eyes, which Emma didn't see.

'I get day release for catering college and have also gone on secondment to other kitchens. They pay all the costs and expenses, not just for me but everyone on the estate. I know they are looking for more staff for the kitchen and house and there is the lab and visitor centre, which will both need catering, so there's plenty going on. Anything else?' Holly asked the three of them. There was no answer, so she quietly took their used plates and headed to the kitchen.

'Not quite slave labour then, Emma. It doesn't sound like it needs a revolution or that Holly needs rescuing,' said Simon, trying to stifle his amusement at Emma's deflated face, having thought she had found a new cause.

'Isn't Dan the lad who has got one of the daughters up the spout?' asked Simon as he swigged his lemonade and wiped his mouth with the back of his hand.

'Shh,' Emma hissed, as she slapped his arm again. 'Keep your voice down.'

'Fuck! What did I say? Oops, sorry. Had a chat with him last night, seemed a good fella, very young, but decent and he seemed pretty happy with his lot. And...'

'God, what are you going to say now?' interrupted Emma.

'Isn't Pen who we met last night His Lordship's daughter? And now shacking up with her maid who was also there last night?'

'For God's sake, Simon.' Emma was now clearly annoyed with him.

Fran gently raised her hand to try to calm things down. 'And Graham's boyfriend is in the process of moving in. Several members of the royal family stayed here last weekend and two people died near here in mysterious circumstances a few weeks ago. Now you've got all the gossip, I think.'

'Fuck! It all goes on here, it's like being at home,' said Simon in surprise.

'But it's green with clear air, not grey and grubby with air that chokes you. And the food's a lot better,' added Emma

'And the room's a lot bigger and more comfortable,' said Simon

'... and a lot cleaner!' added Emma with a smirk.

'Fuck! This is a good gig,' Simon said quietly, almost to himself.

Fran laughed as Emma shook Simon by his arm.

'Sorry, I've got to go,' Fran said as she glanced at the time and started to stand up. 'What are you guys doing this afternoon?'

'Trying to stay cool,' said Emma, still hanging on Simon's arm.

'Fancy a swim later, about three o'clock?'

'Sounds good, but I don't have any trunks,' said Simon.

'Skinny dipping, you won't even need a towel in this heat.'

'Oh! OK,' Emma said, looking a bit unsure.

'See you both in the main hall at three then.' And Fran walked away to meet Pen.

Pen was talking to Anna in the hall. She broke off the conversation when she saw Fran. Anna looked irritated and animated at the conversation.

'Everything alright?'

'Yes, same problem, kitchen and house need more staff, but you can't just conjure them up. We have advertised, so, hopefully, it should be sorted out soon.' Pen looked thoughtful as she turned and walked up the main stairs. 'I thought I'd show you my rooms, Lewis and Charlotte's, and finally Cath's. They're all a bit different and will give you a good idea of what can be done. Then we'll have a look at the old rooms which haven't been touched for a hundred years or more, which is where we would build any new suite for you and Tom.'

Viewing the three sets of rooms didn't take long. Fran agreed with Pen that Lewis and Charlotte's were the nicest. You entered into a comfortable reception-sitting room, and the main bedroom was off the sitting room with a smaller bedroom off that. The latter was originally for the children when they were babies, now Charlotte used it to escape Lewis's snoring or Lewis would use it if getting up very early, which he did often. There was a large bathroom off the main bedroom and two large walk-in wardrobes, one for each of them. There was a study off the reception room as well a second small bathroom and the walk-in strong room where all the family valuables were kept.

'I don't think we will need a strong room, Pen, but two studies, although one would be my hobby room.'

'OK, I will make a note of that and get the architects working on it. Now you have two options of where to put the rooms in the house. It's all about windows. If you go for the end of the house, you will have two sides of windows for the reception room. One wall will have Juliet balconies. The other option is standard windows on one side only. Both have views over the Vale.'

'Juliet balconies please,' an excited Fran replied.

'Once we agree the plans you will need to choose fixtures and fittings, furniture and fabrics etc.'

'How exciting.'

'I assume this means you're not interested in Henge Cottages or the Josephs' farmhouse?'

'That's right, Pen, this seems to be best option. Tom will be pleased; it was me who was nervous about living in the house,' Fran said, feeling this was the right decision and glad it was now made.

'Understand,' Pen quietly replied as she closed her notebook. 'I think we are all done then. I'll get back to you probably in about four weeks. They are looking at changing Cath's room around first with the baby coming.'

'Dan mentioned that when I was chatting to him this morning.'

'They may yet have one of the Henge Cottages, but I suspect Cath would miss all the help she would get being in the main house.'

'Everything alright with you and Jackie?'

'Yes, the initial excitement and gossip has calmed

down, although I think Cath has made Jackie a bit broody, something I'd never considered.'

'Are you considering children, then?'

'Possibly, but not until we get settled in our own place.'

'That's fair enough.'

'What about you and Tom?'

'I guess, some time. We haven't really discussed it, but I think at least two- or three-years' time.'

'Could be a nice bundle of cousins crashing round the house and estate together in future then,' Pen said warmly, her face soft and smiling as she imagined the house alive with small children. 'Father will love it, but it will drive him mad at the same time.'

'Sorry, Pen, must go, going for a swim with Simon and Emma.'

'I spoke to them last night, they seemed very surprised about Jackie and me, but they seem nice. Simon has a twinkle in his eye and is weirdly attractive, I think because he needs looking after, mothering—he's a bit of a mess.'

'I know what you mean, he's intriguing.'

'I might join you for a swim. I assume you'll swim in the pool under the willows?'

'Yes, shall we see you there?'

'That's probably best, see you in a little while, hopefully'

~ 42 ~

Fran decided to pop in and see Tom and pick up her hat before walking into the heat of the afternoon. To her surprise Tom was wandering about. He'd clearly showered.

'I'm going for a swim at the willows,' said Fran. 'You're looking a lot better.'

'Lunch, a snooze, then a shower did the trick. Father popped in to see me, mainly to laugh at my terrible state, I think. Who you swimming with?'

'Simon and Emma. Pen is intending to join us, you coming?'

'Not today. Although I love the place. I understand it's too dangerous to swim in the river now, which is a shame.' Tom paused. Fran sensed he had something to tell her; he had that hesitant face on. 'Father wants me to join him at a meeting on Friday afternoon with Mark Clifford, Reginald's son. Father thinks he wants to do a deal to return the farm to the estate.'

'But—' Fran said with alarm before Tom continued.

'I know, your parents are here. Father suggested we take Charles with us; thought he might like to see some business being done. Give you the afternoon with your mother.'

Fran sighed. 'I understand how potentially important this meeting is. Just be aware, if you take Dad, he will think he is part of the team. Wouldn't be surprised if he charges you a fee for his time. Be nice to spend time with Mum and show her the house, I know she is dying to have a look around, which would bore Dad to death, and just put him in a bad mood.'

'Thanks, Fran,' Tom said, walking over to her and kissing her cheek. 'While I remember, it's the archers' muster this Sunday morning so your parents should come to that.'

'Forgot about that, I assume I'm your shield maiden?'

'Of course, it wouldn't be anyone else, but Isaac's thinking the shield maidens become a separate section. He's spent a lot of time with Duncan discussing how it might work. Have you, the mage, leading the screaming Valkyries.'

'Really?'

'Really, Fran. He mentioned it the other day. I don't think he has decided yet.'

'He didn't mention it to me this morning. Right, I must be off, Simon and Emma will be waiting.'

~ 43 ~

Emma was waiting in the hall, enjoying what little cool its flagstones offered before they ventured into the afternoon furnace of the browned Vale.

'No Simon?' Fran asked as she walked out onto the Vale, pausing for Emma.

'How far is it?' asked Emma.

'Not far, about fifteen minutes, just down the Vale.'

'Simon decided he couldn't face skinny dipping. He's such a child at times, well, most of the time. I left him on his laptop muttering—and fiddling with code, so he told me. Probably looking at porn, knowing him.'

The late afternoon heat was shimmering above the ground as they headed towards the trees.

'God, it's hot,' said Emma, wiping sweat from her face.

'Don't worry, it's worth the walk. I had a dip there yesterday,' said Fran.

'Global warming, I guess?'

'You're in the right place if that's a cause you're interested in, Emma.'

'Actually, Fran, I was going to ask if there's any work here.' Emma paused. 'I went to catering college after

school, landed up working in the café where I met Simon.'
She rolled her eyes as she mentioned Simon's name. 'If I
had got a job at a swanky restaurant, I could have been
swept off to exotic destinations in some rich punter's
private jet. Simon says I'd get bored with champagne and
caviar and be craving greasy chips and deep-fried pizza in
a couple of days.'

'Oh dear! How are things between you two?'

'A bit strained. I don't think he really wants me here.
He thinks I'm cramping his style.' Emma looked sour until
the heat caused her to wipe her face again.

This is going well, Fran thought, pleased to see the willow
coming into sight.

'Emma, there are jobs in the kitchen or in the house,
fancy any of those?'

Emma blew out a long hot breath. 'I spoke to Rachel
after lunch and she put me right on a few things, as you
suggested.'

'The kitchen is desperate for staff, talk to Pen,' Fran
said. 'She might join us for a swim.'

They walked up to the willow.

'I can hear the river,' Emma said.

'The river runs too fast to swim in safely so we use the
pool under the willow.'

Fran led the way.

'Hello, Fran.' Naomi stood naked and wet in front of
them, water still sliding off her smooth shining skin. 'It's
great in the water, such a relief.' Naomi turned as she dried
in the sun and then started to dress; her hair still wet. 'Just
so you are aware, my brother is lurking somewhere.'

Fran followed Emma. As she caught her up, the branch in front of them rustled.

'Hi!' Naomi's brother, equally naked, stepped into the open. Fran and Emma stopped in surprise.

I've seen naked men before, Emma thought to herself, *but...* Emma noticed a drop of water fall from his loose dark hair, drop to his shoulder, stopped for a moment, shudder and then run slowly down his chest, then accelerate down his taut, muscled stomach. Emma shook her gaze from the water drop as it left his stomach and continued down. She wiped her brow again, feeling hotter now than she had walking down the Vale.

'Nice to meet you, ladies. I'm Noah, no doubt see you again soon.'

'See you've found my brother.' Naomi was now dressed, her long legs carrying her next to Fran and Emma in a couple of strides. 'He finally got home this morning.' Naomi raised her voice. 'Noah, you need to stop teasing and get dressed.' She dropped her voice again to speak to Fran and Emma. 'Need to get back as he hasn't seen Dad yet. See you all at the barbeque tomorrow?'

'Yes, nice to meet you,' Fran said, stepping out of Noah's way as he went for his clothes. He brushed past Emma who shook her head.

Fran and Emma undressed, and Fran led the way to the pool.

Fran stood at the edge and curled her toes. She jumped in, feeling the cool water run up her body, relieving the heat, revitalising her skin and senses as she sank and then gracefully rose to the surface.

'Just jump in as I did, the water's fantastic.'

Emma stood at the edge ready when suddenly a naked Pen appeared, went straight to the edge and jumped in.

Having seen Pen break the surface, Emma followed.

Emma felt the delicious shock of the cold water rinse her body. She could feel her skin tingle and tighten as she broke the surface and took her first breath.

Fran and Pen floated in the water.

'No Simon, Emma?' Pen asked.

'No, skinny dipping frightened him off, he's working. Sorry, Simon's an idiot, more of a child than a man.'

Everyone laughed at Simon's expense, as the three of them enjoyed the cool of the water.

'How do we get out?' Emma asked, beginning to feel a little chilled.

'By magic,' said Fran, raising her arms in the air.

Emma watched, open-mouthed, as the branch descended and then lifted Fran on to the bank.

'Raise your arms, Emma, it's quite safe.'

Emma swung up in the air and towards the bank.

'Amazing! How? What?' Emma spluttered to Fran when she'd landed, but went quiet as she watched Pen rise out of the water, her long dark hair trailing behind her. She looked like a mythical figure from a classical painting, her porcelain skin contrasting with her dark shining hair, sparkling as the water flowed off it. She seemed to move in slow motion, head tilted back, against a backdrop of the shimmering green of willow leaves, with shards of sun making the water draining from her sparkle.

As they walked back up the Vale, Fran and Pen explained to Emma what had happened with the willow.

'Magic, real magic,' Emma exclaimed. She liked the idea of karma, and spirits communing with the land. 'You spoke with the spirit of Tom's grandmother?' she said with wonder in her voice.

'Yes, there are many buried in the woods, including Naomi's mother with a hawthorn tree.'

Pen was keen to talk further about a job in the kitchen for Emma and suggested a chat with Chef, Mr Balfour, would be the next step. Emma agreed.

Pen asked if she would need accommodation. Emma considered for a moment then told Pen that it would probably be best. *She and Simon may have run their course,* Emma thought to herself, wondering if Noah was single.

~ 44 ~

Thursday, 10th July, evening. Henry was in a good mood. His old school friend, Christian, had come up trumps, got him a job as a land agent and said he could have one of their rental cottages from the beginning of September, until the next spring. To celebrate, he was meeting Christian at The Oak. Thursday nights were usually lively. Christian's family had several businesses; soft fruit farming, the land agents he was going to work for with Christian and twenty-four holiday rental chalets they'd built up over a number of years.

Henry put on his jacket and admired himself in the mirror, deciding that he was ready for the evening. He hesitated momentarily and opened the top drawer of the chest of drawers in front of him that the mirror sat on and pulled out an old cigar box. He opened its lid and saw the clear phials rolling about. He picked one up and inspected it closely. *Should still be alright*, he thought, as he rolled it in his fingers, then put it in his jacket's side pocket, patting the pocket's flap for good measure.

Henry's father was sitting at the kitchen table, head in his hands, gazing at a letter from the bank. It wasn't a surprise; the meeting with the bank had not gone well. Depositing the fifteen thousand pounds from the sale of the engagement ring had only helped slightly and bought him an extra month at best. The letter was clear— proceed with the sale or be repossessed.

The accounts Tyler was looking at were far worse than he had expected. Costs were running out of control. He'd sat down with Bull, the farm manager, in the afternoon and explained the situation. He'd been quite understanding and had only blanched when Tyler told him he could only pay salaries up to the end of July; after that he didn't know. Bull's only suggestion was to set a fire that destroyed the crops, at least one of the barns and killed what livestock they had left. Insurance would pick up the tab and they should be able to engineer a substantial claim, although they might need cash for Sergeant Bennett and the loss assessor. With land so dry and hot, a fire would be no surprise, according to Bull, convinced this was the best way forward.

Tyler told Bull no, although it was a better idea than anyone else had come up with so far. Before Bull left, Tyler told him he would try and talk to the buyer of the farm about keeping jobs and staff. Bull thanked Tyler, but walked off thinking his time at Long Farm was probably over.

Henry entered the kitchen.

'You look smart, dear, where are you off to?' asked his mother as she dried plates at the sink.

'Meeting Christian at The Oak.'

'Christian from your old school?'

'Yes, that's the one.'

'They farm soft fruit, don't they?' Henry's father muttered, lifting his head from the letter and accounts, which didn't get better no matter how many times he read them.

'Yes, that's right, and run a holiday business and the land agents as well, so nicely diversified. Perhaps something we should have considered some time ago?'

'Bloody easy to say that now,' said an irritated Tyler. 'But we've run out of options so we have no choice and will be proceeding with the sale.'

'Giving up, you mean.'

'I'm too old to start again, and you've no interest in rolling up your sleeves and doing the hard work. You've never shown any interest in getting your hands dirty.'

Henry ran his finger along the line of hooks with various keys on them. 'I'll take the pickup tonight,' he said as he lifted the keys from the hook on the wall.

'OK, have a good evening.' Tyler walked over and opened the front door to let Henry out.

'Watching the football, Dad?'

'Yes, hopefully they'll win and cheer me up.'

Henry walked to the pickup. He still liked the red and white colour scheme which his dad detested. He got in and eased himself into the comfy driving seat, glancing around the cabin. *Plenty of room in here, ideal,* Henry thought, as he started the engine and drove to the pub.

Henry pulled into The Oak car park. It was already crowded. His phone pinged. A message from Christian; he was already inside, what did Henry want to drink? 'Beer', Henry messaged back. The pub was already busy when

Henry entered, with lots of shouting and music blaring. A lot of people were already drunk, which was good.

Henry found Christian at the bar. It was almost impossible to talk with the loud music and shouted conversations roaring through the pub.

Henry saw her standing behind Christian and decided to watch for a while to see if she was with anyone.

It was Henry's turn to get a drink and he squeezed to the bar next to the girl.

'What can I get you?'

'Guess.'

'Do I get a prize if I guess right?'

'We'll see.'

'Vodka and orange.' He'd already spied her drink.

'Correct.'

Henry caught the barman's eye. 'Two beers and a vodka and orange. Large?'

'Why not, as you're buying,' she said grinning.

Henry tapped his card for the drinks, passed a beer to Christian, but stayed standing next to the girl. Christian winked at Henry.

'What's your name?'

'Chloe.'

'Henry. Nice to meet you, you here on your own?'

'Hi, Henry, thanks for the drink. No, I'm here with girls I work with, the loud group at the other end of the bar.'

'You're not joining them, then?'

'No, they will get blind drunk as usual; most will wake tomorrow with a bad head. It will be a slow day packing on the farm tomorrow.'

'What farm do you work at?'

'Pollards.'

'Vegetables, if I remember right? Quite a way from here.'

'Yes, and we clean and pack veg for all the other growers in the area. Yes, some distance, but there aren't many fun places to go for an evening out.'

Chloe was now close to Henry, as the growing crowd pushed them together.

'What do you do at the farm?'

'I'm a packing manager, most of the other girls over there, work on the packing line.'

'Is that why you are here? You're the boss?'

'Sort of, we arrange a team social every few months, so I have to attend, my main job is to make sure we get everyone back on the minibus at the end of the evening. This is the venue I dread, it's such a cattle market.'

'That's young farmers for you.' Henry shrugged.

'The venue doesn't help, and the T-shirt competition is worse than the strippers they used to have.'

'You've been coming here for a while, then?'

'We seem to land up here roughly once a year. As I said, not many places to go.'

Suddenly there was an announcement from behind the bar. 'T-shirt competition in half an hour. See the bar staff for your T-shirt, and free drink for each contestant. Fifty pounds cash for the winner and free drinks all night.' A cheer went up from the crowd.

'Oh God, looks like my girls are keen on entering.'

'You're not?'

'Fuck no; I don't really need the fifty quid and you seem happy to buy my drinks.' She laughed, throwing her head back.

'I think you'd stand a good chance of winning by the look of things,' Henry said glancing down at her chest.

'Cheeky, but I'm worth more than fifty quid.'

'I'll give you a definite fifty quid just for entering and keep buying you drinks.'

'You're a bad man, Henry, but I'm easily worth more than fifty,' she said coyly. Her head dropped forward, and she looked at Henry through her fringe.

'A hundred pounds.'

'OK, you're on, let's see the money.'

Henry got his wallet out and peeled out five twenty-pound notes. He passed Chloe the money and she made a show of counting it.

Henry waved at the barman. 'Need a T-shirt here, mate.'

'What size?'

'Medium.'

'Large possibly,' the barman said, glancing at Chloe. 'I'll give you one of each and you can decide.'

'*God, this is so demeaning, what the fuck am I doing?*' Chloe said to herself as she set off to the toilets to decide on which T-shirt to wear.

Chloe squeezed into the toilets. She joined the many pulling off their tops and squeezing into The Oak T-shirts. *Fuck this,* Chloe thought to herself. And she turned round and stalked out of the toilets.

Henry ordered more drinks. He slipped his hand in his

pocket and held the phial in his fingers. He had to make sure he wasn't spotted.

The barman put the drinks on the bar. Henry took a long sip of his beer. He picked up one of the wooden stirrers and managed to hold the stirrer and the phial in one hand. Henry checked the barman was distracted serving. He managed to break off the top of the phial and empty it into Chloe's drink. Once done, he immediately dropped the phial on the floor and then stirred the drink with the wooden stirrer.

'What you doing, mate?'

Henry looked over his shoulder at the looming figure behind him.

'Nothing, just mixing the vodka and orange.' Henry lifted the stirrer so the figure behind him could see it.

'Not that, mate, what you added. I saw you.'

'Why don't you fuck off and mind your own business.'

The man behind him pushed Henry and he bounced gently into the bar.

'I saw you, mate, so don't fuck me about. I tell you what, you drink that and I'll buy another for the lady.'

Henry noticed a number of grinning faces behind his accuser.

Fuck, I'm in trouble here, thought Henry.

The blow came from nowhere, but was fast and effective. Henry's accuser looked confused for a moment and swayed, his eyes rolling as he fell back into his mates.

Henry turned to see Christian standing beside him, rubbing the knuckle of his fist.

'Outnumbered, thought it best to get in first.'

Henry wasn't so sure. He was quite happy to drink the vodka and orange and keep talking, but it was too late now.

The music stopped, the harsh main lights came on and two doormen appeared with a couple of bar staff to see the friends of Henry's accuser all take a step forward as one towards Henry and Christian. Christian lashed out again at the man nearest to him. Henry watched his nose explode in blood as he crumpled towards the floor. It all got very frantic, with the doormen forcing themselves between Henry, Christian and everyone else.

One of the boys leant through the pushing and shoving melee and pushed his face towards Christian. 'You're fucking dead, pal.'

'Not yet.' And Christian drove up a fast upper cut into the jaw of the taunting face.

'Can you stop doing that?' Henry almost shouted above the pushing and shoving chaos.

'I thought it was all going rather well,' said Christian as the man fell to his knees, clutching his jaw with both hands. 'To be honest, Henry, I thought we'd get one shot in and then we'd get a kicking.'

'Stop, enough now.' Henry could sense Christian was readying himself up for another shot. 'Still time for us to get hurt,' Henry said with feeling. Unlike Christian, Henry had never boxed at school, at which Christian had excelled and had continued.

'Right, you lot, you're all out, you can carry your friends out.' One of the doormen ordered the lads to leave.

'What about them?' said one, pointing at Christian and Henry

'Don't muck us about, mate, we're telling you guys to go. Right.'

'These two need an ambulance,' said one, pointing at his two friends holding their faces.

'You can drive them to A&E. Be quicker, and you have nothing else to do now this evening,' the doorman said, laughing.

The doormen half escorted; half pushed the group of blokes out of the pub.

'Fuck, they'll be loitering in the car park,' said Henry.

'No, they won't. The doormen will make sure they leave, we've made that mistake in the past,' said the barman. 'By the way, mate, nice punching. When I saw what was unfolding from behind the bar, I thought you were both dead-meat, and pushed the panic button just as you landed your first punch.'

'Christ, I leave you for a few minutes and it all kicks off. Where are those farm boys from?' Chloe asked the barman.

'Sorry, don't know, but fairly local. They are regulars, never had any trouble with them before.'

Suddenly, the lights dimmed and the music was back blaring out. Chloe, Henry and Christian stood at the bar as if nothing had happened.

Chloe took Henry's hand and pushed into it the hundred pounds he'd not long given her.

'What's this?'

'I'm not doing it. So, you get your money back, but you can still buy my drinks.'

'Fair enough.'

'Is that my drink?' said Chloe as she reached for the vodka and orange on the bar.

'Yes.'

'Henry, sorry I've got to go,' said Christian.

'OK, mate no problem, see you Monday at the office...and again thank you for all your help.'

'No problem, isn't that what friends are for?' Christian slapped Henry on the back as he walked towards the door. Henry watched him leave. A good-looking brunette attached herself to Christian on his way out. *You dark horse,* Christian, Henry thought.

Chloe drank half her drink, paused and then downed the rest.

'Another?' asked Henry as he waved at the barman, who quickly placed another vodka and orange on the bar. *This is too easy*, thought Henry, wondering how long before Chloe would start to wobble.

The lights flickered and the manager announced the start of the T-shirt competition. Would all competitors please come to the end of the bar? Each competitor downed a shot as they climbed the steps to stand on the bar. Once on the bar they were sprayed with water from canisters held by various members of the enthusiastic crowd. There was an almost feral atmosphere. Pounding music and manic introductions and commentary for each contestant further charged the atmosphere and baying crowd.

'Oh fuck. That's Mary.'

'Is that a problem?'

'She's only sixteen, been working with us for us a month and here she is flashing her tits to the crowd.'

'Well, she seems to be enjoying herself.'

'Fuck off, Henry, she has no idea what she's doing.' Chloe lurched forward into Henry, one hand on the bar, her other on Henry's chest. 'Sorry, I feel a bit light-headed and giddy, suddenly. I haven't eaten much today.'

'Do you want to get some air?' *She suspects nothing*, Henry smiled to himself.

'Yes, that's a good idea.' They walked to the pub door, Chloe hanging on Henry's arm.

Outside, Henry guided Chloe to a bench and sat her down.

'Sorry, Henry, I really don't feel very good.' She made a long sigh as her chin sunk to her chest and she passed out.

Henry could see his pickup not far away.

'Come on, Chloe, let's get you to the car.' Henry half lifted her off the bench to walk to his car. Henry was always surprised how, despite the contents of the phial, the girls could still move and follow simple instructions, didn't lose all function, but then remembered little the next day. *Clever*, Henry thought.

He eased her into the passenger seat and pulled the safety belt round her.

'What are you doing?'

'Strapping you in to take you home, you're not well.'

'What about the others?'

'I spoke to the older one.' *There's always an older one in the group,* thought Henry.

'Margaret.'

'That's her. Told her you're not well and I'm taking you home. She said she'd get the girls home. She wanted to see my ID and she photographed my driving licence; in case I kidnap you.' Henry laughed; the irony completely lost on Chloe.

Chloe chuckled. 'Typical.' And her chin sank to her chest as she passed out again.

Henry climbed into the driver's side and checked her again—out cold—before he started the engine and drove out of the pub car park.

He drove sensibly back to the farm. The police seemed a bit sharper these days. Last thing he needed now was to be stopped for something silly.

He turned into the farm and into the first barn.

Henry sat in silence with the engine off. He then heard a murmur next to him and saw Chloe's head start to lift. Her eyes were fluttering, not able to focus. Henry leant over and undid her seat belt, dragging his hand over her breast as he did.

'What...what...are you doing?' she murmured, confused, still trying to focus.

'Just relax,' Henry said as he let her seat back into full recline before he did the same to his own.

Henry started to pull up her top.

'No. What the fuck are you doing?'

'Shut up, you silly bitch,' Henry spat as he roughly pushed her face, then continued removing her top.

*

Tyler was sitting in the kitchen enjoying the football. They were winning two nil.

Maria was sitting with Tyler, sewing, taking only the vaguest interest in the game, but pleased it was lightening his mood. She was quite happy to leave the farm and was looking forward to the smallholding in Devon.

'What was that?' Maria said.

'What?' Tyler asked absorbed in the football.

'That noise, sounded like a scream.'

'Probably crowd noise from the game.'

'I don't know. Tyler. Can you just turn the sound off for a moment, please.'

'Of course.' Tyler picked up the remote and muted the game.

Tyler and Maria sat in silence for a minute.

'See, I told you it's from the game.' Tyler picked up the remote to turn the sound back on, when they heard a scream.

'That's it,' said Maria, now worried.

'Fuck!' was all Tyler said as he got up, took the keys from his pocket and walked to the gun cupboard. As he unlocked it, they heard another scream. They stopped still, looking at each other, sharing worry and a memory from the past. Tyler took out his shotgun, broke it open and loaded two cartridges, putting another two in his pocket.

'Maria, message Bull, tell him we have intruders in barn number one and to get up

here quick. Tell him I've gone to investigate.'

'Tyler, do be careful, why don't you wait until Bull and some of the men are here?'

'Don't like the sound of that screaming. I'll be alright.' He lifted the shotgun slightly for emphasis.

Tyler opened the front door, his wife behind him. The night greeted him with another scream that suddenly cut off.

'Maria, go and message Bull as I asked, please.' He glanced at the TV from the front door to see another goal go in. Three nil. *Well, it would have been a great evening,* Tyler thought as he steadily crossed the yard towards the barn. The nearer he got, the more desperate screaming he could hear.

Tyler walked cautiously into the barn, the shotgun broken open under his arm, its weight making him feel secure. He spotted the red and white pickup immediately and another shout and scream burst into the night from the truck.

'Dear Heaven, not again,' Tyler said out loud to himself as he walked towards the pickup.

Another scream was followed by a sound he didn't recognise and then long sobs. As he neared the truck, he heard his son.

'Just relax, it's your own fault. You're making this difficult.'

'I want you to stop, don't you understand, you fucking idiot?'

Tyler now realised what the sounds were. They were blows his son was administering.

Tyler took a deep breath and stepped to the open driver's door.

'That's enough, Henry, leave her alone. Get out of the car and we can sort this out.'

Henry's enraged face turned towards his father. 'Why don't you fuck off and leave me to finish my business.'

'Enough is enough,' Tyler said as he leant into the car, grabbed Henry and pulled him out of the truck. Tyler may not have been as strong as he once was, but he still worked every day on the farm, something they should have insisted Henry had done from an early age.

Tyler dragged Henry out of the door and the momentum sent him sprawling across the barn floor. Henry lay still for a moment, stunned by what had just happened, then jumped up and looked at his father, fury in his eyes.

'This is your mess, son, but if you stop now there's a good chance, we can sort it out, no harm done.'

As he finished talking, Tyler heard a crying wail from the car. He glanced over his shoulder and saw Chloe's bruised and battered face with tears rolling down her cheeks, trying to find her clothes and cover herself up. Tyler reached into the truck and picked up a blanket and threw it at Chloe, who looked up and tried to smile in thanks.

Henry stared at his father and with a roar he started to advance forward. Tyler had the shotgun shut in a moment; the safety flicked off. 'Back off, you fool.'

'That's the problem, you think I'm an idiot.'

'Well, to be fair you do little do prove us wrong.'

With that Henry sprung forward and was greeted by

one barrel of the twelve bore, which blew him backwards against the barn wall. Blood splattering up behind him. Henry slid to the floor, leaving a smear of blood on the wall.

'What have I done?' Tyler said out loud in shock. He was still for a moment, as he stood struck by the look of surprise fixed on Henry's face. The barn was curiously quiet now, just whimpering from the pickup, which tore at Tyler's heart, and not for the first time he asked himself, *where did we go wrong with our boy?*

Bull had been walking up to the barn when he heard the shot. The shot also brought Maria running from the house.

Bull ran into the barn and saw Henry lying on the floor covered in blood. Bull knelt next to Henry. He was a mess, but still alive, just.

Bull approached Tyler. 'We can deal with this. He's still alive, we need an ambulance.'

Tyler bit his bottom lip, levelled the gun at Henry's prone body and fired the second

barrel. 'I should have done this eight years ago. Now it's over, thank God.' Tears ran down Tyler's cheek as he looked at his son in a bloody heap.

Bull looked round in surprise; he walked back to Henry's body.

'He's dead now, boss. I think we can still sort this out.'

'No, Bull, we need an ambulance for the girl, and the police, no excuses this time.'

Maria entered the barn and saw her son. 'My boy, my beautiful boy. What have you done?' she wailed as the shock hit her and she sank to her knees on the dusty barn floor sobbing.

'Stop your crying, woman, there is someone in the pickup who needs your help. Henry is beyond help now and has been for years.'

Maria flashed Tyler a look and then, hearing the crying from the pickup, levered herself up from the floor and walked with a slight stumble to the truck and the girl.

Bull walked up to Tyler. 'Boss, we can still fix this if we are smart. I just need a bit of time, a couple of hours. A terrible accident. Leave it to me.'

'No, Bull, not again. I suspect your solution doesn't end well for the poor girl.'

'Needs must, boss. Just say the word.'

'Thank you, Bull, but I have to say no. I found it hard enough to live with last time, I can't go through that again.' Tyler put his hand in his pocket and pulled out his phone.

'Hello, yes, we need police and an ambulance.'

When he'd finished the call, Tyler looked at Bull. 'If this makes things difficult for you, then just go, I'll not mention you were here this evening.'

'Thanks, boss. I think it would be a good time to disappear. I can't help Henry this time.'

'This time' echoed in Tyler's mind. *How many times had Henry needed Bull's help*, Tyler wondered, not daring to think what this might mean.

Maria carefully opened the passenger door of the pickup and peered inside. She lifted a nervous hand and placed it gently on the arm she could see. As she did,

Chloe raised her head and looked with fear at Maria. Chloe's faced was badly scuffed and bruised, her left eyebrow cut and bleeding. Her lip, torn, and bleeding as well. Her nose leaked snot and blood as she sobbed, her eyes soaking her face with tears of fear and pain. Maria looked in horror at the disfigured face.

'Has he gone? Has he gone?' Chloe kept repeating.

'Yes, dear, he's gone, he won't hurt you or anyone anymore.'

'Thank God.' And Chloe's face relaxed, hoping the worst was over. Maria stroked her head gently as she heard sirens approaching.

~ 45 ~

Friday, 11th July. Fran took her phone into the dining room for breakfast, checking several times the sound was off, but as she sat looking at it, she caught Tom's glance and checked it was on silent one more time. Lewis hated phones at the table of any meal and she'd seen Tom's father remind people of his 'no phones' rule on several occasions. Fran didn't disagree with this policy and only had it close today in case, as was quite likely, her mother called to update their arrival time. On cue Fran's phone lit up, showing her mother's number. Fran picked up the phone and walked out to the hall then out onto the Vale and called her mother back.

'Hello, darling,' a cheerful Wendy answered. 'Just called to say your father's call was much shorter than expected and we will be leaving soon. Charles thinks we will be with you at about twelve as originally planned.'

'That's great, Mum. How's Dad?'

'In a surprisingly good mood, said he's looking forward to the weekend. OK, will message you when we are near.'

'See you later, Mum. Bye.'

Fran checked the phone was on silent again and

returned to the dining room but she bumped into Pen in the hall, her hand over her mouth and eyes wide.

'Fran, come and join us, I have something I'd like to share.' Pen sounded a bit muffled behind her hand but her wide eyes expressed urgency and shock at the same time. Fran followed Pen into the drawing room. 'I've asked Jackie and Rachel to join us.'

'What is it?' Fran asked, beginning to feel concerned.

'I'll tell you when we are all here.'

Jackie, followed by Rachel, came through the drawing room door.

'Please sit down. I have news that affects all of us in different ways,' Pen said as everyone sat down, Rachel on one side of Pen and Jackie on the other, all on the small sofa. Fran sat opposite, on a chair pulled close, wondering why she was there.

Pen reached out to hold Jackie's and Rachel's hands. Fran didn't really know why but she also reached and held Jackie's and Rachel's other hands and the four sat in their circle awaiting Pen's news.

Pen's face was sombre. She took a deep breath as she started to talk at a slow, measured pace.

'Last night there was an incident at Long Farm.'

At the mention of Long Farm, Fran felt Rachel's grip tighten.

Pen continued, 'I don't have any details, but whatever happened, Henry

Campbell-Blyth is dead.'

The room was heavy with silence as the news sunk in. Rachel threw her head back and started to laugh. Her manic laughter continued growing in volume. 'None of you have any idea how long I've dreamt of him being dead, I wished it and dreamed it every day for eight years. Finally, I am released from the curse that is Henry fucking Campbell-Blyth.'

'We all are,' Jackie said, beginning to laugh as well.

A feeling of relief and a release of tension now pervaded the room, as Jackie joined Rachel in laughing. A laughter that had been stored deep, waiting for this moment. Fran could see that Pen had tears, not laughter, her chin on her chest.

'Ms Penelope, I'm sorry, I can't shed a tear for him, no matter the manner of his death.' Rachel stood up, letting go of Pen and Fran's hand, breaking their circle. 'Sorry, there is much to do, we have guests arriving.' Rachel turned briefly to Fran. 'We've put your parents in Beeches, it's a room like yours.' And Rachel left the drawing room.

'Why am I crying and not laughing like her?' Pen said almost under her breath as Rachel walked out.

'People react in different ways to such news,' said Jackie, now holding both Pen's hands.

'It might be about closure. Perhaps you feel you've closed that chapter in your life already and moved on, but Rachel feels she has just been stalled and not been able to move on until the news this morning,' Fran said.

'Despite everything he did to me and the injuries he caused, I can't muster the hate that Rachel has, although I do feel great relief and that a cloud has lifted now he has gone.' Pen squeezed Jackie's hands as she gazed at her.

Fran stood up to return to breakfast.

'Let's hope he doesn't return and haunt us all. He's a spiteful bastard,' spat Jackie.

Fran left and Pen looked at Jackie.

'You mentioned children the other day. It's not something I'd really ever thought of, but the idea has settled in me, so any thoughts on how we might go about it?'

Jackie's face exploded in a smile.

Yes, Pen thought, *love is the difference.*

'I read an article on another lesbian couple's experience; I'll dig it out. Perhaps we can chat further, once you've had a read.'

'Perfect,' said Pen, smiling.

~ 46 ~

Fran walked back to the dining room feeling worried, wondering if Henry's spirit could still bring trouble.

'You've been some time,' Tom said as Fran sat back down. 'Your parents alright?'

'Yes, they're fine, be here about midday. Pen had some shocking news she wanted to share.'

Tom, and Fred Connell, who had been chatting in Fran's absence, leant forward, clearly intrigued.

'Henry Campbell-Blyth is dead. Something happened at Long Farm last night.'

Both men sat back in surprise.

'How did Pen know that?' Tom asked, looking surprised.

'I don't know.'

Lewis came sweeping into the dining room, scanning the faces and stopping when he saw Tom and Fred. He walked over, looking purposeful. 'Henry Campbell-Blyth is dead. His father shot him last night and a girl is in hospital, attacked by Henry. Thought you'd want to know before you hear it on the news.'

'How do you know?' asked Tom.

'A courtesy call from Inspector Collins as it is national

news, so the press might be nosing about. Collins might also need to come and talk to some of us as part of her enquires. I've already told Pen.'

'Should we put someone on the main gate?' suggested Tom.

'Good idea.' Lewis turned and found Graham behind him. 'Graham, please speak to Duncan, we need someone on the main entrance. All visitors to be sent to you and met at the house.'

'Don't forget Fran's parents are visiting this weekend,' said Tom.

'I'll get it sorted,' said Graham as he walked out the dining room.

*

Wendy messaged Fran that they were just turning into the tree-lined drive of the estate. As they pulled up to the top of the drive, two men stepped out.

'What's all this then?' said Charles as his window slid down.

'Hello, sir. I assume you're Fran's parents, Mr and Mrs Clarke?'

'Yes, that's right, everything OK?'

'Nice to meet you, sir, I'm Rupert, a forester on the estate, and this is George, an apprentice. Everything is fine here, sir, but there's been an unfortunate incident on a nearby farm.'

'The shooting? Yes, I heard on the news. Was that near here, then?'

'Not that near, but we've been warned the press are

about and we don't really want them poking around the estate.'

'Understand, hence why you two are here, I guess.'

'Yes, sir, now if you go to your right, past the signpost to Woodcoombe, the drive winds gently uphill to the left. The Vale will be on your right.' Rupert pointed as he leant towards the car's open window. 'But it's not very green now, mainly brown and dusty; it's this bloody heat. You will see the house when you are about halfway up. Stop by the door, someone will meet you. You can't really go wrong, sir.'

'OK, thank you.' Charles smiled as he pushed the car into gear and smoothly moved off as instructed, his window gracefully closing as the air conditioning struggled to quell the invading heat.

'I think they should call her Francesca and not Fran,' Wendy said as she watched the brown of the Vale slide past them. 'Far too familiar for my liking.'

'Perhaps our daughter has asked to be called Fran, you know she prefers that.'

'That's not the point, Charles, she has a position to maintain now.'

'For fuck's sake,' Charles said under his breath.

'I heard that, Charles.'

'Please don't start as soon as we get there, perhaps discuss it with her quietly, before you get all uptight about it.'

'OK, I will.'

Charles shook his head and sighed in frustration.

'Here's the house, dear,' he announced as it came into view.

'Beautiful,' Wendy said as they got nearer. 'Bigger than I thought it would be.'

Rachel was waiting by the door and stepped onto the drive as Charles brought the car to a stop. Wendy stepped from the car into the midday heat. 'Hello, Mrs Clarke, Ms Francesca will be down in a moment. She knows you are here.'

'At last, someone who uses her proper name.'

'She has asked everyone to use Fran and not Francesca. She doesn't seem to like using her full name.'

'Told you, dear,' Charles quietly said to Wendy as he joined his wife and Rachel.

'Mr Clarke, nice to meet you. I'm Rachel, Francesca's and Tom's maid, and will be looking after you during your stay.' Rachel shook hands with Charles. 'Shall we wait inside and get out of the heat?'

'That sounds like a good idea, darling,' said Wendy. 'They have a maid!' she half whispered to Charles as they followed Rachel into the hall and its slightly cooler air.

'Hello Mum, hello Dad,' said Fran as she skipped down the main stairs. 'Shall we get your things from the car and show you to your room?'

'One question, sir,' asked Rachel. 'Is your car electric?'

'Good heavens, no,' Charles said gruffly. 'Why do you ask?'

'We have charging facilities and it makes a difference to where they park your car. If I could have your keys, please.'

'I'll just get our bags out first.' Charles pushed a button on the car key fob and the boot silently opened. The four of them walked to the back of the car and collected Charles and Wendy's things.

'You're only here for two nights, Mum!' Fran said, feeling the weight of her mother's bags.

'You never know what you might need, darling, so there's a lot of 'just in case' stuff.'

Isaac strolled up. 'Can I have your keys please sir, and I'll park your car; you shouldn't be needing it during your stay.' He stood with his hand held out and Charles with some reluctance dropped the keys into it.

'Don't worry, sir, I'll look after it. We can even top up the tank for you before you leave.'

Isaac eased himself into the driver's seat and then drove the car up the hill to the sheds, which couldn't be seen from the house.

'Shall we get out of this heat?' said Charles, with a shrug, as he watched his car disappear.

'This is the main staircase that leads to your room.' Fran led the way, heaving one of her mother's bags. 'You're in Beech on the first floor.'

'It's the latest room to have been renovated,' said Rachel.

'I guess renovation is a constant battle in a house like this,' Charles said.

'Indeed, sir.'

They got to the first-floor landing and Rachel showed them to the door with Beech painted on it. 'Here we are,' she said, holding the door open.

'This is beautiful,' said Wendy almost in a sigh. 'It's like a hotel.'

'It's pretty well the same as Ms Francesca's and Tom's room, but they will be moving to their new apartment when it's built, probably by the end of the year.'

'That sounds exciting, darling.'

'We can talk more about that this afternoon, Mum; we don't want to bore Dad to death with decorating talk.'

Charles rolled his eyes, relieved at being excluded. He walked to the window and looked at the view down the Vale.

'Some view, but it's all very brown. Expected it to be greener.'

'It's the weather, Dad, it's been hot and dry for so long. The evidence here is certainly that the weather patterns have changed over recent years and it's having a detrimental effect on the land and the life within it.'

'So, we all have to change due to bit of hot weather,' Charles said sarcastically, shaking his head, knowing this would irritate his daughter.

'I don't expect you to understand, Dad, just stating a fact.'

'Now you two, let's not start the visit with an argument,' Wendy said as she emerged from the walk-in wardrobe.

'I will unpack for you, if you have anything that needs pressing or washing, please let me know,' said Rachel as she followed Wendy out of the wardrobe.

'Lunch is at one o'clock, so we've got half an hour. Why don't I show you around a bit before we go to the dining room?' suggested Fran.

'Are you doing all the unpacking, Rachel?' asked Wendy, relishing having staff run round after her. She looked at Charles, who just shrugged.

'It's no problem, madam, everything will be put in the wardrobe,' Rachel replied as she heaved one of Wendy's bags on to the bed and unzipped it.

Fran led her parents out of the room.

'I felt awkward the first time I visited here, but please don't be, it's part of their job. This is the first floor where all the family live and the principal guest suites are situated.' Fran walked to the top of the main staircase and continued round the landing to the back stairs. 'The main stairs only go to the first floor; you need to use these stairs to get to the second and third floors where there are more rooms. Tom's partner Simon moved onto the second floor earlier this week and seems quite happy. The third floor is all single rooms, originally the servants' quarters, now used by staff who stay overnight. All the rooms and floors are in the process of being renovated and updated to make the best use of the space.'

'How many actually live here then?' asked Charles.

Fran thought for a moment. 'Well, all the family, seven people, including Tom and me. Then there is Graham, Lewis's personal assistant, and his partner; Simon and Emma; Mr Balfour the Chef. So that's another five and I've probably missed a couple so let's say around fourteen, plus staff staying overnight depending on what's going on. There always seem to be guests as well. There are also properties across the estate which are used by employees, both current and retired.

'Now these are the back stairs, they take you down to the ground floor corridor and up to the second and third floor. We're going down.' Fran led the way. 'I know you guys won't really have any need to be down here this weekend, but I'll show you round anyway. The room at the end is the sitting room with doors out to the Vale. It's nice, but not used much, as all the family have such good facilities in their suites.' Fran opened the door to the sitting room and walked in, followed by Wendy and Charles. Fran was surprised to see a number of people busy in the room.

'Hi, Fran, nice to see you, you must be Fran's parents?' Charlotte appeared from behind a table with glasses laid out across it.

'Mum, Dad. This is Charlotte, Tom's mother.'

'Your Ladyship, lovely to meet you, Wendy Clarke.' Wendy introduced herself awkwardly with a slight hint of a curtsey.

'Please Wendy, just Charlotte. No need for any titles here and there's certainly never any need to curtsey.'

'Oh, sorry.' Wendy felt disappointed and embarrassed.

'Charles Clarke, pleased to meet you.' Charles pushed his hand out to shake hands.

'A pleasure to meet you both.' Charlotte shook hands with Charles. 'It's all hands to the pumps getting ready for the barbeque tonight. I haven't been in this room for a long time. I'd quite forgotten how lovely it is. We're setting up the bar in here for tonight.'

'Do you need any help this afternoon?' asked Fran.

'No thank you, dear. I think everything is pretty well

sorted out. Although Chef has had a bit of a panic this morning when he was told they would not be cooking the beef and lamb over the fire pits, as planned, and they would need to be cooked in the kitchen instead. The poor girls are going to be melting down there.'

'Why's that, Charlotte?' asked Charles. Wendy shot Charles a glance, not happy at his tone.

'The fire risk, they would usually split the beef and lamb carcass, mount then on racks and roast them over an open fire pit for hours, a job for the apprentices overseen by the kitchen, but everything, the land, trees, the house, are tinder dry. The pork is still being cooked on a spit and if you poke your heads outside you will smell it.'

'Is it really that much of a risk?' Charles questioned, receiving another, more pointed, glance from Wendy.

'Charles, I'm sure you've noticed the weather. One stray spark and everything goes up, so we have to be sensible. Not something you always hear around here.'

'Oh, I see, didn't think it was that bad.'

'Well, Charles, I'm afraid it is, it's proving deadly to some parts of the estate and across the country, looking at the news. It's such a shame. The weather and seasons are changing.'

Fran decided it was time to move on. 'Thanks, Charlotte, we will see you at lunch. I'm just giving Mum and Dad a quick tour.'

'Yes, Fran, see you then,' Charlotte said, glancing at her watch, 'which will not be long.' Charlotte turned away to speak to someone holding a box in front of them.

'I didn't expect to find Tom's mother setting up a bar,' Wendy said, sounding slightly disappointed.

'Why not, Mum? Everyone here mucks in as needed.'

'She's a lady.'

'For God's sake, Mum, she doesn't spend all day sitting around in a tiara, there's a lot going on here.'

'Enough of that language thank you, Francesca!' Wendy snapped. Charles rolled his eyes.

Fran sighed and rolled her shoulders in irritation and to ease the tension building, as she led Charles and Wendy out of the sitting room.

'I'm not sure what all these doors are.' Fran tried the first door on her left. She popped her head in to find a small dining room, which looked dusty and unused. 'Nothing in there,' she said as she shut the door. The next doors on the left and right were both locked. Fran then peeped into the next door on the right, half-open. 'Hi, Simon, are you working?'

'Hi, Fran,' Simon said, standing up.

'Just giving my parents a quick tour before lunch.'

Simon nodded in understanding.

Charles entered the room with a smile. 'Nice to meet you, I'm Charles.' Again, he pushed out his hand to shake hands.

'Simon is Tom's partner on his project and moved into the house earlier this week.'

'How do you like our new office?' Simon waved his hand vaguely for effect.

'Where were you before?' Charles asked. Fran was surprised at her dad's interest.

'We had a cupboard at the university, nothing like this, but we can work anywhere, really. It was decided we should move here now we are nearly finished for security reasons.'

'I can see that.'

'What can you see, Dad?' Fran asked, wondering why her father was taking such an interest.

'Well, I imagine there are people always coming and going and minimal security at the university, anyone could walk in.'

'Exactly what everyone said,' Simon agreed, 'and so I landed up out here while we finish up.'

'Nice to meet you, Simon. We'll leave you to finish up whatever you are doing.'

'Just shutting everything down. I've been running, hopefully, the last line of code for the main program. Had a bit of trouble getting it right, but it seems OK now, which is good news, and we can move on to finishing the reporting functionality.'

Charles watched Simon place the black laptop on top of a white laptop and push them to the side of the desk. 'All done, lunch time.' And Simon got up and followed Fran and her parents out of the office.

Charles paused as he followed Fran down the corridor. 'Simon, don't you lock your office?'

'No reason to; no strangers to worry about around here.'

'I guess not,' Charles replied.

'You alright, Dad?' a concerned Fran asked, seeing her

father stand still for a moment with his hand on the wall to steady himself.

'Yes, yes, just felt slightly giddy.'

'Have you taken your tablets this morning? Bet you haven't drunk much water,' said Wendy, walking back to take Charles' arm.

'Don't fuss, woman, I'm alright! It's probably the heat,' Charles said in irritation.

'This is the library, we don't really have time now, but I will show and explain to you the Royal Charter, *The Book of the Dead* and *The Map of Souls* another time. And this room is Lewis's office-study and next to it is Graham's office. On the left are the back stairs we came down and now we're back in the hall.'

'Thank you, darling, very interesting, but a lot to take in.'

'There's no shortage of history and things to take in here, makes your head spin at times.'

'I can imagine,' said Wendy, still holding Charles' arm as they followed Fran into the dining room.

~ 47 ~

The dining room was already busy. Fran was aware all the family had been asked to attend. Lewis rushed up to Fran.

'These must be your parents, Fran. Lovely to meet you both. I think we've actually got the whole family out.'

'My Dad, Charles, and Mum, Wendy,' Fran introduced.

Charles enthusiastically stepped forward, untangling himself from Wendy's firm hold on his arm. Wendy looked concerned, but Charles seemed fine as he stepped forward to shake hands with Lewis. Then Lewis stepped forward and kissed Wendy on both cheeks, which made her smile and very slightly blush, which Fran noticed, but couldn't decide what she thought about that.

'Come and meet the family.' Lewis gently guided Charles and Wendy to the assembled clan.

'We met earlier,' said Charlotte with a broad grin.

Fran watched as her parents were introduced to Cath and Dan and the new arrival was explained, with patted tummy and lots of smiles. Fran was amused at her mother's strained expression, like she was sucking lemons, which only tightened when she was introduced to Pen and

Jackie, and she realised their relationship. She looked a bit lighter after meeting Jen, but the look returned on being introduced to Graham and his partner Stephen.

Then her parents were introduced to Isaac, Naomi and Noah, which her mother, thankfully, seemed to navigate without some casual racial slur, to Fran's relief and surprise, although Naomi did raise her eyebrows at one point. I'll ask Naomi later, Fran decided, and apologise if needed. Charles was quiet and nodded, insisting on shaking hands with everyone he met. The look of surprise as the looming figure of Duncan arrived and introduced himself to her parents was priceless. A bit awkward, but introductions had been made without any incident or obvious insult, to Fran's relief.

'Lunch, everyone,' Lewis announced.

Charles was sat next to Lewis with Tom looking pensive on Charles' other side. Wendy was next to Charlotte. Fran sat on her other side with Jen next to her. Fran noticed Fred Connell sitting next to Tom. He was never short of things to say and would keep her father in check better than she would.

Lewis stood up, raised a glass and toasted Charles and Wendy and welcomed them to the family, which made Wendy beam as Lewis said he looked forward to them being regular visitors. Fran was not so sure that would be such a good idea.

Wendy leant into Fran and whispered, 'Lovely welcome, but they're a bit dysfunctional, perhaps they think we might help steady the ship.'

'What do you mean, Mum?'

'Well, unmarried, teenage, pregnant daughter, another daughter living with another woman, that Graham and his boyfriend.'

'Partner! And he's not family,' Fran snapped back in a whisper, her irritation increasing.

'Whatever you call him, it's not right that a family like this has to go through these types of problems and worries.'

'Why is any of this a problem?'

'Well, you'd have thought living out here they would escape so many of the things we have to tolerate.'

'I don't think you'll find Charlotte and Lewis are particularly worried as long as their children are happy, whatever direction they might take. None of those you mention do anyone any harm. Pen has had a very rough time and I think, like others do, that the baby could be the making of Cath.'

'And that's another thing. No one seems to be called by their proper name, how very disappointing. I guess that's why you felt pressure to shorten yours?'

'No, Mum, I asked them to call me Fran, as I have you a hundred times over the years. The only one to call me Francesca is Isaac, but he insists on calling everyone by their full name.'

'Isaac. Ah yes, that funny little black man with his two children.'

'What's so funny about him?' Fran asked, worried at what the reply might be.

'He seems to think he runs the place; how could anyone believe that? Talks about trees and talking to his wife who he says has been dead for some years. He likes you, though, says you have untapped talent, whatever that means. His children seem nice, but perhaps a bit unrealistic about their prospects.'

'Is that because they're black?'

'Well, darling, your background makes a lot of difference. Let's be fair, your Tom would never be allowed to marry that Naomi.'

'Mother, you have no idea how wrong you are.'

'Not sure what you mean, darling, but Lewis and Charlotte must be relieved to have you in the family.'

'Because I'm white?'

'Or any shade, darling. You're going to be nobility.'

'We're walking the woods with Isaac tomorrow morning.'

'He mentioned that, said he would introduce us to the land.'

'It's important you and Dad have an understanding how the people, the land and the life within it are linked.'

'Francesca, what are you talking about?'

'The more you stay here the more you will see and, hopefully, understand, although I have my doubts.'

'You don't think your father and I are open to new and different ideas?'

'In a nutshell, Mum, no.'

Wendy turned to face forward with a huff and scanned the diners, who were all chatting, realising there was a lot of laughter and smiles floating across the gathered throng.

'Good afternoon, madam.'

'Emma!' Fran said in surprise. 'What are you doing?'

'Working in the kitchen. I met with Chef yesterday and he said that with the barbeque they could do with more help so why not work for the day and see what I think. He's paying me.'

'How are you finding it?'

'It's good; hard work though, cooking for the family, guests and staff, it's a constant stream of food going out. The girls are nice. Gail, Holly and Olivia have given me a crash course in how I should behave, especially as I volunteered to serve lunch.' Emma bent down and whispered in Fran's ear with a laugh, 'Wondered if you'd murdered your parents yet?'

'Not yet, but it's shaping up to be a long weekend.'

'Better go, Anna is giving me the eye. Have you had a chance to look at the menu yet?'

'Sorry, no, give us a couple of minutes.'

'No problem, I think everyone else thinks it's just the normal lunch buffet.'

Emma walked round and spoke to Anna. Fran was concerned that Emma might say something she'd regret, knowing her rebellious attitude. But they spoke briefly and parted with smiles. Anna stepped forward and clapped her hands.

'Ladies and gentlemen, can I please draw attention to the lunch menu on the table. We do not have the usual buffet today as we have special guests, Francesca's parents. Thank you everyone, the girls will be round in a minute to take your order.'

Wendy leant into Fran. 'Special guests, at least some-one can get your name right, even if it is just a servant.'

'Mother.' Fran was now very irritated. 'Show some re-spect and, as I told you, they are never called servants.'

Wendy didn't reply but sat tight-lipped as she surveyed the menu card.

Lunch progressed smoothly. Options were selected and three courses delivered with the staff's usual polite, quiet efficiency. Fran noticed Tom decline a glass of wine. He was treating the meeting at Clifford's Farm that afternoon very seriously, which she knew it was.

A convivial air of chatter and laughter continued through the room as lunch progressed. Simon was talking with Graham and Stephen. Simon kept looking at Emma quizzically as she busied herself delivering lunch. *Things are not good there*, Fran thought to herself.

Fred leant over towards Charles. 'Charles, you're com-ing to the meeting this afternoon?'

'Yes, I believe so, anything I need to know?'

'It's potentially the most important meeting for the family and estate for a thousand years: the return of Clif-ford's land to the Woodcoombe Estate, bringing the estate back to its original size.'

'I see,' Charles said, nodding. 'How much land are we talking about?'

'I think Clifford's is about nine hundred acres, but I'm not sure anyone knows exactly.'

'The amount of the land isn't the issue here,' Tom added. 'It's more about the principle of pulling all the parts of the estate back together after such a long time. Charles,

I'll talk you through the history later.' Tom looked at his father. 'What time are we due at Clifford's?'

'Two-thirty. The car is outside, so if we leave at two-fifteen, we should be there on time.'

Tom looked at his watch. 'So, we need to go in ten minutes?'

'Yes,' Lewis replied with a nod.

~ 48 ~

At two-fifteen Lewis stood up and clinked his glass with a fork to get everyone's attention.

'Sorry, we have to leave. As most of you know we have a meeting at Clifford's Farm. See you tonight at the barbeque, hopefully we will have something to celebrate.'

Isaac stood up and waved at Duncan, who stood as well, and both started to chant in a slow rhythm, their voices rising with each line. Duncan was banging the table with a steady beat. Others around the table began to join in, either clapping or banging on the table.

'We give our fealty to lord, liege and land.

Our blood runs deep, strong and true in root and vein.

By the bow, by the land we stand, strong, united, until the end.

By our blood and the spirits of man and land our promise is made.'

There was a huge cheer and loud clapping at the end of the promise, as Lewis led Tom, Fred and Charles out of the room. Lewis paused by the door and raised his hand for silence.

'Thank you, everyone, for that send-off. I trust we will

not fail and will be celebrating tonight.' With his hand still in the air Lewis took a deep breath and roared out a single line from the promise.

'By the bow, by the land we stand, strong, united, until the end.'

It brought more cheering and clapping. Charles looked a bit bemused as he walked out. Fran saw Emma standing open-mouthed.

'What was all that about?' Wendy asked Fran in a low voice.

'That's the promise of the bowmen, Mum. I'd best describe it as the family and estate motto. It shows the relationship between the people, the land and all the life within it.'

'How very quaint, darling. Do they have to shout it every time?'

'It's their passion and the belief in the words and its meaning.'

'What are you talking about? It sounds like a nursery rhyme.'

'I would suggest more of a prayer, Mum.'

'Don't talk such rubbish, Francesca, what an ungodly thing to say.'

Charlotte stood up. 'Thank you, everyone, now I think we have cheese and coffee to come, so please remain seated.'

Everyone took their seats. Her mother seemed to settle after the excitement of the promise and Lewis and the others leaving for their meeting.

'Tom, you drive. Fred, Charles, you two get in the back, it's only a few minutes.'

It took ten minutes to drive to Clifford's Farm. The front door opened as Tom came to a halt and a man of about thirty walked out of the door holding a small child, followed by a blonde woman holding the hands of two older children.

'Mark, I assume?'

'Yes, Lord Woodcoombe, very nice to meet you, I see you've come mob-handed.' Mark looked quizzically at Tom, Fred and Charles standing by the car.

'Sorry, yes. My son, Tom, Fred who works for me and Charles, who's just an observer. We're taking this meeting very seriously. Please call me Lewis.'

'Glad to hear it. My wife Amelia, who has Fraser and Brodie. I have our youngest, Freya, here. She's very shy and probably needs a sleep. Shall we go in?'

Amelia led the boys inside. 'Now you two go and play, Daddy has important visitors.' The boys scuttled through a door off the hall into what looked like the kitchen. Amelia walked over to Mark and took the sleepy Freya.

'Tea for all of you?'

'Yes, please, that would be great,' said Lewis as he made a funny face at the shy Freya now trying to hide her face in her mother's neck.

Amelia followed the boys into the kitchen and Mark led the way into a sitting room.

'Please take a seat,' invited Mark, standing in front of the old, original, wide fireplace. The room was low-beamed and a little cramped with lots of soft furnishings, making the room inviting, comfortable and soft—that was the best way Tom could describe it. *Fran would love this*, he thought.

'Shall I start?' a now nervous-looking Mark said, standing uneasily.

'Yes please, Mark,' Lewis said as he sat down.

'You might have guessed my father would be spinning in his grave if he knew I was having this conversation.'

Lewis laughed lightly and waved Mark to carry on.

'The facts of the matter are simple. The farm has a lot of problems, mostly of our own making. The soil's terrible and, despite flooding the place with chemicals, our yields continue to drop alarmingly. Our land can't cope with the changing climate, baked then flooded: we have no resilience in the ground. Whatever my father might have said about Joseph, his land is coping with all the weather changes better than ours, seems to retain moisture a lot better and equally manage the heavy rainfalls we now get better than us. They don't get the top soil runoff that we get here. We're also under investigation by DEFRA for the chemical runoff from our land, following recent events and the demise of Father and Joseph.'

Charles raised his eyebrows in surprise.

Lewis stood up. 'Understand, Mark, so what do you want?'

Mark stood up straight in front of Lewis. 'To do a deal with you.'

'Go on, please.' Lewis sat back down. Fred sat forward on the edge of his chair, listening intently wondering what Mark would ask for.

'I have a young family, and they have to be my priority. So, I want to keep the house, an annual salary, and the children to have access to the education fund when they are older.' Mark stopped and looked at Lewis.

'OK, Mark, what do we get?'

'I'll pass the farm back and help work on it. I've been told it's a three-year job getting the soil sorted. Over that time, we can work out how we best use the combined capacity of the two farms and the estate.'

Fred clapped his hands. 'Excellent, sounds like a plan.'

Lewis shot Fred a glance and Fred eased quietly back in his seat. 'Thank you, Mark, and as you may have gathered that seems to fits well with our plans.' Lewis glanced at Fred again, but this time with a wink. 'What about your staff?'

'I think you should decide on who you want to keep. They're all good men and we have one woman, Meg, who I think will adapt to the changes better than the men.'

'Is she at college?'

'Finished last year and then came here permanently. She's up on all the latest trends and ideas, very keen.'

The door opened and Amelia walked in with tea and cake and placed it on a small table and started to pour. Mark reached to the fireplace behind him and took an envelope and offered it to Lewis. 'This is a more detailed list of what we want.'

Lewis took it, scanned the list and passed it to Fred, who read it and then nodded to Lewis.

'Mark, I think we have the basis for a deal. Would you let me take this away and come back with a more formal response? It won't take us long.'

Amelia looked up from pouring and handing out the tea. She passed a mug to Lewis and then one to her husband, who she then gave a brief hug.

'How's it going?' she asked in a jolly, questioning voice with a hint of concern.

'Well, I think, we seem to have the basis of an agreement that works for everyone,' Mark said, looking relieved.

'Oh good, it's been such a worry since Mark's father died, so tragic.' Amelia gave Mark a squeeze as she went back to the tray and offered everyone cake.

'You can't beat homemade cake,' Fred said enthusiastically, spraying crumbs in his lap as he spoke. 'Sorry,' he added, seeing the mess he was making.

'We will come back quickly with something formal, which I feel sure will be acceptable to all parties.' Lewis paused. 'Amelia, are you from a farming family? That's not a local accent I detect.'

'I'm originally from the Scottish Highlands. My family

have land up there. A lot of sheep on the uplands, some barley and oats lower down, and a few cows. We also have a managed woodland of Douglas fir. My two brothers run it all now. Their latest venture is six holiday cabins, which they tell me is working really well.'

'How did you two meet?'

'I was working on a nearby estate in Scotland and played for the local rugby team.,' said Mark. 'We met at a party at the rugby club and I eventually managed to convince her to join me down south.'

'We try to go back pretty regularly; all my family are there. It's very different; I miss the wild spaces,' said Amelia.

Lewis finished his tea. 'Thank you both, we will leave you in peace and get back to you very soon, lovely to meet you. Come on, Fred, you've made enough mess for all four of us.'

'Amelia, lovely cake. I'm sorry about the mess, I really am quite housetrained.'

'Don't worry, glad you liked it.'

There followed a lot of shaking of hands, but soon Tom was driving them back to the house.

Once Mark had seen the four drive off, he turned to his wife. 'I think we've done it; I think it will all work out.'

'I'm so pleased, although part of me would have been happy to return to Scotland,' Amelia said a bit wistfully as she hugged Mark. The future was looking a bit clearer now.

*

'Shall we walk down to the house from the shed? I can park this up and put it on charge,' asked Tom.

'Good idea, Tom,' said Lewis. 'What do you think, Fred? All seems pretty straightforward.'

'I think his wife is more worried than him. She looked relieved when she heard a deal could be done.'

'Fred, do you have time when we get back to firm up a deal so we can get it typed up and back to Mark quickly? Tom, can you join us as well, please?'

'Yes, let's sit down as soon as we are back, it shouldn't take too long.'

Tom steered into the shed. Charles looked out and saw his car in the corner with a cover over the top.

'Is that your car?' asked Lewis. 'Isaac said it was nice.'

'I think so, but I don't get to drive it often. Living in the city I suppose it doesn't really make much sense. Thanks for covering it.'

'Don't thank me, thank Isaac, stops the pigeons shitting on it.'

Tom got out and plugged in the Land Rover to charge. They then all walked down the slight hill to the house.

'Christ, it's still hot!' said Fred, beginning to regret the wedge of cake on top of his lunch.

'It will break soon, so the boys tell me. Then we will have a serious downpour and, no doubt, local flooding again. This weather is fucking mad. Sorry, Charles, but the changing weather is becoming a serious problem. It's affecting everyone, as I'm sure you see in the papers, although they only have the loosest grasp of what's really going on.'

Charles didn't say anything; these were problems his company and their customers religiously ignored and worked against. They were not good for business.

~ 50 ~

It didn't take long to stroll down to the house. Lewis, Tom and Fred went into Lewis's study, and Charles decided to go back to his room.

Lewis sat behind his desk and looked at Mark's list. He picked up a pen and addressed Fred and Tom. 'Right, shall we go through this and get it sorted out?'

The two men nodded in agreement and Lewis read the list out loud, making amendments as they went.

'What's the score with the two Joseph brothers? Be handy to have them about to manage the regeneration of Clifford's fields,' said Fred.

Lewis leant back in his chair. 'Old Ted Joseph would have loved that; he'd be beside himself with joy seeing Clifford having to change. I'll see if Pen is about, she might know.'

*

Pen's phone rang.

'Hello, Dad. No, I'm with Mum, Fran and Wendy. We're talking about Tom and Fran's options for their apartment. You can join us if you'd like... I'll take that as a no then.

'How did the meeting go? That sounds good... Seems

there are some problems with the Canadian jobs and the boys probably won't go now until the new year. I also think they're concerned at leaving their mum on her own... Yes, I think they might stay if asked, depends on the job. Yes, regenerating Clifford's land and running the combined farming land would I think be tempting. Nick Hughes would be pleased. He only said to me the other day in many ways he was dreading Clifford's land returning to the estate with so much already going on... OK, catch up later. Bye.'

'Was that your dad?'

'Yes, the meeting went well. It's now all about the detail, but he sounded very positive. He's with Fred and Tom discussing it now.'

'That's good news,' Charlotte said enthusiastically. 'Imagine the estate whole again after over a thousand years.'

'When it's done, we must tell Lord Brandon,' Pen said quietly.

'Tell who? There's another lord?' Wendy questioned, looking confused.

'Brandon was lord a thousand years ago and would have been impacted by the loss of the land,' Charlotte explained.

Wendy looked perplexed. 'How do you tell someone who has been dead for a thousand years?'

'The flesh may be dead, but the spirit lives on,' answered Fran, looking at Charlotte, who warmly nodded her agreement.

Wendy looked at Fran open-mouthed. 'What did you

say, what nonsense was that?' she said, shock and tension showing on her face.

'Wendy, Fran is right, there is much here you have not seen or had a chance to understand,' Charlotte said, learning forward towards Wendy, who looked very unhappy.

*

Charles felt slightly giddy again. He breathed deeply and felt hot, and decided he would go straight to the bedroom to lie down. He went up the back stairs as they were nearest, breathing heavily as he climbed slowly, feeling quite out of breath when he got to the first-floor landing. He reached their bedroom and went in, got some water and sat in one of the comfy chairs with relief and a deep sigh.

*

'Sir.' Graham came into the room. 'Sorry if I'm interrupting, I've just taken a call from

Inspector Collins. She'd like to visit on Monday to interview family and staff in

respect of the ongoing enquiries into the death of Henry Campbell-Blyth. If you have any questions, she's said please call her straight back.'

Lewis looked serious. 'Gents, I think we are done here for the moment, I'll get this typed up.' Fred and Tom got up to leave. 'Tom, please stay. Graham, can you track down Charlotte and ask her to join us, please. Lastly, this needs typing up please.'

'Of course, sir.'

*

Graham went back into his own office. He tried Charlotte's mobile, but not unusually it was not available, so he put a staff-wide message out asking for Charlotte to call him. As he waited, he looked at the scrawled page Lewis had given him and decided this was a job for another day, not Friday afternoon in the heat. Tomorrow morning, it wouldn't take five minutes. Graham's house phone rang.

'Hello, Graham speaking... Hello, Charlotte, thanks for calling. Lewis has asked if you could join him in his study. There's been a call from the police about Henry Campbell-Blyth... Yes, I did try your mobile, but it's either off or out of battery...don't worry, it easily happens, I'll tell Lewis you're on your way.'

Charlotte felt a bit embarrassed and stupid. Her phone was once again not working; Lewis had been annoyed the last time it had happened earlier in the week. She left Pen, Fran and Wendy discussing fabrics and colour schemes. Charlotte found Wendy hard work, and had picked up the friction between her and Fran, which was a shame, and she felt sorry for Fran. She decided the outcome would probably be they would not see Wendy and Charles as much as they might have done.

'Sorry, have you been waiting long?' Charlotte bustled into Lewis's study and sat down. 'Hi, Tom, good meeting, I understand?'

'Yes, Mum, certainly the basis of an agreement there.'

'Charlotte,' Lewis interrupted, 'the police want to do some interviews in relation to Henry's death. I thought it would be a good idea if you were here when I call the Inspector back.'

Charlotte nodded and Lewis put his phone on speaker and dialled the Inspector. A couple of rings and the call was answered.

'Inspector Collins.'

'Lewis Woodcoombe, returning your call.'

'Thank you, I'd like to come to the estate on Monday morning and conduct some interviews in relation to our investigation. Let me give you more details. We have identified eight attacks on women in the area by Henry, mostly through forensics. Two of the girls were unsolved deaths, and they were both in the local papers. One was certainly killed, murdered after the rape.' The Inspector paused for breath. One girl was a seasonal worker and another a girl from Australia, backpacking round Europe.

'Eight girls!' exclaimed Lewis.

'Yes, at least, we are still looking at other cases and there will be some incidents unreported that will inevitably come out with all the press attention. This is a major case, hence it's in the national papers. We'd like to interview your daughter, Penelope, who we believe was engaged to Henry, and Rachel Provo, who works for you. Now, this is the tricky bit. We'd like to talk to anyone else who had any kind of incident with Henry. We are trying to build a full picture of his activities. I will be conducting the interviews accompanied by a female detective constable and a specialist female doctor to offer assistance and support should it be needed.'

'Charlotte here, Inspector, so you want us to ask all the staff if they had any incidents with Henry?'

'Yes, please, family and staff. We quite expect there will have been other incidents with the amount of time he spent with you.'

Charlotte didn't know what to say, but she felt a cold shiver at the thought of what might have happened.

'Thank you, Inspector, I think we understand, we'll make sure you have some private space. What time on Monday?'

'We'd like to start at ten o'clock. We will get to you at about nine o'clock as you will probably have further questions.'

'Thank you, Inspector, see you Monday,' Charlotte said with a slight quiver in her voice.

'Thank you, everyone, I know this is difficult, and really appreciate your help and understanding.' The line went dead.

'Charlotte, you OK dealing with this?' Lewis said gently with concern.

Tom remained silent.

'Yes, I'll talk to Pen and Rachel. This is not going to be easy for either of them, or anyone else.'

'Or you, my dear, having to listen to all this stuff.'

'Lewis, can we gather all the female members of staff across the estate and family so I can talk to them together?'

'I'll ask Graham to organise. When do you want to meet?'

'As soon as possible. Tomorrow morning ideally, say nine-thirty.'

~ 51 ~

Charles could see the barbeque being set up by staff from their bedroom window. At seven o'clock people started arriving. The drawing room and sitting room French doors were all open, as was the small dining room Fran had discovered in the morning. Trays of welcome drinks were held by the girls. Emma held a tray of champagne flutes, bubbly and golden, that sparkled in the sun which was already heading for the horizon.

Wendy had decided they would leave their room at seven-fifteen. She didn't want to be standing around looking lost. She had moaned about what to wear and was horrified when Charles told her there were men and women wearing shorts, and incredulous when he added one of the girls was wearing a crop top. As he stood at the window, he could hear Wendy still complaining, muttering and moaning as she paced up and down their room, angry at what, he didn't know, but she clearly wasn't happy about the barbeque. He couldn't hear what she was saying, just her droning, complaining tone.

'Come on, Charles,' Wendy called. 'Time to go.' As she walked to the door, Charles followed. They walked together down the main stairs into the hall and onto the Vale, joining the happy, humming barbeque throng, which rang with the sound of clinking glasses and greetings in the warm early evening light.

Wendy took a glass of champagne, and a soft drink for Charles, which Charles frowned at. *Should never have mentioned I felt giddy again*, he thought.

Charlotte came over with Jen who Charles realised was wearing the crop top he'd seen earlier, which had so irritated Wendy.

'What's the meeting about tomorrow? I assume it doesn't involve us.'

'No, just female family and staff who may have come into contact with Henry,' answered Charlotte.

Charles noticed Jen looked uneasy and fidgeted with her glass at the mention of Henry's name.

'Terrible business. I was listening to it on the news earlier, eight girls, two dead,' Wendy said almost dismissively. 'Perhaps if they had been a bit more careful...some girls seem to go out of their way to attract the wrong attention,' she said, glancing at Jen in her crop top and short shorts with a disapproving look.

'Yes, of course, Wendy, country girls just sit around bored, waiting to be raped,' Charlotte spat back.

Jen stood listening, looking embarrassed and uneasy, shifting her weight from leg to leg. Charles looked equally uneasy at his wife's opinions and he hoped she wouldn't make it worse.

'Those girls just need to get jobs and knuckle down,

stop spending what money they have on drink and drugs,' Wendy casually added.

Charlotte swirled around and took Jen's arm, clearly angry.

'Come on, Jen, let's find your father. Have a good evening, Wendy, your empathy and concern does you proud.'

With that, Charlotte walked off into the crowd, towing Jen behind her.

'How rude,' was all Wendy could say, clearly surprised.

Charles rolled his eyes; it was only a matter of time before his wife offended someone, he thought, and now she had, in some style.

'What do you think, Charles?'

'Trouble is, you believe everything you read in the *Daily Messenger*. It can be quite extreme at times.'

'You're supposed to support me, Charles, not come to her defence,' said Wendy.

'Not when you're wrong, Wendy, and you just cause offence.'

'Hello, Charles, I was just looking for you.' A cheerful Fred Connell stepped from the growing crowd. 'Sorry, am I interrupting anything?'

'No, no, I was just telling Charles I have a headache. I'm going back to our room and will see him later.' Wendy paused and glanced down at the bottle of red wine and two glasses Fred carried. 'Charles, don't drink too much and don't forget your pills at nine o'clock.'

'Don't worry, I'll look after him,' the ever-cheerful Fred said with a grin.

Wendy walked off towards the house without another word.

'Sorry, Charles, did I come at a bad time?' Fred asked, watching Wendy walking purposefully away.

'No, you probably saved one of us, probably me, from saying something they'd really regret.'

'Ah, good, shall we find somewhere to sit? We can then give this a try.' Fred raised the bottle and waved it gently in front of Charles. 'This way,' he said, heading towards the sitting room doors. Charles followed, pleased to be rescued, wondering how things might play out with Wendy later or, most likely, in the morning.

'Dad.' Charles stopped and saw Fran squeezing through the crowd towards him.

'What's happened? I've just been talking with Jen and it seems Mum and Charlotte have had a bit of a dust up?'

'A misunderstanding, your mother was very insensitive, you know how she can get, especially on things she doesn't really understand and only has half an idea about.' Charles put his hand on Fran's arm and gave it a squeeze. 'I'm sure we can fix it.'

'Maybe, Dad, but I've never seen Charlotte so annoyed or so upset, she is usually so tolerant and understanding.'

'That's something else that annoys your mother. I'm sure you can guess her reaction to some of the things going on here?'

'Yes,' said Fran weakly. 'I can imagine.'

'The important thing is to make sure none of this impacts you and Tom. It'll look better in the morning; these things always do.'

'Thanks, Dad, where are you two off to?' Fran curiously asked her dad and Fred, who looked back at her like two naughty school boys caught getting up to no good.

'We're off to find a seat and test His Lordship's wine for him,' Fred said with a grin, waving the bottle again.

'I could do with a sit down and the wine is tempting. I have my pills, don't worry, I won't be late to bed.'

'Love you, Dad.' Fran turned and disappeared back into the crowd.

'She's a great girl.'

'Thank you, Fred. You're right. Although we don't always see eye to eye, which on reflection is usually my fault.'

Fred slapped Charles on the back as the two walked towards the sitting room doors. Fred led the way inside to two comfy chairs. There weren't many people in the sitting room, mainly people popping into the bar.

'Here we go,' Fred said as he placed the two glasses, he'd been carrying on the small table and reverently poured the silky, deeply coloured red liquid. 'It's a 2005 Bordeaux.'

'Assume that was a good year, Fred?'

'Yes, and fortunately Lewis doesn't mind me choosing the odd bottle from the cellar.'

Charles picked up the glass, swirled the wine and watched the fine liquid flow smoothly around the inside of his glass. He raised the glass to his nose and inhaled its aroma then took a long sip, a rich, smooth, delicate, slightly peppery taste of blackberry and plum caressing his palate. He relaxed in his chair, allowing the red liquid to flow into him as he took another sip and sighed with satisfaction.

'I told you it was good,' an equally satisfied Fred said as he took another sip.

'You work at Cotton's; don't you run one of the investment divisions?'

Charles looked up at Fred in surprise. 'Yes, that's right, how do you know that?'

'Lewis asked me to do a bit of research on you, which proved rather interesting.'

'Do you always do that on your guests?'

'Charles, it's very basic stuff. For example, we're doing a bit of research into Amelia's family in Scotland. Might be interesting, especially as she sounded like she would be happy to return there. It's just good to know these things. You never know when it may be

useful.'

'So, what have you found out about me then?' Charles said, now leaning forward in his chair, intrigued at what Fred might say.

'You run the UK/Europe team, which has got progressively more difficult since Brexit, but you've turned in record profits for the last five years. You really should be on the main board, but for some reason you're not. I noticed your name is on nearly all the major investment prospectuses and papers Cotton's issues, which is interesting. I found you responded to Thomas's original paper on natural resource economics some years ago. You were quite dismissive at the time, but I guess it's different now?' Fred paused to sip his wine.

'My main job, other than running my team, is getting any capital-raising projects for clients in shape for market.'

'You certainly do that, Charles; I couldn't find one you had been involved with that had failed. But my real interest is the environmental aspect you seem particularly good at greenwashing.'

Charles sat up in a bit of a huff. 'We take a realistic approach and factor in environmental costs to the overall costs. If we listened to our green friends the projects would become uneconomic.'

'Listen,' Fred said, 'you've turned a complete deaf ear to the issues. The world is changing and I see even the Australian government is raising questions about some of the projects Cotton's have handled.'

'Yes, you're right, it's getting more difficult; public opinion is starting to drive politics and business sentiment everywhere.'

'It doesn't help the way some of your clients' work. The Harold incident where they paid a bunch of local rednecks to burn out the local native population, then moved straight in and started to strip-mine their sacred tribal lands, before the authorities could act.'

'Allegedly paid,' Charles fired back, wondering where Fred was going.

'Well, the government took a different view of your client, as did public opinion. Then there's the bearded brown moth episode on the North Coast. You said all the right things in the prospectus about preservation and then your client did nothing about it and additionally pushed tons of spoil into the ocean that affected the reefs. The government acted that time after your customer wiped out their habitat and damaged the reef.'

'An operational issue, not our problem,' Charles responded.

'Something went wrong. I particularly liked the company's defence lawyer's first comment at the enquiry. 'We're talking about a bug nobody has heard of and even fewer people care about.' No wonder they got stuck with a record fine. Charles, there is a definite pattern, you build in some spurious environmental costs, with a greenwashed report, but your customer often has little or no intention of spending the money or doing anything.'

'I have to admit, Fred, I'm not always happy with the way our customers act, but we are not the only arbiter on how or if any project should proceed. I have felt at times like I've got blood on my hands, which no one should have to carry. To be honest, I'm tired and I think it's probably time to retire.' Charles looked at his watch. Time for his pills. 'Fred, could you get me a glass of water, please?'

'Of course, old boy.'

Charles could have taken his tablets with his wine but that felt wrong, even though they all landed up in the same place.

'Interesting chat, Fred, but I really need my bed now.' With that, Charles got up and turned to Fred. 'Goodnight, Fred we must talk again sometime.'

Charles walked out of the sitting room into the corridor

he'd walked down with Fran earlier in the day. He passed Simon and Tom's office and paused for a moment thinking about his morning call with Marcus Cotton. *You could just walk away*, he thought to himself. He went up the back stairs to the first floor and their room. As he eased the door open, he could hear Wendy's gentle nasal snore. He quietly undressed and slipped into bed. Wendy stirred slightly. 'Is that you, Robert?' she muttered and then returned to her snoring.

Who the fuck is Robert? Charles thought, but didn't feel any concern. Perhaps he would need more courage than he thought over the next few days. Charles settled into his pillow with a feeling everything was changing around him.

~ 52 ~

Saturday, 12th July. Fran hadn't expected a call from her mother, especially one asking if she had a small bag she could borrow.

She dressed quickly and walked the short distance to her parents' room. When she entered, she found her mum dressed and a small pile of clothes on the bed. 'That's what I'm taking. My other clothes can follow in due course.' Fran noticed a determined, resolute tone in her mother's voice and look on her face.

'What's going on, Mum?' said Fran.

'I'm leaving! After last night and everything else I think it's for the best for everyone, especially you.'

'Don't be silly, Mum, it was just a misunderstanding, which can easily be sorted out.'

'No, I went too far, not only with Charlotte, but with your father, wherever he is.'

Fran looked around the room. 'Where is Dad?' a now concerned Fran asked.

'I don't know. He left an odd note before I was awake this morning.'

'Can I read it?'

'Yes, please do, perhaps you can make sense of it.'

Fran picked up the folded paper with 'Wendy' written on one side.

'It says he's gone for an early breakfast, something he has to do. What's wrong with that?'

'God knows, he doesn't talk to me anymore.'

'Stay and talk it through with Dad, where would you go, Mum?'

'I'm going to stay with Miriam for a couple of nights, then go back home and try and talk to your father about where he and I are going.'

'Crickey, didn't realise you two had problems and it was this bad,' Fran said sadly.

'I don't think your father does either.'

'How are you getting back?'

'On the train, next one's in half an hour.'

'While you pack your bag, I'll go and get my car and drive you to the station. Meet you outside in five minutes.'

'OK, darling.'

It took Fran a bit longer than she expected to fetch the car and she found her mother
standing outside. As Fran drove, she wondered aloud, 'What shall I tell Dad?'

'Tell him whatever you like. I'd be interested in what he says. Please give my apologies to Charlotte and Lewis, make up some excuse if you have to.'

Fran didn't reply, but felt angry at her mother, a feeling she usually reserved for her dad. They pulled up at the station and Fran accompanied Wendy as she bought her ticket and walked to the London platform. They only had to wait five minutes for the train. Fran saw her mother safely into the carriage and waved as the train pulled away. 'I'll call you later to make sure you got to London alright,' were Fran's last words before the door to the carriage closed. She now wanted to see her dad, and find out what was going on.

*

Wendy watched Fran wave and disappear as the train pulled away and the view gave way to green sprawling countryside. She sighed deeply, feeling a sense of relief at having made a decision. *No going back now*, she realised with a feeling of anxiety and excitement. She took her phone out of her bag. No messages. She went to her contacts, scrolled down, pressed a number and waited for it to be answered.

'Hello... Robert... I'm on a train to London, could you pick me up from the station? Oh, sorry, I'll hang on while you serve him...I've left him...Can I stay at yours for a few days? OK. I'll get a taxi from the station to the shop... Robert, you're so naughty, I'll see you soon.'

Wendy giggled at what Robert had said. As she put her phone back in her bag she sighed again, but this time more from contentment than anxiety. Robert didn't say no, in fact he said she could stay as long as she wanted. It would be different to the monthly book club meetings with furtive glances across the upstairs room at the Goose and Duck, and the quick, secret, fleeting touch during the break or at the end of the evening. Her Sunday morning visits to his flat above his shop, when everyone thought she was playing tennis, were the most exciting.

Wendy sat watching the countryside slide by, the city outskirts gradually replacing the green fields, and finally London arrived.

Charles walked into the dining room and saw Lewis, Fred and Tom sitting at the table.

'Good morning, do you mind if I join you?'

'Not at all, Charles, please take a seat,' said Lewis waving Olivia over to take Charles' breakfast order.

They sat in silence as Charles ordered boiled eggs and a coffee. No one spoke until Olivia had vanished to the kitchen to wrestle with the coffee machine again.

'Charles, we're just finalising the letter to Clifford, confirming everything from our meeting,' Fred said, leaning forward over the table and waving his last piece of toast in the air.

'We've had it typed up and we're just giving it a final review before it's delivered,' added Lewis, clearly pleased.

'You've given him everything he's asked for?'

'Yes, Charles, and a little bit more, this is a big moment,' Lewis said.

Olivia returned with Charles' coffee and boiled eggs and placed them on the table.

'Can I get anyone anything else?' she asked brightly.

'Another tea for me, please, anyone else?' Lewis replied.

Both Tom and Fred said no and Olivia turned to serve someone else.

'Are you alright, Charles?' Fred asked with concern as Charles struggled to peel one of his eggs.

'Not really, I didn't sleep well and I'm not feeling a hundred per cent. As I said last night, I feel some of my deals have left me with blood on my hands, which is not a good feeling and I want to atone, so Fred, I'm on my own road to Damascus. Had a very odd call with my boss, Marcus Cotton, before we drove here yesterday which I'm still processing.'

Charles finished his coffee, but left one boiled egg and his toast untouched, got up and left the dining room.

Tom followed Charles, leaving Lewis and Fred in deep conversation.

*

Fran returned to the estate, worrying at what was going on. She parked her car and walked quickly back to the house. She called Tom on the way.

'Tom, did you see Dad this morning? How did he seem?'

'I had breakfast with him, just helped him back to his room, he's not feeling too good. I left him on his bed resting, no sign of Wendy.'

'Thanks, Tom, I'll go straight to his room, be there in five.' Fran speeded up as she neared the house.

Fran found Tom sitting looking thoughtful in her parents' bedroom. She told Tom about her mother leaving. Tom looked shocked.

Charles was sitting looking tired and confused.

'Where's your mother?' he asked, looking up at Fran.

Fran swallowed hard before speaking. 'Dad, Mum has left.' She didn't really know how else to tell him and, as the news fell out of her mouth, it made her wince.

Charles' shoulders sagged down further. 'Home?'

'She said she's going to stay with Miriam for a couple of nights, then come home to talk.'

'Miriam,' Charles said slowly, rolling the name in his mind. 'Ah yes, that's who she plays tennis with on Sunday mornings.'

'Tennis?' said a surprised Fran.

'Yes, she started about six months ago, someone she met at her book club.'

Fran looked perplexed. 'A bit athletic for Mum, and she's never mentioned it to me.'

'Well, she comes home sweaty and tired early Sunday afternoon, so something is going on and it seems to do her good. I can imagine she loves the tennis set down there; a couple of gins and a gossip after a game is probably what she enjoys best.' Charles forced a smile, finding it as hard as Fran to visualise Wendy running around a court.

'All a bit odd,' Fran said thoughtfully, sitting next to her father, holding his hand with one hand, stroking it gently with the other.

'Is it? It's been pretty strained between us for some time. It's my fault, the job is constant.'

'Mum said you'd mentioned retiring?'

'Yes, I think it's time to go. I actually think they want

me out. Your mother seemed quite concerned when I suggested we go on a long cruise.'

Fran didn't say anything, just squeezed her father's hand, which he appreciated as he closed his eyes. He felt so tired.

'Let's get you back to our room to rest. Have you eaten?'

'Had a coffee and boiled egg with Tom, I'm just tired.'

Fran and Tom helped Charles back to their room. Fran got him to lie down on the bed and covered him with a blanket. 'Have you had your pills?' Fran asked gently.

'No,' Charles rasped as he fought sleep.

Tom fetched Charles' pills. There was a note in Wendy's handwriting which detailed Charles' pills to be taken twice a day. Tom waved a concerned Fran over as he sorted out the morning dose. 'Fran, you'd better check this.'

'OK, yes, we don't want to poison him by accident.' They smiled weakly at Fran's bad joke.

Tom left Fran watching her father sleep, reading again her mother's pill note. Charles had a consultant's appointment on Tuesday morning, which he needed taking to. Fran and Tom discussed it quickly and decided Fran could drive Charles back on Monday evening, stay over and take him to his appointment. Tom would drive the mini back at the same time and see the removers into the flat on Tuesday morning.

Tom left. Fran sat quietly with her father, watching his steady breathing, his face relaxing as he slept. She suddenly remembered they were supposed to be meeting

Isaac at eleven. She glanced at her watch, then decided she could leave her father asleep for a while and hurried out the room.

Isaac was lounging casually against the wall as usual, seemingly untroubled by either the heat or the wait.

'Hello, Francesca.' He paused and looked up at the sky. 'The weather's changing, we could see rain.'

'Really?' Fran looked at the sky. To her it looked as clear and blue as usual.

'Trouble is, Francesca, we get too much all at once and it causes floods and is as much a problem as the heat.'

'Isaac, I'm sorry, my parents won't be able to make it today, Dad's not feeling well.'

'Your mother?'

'She's left.'

'Oh, I hope everything is alright.'

'Yes, fine thank you,' Fran lied.

'Would you like to walk with me? 'Isaac asked sympathetically.

'Sorry, not today, I have to get back and look after dad. Providing he's alright we'll be at the muster tomorrow.'

Isaac smiled warmly as he left Fran and walked towards the woods on his own.

~ 54 ~

Charles felt a bit groggy when he woke. He'd slept heavily. First time he'd slept well for some time. He saw Fran sitting smiling at him.

'How you feeling, sleepy head?'

'Much better, but still tired. I think worry eats away at you.' Charles yawned and sat up. Fran pushed his pillows up behind him as he sat back.

'What's worrying you, Dad?' Fran sat on the side of the bed and took her father's hand.

'Your mother, work, and you.' Charles closed his eyes and sighed.

'I didn't realise you and Mum had problems. What's up with work? Don't worry about me, I'm OK.'

Charles opened his eyes and squeezed her hand. 'Ever since I started talking about retiring your mother's been in a panic and we just don't seem to talk anymore. Work is getting more and more difficult and our clients more desperate. I have ghosts haunting me from the things I've done. I need to get out. I feel I'm losing you sometimes. I have treated Tom terribly.'

'Dad, stop, I'm sure it can all be solved, and don't

worry about me or Tom. What's this about work? You could easily retire.' Fran leant forward and kissed Charles on the forehead warmly. 'Now rest.'

'No, first I must explain. I've done things for clients who really don't care who they hurt or what they do, as long as they make a turn. Now these events are haunting me. Last night Fred reminded me of few things that have happened directly due to our success in securing capital for certain clients. We know perfectly well what they're like, but we don't care, it's all about the money and nothing else.'

'Dad, I'm so sorry, I never realised. What are you going to do about it?'

'Retire, and try to atone.'

'Why don't you talk to Fred about this and what to do?'

Charles laughed. 'Already spoken to Fred and Lewis and I'm on the road to Damascus.'

'What!' Fran said. 'But before you go anywhere, we have to get you well. Are you hungry? Have you eaten much today?'

'Not really. I can't face going down to the dining room for lunch.' Charles squeezed Fran's hand.

'Don't worry, Dad, we can sort everything out. I'll pop down to the kitchen and get something for the two of us.'

'Are you sure?'

'No problem.' Fran stood up, sliding her hand out of her father's light grip.

Fran walked down the main stairs, bumping into Naomi in the hall.

'You, OK? How's your father?' Naomi asked.

'I'm OK, Dad's just tired, I think. I'm going to the kitchen to get some food for us.'

'I'll come with you, give you a hand.'

Fran and Naomi carried trays from the kitchen back to Charles' room. They met Tom on the stairs on their way.

'What's that in your hand?' an inquisitive Fran asked Tom.

Tom lifted the envelope and waved it gently in the air. 'It's our letter to Mark Clifford confirming everything we agreed. Dad asked me to deliver it. I was thinking of walking there and back. Wondered if you'd like to come, if your father's alright.'

'Fran, you go, I can sit with your father,' Naomi said warmly. 'You two go.'

'Are you sure?'

'Yes. I've got nothing planned, so I insist, providing your father is happy.'

'I'm sure he'll be fine.'

'Let's eat first, you two have enough food there for an army,' said Tom.

They found Charles sitting up looking quite awake when they got back to their room. Fran held his arm as he walked from the bed to a chair.

'Good heavens, that's a lot of food,' Charles said as he surveyed the trays.

There was a knock on the door and, when Tom opened it, Olivia entered with another tray.

'Selection of soft drinks and also some desserts, if you have any room after you've finished that lot.' Olivia placed the tray down and left the room, with a casual wave.

'That was good of her,' Fran said as everyone started to tuck in.

Tom took a can of cola and asked what they would like to drink.

Fran was pleased to see her father eating and looking more relaxed. He certainly didn't look as haggard as he had done earlier.

'Dad, after lunch I'm going for a walk with Tom, but Naomi is going to sit with you.'

'OK, that will be nice, you two go.'

Fran was surprised. She thought he'd insist he could be left alone, which might be true, but she didn't want to find out he was wrong.

'OK, Dad, we'll take the trays back down as we go. Do you guys want us to have tea or something sent up?'

'Any chance of a coffee, do you think? 'Charles turned his head to Naomi. 'What would you like?'

'I'll stick to water, but thank you for asking.'

Fran and Tom gathered all the plates and carried the trays down to the kitchen and requested a coffee for Charles.

Olivia went to wrestle with the coffee machine again. *I will master this*, she said to herself.

~ 55 ~

Fran and Tom stepped out from the house onto the drive, turning right up the slight hill past the two sheds on the right, purposely out of sight from the house. Tom took Fran's hand and squeezed it.

'You, OK?'

'Yes, a bit worried about Dad and Mum. I'm also looking forward to getting the move out of the way this week. It's just a shame all this is going on at the same time. That reminds me, I said I'd call Mum to make sure she got back to London safely.' Fran glanced at her phone. 'She must be there by now.'

Fran pressed her mother's number and waited for her to answer. 'Hi, Mum... are you at Miriam's?... Good, your journey was alright then...What are you doing now?... Cup of tea, nice...We'll be driving back late afternoon/early evening Monday. I'll take Dad to his appointment Tuesday morning... Yes, I'll let you know how it goes.' Fran was getting increasingly exasperated with her mother. 'When will you be home?... What do you mean, you don't know? Would have been good if you could be home when we get back from seeing the consultant...You don't know...I don't understand. OK, I'll call you and let you know how it went...Who was that? She has a deep voice and that's an odd thing to say... This is all very strange, Mum. I will call again and update you on Dad...Bye...Love you.

'That sounded a bit strange?' Tom said as Fran put her phone in her back pocket.

'Fuck knows what's going on, she doesn't really seem very interested in how Dad is and just assumes I will look after him.'

'*We* will look after him, it's not all down to you. You have another family now, who will help you and your dad.'

'Thank you. Now let's deliver that letter.' Fran took Tom's hand and they speeded up.

'This is where they found the bodies,' Tom said, pointing to a cleared part of the hedgerow.

'Looks pretty yucky,' Fran said as she peered down at the fetid water, sitting still and quiet with a shiny layer of scum on top reflecting the sky like a badly tarnished mirror. 'What a horrible way to go.'

They came to the entrance to Clifford's Farm marked by a small signpost. Fran and Tom walked up the drive towards the farmhouse.

'Wow, that looks a great place,' Fran said enthusiastically, a broad smile across her face.

'Forget it, it's part of the deal. I thought you'd like it; you'll love the inside.'

The front door opened as they approached.

'Sorry, saw you walking up the drive, nice to see you again, Tom.'

'This is Francesca, my fiancée.'

'You must be Mark. Nice to meet you, please call me Fran, everyone does.' Fran took half a step forward to shake hands. 'And who are you?' Fran bent down and smiled at the little man hiding behind Mark's legs.

'Come on, Fraser. Come out and say hello,' Mark gently coaxed.

Fran bent down further and pushed out her hand. 'Hello, Fraser, are we going to be friends?'

Fraser slowly moved out from behind his father, but looked suspiciously at Fran's extended hand.

'Say hello, Fraser.'

'Hello,' a nervous Fraser shouted out, and then scuttled back behind his father's legs.

'Sorry, he's usually very friendly, but clearly not to-day.'

'We all have days like that,' Fran said.

'I have this for you.' Tom held out the envelope, which Mark took. 'Should have

everything we discussed the other day. Any problems or questions, don't hesitate to call me.'

Mark looked excited as he held the envelope. 'Sorry, I should have asked before—do you want to come in? I can look at this while you are here.'

'No, sorry, we have to get back,' Fran said before Tom could say anything.

'OK, no problem, I will call you if there are any questions.'

'Thanks, Mark, can we get back across the fields?'

'Yes, there's a path runs along the hedgerow this side of the ditch, but you have to cross White Lady's Field. And you will have to walk down all the way to Joseph's Farm before you can turn up to your place.'

'OK, thanks, Mark. We'll go back the way we came, it will be quicker,' Tom said.

It seemed faster going back than getting there and Fran and Tom walked back into house, feeling a bit hot and sticky. It was still warm; stormy, Tom had said, but only the faintest wisps of cloud offering no relief from the sun and heat. No sign of rain.

They found Naomi reading a magazine and Charles back on the bed sleeping again.

'All, OK?' Fran asked.

Naomi looked at her phone to check the time before answering. 'I thought you'd be longer. He's been no trouble; he was fascinated by my family's history and connection to the estate. We then talked about the woods and the connection with it. He sounded disappointed to have missed the walk with my dad today. He then got tired, so I helped him back onto the bed and he's been asleep for a good half an hour.'

Fran looked at her father sleeping peacefully in relief. There was a knock on the door.

'Come in,' Tom responded.

Rachel entered. 'Do you need anything?'

'Tea would be good, please,' Tom quickly replied.

'Tea for three?'

Everyone nodded as Rachel left.

'Guess we'll be having dinner in here tonight?' Tom said, looking at the sleeping Charles.

'We can tell Rachel when she comes back with the tea,' Fran suggested.

Rachel returned with tea and biscuits.

'Thank you, Rachel, three of us for dinner in here this evening please, I don't think Fran's dad will be up to the dining room tonight.'

'No problem and quite understand.'

'Thank you,' said Tom as Rachel left the room.

Naomi left after a cup of tea. Fran sat next to her sleeping father. Tom fidgeted, unable to settle.

'What are you reading?' Fran asked, seeing Tom sitting in a comfy chair looking focused.

'It's Fred's draft plan for the estate following his conversations with Dad, he gave it to us this morning at breakfast. It's become obvious we need a clear plan of what we are doing. Especially important now with the return of Joseph's and Clifford's Farms. Lots to do.'

'So, what does he say then?' a now curious Fran asked, putting down her magazine to listen.

'Fred proposes our plans should spin off three things: water, energy and food.'

Fran nodded, not noticing her father stir and open his eyes.

Tom continued, flicking back through the report to remind himself of the key points. 'Water. Restore the old lake, dig another, divert the river back to its original course through the estate, let it meander, like it used to do. Introduce beavers at the head of the cut and above

Woodcoombe Village to further control the flow of the river. The beavers would, at first glance, seem the most difficult part of the plan. But all this and other measures should slow the river and help reduce and stop the flooding at Woodend, New Wood, the estate and further down towards the sea. And store water for the estate in the lakes.' Tom stopped and drew a breath. Fran didn't know what to say.

'So, who will pay for all that, then?' Charles said sleepily as he tried to lever himself up from his sleeping position.

'You're clearly feeling better, Dad,' Fran mocked lightly, pleased to hear her father sound more like himself.

'Good question, Charles. With all of this, most of the money will come from the family and charity. We may get government funding as well, for flood prevention. The council might also have flood prevention funds for some bits. There's more to the plan.'

'Go on, Tom, it's really interesting.' Charles waved as Fran arranged his pillows and helped him sit up.

'Energy. While Lewis's original idea of a giant industrial turbine has been turned down several times, we believe, with the addition of Joseph's and Clifford's land, we could install three, maybe four, smaller turbines which could only be seen on the estate. With the prevailing southwest wind coming up the Vale they should produce more than enough power for the whole estate and possibly beyond. We can store it and even earn income, passing surplus on to the national grid. In theory this all adds up. We need to get into the detail, but it all sounds promising.' Tom stopped and looked at Fran and Charles, who were staring at him.

'Yes, all very interesting, but what you really need is a mine. You're sure there's no coal deposits hidden away somewhere under your land? I also understand peat burns really well. Fracking?'

Fran playfully slapped her father, and he pulled away in mock fear.

'I think you're missing the point, Dad.'

'I'm only joking, at Cotton's we would decline working on renewable energy projects, as it felt like working with the enemy.'

'There's more,' Tom continued, now on a roll. 'Food. With the return to the estate of Joseph's and Clifford's Farms, and we mustn't forget the purchase of Long Farm, which will be renamed, we believe we can become food self-sufficient within the next five years. The intention is for organic regenerative farming with very high eco-logical standards and requirements, so in many ways Joseph's Farm is the template for the future.'

'So, from what I understand listening to your father and Fred you're going back to go forward.'

'You're right, Charles, but with some up-to-date think-ing and science sprinkled into the mix it's estimated it will take three years to get Clifford's fields to where we want them. We can consolidate the livestock farming and integrate that with the wilding introductions being considered.'

'Do we have the knowledge to do this to the land?' asked a curious Fran.

'We think the Joseph brothers might stay. Their Canada plans seem to have faltered. There are others we can bring in who Fred's team have already spoken to for advice and opinions. Some of the lab projects will support this work.'

'How big is Fred's team?' asked Charles.

'Six strong, I believe. One last thing before I shut up, which I think is interesting, we will possibly need our own mill and bakery. We could build a windmill, a watermill or power it from the wind turbines. It's amazing what new options start popping up with this plan.'

Tom and Fran moved the table to the window and brought up three chairs so they could sit together at dinner.

There was a knock at the door and Anna came in. 'This was hand-delivered for you, sir,' she said, handing an envelope to Tom. He opened it and, to his delight, he saw the Clifford offer letter, agreed and counter-signed.

'Is that what I think it is?' Fran asked excitedly.

'Yes, all agreed and signed.'

'We should invite the whole family over for lunch or something.'

'Good idea, but first I must tell my father.' Tom got up and briskly left the room.

'That's the meeting you went to, Dad, it's all agreed, the deal is done.'

'That's good, it seemed very important to everyone.'

'You have no idea how important.'

Tom returned in ten minutes. 'I've left Dad bouncing at the news. Charles, I got you this as I think you're going to the mustering tomorrow.' Tom passed Charles a book; a *History of the Royal Archers*.

'Thanks, Tom, Naomi talked a bit about this when you two were out, very intriguing. Tell me, why are the archers still maintained?'

'It's a requirement of the Royal Charter. In theory, if we don't, we could lose all the land, but it's a key part of our history and who we are.'

'Could I have a look through it? There's much I don't know,' Fran asked.

Charles muttered yes, already flicking through the pages.

'I'll get another copy; we have boxes of them. Something to drink with dinner? We have something to celebrate. Some bubbly?'

'I'd prefer a glass of red, if I'm honest,' Charles said.

'You're clearly feeling better, Dad. Some bubbles would be nice, Tom.'

'Bubbles and red wine coming up.' Tom got up and left the room again.

He returned with a half-bottle of champagne covered in condensation from its chilling, and a half-bottle of red wine.

Charles looked at the small bottle sadly.

'Father tells me that's as good as any wine in the cellar, ideal for a couple of glasses in the evening.' Tom watched Charles examine the label with a shrug and smile before Tom uncorked the bottle.

'You're definitely better then,' Fran said to her father as she held ready two glasses as Tom opened the champagne.

'To the estate, Woodcoombe,' Tom toasted.

'Woodcoombe,' Fran and Charles responded.

'Let me see if I can remember...' Fran said.

> 'We give our fealty to lord, liege and land.
>
> Our blood runs deep, strong and true in root and vein.
>
> By the bow, by the land we stand, united, until the end.
>
> By our blood and the spirits of man and land our promise is made.'

'Hooray!' Tom shouted. 'Well done, well remembered.'

Charles looked confused. 'I'm sure that's in the book you gave me.'

'Yes, it is. I've got you a copy, Fran.' Tom pointed to the book sitting on the table.

There was a knock on the door. Tom opened it and Rachel and Olivia glided in with dinner.

The three of them sat down. The dinner conversation was driven by Charles asking lots of questions about Fred's plan. Fran had never seen Tom so relaxed with her dad. They talked all through dinner and after, until her father looked tired.

'Time for bed, I think,' said Fran. 'Will you be OK on your own?'

'What? Yes, I think so.' Charles replied, a bit tired and confused. 'I've got my phone if there's a problem.'

'OK, leave your door unlocked and I will look in later just to check.'

'See you in the morning. Thank you, love you. Goodnight.'

*

As ever, Fran fell asleep quickly. Tom looked through the archer's history book he'd brought up for Fran. There was always some fact he'd forgotten. Before he went to sleep, he quickly checked on Charles, who was sleeping peacefully.

~ 56 ~

Sunday, 13th July. Tom woke early, before the alarm, and got up and checked on Fran's father again, who was still sleeping peacefully.

Fran was woken by Tom moving about. She stretched and then stumbled, still half asleep, to have a shower. When she came out of the bathroom her phone rang. 'Dad,' she said as she picked it up. She chatted for a moment and then put the phone down thoughtfully. 'He wanted to know where Mum was, which was a bit awkward. I've told him we're going to breakfast before we go to the range and the mustering.'

'I'll bring your car down and put a collapsible chair in the boot for your dad. He won't want to stand for too long.'

'Thanks, Tom, that would be great.'

When Tom had left to get the car, Fran looked at her phone, wondering if it was too early to call her mum. Fran pushed her number and waited for an answer.

'Hello, Wendy's phone.'

'Sorry, who's that? It's her daughter.'

'You, must be Francesca, hello. She's in the shower at the moment, she won't be a moment.'

'Who are you, Miriam's husband?'

'Not exactly, here she comes.'

Fran listened, a bit confused, and heard the same man's voice say, 'It's your daughter, here's the phone, I'll get you a dressing gown.'

'What's going on, Mum?'

Wendy stuttered, 'What, do you mean?'

'Who's that man? What are you doing?'

'He's a relative of Miriam's and also staying.'

'You two sound like you are getting on alright.'

'Don't take that tone with me, young lady. I can understand it might sound a bit odd to you, but everything is alright.'

Fran heard her mother laughing and then saying, 'Stop it, stop it! Wait a minute. I'll be finished soon.'

Fran ended the call as she felt a bit sick at what she was hearing. What was going on, who was this man and what was he doing? Fran felt nauseous again as uninvited possible answers flashed in her mind.

*

To Charles' annoyance, Fran insisted on holding his arm as they descended the main stairs to breakfast. It was busy, as so many were going to the mustering. Fran helped her dad to sit down and got him a plate of food and a coffee from the pot.

'No chance of a proper coffee?' Charles asked. He looked into the cup, disappointed.

'Sorry, not today, dad. Good morning, Charlotte, how are you?'

'Morning Fran, not bad thank you. Assume you're off to the mustering? I'm coming to watch. Trying to get organised for the interviews with the police tomorrow.'

'Can I help in any way?' Fran asked.

'If you could be about, it would be helpful. To my surprise Jen has come forward, which is a worry as she won't speak to me about what happened, so my fears have run wild.' Concern was etched on Charlotte's face.

Fran stepped forward and gave her a hug.

'Thank you, I think I might need more of those to-morrow.'

Fran sat down with her dad to eat and watched Charlotte walk to her seat, trying to appear her usual cheerful self, but Fran noticed she looked tight, and kept rolling her neck as if it was stiff or achy, and she rubbed her forehead, stressed. Fran wondered what secret Jen was holding.

Tom returned from getting the car and had a quick breakfast.

*

Fran drove to the range, her father next to her, Tom in the back. She was surprised to see so many people gathered already. She parked and Tom got the chair out of the back. Fran took her father's arm again, to his irri-tation, as they walked across the range.

'Can my dad join you?' Fran asked a sitting Cath.

'Of course, no problem, glad I'm not the only person sitting. Dan said in my condition I shouldn't be standing for hours. Bad enough I'm not allowed to take part and be a shield maiden, although I guess I'm not a maiden any-more.' Cath laughed at her own joke. Charles, looked embarrassed as he sat down in the chair Tom had set up.

'Hi, everyone.' Holly walked up with Cody trotting along beside her. 'Would you mind looking after Cody while I'm at the muster? He's had a walk and done his business so shouldn't be any problem.'

'Hello, boy.' Charles leant forward and tickled Cody behind his ears as he reached up with his other hand to take the lead. Cody backed himself under Charles' chair and made himself comfortable.

'Right, that's sorted, thank you so much, he's a very good dog.' Holly turned and walked towards the gathering crowd.

'Fran!' Cath called, getting up from her seat.

'Yes? Crikey, you're showing now, Cath.'

'Since I discovered I'm pregnant it seems to have popped out. Dan is so excited, I'm

worried he might burst. Fran, can I ask you something?'

'Of course, fire away.'

'Please, tell me if this is a problem.'

'Whatever it is, I'm sure it won't be.'

'We'd like to use Pen's September date to get married, unless you are going to use it.'

'That's not a problem. We're thinking next year, so no issue at all, Cath.'

'Brilliant, thank you, Dan will be so excited.'

Cath sat down and turned to Charles.

'And you must come too, Mr Clarke.'

Charles looked flustered; he'd been quite happy just eavesdropping on the conversation. 'Only if you call me Charles and I can bring my new friend,' Charles said as he stroked Cody.

'Charles, you can bring whoever you like.'

'Dad, I must go, they're starting soon.' Charles took Fran's hand and pulled her nearer. 'Any thoughts when you and Tom might get married?' he asked quietly.

'We haven't set an actual date. Broadly thinking late spring, early summer next year, give us time to settle in here.'

'Just wondered. I think I'll last that long.'

'Don't talk like that, there's plenty of life left in you yet. Sorry, Dad, I have to go.'

'See you later, have fun.'

Fran walked away thoughtfully. It was the first time she'd heard her Dad talk like that. Perhaps he was more worried than she thought. Maybe now rested he'd been thinking about the situation. She was surprised then that he hadn't mentioned her mum. Maybe that was next?

As Fran walked, she saw Isaac waving. He came over to her and Tom.

'Hi, you two, I wanted to catch you before we started. There's a couple of people I'd like you to meet.'

Isaac steered Fran and Tom to a small group of men talking to Pen and Naomi.

'Gentlemen, can I introduce you to Lord Lewis's son, Thomas, and his fiancée, Francesca. As heir, Thomas is captain of the archers. He has just returned to the estate, having been away for a while.'

'Nice to meet you both. I'm Captain Smith; I look after all the reservist and territorial units in the south of England. The General nudged me to visit before his formal inspection, additionally after the King's recent visit. He asked if the archers could be used in ceremonial duties. *The Scottish Royal Company of Archers* already undertake ceremonial duties, no reason why we can't have an English company.'

'Nice to meet you, Captain,' Fran said as she shook hands.

'And this is my wife, Klara, who's from Sweden, but her ancestors were Danish and could have been part of the raiding party that pursued Ethelred, but more likely would have been part of the Viking hordes and at the Battle of Stamford Bridge, so she has come along to have a look at what's going on.'

'Hello, Klara, please call me Fran'

'Nice to meet you, Fran,' Klara replied.

Isaac shuffled forward.

'This is Gregory Hepton, who represents all the re-enactment groups taking part.'

'I have already been through most of the details and health and safety issues for Ethelred and the Danish raiding party,' said Gregory. 'We can then plan the Battle of Stamford Bridge re-enactment in detail for next year.'

'I agree with Gregory, the re-enactment is a far more complicated thing to stage safely than any of us thought,' said Pen. Naomi nodded in agreement beside her.

'Thank you, Mr Hepton, that sounds very exciting,' said Tom with a grin.

'Right, let's get the mustering going,' Isaac said, clearly fed up with all the talking.

Isaac stood on a wooden box while Duncan quietened everyone down. Then Isaac explained the plans to the eager faces. 'This is the first muster of shield maidens; the armourer has, hopefully, organised enough spears for everyone today. The bowyer has confirmed that he can make bows for the maidens, but the fletcher will need help making sure there are enough arrows. Ladies, you will need to be a bit patient while we get everything sorted out. But we do want you to be part of the inspection this year.'

Isaac called the archers to form their companies and the shield maidens to stand in front of their archer. There followed a great shuffling around of people finding and taking their places.

'Each shield maiden will need a spear,' Isaac instructed.

Fran's first thought on being handed the spear was that it was bigger and heavier than she expected, but she could do it and was determined not to prove right those doubting archers, who were looking on, smirking.

She found once she had the balance right on her shoulder, the spear was pretty easy to carry. Fran watched some of the others getting organised. Holly was in front of Eddy with a look of determination on her face. Eddy leant forward, put a hand on her shoulder and said something that clearly encouraged her. The forester next to him gave him a playful slap and said something to Eddy through gritted teeth. Not everyone was happy about the shield maidens. Eddy spat something back. Fran saw Noah standing straight and strong in one of the flank companies. To her surprise she saw Emma was his shield maiden. *How'd she manage that?* Fran thought.

They were shown how they would need to place the spear firmly on the ground when instructed and lean the spear forward. The best way was to raise it up and drop it, anchoring the end into the earth. Once done, they would lean the spears forward to create a spear wall in front of the archers.

Tom was very encouraging and soon his company had all its shield maidens organised. Fran looked at all the ladies lined up. They might not be perfect, but they'd all done it and looked determined to carry on. To Fran's disappointment, she saw some in the other companies give up and be replaced. There was, as Isaac had said to her, a surplus of potential shield maidens.

'Spears up,' Tom called.

Fran lifted the spear up on to her shoulder; the others followed her. The archers stood behind their shield maidens; bows slung over their right shoulder.

'Eyes up. All facing this way please,' Tom ordered.

The centre company stood in a line like a strange school crocodile of children with spears and bows rather than bags and coats.

'Steady pace, follow my lead.' Tom started to walk, holding a wooden staff straight above his head. As he led the company forward, he then held the staff out to his left and gently started to turn the column left. Tom glanced over his shoulder and was delighted to see they had lost no one and the company looked pretty good, not perfect, but better than he expected for a first time. He caught Fran's eye and winked at her as she strained with the spear. Tom brought the staff straight above his head again and the column straightened up as they started to march forward, the large number of spectators now lining the range.

Fran was suddenly aware the crowd was clapping. She saw Charlotte and Cath bouncing up and down excitedly. *So much for Cath taking it easy*, Fran thought. Fran felt suddenly emotional. Maidens were now part of two thousand years of history and tradition.

'Halt!' Tom ordered. 'Face right.' Archers and maidens swivelled and now faced the excited crowd.

'Spears set.' Fran slipped the spear from her shoulder with relief. *That's going to be sore in the morning*, she thought, as she raised the spear up then drove its end into the dry ground with a satisfying thump. She then leant forward, lowering the tip in front of the archers. Only one spear was dropped, but quickly picked up

'Archers, stand ready,' Tom said, then walked down the line to inspect the company. *Brilliant,* he thought, and then took his position behind Fran in the middle of the line. He dropped his staff to the ground, raised his hands and started to clap. He looked left and right and nodded to the other archers to join in, who all, having shouldered their bows, did. The crowd joined in enthusiastically. The left flank company came into position and its archers started to clap. The right company arrived looking bit more ragged. Fran saw Gail next to Olivia. Both looked red-faced from the effort, but still determined.

Isaac turned to Captain Smith. 'Would you like to do a quick inspection?'

'Be a pleasure,' the captain replied, 'I can then tell the General everything is in order for the open day and his formal inspection.'

It was a short walk to where the companies were drawn up in front of the crowd.

'Spears, stand easy.' The maidens had to raise the spears up and a couple were dropped with the effort, but quickly recovered. Isaac and the Captain began their inspection. Freya and Gregory walked behind Isaac and the Captain. Gregory looked very excited.

As Isaac and the Captain reached the middle company Fran started in a clear voice heard by all.

>'We give our fealty to lord, liege and land.
>
>Our blood runs deep strong and true in root and vein.'

*

Duncan walked purposely out in front of his companies and urged the archers to join in. Duncan bellowed out the next two lines. Most archers joined in, a few stayed resolutely silent, but the enthusiastic crowd more than made up for any archers' missing voices.

>'By the bow, by the land we stand, united, until the end.
>
>By our blood and the spirits of man and land our promise is made.'

As ever, the promise ended with a huge cheer as well as more clapping from the crowd.

Fran shouted, 'Woodcoombe Valkyries!' and the girls joined in with shouts and screams. The archers looked shocked and stood in silence, some grinning, some shaking their heads in disbelief.

Isaac walked up to Fran. 'I like the Valkyries, we need to sort out the right weapons as well as uniform, not a costume.'

'Yes,' said Fran. 'A good start but let's have a think about next steps. I have some ideas.'

Fran turned from Isaac, feeling the spirits drawn to the archers' passion again. 'Let trees shake and bow to the promise made here today,' she commanded the spirits swirling on the range.

The spirits! Suddenly, Fran had a burst of understanding. These were the spirits of those who had gone before, the spirits who, hundreds of years ago, no, thousands, Fran corrected herself, decided to make their home here and carve out a life on this land. Hunted, felled trees, ploughed and harvested by hand, bore and raised children, watched the sun rise and fall, the moon wax and wane, who felt, lived and died with every twist and turn nature made, fought flood, drought, fire and disease and even battles to survive. Men and women, side by side. Family. But they had found a way to thrive by living with the land and all its elements, they'd learnt its ways, they respected it and lived with it, worshipped it, honoured it, believed in its power and spirits to help them thrive, their families thrived and multiplied. These were the

most powerful spirits of man. Fran felt overwhelmed by
what this meant.

As she looked around, Fran saw a couple of shadowy,
raggedy figures shuffling behind the Captain with his pips
and smart uniform, faint echoes from a distant, vanished
past; a man and a woman, perhaps man and wife, who had
stood together to take on the challenges of those distant
times and, as family, overcame adversity together.

Captain Smith looked up, glanced twice, surprised to
see the trees shake and seemingly reach over the crowd
towards the range and the bowmen and maidens. He
glanced behind him, thinking something had caught his
eye, but there was nothing there. He shrugged and
walked on.

'There's more at work here than you can imagine,'
Isaac said to the Captain, while giving Fran an approving
nod.

'I understand now.' Fran managed to croak out, still
watching the ragged pair.

'I know, I feel them too. Don't fear them, they are
pleased,' said Isaac who now stood next to Fran.

Charlotte bounced over. 'Brilliant,' she said, clapping
her hands. 'You can feel the spirits.'

'Can you hold this, please?' Fran leant her spear over
towards Charlotte. Fran then walked out of the line towards the ragged couple, stopped and bowed her head.
The two figures stopped and bowed back. The trees shook
and shivered. Tom and Duncan, followed by Isaac,
followed Fran's lead and also bowed. Behind them the
archers and maidens did the same.

The Captain looked confused. Charlotte looked at him and said, 'They honour the past, the ones that have come before and whose spirits are with us today.'

The Captains wife stepped up to him and took his arm. 'What is that I can feel?' she said, not in fear, but excitement as she held his arm tightly.

'I don't know, but it's beyond my understanding,' the Captain said quizzically.

The spirits faded and evaporated into the air. Fran walked back to Charlotte, who was still holding her spear.

'They've gone now,' Fran said as she took her spear back.

The trees shook and hundreds of birds flew out of the woods and swooped and dived over the gathered crowd. Everyone looked up and started laughing at the joyous sight above.

'Perhaps we do have Merlin's child,' Isaac said quietly to himself as he looked up with a smile, suddenly realising the White Lady was floating next to him.

'Perhaps she is, perhaps she is,' she repeated. 'Don't forget your promise to bring her to me, she is indeed a strong mage.'

Isaac watched the White Lady swirl gently and disappear into the air, realising he was the only one who could see her.

Tom and Fran bumped into Charlotte outside the house.

'Tom,' Charlotte said excitedly, 'today was brilliant, all the girls did a great job. Fran leading the promise will no doubt ruffle the feathers of some of the men, but some-times things need to be shaken up a bit.'

'I did wonder that, Mum, but I'm pleased it went so well,' said Tom.

'Thanks, Tom, but everyone's going to ache to-morrow,' Fran said, rubbing her shoulder, which was stiffening up, wondering if ice or a hot bath was the best remedy. *Bath*, she decided.

'Fran, could we meet at nine tomorrow? Could you help look after whoever might be waiting? Be warned, I think it's going to be a tough morning.' Charlotte looked strained and anxious again.

~ 57 ~

Monday, 14th July. Fran was in the dining room, already feeling tense about the day ahead, when Charlotte walked into breakfast looking tired and anxious. Fran went to talk to her. 'You wanted a quick chat before we get started,' she said as breezily as possibly, sure she'd failed to lift Charlotte's veil of anxiety.

'Yes,' Charlotte said almost mechanically. 'Sorry, I didn't sleep at all well last night, then fell into a deep sleep in the early hours. Still trying to wake up.' Charlotte yawned involuntarily which only emphasised her tired, watery eyes. 'Sorry, we start at ten, first in is Pen—Jackie is going in with her—then Holly, Rachel and, lastly, Jen. I'll definitely go in with Jen. Could you make sure everyone is here on time and is OK when they come out? The interviews are taking place in the drawing room and everyone will meet in the sitting room.'

'Understood, and I'll do my best to look after everyone.'

'Thank you, Fran, you should come to the briefing with the Inspector, I'll give you a wave when she arrives.'

Fran returned to sit with Tom and her father. She

decided Charlotte's anxiety must be contagious. She felt a creeping dread of what the morning might hold.

Tom was chatting with Charles about the plans for the estate he'd revealed the previous afternoon. Charles was quietly eating his boiled eggs and toast and a 'proper coffee' as he referred to the cappuccino Olivia had brought him.

Tom saw his mother get up and slowly leave the dining room, waving at Fran, who was playing with her untouched yoghurt and fruit. Tom gave her a slight nudge. She looked up, nodded at Charlotte, dropped her spoon into her bowl and pushed her chair back.

'Bye, you two, got to go.'

Tom caught her arm and squeezed it. 'Hope your morning goes OK.'

Fran bent down and kissed the top of Tom's head and then stood behind her father. She patted his shoulder, kissing him on the head as well.

'Thank you,' her father said, as he buttered his last piece of toast.

Fran followed Charlotte out of the dining room. She saw the Inspector with two other women, standing in the hall admiring the main staircase.

'Good morning, Inspector.' Charlotte tried to sound light, but failed. Her words seemed to hang heavy in the hall.

'Good morning, Your Ladyship.'

'Please, all of you, call me Charlotte, and this is Fran, my son's fiancée.'

'Charlotte,' the Inspector continued, 'can I introduce

Doctor Grace Jarvis. I was lucky enough to be able to draft her in. And this is constable Kate Fuller, she is just finishing her first stage of training in these matters and is here to help, listen and gain valuable experience, I hope that's alright with you.' The Inspector looked at Charlotte who nodded her agreement. 'When based in Birmingham I undertook all stages of the training and worked successfully on a number of such cases, several times with the help of Grace. We are all here to help and give support to you and the interviewees. These things can be difficult.' The Inspector finished her introductions, hoping she had reassured Charlotte, but Charlotte's face was as tight and stressed as when they first started.

'Oh dear,' was all Charlotte could say. Fran said nothing, but could feel the weight of the morning increasing.

'We also need to look after you two. Please call me Grace.'

'First names only, we don't want to be any more intimidating than we need to be, the interview will be stressful enough as it is. My first name is Hazel.' The Inspector paused. 'Is your husband around? I have some news you will both find interesting.'

Charlotte saw Gail moving through the hall. 'Gail, can you find Lewis and ask him to join us. Tell him it's urgent, please.'

'Yes, ma'am.' Gail scuttled off to the dining room.

'Please follow me, I thought this would be a good room for the interviews.' Charlotte led everyone into the drawing room. Fran, feeling nervous, brought up the rear.

'Perfect, what a lovely room,' Grace said, looking round. 'Are these all-family pictures?'

'Pictures of the estate at different times in history. We don't really go in for portraits, the few there are hang in the hall,' Charlotte said, looking relieved as Lewis walked in.

'Good morning, everyone,' Lewis said, looking around questioningly.

'Lewis, the Inspector has some news.'

'We've uncovered two more victims of Henry's. One's dead—suicide—the other found she was pregnant, left the area to have the child then had it adopted, never came back. There are also two others we are still investigating, and one girl had a near miss after he'd drugged her, she collapsed in The Oak and her friends wisely stepped in. It was reported at the time, but not followed up. Which brings me to my other news. Sergeant Bennett has been suspended subject to investigation. We think he purposely dropped any complaint or investigations involving Henry. We also think he took bribes. We're just looking into his finances. I may as well tell you; the news has already washed through the station like a tornado and I have no doubt will be well-worn gossip across the area by this afternoon, but if you should be asked, you didn't hear it from me.'

Lewis stood still, shock on his face. 'Yes, you're right such news will travel fast. Bennett was a well-known figure in these parts. So, thirteen women, including the girl who collapsed in The Oak, three dead. Bennett always had his own way with the law, which in many ways worked well around here, but I never thought he would go that far.' Lewis shook his head and rubbed his chin as the news sunk in. 'What about Tyler?' he enquired.

'Still trying to finalise the exact order of events. As of this moment the CPS seem to think manslaughter, but they haven't made a final decision yet. Given the circumstances, his health and age, he may even get away with a suspended sentence.'

'His health?' Lewis questioned. Lewis could only remember him being in the best of health.

'He's had a heart attack or mild stroke, waiting for the medical report to pass to the CPS. I visited him, he is bed bound in hospital and can only move in a wheelchair.

'Poor chap. OK, thank you, Inspector.'

'One more thing, we'd like to interview Long Farm's manager, who seems to be simply known as Bull, any idea where he might be?'

'Sorry, no, but he has a certain reputation. I understand he has a couple of goons who are always close to him. None of them are to be messed with.'

'Thank you, Lewis. As far as we can find, Bull and his two associates came to the UK illegally about fifteen years ago, from Albania we think. We can only really track them from when they started at Long Farm. We have questioned his two associates already and they're being held in custody due to their immigration status, but Bull seems to have disappeared on the night of the shooting.'

'Sorry, Inspector, I can't help you, but feel free to talk to anyone here. I would suggest you start with Duncan, Poacher John and

Rupert. Talk to Graham, he will sort it out for you. Sorry, if there's nothing else, I have to go.'

Grace said she would sit in with the Inspector for all the interviews.

Charlotte joined Fran and Kate in the sitting room. They all sat awkwardly in silence; tension and worry filled the room. The sitting room door opened and Pen and Jackie walked in. Kate jumped up and led them to the drawing room.

The Inspector introduced herself and Grace and gave an update on the investigation and said that the interview would be recorded.

'Any questions?' the Inspector asked.

There were none and Pen sat nervously holding Jackie's hand.

After forty minutes Pen and Jackie came out, both visibly upset, holding each other tightly. Grace accompanied them into the sitting room.

'Sorry, could you give us some time in here, please?'

'Can I stay, please?' said Charlotte, seeing her daughter was upset.

Grace looked at Pen. 'Your decision.'

'I'm OK, just the shock going over everything and hearing details from Jackie I never knew, bit of a shock. I'll catch you later.'

We're running out of rooms, Fran thought, as she steered a reluctant Charlotte out of the sitting room. The small dining room came to mind and she found the door was open. The room had been cleared and cleaned after the barbeque on Friday. Fran kept the door open to intercept Holly so she didn't crash into the sitting room.

Charlotte sat bent forward on her chair, sobbing and muttering under her breath, 'I should be with Penelope...my child... my baby.'

Fran didn't know what to say or do; she couldn't find any words. Then she leant over Charlotte and wrapped her arms around her. Fran felt Charlotte sink into her embrace and relax, and her shaking and sobbing stopping. Her red eyes opened and she forced a weak smile. 'Holly will be here in a moment. I don't want her to see me like this,' Charlotte said, glancing at the door. 'God, we've only just started and I'm already a mess,' she said, standing up.

Charlotte and Holly went into the drawing room and were out in fifteen minutes. Hearing how Holly had wrenched Henry's arm raised the only smiles of the morning. Grace again came out with them and chatted with Holly in the sitting room.

Rachel arrived and sat waiting in the small dining room kneading her hands in nervous anticipation, not looking forward to having to relive that evening of so many years ago. She then went into the drawing room with Charlotte to meet the Inspector and Grace.

To Rachel's surprise and relief, questions didn't linger on the events with Henry, but instead on the police procedures afterwards. Rachel advised that Bennett had told her she shouldn't have led Henry on and it was her own fault as she'd changed her mind. When she protested, Bennett told her if she didn't behave, she would be charged with wasting police time and anything else he could think of. Lastly, she confirmed her house in New Wood had been paid for by Tyler Campbell-Blyth, Henry's father, in exchange for her silence.

Rachel finished and spoke with Grace in the sitting room for a while. Charlotte and Fran sat in the small dining room waiting for Jen to arrive. Fran could feel the dread rising like a dark tide as she waited with Charlotte, the only sound the distant mumbling sounds of the house going about its normal business. *Nothing normal in this room today,* Fran thought.

Jen arrived, just as Grace walked into the small dining room.

'Ready, then?' Grace asked lightly.

'Just a minute,' Charlotte answered as she took Jen's hands and clasped them to her chest. 'Jen, are you ready? I'll be with you. Don't worry, whatever happened remember, we love you.'

Jen lifted her head up to look directly in her mother's eyes. 'Thanks, I've been such a fool.' Charlotte didn't say anything, just leant forward and kissed Jen on the forehead.

Jen and Charlotte followed Grace into the drawing room. The Inspector stood as they walked in.

'You must be Jennifer?' Hazel asked, reaching forward to shake hands.

'Please call me Jen.'

'Of course, Jen, please have a seat. Now I'm going to ask you some questions which are all to do with our current investigations into Henry Campbell-Blyth. We appreciate you coming forward. Just so you know, I will be recording our conversation, is that alright?'

'Yes, that's fine,' a serious, resolute-faced Jen answered.

'Thank you, Jen, if you would like us to stop at any time, just say.'

'OK. Understood.'

Charlotte was surprised how calm Jen seemed, but she thought she could detect a slight twitch in her neck.

Hazel said, 'When did you first meet Henry?'

'As family or relationship?' Jen's question made Charlotte's heart miss a beat. Grace made some notes.

'You choose, Jen, whatever you feel most comfortable with,' Hazel answered.

'He'd been seeing my sister.'

'Penelope?' Hazel interrupted.

'Yes.' Jen paused and fell silent.

'You alright, do you want to stop?' Hazel asked with concern at the dark face in front of her.

'No, no.' Jen paused again and took a deep breath, looking determined. 'He'd been seeing my sister for about three months and he'd started staying at the house. He talked to me, saying how pretty I was. He told me Pen and I looked very similar, but I was the prettier. He would talk to me like this often. No one had called me pretty before.' Jen glanced at Charlotte. 'Well, not in that way. He said when he was with my sister, he would often pretend it was me, I was much nicer and prettier than her, and I believed him, feeling flattered.'

The room was quiet, but to Charlotte the silence screamed out her worst fears.

'You sure you're OK to carry on?' Hazel asked, glancing at Grace, whose face for the first time this morning showed signs of concern.

'Yes, I'm OK. He would ask me about boyfriends. I told him there'd been a couple, but they hadn't lasted long. He asked what had happened with them, had I been intimate.'

Grace let out a big sigh. 'Hazel, would you mind if I took over?'

'Please do, Grace,' a relieved Hazel agreed. A skilfully groomed innocent was always the worst victim.

Jen was sitting very upright, facing Grace.

'Can you tell us what happened?' Grace gently asked in a low, soothing voice that glided through the tense emotional silence.

'It was my fault, I asked him to the first time. He instigated the second time, but I didn't say no, it was exciting.' For the first time Jen's face flickered with upset. She carried on. 'I was very naïve. I was intrigued, flattered by this man, not a boy, who liked me and thought I was prettier than my sister, who treated me like a woman, not a child.' Jen stopped.

'How old were you when this happened?' Hazel asked gently.

'Sixteen,' Jen answered, but there were no tears. 'It went on for about three months, then he simply stopped trying to see me.'

Charlotte's head fell forward, her hair covering her

face, and she let out a low whimper of despair. Grace waved Kate over and whispered in her ear, 'Please take Charlotte into the sitting room.' Kate smoothly walked over to the bent-over Charlotte, put her arms around her and very quietly asked her to stand. Charlotte offered no resistance.

*

Fran sat up as the sitting room door opened and saw Charlotte being led in, wrapped in Kate's arms. 'What's happened?' Fran said as Charlotte sat down.

'The worst,' was all Charlotte could say, in a quivering voice between sobs. 'My poor babies. Why was I so blind to what was going on with both of them?' And she put her face in her hands again.

~ 58 ~

Friday, 18th July. Charlotte picked up her book and left her room to walk down to the drawing room. It was three o'clock on Friday afternoon. After what had been a most difficult week, Charlotte had decided she needed to rescue some of her old routine, although she knew things would never be quite the same again.

Grace and Kate had stayed until late afternoon Monday after seeing everyone who'd been involved to make sure they were alright. Grace had returned Wednesday and Friday mornings and held more sessions, and said she would come back Monday and Thursday mornings the following week. After that her secondment ended and she was off back home, but said she would continue to help, especially Jen. Charlotte had been pleased with Grace's help; she'd felt lost after Monday morning. The sessions had helped Jen especially, who'd decided to defer university for a year and was reconsidering what she wanted to do going forward.

Charlotte walked down the main stairs and into the hall, the girls, as ever, buzzing around. *God*, Charlotte thought, *this house never sleeps and it's only going to get worse!* Olivia came past.

'Good afternoon, madam. I'm just going to get your tea; will you want anything else?'

'Could you put a mug on the tray? Lewis said he might join me later and he prefers that to a cup. And some extra hot water to refresh the pot.'

'No problem, madam.'

'Thank you, Olivia,' Charlotte said, turning to walk to the drawing room as Olivia disappeared behind the stairs to the kitchen.

Charlotte opened the French doors. It was still warm, but not the scorching heat of before. There'd been some light rain which had allowed the Vale to recover some of its green, but it was still very dry. The trees looked sad, slouching and losing their leaves; a false autumn, she'd been told, as the trees hunkered down after so long without rain. Everyone was saying the rain would come soon.

Olivia entered and placed a tea tray next to Charlotte.

'Thank you, Olivia,' Charlotte said as she sat down.

'You're welcome, madam,' Olivia replied as she left the room. 'I'll be back in an hour with a fresh pot and some cake. I know His Lordship likes a piece with his afternoon cuppa.'

Poor Fran, Charlotte thought with a sigh, got her caught up with the Henry fiasco this week; we shouldn't have involved her. At least her father's hospital appointment went OK; change of prescription, less stress and more exercise. She hadn't expected him to return to the estate with Fran on Tuesday, although in the circumstances, there seemed to be no other choice, and he wasn't much trouble. Wendy appeared to have left him. Charlotte hadn't really warmed to her when she stayed, she seemed disapproving and disappointed most of the time.

All very strange, Charlotte thought to herself, as she picked up the book lying in her lap. She read the blurb. A historical romance, it sounded like. She opened a page at random in the second half of the book. The page contained heavy breathing, tearing lace and whispered words, heaving bodies, sweat and references to moistness which shouldn't appear on any page. Charlotte shut the book with a slap and dropped it in the bin in disgust.

She sat up to pour her first cup and picked up a magazine someone had left and browsed the articles, scanning some, reading others. She wondered if she should subscribe to something. She wasn't having much luck with books at the moment.

Lewis appeared at the French doors earlier than Charlotte had expected. He'd been walking in the woods after lunch. Charlotte had accompanied him yesterday; it was, as ever, calming. Deep breaths brought relief and healing. Lewis had walked the woods every day this week. He'd been very troubled after the revelations from the police interviews. Lewis had had a grave face all week, which only today seemed to be lifting. Charlotte had already decided if Tyler hadn't pulled the trigger, she would have happily shot Henry with both barrels, surprising herself at how comfortable she'd felt with such thoughts. Grace had told her it was quite natural. *Maternal*

protection was one thing, but maternal murder was quite
another. Don't mess with the lioness's cubs, she thought with
a wry smile.

Lewis picked up the mug with a flourish, poured himself a tea and sat down opposite Charlotte with a sigh.

'Jen and I are going to London for a week soon,' said
Charlotte, 'to get away and have a break, visit museums,
galleries, restaurants, catch some shows and no doubt
some retail therapy. It's easy for Grace to get to London
so we can meet up with her as well. Why don't you come
with us?'

'That's a good idea. I have a few people I need to see,
so it'll still give you two some time alone.'

'You don't fancy a bit of shopping then? It's always
nice to have someone to carry the bags,' teased Charlotte.

Lewis shuddered in mock horror.

'Tom and Fran's move to the estate is good,' Charlotte
said. 'Hopefully they'll have a quieter time while they
settle in.'

'Poor Fran is having quite a time with her mother. I
found her an odd woman,' said Lewis as he sipped his tea.

'Yes, I didn't really warm to her,' Charlotte added.

Lewis got up from his seat, went over to the French
doors and looked down the Vale and across to the trees.
He waved at Charlotte to join him.

Charlotte put her cup down and walked over to stand
behind Lewis, who was staring towards the woods. Then
she saw them gliding up over the trees and onto Vale
towards the house. Lewis took a step out. Charlotte

moved to stand beside him. They both looked up at the graceful sight of the large birds' effortless flight.

'Red kites,' Lewis almost whispered. 'I'd heard a pair had been spotted.'

'Beautiful,' was all Charlotte could say as they glided low and near and then, with a few pumps of their wings, rose up and glided back towards the trees, banking up, turning back towards them again.

'Beautiful colour,' Charlotte said, captivated. The birds' wing feathers ruffled as they glided on the air, and they swooped close again then rose once more into the blue sky.

Lewis put his arm around Charlotte's shoulder and squeezed. She looked up at him and stretched on her toes to kiss his cheek.

Lewis stood thoughtfully looking down the Vale. 'We've done something right if they've returned.'

~ 59 ~

Wednesday, 30th July. The police finally closed the case on Henry Campbell-Blyth. There was a total of fourteen victims: three dead, the survivors damaged and scared, many others affected. Collateral damage; family and friends left lost in the wake of Henry's actions.

There'd been much talk on how to mark Henry's funeral. Charlotte was happy to just ignore it. Others, like Rachel, wanted to mark the occasion, get some closure. The funeral was being held at Woodcoombe Village church; Henry would be buried in the Campbell-Blyth family plot. The church and cemetery could be seen from the old road to Woodcoombe Village, which led to the Foresters' pub. They'd decided they would meet at ten o'clock on the Vale outside the hallway and walk together up the Vale, to the top of the estate to watch Henry being interred. They'd agreed none of them would wear black as none were in mourning. Rachel wore a scarlet dress; Charlotte had a lime green outfit. Everyone else wore bright coloured combinations, mainly summer dresses— it was still hot and dry. The eight of them set off from the house looking more like a carnival procession than a funeral cortege. Rachel and Jen carried wicker baskets.

The conversation was light but nervous as they walked up the Vale. Jackie held Pen's arm. Holly was talking enthusiastically to Naomi on how things were going with Eddy and that they were now officially an item. Jen walked quietly on her own listening to the chatter around her, wondering about Charlie, who she'd met fleetingly at the art college open day. She'd taken art as one of her four A levels and was now considering a more artistic direction than following her brother Tom, studying mathematics.

Isaac and Poacher John watched them moving up the Vale towards them. John had joined Isaac to find the best spot from which they could see the cemetery. They had found a place with a good view, but also where they could easily slip into the field between the estate and church if they wanted to get nearer.

'Good morning, ladies. You can see from here or you can get into the field if you want to be closer,' said Isaac cheerily, as the colourful parade approached.

'I think we're fine here,' said Charlotte. Everyone seemed to agree.

Rachel and Holly put the wicker baskets down. John moved them under the hedge to give them some shade and help keep them cool.

'Eleven o'clock. They will be starting soon. Look, you can see the cars arriving,' pointed John.

'Just about, we're not really near enough,' said Rachel, straining her eyes.

'Thought you wanted to see him buried, not read the bloody hymns,' John retorted.

'Yes, but it's tempting to make a scene after eight years,' Rachel bitterly replied.

'It's not about him, it's about us and everyone else he's affected. We're here for them as well,' said Charlotte.

Everyone nodded in agreement. The light conversation between them faded. Charlotte took Rachel's hand. They all quietly joined hands and stood in a line looking down over the cemetery from behind the thin hedge that ran along the border of the estate. They went quiet as they waited for the coffin to appear. Everyone stood with their thoughts. Charlotte started to sing gently. Jen and Pen joined in and then Fran realised she somehow knew the words and added her voice. The sad, thoughtful song brought a calm to the group, a gentle flowing soothing lilt. Hands linked, they swayed gently to the mystical harmony resonating gently through the warm air.

'Here he comes,' announced John.

The singing stopped. Everyone could clearly see the coffin leading the few mourners towards the grave.

'That must be old Tyler in the wheel chair.' John commented out loud

They watched as the coffin was placed on the ground. There were more words, then the coffin was lifted again and lowered carefully down.

The air around them went cold.

Fran was suddenly aware of Henry's spirit, full of spite, hate, anger and loathing. She could only see Henry's face leering. Fuck you! it said, as he had at the dinner when she'd first seen him. His face was close. Fran shuddered. The air turned icy cold and it felt as if he was touching her. It took a big effort to reclaim her senses. *No!* she shouted in her head. *Get out, you have no place here.* But the vision in her head hadn't stopped; instead, Henry's laughter got louder. Fran took a deep breath, pulled all the spirits she could muster and shouted *NO, YOU HAVE NO PLACE HERE, BE GONE NOW!* And suddenly her head was clear, he'd vanished.

Fran looked at Charlotte. She was standing next to her with her arms tight by her side, shaking from head to toe, her face twisted. Fran took Charlotte's hand and placed her other hand on the side of Charlotte's head. Charlotte's vision flickered into Fran's mind, each of her daughters in turn in Henry's arms as he laughed mockingly, and the same piercing cold feeling. Fran squeezed Charlotte's hand. 'Listen. We have to get him out of your head. We'll do this together, find something to drive him out, something to focus on.' Charlotte squeezed Fran's hand in response.

'ENOUGH,' Charlotte shouted.

Fran felt a surge of energy and saw Charlotte conjure a shotgun into the vision and without hesitation pull both barrels. Immediately, Henry disappeared. Charlotte stopped shaking. 'He's gone, I knew I would pull the trigger, knew I would do it; he will never hurt my babies again.'

Fran looked around. Everyone was affected. Fran grabbed Rachel's hand and found she was fighting the vision as hard as she could, but her strength was fading.

She was laughing in Henry's raging face. NEVER AGAIN, she screamed, to little effect, her fear fuelling him.

Fran told Rachel her life was not worth losing to this, having survived so long with so much pain. So near to being free. 'You're stronger than this,' Fran said, but she could feel her life force ebbing. Fran channelled all the energy she could find and drove Henry out, despite his protesting.

Rachel slumped down on the grass, exhausted by the fight. 'The bastard was never going to have his way with me again, I'd have rather died.' Fran knew that was true; Rachel's life force had been fading quickly.

Fran took a deep breath. She expelled Henry's presence from everyone's head. Naomi was in flames, watching her father and brother also burning while Henry laughed, leered, mocked and abused her.

Holly was weaker, younger and needed most help to expel Henry. Pen and Jackie had the same vision of being taunted by Henry together. Fran held both their hands and told them hate couldn't conquer their love and devotion, and together they threw Henry out.

Jen was quietly strong and her horror was of being with him in different rooms of the house. Fran helped her lock him out of whichever room she found herself in. They laughed at Henry's vain attempts to break in. Together they drove him out.

Finally, everyone's horror was over. Fran was exhausted. She glanced around and they all stood or sat depleted and ragged. Holly was in tears, Pen and Jackie clung to each other. Rachel was laid out breathing rapidly, Jen trying to comfort her. Charlotte was slowly walking around checking on everybody, trying to be strong.

Fran looked to the sky, knowing Henry was still there. She felt him near her and suddenly she was knocked back onto the ground, losing her white sun hat. Henry only had to concentrate on her now.

You stupid fucking bitch, echoed in her head. *I'll deal with you and then the others one by one. This is not over.* Henry's voice echoed on the hill.

Fran scrambled to her feet and raised her hands skyward; she needed stronger magic. She uttered words in a tongue she didn't understand, calling for magic she'd never found before.

Isaac and John stood open-mouthed, watching. Isaac had to stop John from rushing in. He'd said there must be something they could do. Isaac shrugged, but then saw a flash of white in the corner of his eye. They both turned and saw the White Lady floating behind them.

'Someone has used the old language and there is much going on here.'

'The young mage we've spoken about uttered the words. She's wrestling an ugly spirit,' Isaac said, pointing to Fran, her arms lifted to the sky, her face a picture of concentration. They heard Fran speak more words they didn't understand.

'Look,' said the White Lady. 'She's tearing the very sky, its fabric. You can see the air folding and sucking in the ugly spirit. She's working the element that holds the universe and everything together. I think you would call it dark matter.'

Isaac, John and the White Lady watched Henry's spirit get sucked into the tear in the sky and then stream back into the grave it had come from. The dry earth for the grave rose into the air and plummeted back down, sealing the grave. The mourners cowered in shock. The last thing they heard was a screamed single word from Henry, *Nooooooo*, as he was entombed in the ground.

Fran stood not moving, her hands still in the air. She uttered more words, then dropped her arms and allowed herself a small smile. It was finished, the warmth returned, the cold banished.

'She's condemned his spirit to his grave for eternity. Strong magic,' the White Lady said, looking at Isaac. John was pale and looked confused.

The White Lady gently drifted over to Fran, who was breathing heavily. Isaac and John followed behind.

Everyone could see the White Lady floating amongst them and listened to what she said. 'Well done, young lady, you really are a strong mage. How did you know the old language?'

'Somehow, I knew what I needed to do and managed to find the dark element. The words just tumbled out, from where I don't know—somewhere deep inside me.'

'You've locked him up for eternity. Only you can release him, which I wouldn't recommend.' The White Lady floated lower and spoke to Fran; no one else could hear. 'Yes, I think you might well be Merlin's child, a mighty mage. You can use the old words and can now weave dark matter, so the Once and Future King could return knowing he will have strong magic at his side. Young mage, we shall talk again. Come to my field soon and I will find you.'

The White Lady rose in the air, twirled and disappeared. John brought out the wicker baskets and everyone sat on the grass. Rachel and Jen opened them, handed out glasses, popped the corks and filled all the glasses. The trees nearby bent over gently and quietly to shade them from the hot midday sun chasing away the cold Henry's spirit had brought.

'To us and the others, who are not here' Charlotte toasted; everyone raised their glasses.

John sipped his dainty glass. He leant into Isaac and whispered, 'I could really do with a pint after all that. Shall we slip off to the Foresters', leave the ladies to it? Pub's just few minutes away.'

'Good idea, John.' Isaac stood up. 'Ladies, we will leave you now. We are so pleased you are all safe.'

As John and Isaac walked down the hill, Isaac paused, shielding his eyes from the sun above scanning the horizon ahead. 'I see clouds, I think it's the rain we keep hoping for, the weather looks like its breaking.'

Two hours later, the ladies stumbled into the house soaking wet from the rain that had washed across the estate from the south west and still rained down as they dripped laughing in the hallway of the house as towels were passed out. It wasn't cold, the air felt refreshed by the downpour, the ladies felt as revived as the land by the

pouring rain. Life would blossom and flow again for all
of them.

About The Author

Mike was born in 1960 in Leigh-on-Sea, where he has lived ever since. Married his beloved Sally in 1991, two children Emily and Toby, who he couldn't be prouder of. He feels so lucky to be cocooned in a family full of love and laughter.

Belfairs High School followed Chalkwell Hall Juniors. An average academic, but loved sport. A County swimmer, a successful judo competitor, a clumsy basketball player. But rugby was his passion, attending England schools summer training at Bisham Abbey two years running.

A member of the Royal Ocean Racing Club sailing many offshore races across the North Sea, English Channel and beyond, including the Fastnet race.

Mike took up cycling as he got older making more great friends and visiting various riding locations around the country.

Mike started in insurance in 1978 after spectacularly failing his A levels. Enjoying steady career progression, he completed his MBA in 2003. After a successful and fun forty-two years in London, he happily retired in 2020.

Unfortunately, six months after retirement, Mike suffered a stroke, leaving him with no movement on his left side. So started his greatest challenge, reteaching his brain and body to do things he'd always taken for granted. Plenty of ambitious goals, including typing one handed to write this book.

Milton Keynes UK
Ingram Content Group UK Ltd.
UKHW022053291023
431569UK00005B/15